The Confessions
of Elisabeth Von S.

The Confessions of Elisabeth Von S.

The Story of a Young Woman's Rise and Fall in Nazi Society

Gillian Freeman

Thomas Congdon Books

E. P. Dutton | New York

First American edition published 1978 by E.P. Dutton, a division of Sequoia-Elsevier
Publishing Company, Inc., New York.

For information contact: .
E.P. Dutton, 2 Park Avenue, New York, N.Y. 10016

Library of Congress Catalog Card Number: 78-60670

ISBN: 0-525-08453-3

10 9 8 7 6 5 4 3 2 1

The Confessions
of Elisabeth Von S.

1933

January 1st
Heil Hitler!
What a year it's going to be. It can't fail. Heil New Year! Heil New
Baby! I thought I might just give birth at the Neudeckers' party last night.
I was drunk by midnight and failed to recognize myself in the mirror.
There was the party going on, it was like being at the movies except
that the scene was in colour, the Christmas tree with the star on top
(not quite straight unless the alcohol put it at a slant!) and the red
apples polished by Christel Neudecker and hung on the branches. I
watched Hugo in the reflection talking to Gregor what's-his-name, the
new leader of our Kulturbund, already having an affair with Elsa who
runs the office, though he only took up the post in December. The
Neudeckers have an Italian maid – very hairy arms – who brought in
spaghetti as well as roast goose. There's been quite a craze for Italian
food this year. I mean *last* year, of course. It wasn't until I was carrying
my plate away from the serving table that I identified myself by my
dress – the almond green voile with the cape. Hugo may feel proud
of approaching fatherhood, but how can he possibly find me attractive?
I look and *feel* like a python that has swallowed a pig, a *living* pig, still
kicking. I can't help hoping it's not a girl.

January 2nd
Well, this year I'm determined to keep up my diary. I know I make it
an annual resolution but 1933 really inspires me. This time last year I
was at school, so all there was to write about was my *Abitur*.* Now I
am IN LOVE, I am MARRIED, PREGNANT. I will be a mother
before the end of January. (Incredible!) Anyway, the diaries themselves defeated me, those apportioned pages, equally divided, so many
lines per day. I was *consumed* by guilt every time I left a blank. It was
like dieting. Break it with one spoonful of whipped cream and it's
impossible to return to the régime. I rather like the significance of this
exercise book – mine by subterfuge – meant for an essay in English for

* The highest school-leaving examination. Elisabeth appears to have passed this one
year ahead of the norm.

the dreadful 'Miss' with the rabbit teeth and the manly shoulders. I swore I had completed my homework and left the book on the bus! (Actually I had met Hugo instead, the *first time* in the summer house!) 'Miss' twitched her whiskers and gave me a lecture that next time . . . etcetera, etcetera. I looked at her with pity, a virgin for life, what a fate, worse than death. Had she known how I spent *my* evening she would have said the same of me! Still, 'to finish the thought' (as she constantly reprimanded me in the margins) *this* kind of diary writing is less demanding, for if there is nothing compelling to write down, nothing worth remembering for my old age (or for my baby to read one day when he is grown up) then I need not struggle to fill a space marked (for example) Thursday, March 4th – or whatever. I wonder why I picked on March 4th. Of course it may not be a Thursday. I must remember to fill in a page for March 4th. It has given me quite a shock to realize that by March 4th my life will have changed *utterly*.

January 5th
Not too bad! Two forgotten days. Not yet forgotten, but by this time next year I will recall that I ate liver for lunch yesterday only because I record it today. (Someone told my mother that pregnant women must eat liver, it makes the baby's liver strong!) I had not intended to leave the last entry at that point, I was all set for a morning's outpouring, but Mutti arrived (with the liver bleeding through the butcher's bag) to deliver a shawl sent by Helga R, the very first chamber-maid we had when we took over the *Gasthof*. She seemed old to me then and she retired when I was ten so she must be a hundred by now! She had worked for the Schmidts, who ran the place before, and spoke of them with religious fervour. Herr Schmidt was God and Frau Schmidt an angel. As for the *young* Schmidts (who were in their forties when *I* met them) they were set before me as shining examples of morality, never greedy, never naughty, never cross, never rude. I spent my childhood under the shadow of Schmidt superiority, but now of course it is we who have ascended to heaven. No employer was ever as good to her as Herr Stofen, no lady as considerate as his wife, no child as clever as her little Liese. No doubt as she knitted away at the shawl (unwearable!) she thought she was preparing swaddling clouts for a holy infant. A similar thought occurred to me at the Neudeckers' party, and I would have *blasphemed* only I remembered in time that Christel N is a Catholic. There was so much talk of birth and rebirth – of Germany – that my hideous stomach seemed positively symbolic bulging beneath

8

the voile, as though I would personally bring forth the Saviour. Luckily I was not too drunk to indulge, although I told Hugo on the way home who thought it was funny. The party ended with a row and Christel crying. She is not only Catholic but communist and when the usual boring arguments started – as they *always* seem to nowadays – she and Gregor almost came to physical blows. I really can't think why she is so against Hitler. She should have gone to the students' meeting. He wore an ordinary blue suit and spoke quietly, and was even humorous (but not comic, a subtle distinction) at the beginning of his talk. I can't think why people who haven't bothered to hear him spread these rumours that he raves and shouts.

Mutti made me promise to rest more, but frankly, at the moment, I seem to do nothing else.

January 6th
The doctor came today and said that the baby's head is in the right place for a normal birth (that is, *down*) and that it could be any time within the next three weeks. I was pleased at the time, but for some reason I have been depressed all afternoon, and afraid of the actual delivery. Everyone tells me such ghastly stories of their confinements, pain, bleeding, deformities, *tearing*. I suppose I have been alone too much this week, Hugo has been studying and out all day.

I can't decide whether to have my hair cut. An American woman has been staying at the *Gasthof* and left a whole lot of magazines which Mutti brought over yesterday. I like the look of short curls, but it would mean going to a hairdresser's, and Hugo likes my braids, especially when I wind them into 'earphones'. No movie stars have braids, though!

January 7th
Absolutely nothing happened all day. I don't even know why I am bothering to write this, except that there is nothing else to do. I wish I had never agreed to live here, it was a mistake. The apartment on the Königstrasse would have been preferable, even if the area was not acceptable to my mother-in-law. (Note to unborn baby: choose your mother-in-law wisely.) She has always hated me, resented me I suppose I mean. Despised me for being from the wrong social class. I'm surprised she wanted me to live on the estate, come to think of it. But then it meant keeping Hugo under her control. 'Come up to the house for an hour or so, my darling. No need to bring Elisabeth. She needs to rest.'

Of course most people think I'm frightfully lucky. It must have been the estate manager's house once. It's about 150 years old Hugo says, and he ought to know. Naturally I had no hand in the decoration, she wouldn't trust my vulgar taste, she makes me feel like an inn-keeper's daughter in a comic opera, only it isn't comic. The only amusing aspect (to me, that is) is that despite all the high-born young ladies imported here for Hugo to make his selection, I was the one he wanted. I was the one who became pregnant in the summer house – the revolving summer house. We turned the front away from the windows of the house. She has never forgiven me for not having had an abortion. Her religious convictions stop conveniently short at my social level, God would have favoured this termination. It wouldn't have sullied the von Stahlenberg blood.

The two fathers were opposed, but also in harmony. My honour and Hugo's had to be acknowledged by marriage; mine because I had been ill-used – very well-used actually! Hugo's because he had to face up – as a gentleman – to his wrong-doings. Mutti needless to say was delighted beyond her wildest dreams. She had always looked up to the von Stahlenbergs. I remember Frau von S called on us once for a reference for a maid (fifteen-year-old Gretel K who had worked for us for a single summer) and how my mother behaved as if a medal had been bestowed on her by Colonel Schreider! Being asked for an opinion on whether or not Gretel emptied chamber-pots efficiently (her capacity was of the lowest in our establishment) she reacted as if a flattering compliment had been made to her.

That was the extent of the contact between the grandmothers-to-be; except when Valerie married and there wasn't room at the big house for all the guests. The von S's farmed them round the village and in the town. We didn't have the high-ups, two young men who were friends of Valerie's husband in his student days, and a cousin who had gone down in the world but wore some fine pearls, a relic of her past. She told my mother that her father had given himself (and the family funds) to God. When she was at the reception I went into her room – I always went into the rooms when the guests were out! – and it smelt stuffy and scented, and her red hair (henna-ed) was thick in the comb on the dressing-table. I think she was probably going bald. We had all been allowed out of school early to watch the wedding procession, the von Stahlenbergs were treated like royalty by the principal who regretted the loss of the monarchy, and told us so daily!

Valerie had eight bridesmaids – the procession was on foot as was customary in the family tradition – and two pages, who carried hassocks embroidered especially with heraldic crests and the initials of the bride and groom. The convent produced them – the von S's keep the nuns busy! They constantly repair the tapestries in the house and make new ones for the von S's to present to neighbouring churches as altar decorations. There was much excitement when one was blessed and sent to African missionaries, a little piece of Germany in the jungle, we said at school. Several of our girls became novices each year, the ones who were best at needlework, of course.

Pause here – the gardener delivered some potatoes, and the maid allotted to us by Frau von S (her spy?) asked him to release a bird trapped in the kitchen flue. It emerged with a broken wing and finally expired in fright having crashed into everything in sight. Feathers all over the place, plus its droppings. I covered the goulash just in time!

Valerie's wedding! When I stood with the school watching them all parade by, Hugo looking so devastatingly handsome, I thought how wonderful to be a member of such a rich and elevated family. Valerie came to *my* wedding, but Hugo's other sister declined. She said in the circumstances she didn't want anything more to do with him. This she later rectified by saying that she would be happy to see him at any time, but not in my company. *Her* husband is a Count, so like me, she took a social step in an upward direction. Although this is not the way she sees it. She has married *well*, and Hugo has married so badly she won't even acknowledge it!

I feel much better having written all this. Hugo should be home soon, anyway.

January 8th
Hugo arrived just as I finished writing. I felt guilty keeping it from him, but one can't share *everything*. I always thought I would have no secrets from my husband, but then it would never have occurred to me that I would hate his mother. Unfortunately *he* loves her!

January 9th
I think if I had travelled abroad my mother-in-law would like me more. My schoolfriend Klara spent her holidays in Vienna and Budapest, it gave her a 'certain something'. I am afraid to give my opinion on so many things because I might seem ignorant. Last night the Neudeckers came to see us – turned up, luckily having eaten – and the three of them talked of nothing but the cinema. Better than politics,

I couldn't have stood another of those scenes with Christel. I felt such a fool not being able to take part. Christel and Karl belong to a film society, I didn't even know that films were made at the beginning of the century. Christel was never a student, so how does she know so much? *I am going to learn.* I nodded agreement each time Hugo made a point. He said that six years ago the German film industry reached a crucial turning point. All those money complications. I'm afraid I just look at the finished product and never think of the big business behind it. I am like most cinema audiences, surely? I didn't dare say it, but I like American movies best.

January 10th
Is the baby departing or arriving? I am ready for its arrival. I keep looking at all those doll's clothes in the nursery; if my sister-in-law Käthe doesn't admit that Hugo is married, does she consider his baby a bastard?

I was so bored I decided to walk home (home being the *Gasthof*) and talk to Vati. Leaving home, I now see my parents quite differently, before they were part of the furniture. I must say that Vati is thoroughly sensible when it comes to politics. *He doesn't become excited!* I ask him a number of questions, and he comes to the *point* and I understand things far better than I do when Hugo explains. Like all his friends, he goes round and round, pretending to examine every point of view although his mind is made up at the start. When we went camping on the Obersalzberg the summer before last, Heidi, Klara and I sneaked off from the awful school sing-songs at night and listened to the students talking round the fire. They cooked far nicer food than we did! Naturally all my ears (well, both!) were for Hugo. Seeing him close to was a thrill in itself. I mean I had seen him *around* since I was a little girl, but he didn't go to the local school, he had a private tutor until he was twelve, and then went away, and I know now that he spent his summer vacations abroad (there is a branch of the family in Paris and some distant connection in England, he went shooting in England, there are photographs of him doing it). Here he was, twenty years old, blue eyes, yellow hair and brown arms and legs – do I sound romantic? I am! – holding forth on the financial state of Germany (the Darmstädter and Nationalbank had collapsed and while we were there on the mountainside in the sunshine all the banks were closed) and the Wall Street Crash. I learned more about current affairs sitting under the stars and gawking at Hugo than I ever did in class. Christel was there too (having an affair with Hugo) and she went on and on about personal belongings being *bourgeois*, and I remember one mad argument about whether or not a true Marxist should go to the hairdresser's. The students accepted our presence without comment, perhaps they found it amusing to impress three schoolgirls – three pretty schoolgirls, in fact. Hitler was staying at the *Haus Wachenfeld*, or so they said, since no one actually saw him. One of the boys, an ardent follower, spent most of the day watching the house, and said there was a constant arrival and departure of official cars, and that Geli Raubel was sunbathing in the garden. Afterwards, when she shot herself – Christel insists she was murdered – no mention was made of her being at the villa at the time we were there, so I think it may have been someone else in the bathing costume!

I don't seem to be able to keep to the point – unlike Vater (see above!) who thinks the NSDAP* is absolutely essential for Germany now. He says that for men like himself, with their own small businesses, there is no worthwhile alternative. It needs Germans to build up Germany again. Money is at the root of everything, even my mother-in-law's dislike of *me*. However 'vulgar', if I had been rich . . .!

I didn't feel very well at midday, and couldn't eat, which caused my mother *much* anxiety. She telephoned Frau von S, who sent the car to take me back. The chauffeur wore his party badge in his lapel, which I had not noticed before.

January 16th
Hugo very excited because the NSDAP won the Lippe elections. He wanted to make love to me (he always does when his emotions are aroused, whatever the cause) but I felt too vast and uncomfortable. He said he wished he could go to Berlin, because Schleicher can't last much longer. I believe he thought I would say, 'You must go if you want,' but I said, 'If only the baby wasn't so near it wouldn't matter if you went away.'

January 17th
How can Christel keep a maid when she is a Marxist?

January 18th
Hugo mentioned Berlin again. I don't really know what to do. I am conscious how much he misses being at the *centre* of things. He is bored

* Nationalsozialistische Deutsche Arbeiterpartei ('Nazi' was a derogatory term never used in the Third Reich).

being stuck here and in a way that's my fault. He often mentions how wonderfully exciting it was being a student in Berlin. He doesn't like staying home with me in 'domestic bliss'; we either visit friends, go to the cinema or else he goes out alone. He said the other night how pointless it seems, having graduated, to spend his days at the Stahlenberg foundry, ostensibly 'learning' but actually doing nothing but sit in an office with files dating back to the 1880s. For this he is nominated 'Herr Direktor', and paid a handsome salary, while his brain rots. He was always destined for this position but he never questioned it until now. I asked him what he would *like* to do. He said, 'Use my mind.'

January 20th

The worst day of my life. It is my fault. It's this Berlin thing. I said everything I meant to keep to myself and of course Hugo said everything back that I didn't want to hear and he probably didn't even mean. I provoked it all. Why why why did I do it? He's out, and I've cried until my head aches and my face burns and my eyes are hidden in red cushions! Suppose he leaves me? What would I do? Where could I live – not back at the *Gasthof*, I couldn't *bear* it, being told what to do, how to look after my own baby. Wouldn't my mother-in-law gloat.

This morning, after breakfast (which I had in bed) Hugo said 'If I do go to Berlin . . .' I said 'I thought you had decided not to go.' He said 'Why should you think that?' Then I said 'Of course I know how boring it is here with me . . .' He protested, but I persisted, it was a kind of perverse, needling jealousy of a life he enjoyed without me. I said, 'I'm sure you wish you hadn't been forced to marry me, what can I do to amuse you, I'm not interesting like Christel or sophisticated like those highborn* daughters of your family friends. But of course, they wouldn't have given you the chance of making them pregnant. They were the ones to marry.'

He didn't answer. I suppose I expected him to say that he loved me, would have married me anyhow, nothing to do with being pregnant. I wanted him to tell me that I *was* interesting and that so-called sophistication was an empty sham; what mattered was the *person*, that my simplicity attracted him, was what he wanted in a wife.

He chose a necktie from the rail inside the wardrobe, and put it on carefully and slowly in front of the mirror. I could see his reflection,

* Literal translation of *hochgeboren* in the sense of *well-bred*, but does not convey the full flavour of the German.

14

it was as if I hadn't spoken. I said, 'I suppose you don't really love me, I was just available and willing.'

He finished tying the wretched knot, then turned and came and sat on the bed. He said 'I do love you, but you're right, I wouldn't have married you unless the situation had arisen. You know that. There's no point in pretending. We'd have gone on having an affair for years, possibly, and eventually I would have married someone approved by my family. We might even have gone on meeting after I was married, managed the occasional weekend away.' It was like being punched in the throat. My breath was literally taken away. Tears just oozed out of my eyes but I didn't make a sound. When I could speak I gasped out 'How dare you assume I'd want to . . . meet you secretly?' His arrogance astounded me. Curiously, before, I'd admired that assured manner, that unquestioned superiority. It had attracted me. Now I found it painfully insulting.

Hugo took my hands. 'Don't cry, Elisabeth. But it's true, you said it yourself. I didn't say I was *sorry* the way things happened. I like being married to you. I think you're going to be an excellent wife.' Well, it was worse every time he spoke. I think he realized how patronizing he appeared. He said 'We're happy together, aren't we? There are areas of our life which are different, you mustn't begrudge me my friends. There are some things we can't share – and you're right, a higher education is one of them. Christel's a silly creature, with her conviction that communism is Germany's answer, but I enjoy her company, I enjoy quarrelling with her. When she waves her arms about and rants on about fascism being the last stage of capitalism, I get a kick out of demolishing her arguments. She can't give me what *you* give me, though.' He put his hand on my stomach which humped up the bedclothes like an extra bolster. I willed the baby to kick his hand away. 'I want to go to Berlin, not because I want to leave you, but because I think something's going to break. It's an historic time, Elisabeth. The Republic is going to collapse, and I want to be in Berlin when it happens. At least test the temperature myself. A couple of my friends are well in with the Movement, quite influential, Moritz . . . you've heard me talk of Moritz?' I nodded. 'He works with Goebbels, he wrote to me last week, inviting me to stay. Schleicher simply can't hang on, he's been behaving like a blinkered horse, can't see what's happening all round him.'

I said 'I want you here when I have the baby.'

Hugo looked at his watch. 'My God, look at the time. I'm supposed to meet Vater in his office. I must fly.' He kissed me on the forehead. 'Don't be upset, Liese. I care about you very much.' At the door he paused and added, 'I can't contribute much to *having* the baby, they won't allow me near you. You'll give birth whether I'm in the next room or Berlin. But don't worry. I'll be back long before then.'

That was this morning. He still isn't home (4pm) and I haven't eaten and I don't know what to do. I've thought of making myself fall downstairs, but that might really hurt the baby, not just bring on my confinement, though it would pay him back if the baby did die. I *know* he'll go to Berlin, and if I try any more to stop him I'll just seem a nagging bitch. I *don't* begrudge him the pleasure of going there – but oh, how I wish he didn't *want* to leave me even for an afternoon. I want to be with *him* all the time.

January 23rd
I'm quite reconciled. He's gone. And I *do* understand. In fact I've come to a number of conclusions which make me more mature, which isn't a bad thing for one approaching motherhood. These are my resolutions.

1. I won't obstruct him. I'll comply and even *suggest*, which will make him like me more.
2. I'll learn to take part in conversations, not keep my ideas to myself, even if they might seem silly to me. He thinks Christel is mad – but he doesn't despise her. I am determined that his friends *respect* me and don't just think of me as a 'wife'.
3. I am going to educate myself. Hugo says my responses are only emotional and not intellectual, and I'm going to really try to reason out my feelings. Hugo says too many Germans follow Hitler because he is compelling when he makes a public address (it's true. I found him compelling) – and that they don't bother to examine what he has said. The NSDAP will give us *stability*.
4. I will read *Mein Kampf*. There's a copy at home, I'll ask Mutti to bring it over. I can read it after the baby is born. After all, I have to spend three weeks in bed.

January 25th
My feet were swollen this morning and I felt dizzy. The doctor came and said I must stay in bed and is sending in a nurse. It is only noon now, and the day seems to have gone on for weeks. I wonder if the baby is

16

going to be born today. I asked the doctor, but he *never* answers a question. He told my mother-in-law to instruct the maid to give me plenty of *Sächsisches Warmbier** and not too much solid food. I'm *hungry*. And a bit afraid.

January 26th
Visitors all day. First (briefly) my mother-in-law, then Mutti, then Frau Brokdorf who had heard from Mutti that I was confined. Then the doctor, who was as uninformative as yesterday, except to say that all was going well. Then the nurse, who couldn't come yesterday after all. She has moved into the small room next to mine, and is a *talker*. She won't rest. If I suggest it, she says, 'I'll have plenty of time to rest when I'm in my little box.' She tells me about other patients, the last one being 'a gentleman with skin like marble' who passed away last Tuesday. His wife was so grateful to Nurse that she gave her a fur coat, not new, but scarcely worn. Klara also heard (on the town grapevine) that I was in bed, and brought all the gossip of the girls who used to be in our class. Heidi has moved to Munich and has a job as secretary to a Jewish businessman. Klara doesn't know *what* business, but says H is well-paid, and has had her hair cut and waved and looks at least twenty-five. Anni has decided to become a nun, not at our convent, but some Order where they are not even allowed to speak. I said, 'Anni never had anything to say.' We laughed so much Nurse came in and said Klara would have to go unless I kept calm! We reminisced about the summer I met Hugo. When she had left I pretended to Nurse that I wanted to sleep, and I shut my eyes and let what I call my 'movie memory' run. If I get myself in the proper mood I can even recall smells and sounds, and I summoned up the school camp, first of all, to start the private process. There were ten tents pitched on a lower slope of the valley looking across the border to Austria. The first night we were there (it was a week in all) a storm blew up, and (this is copied from my school essay which got an A) 'the sky became wild, the fragments of white clouds darkening and joining together, blotting out the last of the setting sun. Lightning flashed so repeatedly that there was almost permanent illumination, like lantern slides, projected one after another onto a screen. The tents creaked horribly as we crouched inside. Klara, Anni, Heidi and I held hands, and when the thunder rolled Klara screamed. I sat at the entrance looking out. The dark

---

* A mixture of warm beer and milk given to pregnant women.

mountains were like paper cut-outs, and gradually the storm passed, and the clouds separated to reveal stars and a new moon, and the grass smelt heavenly from the rain.' 'Miss' who was in charge of us unpacked the food, and detailed four of us to distribute it. There was a stream nearby where we washed the plates and cups when we had finished. It was too damp to light a fire, but we all sat on groundsheets and sang the English songs she had taught us, *God Save the King*, *Strawberry Fair* and *Cockles and Mussels Alive Alive O*, but I never knew what it meant. We were all tired, it had been a long day, first the train ride, then the walk up the steep paths and the tiring business of putting up the tents (we couldn't get ours to stay up!) and then the emotional impact of the storm. One stupid girl cried all through the sing-song, and Heidi said she heard her sobbing in the night.

I woke up very early. I couldn't think where I was, in the customary way, and the first thing I heard was cow bells, and the shout of the cow-herd, driving them to pasture. I crawled to look out of the tentflap, and it was an incredible dawn, the sun came up as I watched and lit the grass and the stream, it was like switching on an electric light. The colours changed in an instant, the air was cool and fresh and I took a deep breath so that I felt it flow down into the recesses of my lungs. The cow-herd was about my own age (fifteen), slight, bronzed, a straw hat on his head and a stick in his hand. His voice, as he called to the meander-ing cows, had only just broken. He saw me, waved his stick, and smiled. I waved back. At that moment I thought that rural life was the only life worth having in the whole world.

The students trudged past us as we were having breakfast, and need-less to say, we all recognized Hugo as coming from the big house. He wore *lederhosen* and a white open-necked shirt, and his brown feet were in sandals. Some of the girls said good morning, and a few of the students stopped, probably glad of the rest, shifted their knapsacks and exchanged a few words under the cold eyes of 'Miss'.

We spent the day doing lessons, English recitations, nature-study and gymnastics (the gymnastics teacher was also with the party), and walked in formation to the village to eat lunch. We passed a little onion-domed church, and several painted houses with overhanging eaves, and a farmyard with a few hens and a tethered goat. We had arrangements to visit the farm, and sat at two long trestle tables especially set out for us by the farmer's wife and two daughters, like story-book characters, plump and rosy-cheeked and smiling. We drank fresh apple juice and ate bread and goat's cheese and sausages.

I said to Klara, 'Isn't it wonderful?' but she said 'What do they do in the winter?' I hadn't thought of that before.

We took our sketchbooks and took up various positions to commit the idyllic views to paper. My hen persisted in looking like a two-legged dog, but the mountain behind, and the inn at the right of the page, with bunches of evergreen tied over the door for the new wine festival, is as good as a photograph. At least, it is to me; whenever I take it out to look at it I feel I am there again.

When we left, the farmhands were coming home, on foot, or riding in carts with metal-rimmed wheels which made a crunching sound on the tracks. The mud from last night's storm had dried hard during the day, and the cart wheels used the same runnels, as if they were railway lines.

As we walked back to our camp we heard a few of the men singing in unison. They were not in tune, but they gave the verses more enthusiasm than we had given *Strawberry Fair*!

The student camp was not far from ours, and we could see the light of their fire when we went to wash the dishes in the stream. Heidi said 'No one can see us, they're all jawing away at their silly debate.' ('Miss' conducted debates, it was part of the curriculum for the school camp. 'Tuesday' it said on the type-written sheet sent to parents, 'Debate on "Sport is a necessary part of a balanced education".') So Heidi, Klara and I walked boldly up the path to where Hugo and his friends were sprawled by their tents, drinking wine out of their tin mugs. We actually had the nerve to sit down close by, and Hugo said, 'Ah, the little schoolgirls! Don't tell me you've given the gymnastics instructress the slip!' They had passed us during the morning when we were touching our toes and jumping up and down on the count.

'She looks like Brigitte Helm,' said one of the boys. 'If we had been taught by a goddess we might have become keener athletes.'

I was amazed, never having thought of Fräulein Willfried as anything but a tyrant, certainly not possessed of sexual charms.

'Did you see her in *At the Edge of the World*?'* asked Karl Neudecker (of course I didn't know his name then). 'Fantastic. The perfect camera face. I couldn't take my eyes off her.'

'She was more spectacular in *Metropolis*.'

'But more sympathetic in the Grune picture. The role suits her personality.'

---

* *Am Rande der Welt* directed by Carl Grune for UFA.

That may not be an exact record of the dialogue, but it was along those lines. We three girls sat enrapt. The discussion continued, analysing Grune's earlier film, *The Street*, Christel condemning him as a man who could not make a popular movie. Personally I had never thought of films as anything but entertainment, good or bad, depending on how it related to me! I liked romance. I still do!

'What do *you* think?' Hugo asked me at one point. I shook my head, blushing, which he couldn't see in the firelight. Months later he said I had embarrased *him* because I hadn't taken my eyes off him the entire evening!

January 27th

A surprise visit from Christel, an offer of friendship I felt, since Hugo is away. I don't really understand her, she had a *von* to her name before she married Karl, and apparently lived in a small castle! Why does she denounce it all? I'm not sure how honest her denouncements are – especially as she doesn't renounce her comfortable life. Apart from the maid and the silver dishes (wedding presents) the apartment is extremely well set up. I wouldn't mind it, although the modern furniture doesn't appeal to me, those so-called 'tubular' chairs aren't comfortable, I like nice deep velvet cushions.

Nurse told Christel she couldn't stay long, my blood pressure was high and I had to be quiet. 'I shan't make a noise,' said Christel. She's a funny looking girl, with that thin intense face and dark hair. There's an Egyptian look about her, what was the name of the princess who found Moses in the bulrushes? Christel reminds me of the illustration in my bible. *As always* she talked about Bolshevism. I was quite surprised that she wants the National Socialists in power. She and Hugo usually want *different* things. I said this, and she explained her reasons which seemed mad to me. 'We have to destroy the Social Democrats and the Socialist trade unions and the most expedient way is to bring Hitler into power. They couldn't last long, Elisabeth. Capitalism would collapse, and we'd take over.'

I wasn't sorry when Nurse came in again and sent Christel home. I didn't put my bedside light on. I lay in the evening light and went over my list of names for the baby.

January 29th

11.50pm. I have just had my first pains. Very slight. I am so afraid. I am writing this in case I die in childbirth. I love Hugo. If my baby lives, look after it. I am going to call Nurse.

January 30th

Twelve hours later. The pains have just begun again. Last night they came for an hour or so and then stopped. This time the doctor is on his way. Why wasn't I told I might bleed? I thought I was having a haemorrhage. Nurse said, 'Oh, that's perfectly normal. Don't fuss.'

January 31st

My son was born late last night! Dark hair . . . but Nurse assures me that it will soon fall out and he'll be as blond as we are. Blue eyes. No neck at present, but no doubt it will emerge! Ten fingers, ten toes, one penis, one small birthmark on the left calf. What a day that was, January 30th 1933. Hugo came home, Hitler was made Chancellor and Elisabeth von Stahlenberg became Michael's mother!

February 4th

Klara came to see me. Michael is the first baby from our lot at school. She said 'Why not Adolf as a second name?' I said it was an *ugly* name, it was enough to have the double birthday – his own and Germany's!

February 5th

For the first time since he came home Hugo talked to me about his visit to Berlin. He stayed with Moritz, who tried to persuade him to throw up everything (not me, of course!) and to live there permanently. At first it did not occur to me that Hugo would even consider it, and I began to say what a crazy idea, etcetera. He cut me short, saying it wasn't so crazy, he was bored to death with the foundry, uninspired by glass manufacture and depressed by the provincial life. All I could think of was how we could *live*. The description of Moritz's two-roomed apartment at the top of a seedy house *depressed me* far more than the life we lead here! I have always lived in the provinces, and in *comfort*. The *Gasthof* is not elegant, no tapestries, paintings or minstrel gallery, but very warm and homey. My bedroom there is more to my taste than the one we have here – although I would not say so – I like the painted furniture and the low ceilings, and my doll collection that *Schwiegermutter*,* as she likes me to call her, would not let me display,

---

* Mother-in-law.

although there is the perfect alcove beside the stove. If Hugo left the family concerns, where would our money come from? I have become used to spending freely on food, for one thing, and clothes. I had to have maternity clothes, I wasn't being unnecessarily extravagant, but I didn't have to think can I afford it, as Mutti always has. I said this to Hugo in a careful way, he has never suggested himself that I liked the idea of marrying him because of the background – but others have. I said, 'What would you do? We have to think of Michael's future.' He said 'The whole point is, there's work for me, really interesting work. Radio, for one thing. Film for another.' I couldn't help pointing out that he'd no experience of either, so what sort of position could he hope to have. I mean, in the family business he's a director, from the word go. Even an idiot gets a good salary if he's related, there's Hugo's cousin Helmut who has a head like a block of wood. They've given him an office and invented a title for him, and he has enough money to staff his house with servants and take a holiday in the Orient. I felt quite chilled at the thought of our security going. I suddenly became deeply attached to this house, I thought of Michael being brought up in a city, smoke, cars, crowds. It wasn't what I wanted, not what I had envisaged. I tried to explain to Hugo, but he said, 'Don't talk nonsense.' Anyway, this time I was not going to risk a scene, so I tried to find out more in a conversational and interested way. It seems that he had made enquiries when he was in Berlin, and even had some sort of preliminary interview. I shall do all I can to discourage him.

February 11th
It's no good. I can't write regularly. I thought, being in bed all this while, I'd keep up long entries, but the days are absolutely squashed with things that have to be done. Nurse is very keen on a hospital-type routine. She bustles in about 6am, with Michael to be fed. That takes ages (he is *so slow*) and then she gives me a ghastly blanket bath. Breakfast follows, and I look at the newspaper. I want to keep up with events, Michael is back for his next feed at ten – and so it goes on, meals, visitors, an afternoon sleep, the doctor, and so on. Tonight Hugo has gone to dinner with his parents, so I have time and privacy.

My father-in-law has been invited to a meeting on February 20th. It is supposed to be a secret, but Hugo told me it's to be at the Reichstag's President's Palace, and *Hitler will be there*. Hugo says he has heard that the head of the United Steel Works has been asked (can't remember his name) and Krupp and others, all leading industrialists. Hugo said he might go to Berlin at the same time. He is going to suggest it tonight. I am hoping his father will say he has to stay here, at the foundry.

February 12th
Christel came today. She was even more tense than usual and made mysterious remarks like 'I may have to go away. I may not be able to stay here.'

February 14th
The von S contingent of cousins made their pilgrimage to the cradle today. I was deferred to, but I felt like the delivery van that brought the goods. I delivered the infant and am no longer of interest!

February 20th
Hugo and his father are in Berlin. Nurse has given me detailed descriptions of all the people she has laid out, their last words of gratitude to her before her macabre services were required, and the undying admiration of the bereaved. I said it must be a pleasant change to look after a new baby, and she said the beginning of life and the end were all the same to her, until she was in her own box she had a duty to serve.

February 23rd
They're back. My father-in-law is entirely committed to the NSDAP, Hugo said. Any doubts he had were wiped away. He gave thousands of marks to the party, the Marxists are going to be eliminated, Hitler said. He told Hugo this on the way home, *in confidence* – but did the chauffeur hear? – and Hugo told *me*, confidentially too. Everyone tells the secrets of others in confidence. It's like the beginning of the human race, two soon become four. If each one at that conference told just one person it will soon be all over Germany! *I* told Christel, who came again to see me. She has always seemed so superior in every way that it gave me a feeling of power to frighten her about Hitler's pronouncements about the Marxists. She said, 'Karl was right not to join the Party.' I said, 'Why did you?' She said 'Because I have to go the whole way. Karl never believed as strongly as I do. God, the people are mad. The NSDAP will destroy the country.'
Christel is the one who is mad!

February 25th
The news today is that the communist headquarters in Berlin were

raided, and the papers found there prove they were *planning a revolution!*

I was allowed out! At last! My legs felt like pieces of straw! I have felt well for weeks, I think it is stupid to keep one in bed so long. Having a child isn't an illness.

February 26th
Nurse has gone!

Terrible row with Hugo's mother. She wants us to engage a nursemaid. *I* want to look after my own child. What would I do here all day alone? I telephoned Mutti – to complain – who said most young wives would give anything for the opportunity. Why did I want to get up in the night when Michael cried?

February 28th
I fed the baby at 6am. He belongs to *me* now. I went back to sleep, to be wakened by Hugo waving a newspaper and saying that the communists had set the Reichstag on fire. I am glad he isn't in Berlin. The communists deserve all they get. I shall be so glad when the elections are over. You can't turn on the wireless without hearing Hitler or Göring or one of the others telling us why we must vote for them. I agree that there has to be a campaign, but I like to hear music when I switch on!! What a relief it will be when the new government is in power. Vater said it is a good thing that the communist plot was discovered, because now the threat is clearly seen by everyone.

March 1st
Mutti came to the house to look after Michael so that I could go with Hugo and some other friends to the rally tonight. Hugo is asleep, but (at 4am) I am still wide awake. The Square was packed, and after the speeches, there was a torchlight parade. The streets were festooned with flags, and we joined the march, singing. I felt *carried away*, it was like taking part in a wonderful dream, my legs didn't even ache, and we must have walked for miles, all round the town more than twice! There were several bonfires and the heat from the flames and the torches made it as warm as a summer night. People came out of their houses and gave us food and glasses of wine, and shook our hands. It rained at about eleven o'clock, and that ended the affair. We had parked the car in Ludwigstrasse, and luckily it was unharmed – we saw several cars damaged by the marchers who became too excited. Eight of us jammed in, and we continued singing all the way home. We

dropped everyone at their front doors. I would have loved to have gone in for more drinks (we were pressed to accept) but I thought of Mutti, anxious to get to bed. Perhaps we *should* have a nursemaid!

March 2nd
The most terrible thing has happened. Christel and Karl were arrested last night and taken to the SA barracks! Apparently while we were singing and marching and listening to the election speeches, storm troopers went into half a dozen houses and made arrests. It never occurred to me that Christel was involved in the Plot, but now I think about it I realize that she must have been, all the talk about 'going away'.

Hugo is very upset, he kept saying 'Why was she such a fool?' There will be a trial and I suppose they will be imprisoned – unless of course they are acquitted. Perhaps it was only Christel who was really in the thick of it. I don't know any of the others personally who were arrested, but Vater says two are Jews and one a schoolmaster.

March 5th
Everyone voting. Surely there is no question of the outcome? Hugo says the Centre Party might be a stumbling block to the NSDAP but I don't believe it. Vater says Chancellor Brüning (well . . . *ex* Chancellor B!) is accusing the NSDAP of starting the Reichstag fire themselves!! No one will swallow *that*. Anyway I spent *my* day casting votes for a nursemaid. Yes, I've succumbed. It dawned on me that if I don't have help, I'll be forced to stay at home when Hugo goes to Berlin or wherever else the whim takes him, just as I was when I was pregnant. I had to decide between Anni, aged 37, stout and kind (from the Black Forest by way of the Königstrasse Hotel where she was housekeeper) and Hannelore, pretty, 20-ish and an experienced nurse. She worked in Nuremberg, second in command in a very grand nursery. My mother-in-law wanted me to take her, so I cast my votes for Anni. My mother-in-law said 'You must make her wear a uniform.' I said 'SA or SS?'

March 6th
A majority of 16. Hugo says it isn't good enough. We had another small argument today. He half accused me of bringing him back from Berlin on the eve of Hitler's appointment as Chancellor! It was too silly to fight. I said he *chose* to return and wasn't it better to be home for

his son's birth. He hugged me and said yes, so everything was back to normal. He said he had made enquiries about the Neudeckers, but no one is sure where they are being held. We're giving a celebration party tomorrow. I've ordered a cake from Konrad's bakery.

I had a long talk with Frau Konrad who has known me since I was small. On the bus going I had the wonderful idea of having the cake made in the shape of a *Hakenkreuz*,* not only would it be easy to cut in equal slices, but it would look so dramatic as a centre-piece for the table. I was disappointed when Frau K dissuaded me. 'I don't have the correct baking tin,' she said, 'and for such an important party it might go wrong.' 'What about a design in icing?' 'Swastikas are black, and black icing isn't appetizing.' Well, I just had the feeling she didn't want to make it like that, and I said to her that if I had had the idea, many others would be bound to have the same thought. She said, 'We are traditional bakers, Liese.' (She has always called me Liese, and I can't correct her, although I do feel now that I should be addressed in my married name.) 'Let me make you my best party cake, like I did for your grandparents' Golden Wedding.'

She insisted I stay for lunch, she has four tables in the window and she wouldn't let me pay her. She made her spinach omelette, and of course I couldn't resist the cherry tart with cream. The taste of it takes me back years! She asked all about Michael, she is a grandmother now, and made comparisons. 'Willi smiled at three weeks, it wasn't wind, he looked at me and smiled.'

When I left her I went to Mann's, and bought six miniature flags, so I shall have my swastikas on the cake after all. I told Hugo and he said life is always a compromise. He had ordered French champagne, and we have our list of forty guests. My figure is back to normal, and I will wear my pink chiffon.

We have some distinguished visitors, including the Bürgermeister. My mother-in-law hinted that *my* parents shouldn't be invited . . . but I pretended I didn't understand. I have made the table plan and put them with the Mansteins so no one will be offended or embarrassed. I think I should be awarded the Hostess Medal for Tact!

March 9th
The party was a triumph, everyone said so. I would like to give a party at least once a month. There were toasts and speeches, and already I have been asked to luncheon by the mayor's wife, who told me to call

* Swastika.

her by her first name – which is the same as mine! How we laughed when I made the same request! Thank heavens I have Anni to look after Michael.

March 10th
Michael gave his first smile. To me, naturally.

March 14th
So much has happened since my party. I suppose I should write 'our' but really it was mine. I have nothing to be ashamed of to the von Stahlenbergs. No one is responsible for their birth, it is what they *become*. Look at the Führer! (I still haven't got round to *Mein Kampf!*) *Schwiegermutter* may try and make me feel less than I am, but whether she likes it or not I am now a von Stahlenberg, and personally I think I have brought fresh air to their stuffy self-satisfied clan. *Schwiegervater* isn't so bad, quite nice if I am honest. Snobbishness is worse in women, and he doesn't look down on the lower orders. I have heard him speak warmly of his workers, as if he valued them as people, whereas *she* thinks of them as servants. She chokes when she has to talk to Mutti, but the other evening *he* made a point of going over to Vati and asking him about business.

Anyway, I had lunch with the *other* Elisabeth – a 'ladies' lunch', eight of us, all wives of important men in our community, although I was a little surprised that Frau Willfried had been included. We had a very pleasant soup, followed by different cold meats and salads.

Hugo is very pleased that Goebbels has been made Minister of Propaganda. He says it is excellent for Moritz, and might be good for *us.* I intend to stay put, life is just beginning to be fun. I have been asked to join the Orphanage Committee.

March 15th
I have ordered tablecloths and napkins to be embroidered at the convent.

March 16th
Anni is wonderful with Michael, and doesn't try to exclude me. I learned from the wives at lunch the other day how some nurses do all they can to take the mother's place. Of course, some mothers are only too pleased to take a back seat. Went to the movies and saw *Das blaue*

*Licht.** It is about a strange blue light which casts a spell over an entire village. Young people climb the mountain to reach it and fall to death. A solitary girl, a kind of gypsy, reaches it safely, and is stoned as a witch. I found it very moving. Her love affair with a Viennese painter, who leads to her death by his discovery and theft of the crystals which *gave* the mysterious light, made me cry. I borrowed Hugo's handkerchief and came out with red eyes.

March 17th

H wants to go to Potsdam for the opening of the first Reichstag of the Third Reich. He is stirred by what he thinks are historic occasions. I suppose it *is* very important, but I'm happy to hear about it on the wireless and see the pictures in the papers. I know it would be thrilling to be there, in the same way that the procession was the other week, but as I'm still feeding M, I can't possibly go. Perhaps I can arrange something, ask people to dinner, so that it isn't convenient for him to be away.

March 18th

I went to the convent to select the embroidery silks. The novices looked sweet, but I have heard they are not always happy, the discipline is strict. The Sister in charge of the workroom told me they had received instructions to greet visitors with the *Deutsche Gruss*† salute, but she did not intend to implement it. I said, 'Heil Hitler!' when I left, she just smiled and said goodbye!

I chose various shades of yellow and orange for a sunflower design.

March 21st

Hugo is in Potsdam! Moritz was involved with the broadcast, and had arranged for Hugo to be in the Garrison Church for the ceremony. Too good to turn down – and Hugo said confidentially that he may have a personal introduction to Goebbels. I listened to it on the radio from beginning to end, it must have been a wonderful sight, all the uniforms, the old field marshals, generals and admirals coming together at such an historical spot. Hindenburg made a short speech, I felt quite emotional. His voice is very feeble, but he talked of a proud, free

---

* *The Blue Light*, 1932, directed and produced by Leni Rienfenstahl (who also starred), Béla Balázs and Hans Schneeberger (the photographer).
† The Nazi salute.

and united Germany, and it is *impossible* not to feel patriotic. Hitler answered him with humility, he said 'We pay you homage' and then the commentator said they shook hands. It must have been a breathtaking scene to witness, and Hugo was right to go. I want to be very careful not to have another baby soon. Apart from what it does to the figure, I believe it is essential I am free to be with Hugo for *all* the reasons I've written about earlier.

March 27th

I have met Moritz at last! What an odd creature he is, nothing like the man in my imagination! I had thought of someone rather *princely* but he is big and *stout*, astonishing for a young man. He is most affected in his manner, and uses a monocle for his left eye. He has a paunch, like a fifty-year-old. He came back with Hugo from Potsdam, and talks of nothing but politics, from breakfast onwards. All the events which have taken place, and I hadn't an inkling! He calls Goebbels brilliant. There was a 'brilliant' NSDAP coup with the Bavarian Government two weeks ago, a 'brilliant new law' (which I couldn't follow and didn't like to ask) and many other 'brilliant' happenings!

An entire evening was spent reminiscing with Hugo in *detail* (he has a photographic memory) over a meeting at the Berlin Stadium when Hitler spoke. Hitler arrived late, the streets were jammed tight. Moritz remembered the conversation he had with the man next to him in the stand, what Hugo said, what he said, and – of course – what Hitler said. He gave an hilarious imitation, he has Hitler's voice to perfection. Goebbels is already moving into his new Ministry, and an architect has been employed. Moritz will have an office there as soon as it is ready. 'You will take your place,' he said to Hugo, and he was obviously mimicking someone, probably from the University, because Hugo laughed and encouraged him to go on. I asked later (when we were in bed) if Moritz meant Hugo would take his place in the Ministry, and he said Mortiz had all kinds of wild plans, but they probably wouldn't come off. I made Hugo be very careful in bed. I am going to see a doctor next week (*not* Dr R, who doesn't believe in interfering with God's will) who runs a special clinic.

March 30th

I wish Moritz would go. He is still on vacation and eats like a goat – *everything* that is put before him! I am sure he would consume paper bags if I chopped them up and put them in a sauce.

April 2nd

He went yesterday, suddenly, after telephoning Berlin. Something to do with May Day being a national holiday. I heard Hugo and his father discussing transport for some of the foundry workers to go to Berlin, but I don't suppose it will affect us much here. I had the guest room thoroughly cleaned after Moritz's departure. There were crumbs everywhere, even under the bed!

Apparently there is a boycott of Jewish shops, announced by Hitler. Hugo's father is against it, and I must say it seems rather unfair. I'm not mad about the chosen people, but I like their merchandise. Who will make Vater's next new suit?

It was astonishing how little Michael responded to the awful Moritz. I am sure his breath must have smelt horribly of onion, beer and pickles, but whenever Moritz picked him up, M beamed! Moritz only took time off from his political analysis to *sing* – and in all languages. *Frère Jacques; Deutschland, Deutschland über alles* and an English song beginning ha ha ha hee hee hee, which made Michael actually chuckle like a grown child. Nurse was right, the dark hair has rubbed off, and now there is a fuzz of soft yellow down. I call him my treasure!

I just read this epistle from the beginning. I forgot March 4th! I didn't even make an entry. My mind is like a coffee strainer. No, that's not true, I have a great deal on my mind, and I cannot . . .

Hugo called me (three hours ago) to go to the movies. The Kultur-bund has a special showing of *Der Rebell*.* The ending was of the 'lump in the throat' variety. Hugo and Gregor had a long discussion after-wards, we all went next door for beer. Hugo was very impressed by the use of flags in close-up, and the flag held by the student when he's shot. He called it a 'deliberate contrivance' in order to arouse national pride *today*, but Gregor (who had his hand up Elsa's skirt under the table, I saw when I dropped my handkerchief!) insisted that Trenker was con-cerned with the *visual effect* only, and that there was no ulterior motive. Both agreed that it was a film with immense contemporary applica-tion – which of course is why the Kulturbund had a special showing for its members. Gregor is quite a lively leader, and has attracted many new members in the four months he has been here. He comes, origin-ally, from Aachen. I asked if he had heard anything of Christel and Karl (their apartment is empty, and I have tried to telephone, but each time the operator has said there is no reply) and he said he understood

* *The Rebel* (Luis Trenker), a thinly disguised pro-Nazi theme.

their crimes were being assembled, and in the meantime they were being held in a special detainment centre. Elsa said, 'We had such fun at their New Year party,' and Gregor said, 'It doesn't look as if they'll be giving any more parties for a while!' Hugo said, 'I was in Berlin with Christel, I knew she was on the wrong track, I did all I could to dissuade her from going along with Marxist ideas.' Elsa said she thought Karl was partly Jewish, which may or may not be true, but Christel is of pure stock, her family were Prussians, and were honoured by Frederick the Great.

We were back late, but I had drawn off enough milk for Michael's feed, and Anni had given it to him. He looked so small and beautiful lying in his crib (he's almost too big for it) and we stood looking at him for about twenty minutes. 'He might have been born anywhere,' Hugo said. 'An Indian village or in an Italian peasant community. But the lucky little so-and-so has picked a winning ticket, Germany in 1933, with parents who haven't made intellectual mistakes like the Neudeckers.'

'All the advantages,' I said.

'And a beautiful mother.'

April 15th

I went to the clinic for my appointment, and found it *closed*. Klara had come with me (although she is not married she had need of its services! She has had a number of lovers and is very much a 'free thinker'), having arranged my visit in the first place. There was a sign on the door with no further information, just *This clinic will not reopen.* Someone had drawn a Star of David on it, and Klara said, 'That's it, of course.' We went to the café a few doors up the street, and Klara asked some questions. I thought it was rather too bold, but the manageress was very open about it. She said that Dr Jakob (it was the first time I realized that the doctor was a woman) had been ordered to close her doors, and told that she was no longer allowed to practise. Apparently she had many American friends and had told the manageress (she came here every day for a snack) that she was going to go to New York and work there. There was opportunity for doctors in her field, she had even left a forwarding address. The manageress wrote it down for us, it was care of The Margaret Sanger Clinic, Brooklyn. I don't suppose I shall ever want to use it, but I thought I would put it down here, just in case. Anyway, it certainly hasn't solved my problem, with an amorous husband. I made Klara promise to find somewhere else for me to be fitted. She says she knows where she can buy a douche, and will get one for me. It is better than nothing, I suppose! I wish Hitler had let the Jews continue working just a few weeks longer!!

May 2nd
Everyone is talking about the celebrations yesterday. Hugo's father flew to Berlin in a private plane, at Dr Goebbels's invitation, and we are waiting for him to come home with all the details . . . and, I hope, some photographs in his camera. We heard Hitler's speech on the radio. The newspaper is full of it today. It must give a great wave of pride and self-esteem to all those workers who suffered in the Depression.

I have decided to take up embroidery. I don't mean on the grand scale, but I would like to make a blouse for myself to wear in the summer. I thought poppies would make a gorgeous blaze of colour, with perhaps cornflowers and sheaves of wheat in between. I could wear it with my dirndl.

May 4th
I *cannot* understand politics! Half the trade-union leaders who attended the Rally have been arrested. I'm *sure* there's a good reason. Even my father-in-law is bewildered. Men he was dining with on Monday, and who had sworn allegiance to the NSDAP, are in prison. Anyhow, the workers are to be protected, even without their unions. I remember Karl Neudecker talked about the unions and their power to help the underprivileged worker. If one thinks about it, then it is right that the unions should hand over that power to the government. If we're to get anywhere in the world, then we have to do it as *one nation*. As Germans first and foremost.

May 5th
Today Mutti telephoned in a great state. The mice were back! That is in spite of the two cats installed after the last invasion. They are too well-fed in the kitchen, but they have such sweet faces no one can resist giving them tid-bits. Herr Brokdorf is going to be called in with all his murderous paraphernalia! Well, he got rid of the beetles once, so I hope his traps and poisons do the trick before one of the guests finds a mouse in her soup.

May 9th
Berlin. We are staying with Moritz's mother, all four of us, Hugo, Michael, Anni and me! This is the result of much wrangling and arranging, because I didn't intend to let Hugo come alone for a second time. Moritz has telephoned and written every week, but Hugo doesn't tell me exactly what is going on, although only a fool would not gather that a job is in the offing. I made it plain, when the invitation came, that I couldn't leave Michael, but that I wouldn't stay cooped up in the house at the mercy of *Schwiegermutter*! I also said from all I'd heard, Moritz's apartment wouldn't accommodate us. He fixed up the rest, a couple of telephone conversations and Moritz said his 'Maman' (he calls her 'Maman' in the French manner, another *pose*) would be delighted to accommodate us. So here we are, established in a huge, gloomy flat in Charlottenburg, with 'Maman' and her two English servants, a man and wife, tremendously pro-Hitler, Gladys and Stanley. Stanley is their surname. Gladys is tall, thin and pale, very English, and Stanley is shorter, and changes his dress several times a day, according to the work he is doing. At night, when he serves the dinner, he wears gloves. 'Maman' is big and heavy, like Moritz, and *dotes* on him. She is extremely cultured, and knows a lot about art, and I am fascinated by the conversations. As usual, I can add very little. I sit and look interested, and try to remember enough so that at least I can write it down here. Moritz's old nurseries have been opened up for Michael, they are *amazing*. The night nursery leads off from the day nursery (M apparently had an English nanny followed by a French governess) and the night nursery contains a mahogany cot and a high bed with mahogany carved head and foot. In the cot my little treasure looks utterly lost! Together the two rooms cover an area the size of the top floor of the *Gasthof*! Schoolbooks (in English and French) are still on the shelves, likewise his toys. He had a collection of music boxes which are arranged in a glass-fronted cabinet, and he (Moritz) unlocked it for us, so that Michael may listen to the assorted waltzes, jigs and folk tunes. Anni ('Maman' insists on calling her 'Nanny') is confined to these quarters, Gladys brings her meals on a tray.

We arrived about three o'clock, having had lunch on the train. 'Maman's' car met us, driven by Stanley in his chauffeur's attire. The car is old, a Minerva, the wheels were almost as high as my shoulders, not a scratch on it and one feels very grand riding along and looking out, sedate and perpendicular!

The apartment building is vast, and Stanley unlocked the door for us with a key that he then pushed through the keyhole and locked us in from the other side. Another key unlocked the lift, and when we stepped out, Gladys was waiting with *her* keys to lock it up again, and then to unlock and lock the heavy front door of the apartment. 'Maman' greeted us, and we took 'English tea' with her in the drawing-room. The curtains are brocade and lace and the furniture mostly Biedermeier (Hugo tells me – I called it heavy and old-fashioned!) but some French pieces. After tea we rested – our bedroom is in keeping with everything else, old, dark and overstuffed – and Moritz joined us for dinner. 'Maman' dominated the table. She was once an actress!* She made no secret of the fact that she was illegitimate and that her mother was English, her father a German aristocrat. She performed first on the stage and then in the movies.

Maman	Thanks to the great Englishman Paul Davidson.
Me	Who is Paul Davidson. . . .
Maman	He elevated the film to art. Through him I met Max Reinhardt. And made some money for the first time.
Moritz	Maman was one of the first actresses to work in the new studios at Tempelhof.
Maman	I gave it all up when the war started. Ernst von Wolzogen† refused to write any more scenarios. He said that the masses preferred the banal. I agreed with him. Anyway, audiences only wanted the American Westerns.
Me	Do you have any photographs of yourself. . . .

At this point we were served with 'pudding', with 'Maman' exclaiming over its texture and promising before I left to show me her albums. After dinner I was tired, and went to bed. Moritz and Hugo went out, which I hadn't anticipated (I would have stayed up!) to go to a night-club. 'One can't be in Berlin and go to bed early,' Hugo said, as he changed his clothes. Tomorrow I shall rest after lunch.

May 11th
4am
I won't be able to sleep tonight. It was lucky I had my rest this after-noon, because we were out from 9 o'clock, watching the students building a bonfire of books in the square opposite the University (in

---

* Under the name of Lotte Fromm, she performed at the *Freie Volksbühne* in 1890 and had a non-speaking role in the film version of Reinhardt's *Sumurun* in 1910.
† The poet.

the Unter den Linden). It appeared as if the library shelves were being cleared and just hurled onto the growing pyramid; sacks, barrows and boxes were emptied out. The word must have spread all over Berlin. Moritz came for us at six, but 'Maman' insisted that we had dinner first, and dinner wasn't ready before 7.45. She asked if it would be possible to drive to the site, but of course it wasn't (the streets were jammed), she was obviously dying to see for herself. Hugo, Moritz and I linked arms so as not to be separated. As far as I could make out, M has been involved in the preparation of the event, because he brought with him several printed proclamations, urging students to destroy any books which are subversive and strike 'at the root of German thought and the German home'.

'Maman' said it was utter nonsense. 'You're certainly not taking any of *my* books, my boy!' 'You'll have to put new covers on them,' said Moritz, 'I'll get you some tomorrow.' 'Maman' was furious. 'Just what books are you going to conceal?' 'All that sexual stuff. Havelock Ellis and Margaret Sanger.' 'If it wasn't for Margaret Sanger you wouldn't be an only child. You'd have had none of the monetary advantages I was able to bestow.'

I hadn't heard of Margaret Sanger until Klara and I tried to go to the clinic. It's always the way, once you learn something new, you hear about it afterwards again and again.

Hugo thought it seemed far-fetched to rid the country symbolically of writers. Moritz said it wasn't symbolic, but actual. Hugo asked 'You mean I won't be able to go out next week and buy *Totem and Taboo* (by Sigmund Freud)?' 'No,' said Moritz, 'nothing by Jews.'

Hugo was upset, I could see. He often quotes Freud in his arguments. M gave quite a speech over dinner on what he calls 'the regimentation of culture'. He went on so long his food was cold, and then he wouldn't eat it, and it was cleared away, which made 'Maman' angry. It was a strange dinner altogether. (I don't mean the food which was very nice!)

By the time we reached the University, the crowd was dense and it was a slow process. Several important members of the Party were there, including Dr Goebbels (Moritz refers to him always as The Doktor), and it was by hitching ourselves to a small official group that we managed to get as close as we did. It must have been midnight when the head of the torchlight parade came into view, to a great, deafening cheer from the onlookers. As the first students reached the square they hurled their torches onto the books to light them. They must have been soaked with petrol because they ignited immediately, the flames seemed to jump from the base to the top, and black smoke made the air quite acrid. From where we stood we felt the heat, and grey flakes of burnt paper floated and descended, some still glowing. I thought it was like a snowstorm in Hell! Singing broke out, and not only singing, because a fight began nearby. The man who started it was knocked to the ground, and I was terrified that he would be trampled to death. Fortunately some Brownshirts were at the spot, and rapidly put an end to the trouble. I saw them taking the man (and others) away from harm. It wasn't the time to make a protest!

I have never seen so many people, the procession went on and on and on, there were literally thousands of students, casting their torches into the fire, and as the books burned, so more were added. One was dropped close to us, and I just managed to pick it up before it was kicked by that continuous surge of marching feet. It was a book I had read when I was pregnant, by Erich Maria Remarque, and I said to Moritz, 'I want to throw this one!' It wasn't that I hadn't enjoyed the book, but the desire to add to the flames was overwhelming, as if by doing it I was making a positive contribution to the future which I *knew* was going to be more wonderful than anything anyone had experienced before. I felt that if I didn't throw at least one volume into that funeral pyre of the past, I would somehow have been letting Germany down. I think the most moving moments of all were when the flames finally sunk down into the ashes (I hope the wind doesn't come up, they will cover the city) and Dr Goebbels spoke. Everyone grew silent. After the din of crackling fire and the shouting and singing that had been going on for so many hours, the quietness was thrilling. He said, 'The soul of the German people can again express itself. These flames illuminate the end of an era and light up the new.'*

What Moritz said at dinner was right. You simply cannot build without first clearing away the debris, you can't allow yourself to be sentimental about the past. In a way it is like getting married and starting with new things, who wants to equip a kitchen with outmoded pots and pans, simply because your mother cooked with them before?

It seemed particularly touching that Michael had slept through the entire evening, the first time he hasn't woken up for a ten o'clock feed. I looked down at him in that outsize cot and thought, 'By the time you've grown up, Freud won't even be remembered!'

* She was quoting from memory. What he actually said was: 'The soul of the German people can again express itself. These flames not only illuminate the final end of an old era; they also light up the new.'

May 12th
We didn't get up until noon. How lucky we are in Berlin at this time, to be able to witness last night's (or should I say morning's?) demonstration. I will never forget the colour of the light from the fire, or the smell, or the noise, as long as I live.

Hugo went with Moritz today actually to *meet* the Doktor. I can't believe it will come off. I had lunch alone with 'Maman' and we had the most marvellous talk. I confessed to her that I felt inferior to the von Stahlenbergs, and she dismissed them as 'Ordinary peasants, my dear, who managed to push their way up. They only received a title because one of them made money. Scarcely *noble*. Education may have given latter generations a sense of self-importance, but it isn't *breeding*. Now, *my* father had genuine aristocratic lineage. Believe me, it makes all the difference. You can spot it in the features, let alone *manner*.' She told me that I had far more to offer – 'you're a fair woman' – which sounded oddly old-fashioned, but cheered me tremendously. She said she had taken to me the moment we met.

May 14th
We are still here! Anni suggested today that if we intend to stay much longer, she would like to take Michael back home. The English couple treat her as a lesser being – I am just beginning to be aware of the hierarchy of servants! In one way I would like to go home too, I find Berlin extremely *oppressive*, claustrophobic almost. All that locking of doors not only in 'Maman's' apartment, but everywhere. I can't decide if one is locked *in* or locked *out*. Such an expanse of iron greyness, too – but on the other hand, there is a feeling of suppressed energy and excitement, and that transmits itself to everyone so that you seem alert and electrically *charged* all the time. At home I often sleep in the afternoons, since I've had the baby that is, but here I not only don't feel tired, I would be terrified to sleep – because I'd *miss* something.

We go out every night to nightclubs – rather we went last night and tonight and Moritz has plans to take us somewhere in the Kleiststrasse tomorrow. I was rather shocked, for two reasons. First I thought it wrong that the cabaret artists should make fun of the Party, and secondly, I was horrified that both Moritz and Hugo should find them so funny. We went to a cellar club the first time, through a street door (locked, of course, until a membership card was produced and shown to the eyes peering through a kind of high letter-box) and down stone stairs, and through a bead curtain. There was a strong smell of wax from the burning candles on the tables, and wine, which was the only thing drunk there. The tables were wooden, and the customers sat on benches, not unlike a beer hall (but no beer!). The air was thick with cigarette smoke. Apart from the endless locking of doors, I will always associate Berlin with burning. I wasn't there when the Reichstag fire happened, but I have dreamt about it. I know how it *smelt*. I have been close to a burning building once in my life, when I was five or six years old. Most people think of fires as smelling nicely of pine cones, or faintly scented wood. I think of them as suffocating and bitter. In one way the pungent odour from the burning books made people more excited, like witchcraft night. The combination of tobacco and candle-wax all helped to make the audience more receptive, more *cruel*. Because the cabaret was cruel, and to me it wasn't amusing at all. For example, there was a song supposedly sung by the ghost of Geli Raubel. Each verse ended with a cry of 'Let me go!' One was about Hitler forcing her to tie him up during their love-making. The 'Let me go' refrain was capped by Hitler's final line, 'If you do, I'll shoot you!' The last verse was about his refusal to allow her to go to Vienna to study singing. She cried out, 'Let me go, let me go, let me go!' Then shot *herself*. Clowns rushed on to the stage, daubed her forehead with red paint, and put her in a coffin. I was really upset by it, I felt sorry for Geli Raubel when I read about her suicide, and I don't like anyone to make a mockery of pain and death. I said this strongly, and Moritz told me I was much too provincial. Hugo said there has to be freedom of speech. All the same, it seems odd to me that it is allowed to go on. If books that are a bad influence are banned, why aren't these songs? I have to add that Moritz wasn't laughing at a sketch about Ernst Roehm, who is chief of the SA and a *personal friend*. I suppose I am very ignorant, but I had to ask Hugo to explain it to me when we came home – the theme was about a concentration camp for 're-education and rehabilitation', but all the criminals were turned away, the only prisoners admitted were 'naughty boys'. Hugo told me that it is generally known that Roehm (and Karl Ernst) are perverts. I had to ask him what he meant by *that*, and he told me. I felt a fool because I had never heard of men being attracted to their own sex. It didn't seem possible, and Hugo told me how they make love (up the back passage). Of course I had known about hero-worship, and at my school girls had crushes on other girls – but I had never related it to *sex*. When he said about men forcing little boys to submit to them I felt physically sick, and could only think of my own son. 'I had a tutor who used to make me do gymnastics in the nude,' Hugo said. 'He always watched me in the bath, and when he thought I wasn't looking, he fondled himself. Naturally I always saw him!'

May 15th
'Maman' played me gramophone records of Richard Tauber. She knows him of course, and went to see him at the Kroll Opera House as his guest six times in *Das Land des Lächelns*!*

May 16th
Anni and Michael went home. We are staying another couple of days because Dr Goebbels has promised to see Hugo definitely this coming week. I wonder just how much influence Moritz really has – and what Hugo hopes will come of it if they do talk. I *hope* he lets Hugo down. I don't like Moritz (although I love 'Maman') and I should loathe to live in Berlin. Even my mother-in-law is preferable to this city.

Already I miss my baby!

Tonight we're going to the movies. 'Maman' is going to accompany us. Thank God it's not another nightclub.

Midnight
We saw *Acht Madels im Boot*† and it made me more determined than ever to visit a clinic! Like me, the heroine married in time to have her baby in wedlock, but I am so nervous every time Hugo makes love to me (very often at present) that I can't recapture my *summer house abandon*! 'Maman' dressed up for the outing as if we were going to visit the Führer himself! She was scathing about the end of the movie. 'As if *marriage* settles everything!' There was a ghastly club leader in the story, dominating and sadistic – she punishes poor pregnant Christa by making her jump off the diving-board ten times. I said she reminded me of one of our teachers. Hugo said he found her sexually attractive!

No Doktor G in evidence today, again. Hugo had lunch with Moritz in a very expensive restaurant, and *paid*. I said I thought M should have paid for himself, and Hugo said, 'We're not exactly paying hotel bills in Berlin, are we?' I said, 'We're not Moritz's guests. I wouldn't complain if you spent three times that amount on "Maman".' Hugo said, 'You're turning into a Jewess.' So I kept quiet after that.

* *The Land of Smiles.*
† Erich Waschneck's *Eight Girls in a Boat*, made in 1932.

I *bought* a blouse today. I've decided I couldn't face stitching away day after day. This one doesn't have poppies, but strawberries and bluebirds on the bodice . . . it goes with the dirndl beautifully, and requires no *effort*!!

May 17th
'Maman' in a great state about Richard Strauss's new opera.* I couldn't make out if the letter she was waving at us at breakfast was from the composer himself, or his librettist, Stefan Zweig. Something to do with an attack by Goebbels on Zweig, saying he was homosexual . . . utter nonsense says 'Maman' . . . and Strauss's collaborations in the past with a Jew. Moritz, who arrived in the middle of her hysterical diatribe, assured her that for certain important Germans in the artistic field, Jewish connections would be overlooked. 'You know perfectly well that he has defended Zweig, Maman. You just want to make a drama out of it.'

May 18th
Hugo met the Doktor at long last. Half an hour in his office, during which he asked Hugo a number of questions, was he married, what did he think of the interior of the Ministry, what did he think of modern art, did he like Munich, what did his work consist of at the foundry, was he merely his father's 'yes-man'? Hugo said he thought he answered well and to the point, and was totally honest throughout. I wanted to know his impressions of the Doktor. He said, 'Horsey little face . . . but charming, doesn't miss anything, I'm certain of that.' No mention of a job, however. At dinner (English roast beef and Yorkshire pudding) Moritz said 'You had better join the party, Hugo "old chap",' (he is always using English sayings, the way Hugo's mother throws French sayings into her conversation).

H	I don't like to be tied to doctrine.
M	Don't give me that crap about intellectual freedom.
H	I feel very strongly about it. Actually so does your boss. Remember that editorial in the *Angriff*? Joining now looks like opportunism.
M	So what?
Me	I think you should join. You believe in the Party. You've said so ever since I've known you.

* *Die schweigsame Frau.*

H	I like to retain the right to change my mind.
M	One always has that, 'old bean'. One doesn't announce the change, that's all.
Maman	How did I give birth to such a cynic?
Me	Moritz, does being a Party member mean he'll get a post with the Ministry?
M	No. But he won't stand much of a chance without. A pause.
Maman	What worries me is that young Franz Strauss is married to a Jewish girl.
Moritz	For God's sake, Maman! We've exhausted *that* subject . . .

'Maman', needless to say, thought otherwise, and held forth on the première of *Der Rosenkavalier* some twenty years ago! She said there was a tremendous fuss about where it should take place, Vienna or Dresden, and that she had acted as a go-between! Reinhardt would never have had a hand in the production if it hadn't been for her. 'His name wasn't even on the programme for the first performance, but *everyone* knew. There should have been some credit for me, if there is any justice in this world.'

Moritz and Hugo have gone out to a cabaret, but I decided to pack my things and have an early night, as we leave tomorrow. Moritz is driving us home – I would so much prefer to have taken the train – and wants to make an early departure. I am in a dilemma about Hugo and the Party. If he joins, as I was pressing him to do at dinner, then he stands a chance of getting the kind of position he wants. He is *bored to death* at home. But if he does work for Goebbels, then *I* will have to leave the house, my parents and friends and possibly end up here, where I will be depressed. Who should one put first, oneself or one's husband? Commonsense makes me realize that if he is happy in his work, then our marriage will go well . . . if he is frustrated by the daily tedium, then he might look for stimulus elsewhere, especially as marriage to me could be *blamed* for the situation. Without responsibility, he would be free to go where he pleased. Then again, if it wasn't the prospect of Berlin, I would love to be in the new German wave. I would like to meet the Doktor myself!

May 19th
I almost forgot to pack my diary! Moritz hasn't arrived yet (10.30) in spite of his insistence we leave before 9.45. They were very late last

night. 'Maman' as usual is up and immaculately dressed. She has the actress Emmy Sonnemann coming for lunch (Hermann Göring's mistress!) and has changed the menu three times. Gladys retains her English calm. 'I knew his wife,' 'Maman' said, 'I'm afraid this one doesn't have the breeding and style.'

Moritz is here, Stanley has just taken the cases down. Oh, I'm so relieved to be going. I will just give 'Maman' her parting gift, and then we're on our way.

(There are no entries for four months.)

September 20th
I feel very ashamed! All those good resolutions to write, and I haven't opened this book since we returned from Berlin. The evening we arrived – I had a sick headache from bumping about in Moritz's car on the country roads – we found the doctor here with Michael. He had a fever and a high temperature. Anni had summoned my mother-in-law down from the big house, and I can imagine the panic and the accusations. She had called the doctor. Both blamed me. 'How could you send a child of that age home with an inexperienced nurse?' were the dear lady's first words to me. 'A great mistake to wean him before nine months,' said the doctor. 'Babies fed on a natural diet of mother's milk seldom fall ill.' 'Oh, my daughter-in-law wanted to enjoy herself in Berlin.' 'I'm afraid the young women of today don't have the responsibility of your generation, Frau von Stahlenberg.'

Of course I was sick with guilt. They were right. I shouldn't have left him with Anni, and I should have gone on breast-feeding. It was true, I had stopped it for my own convenience, and because I wanted my figure back.

He was ill for three weeks, pneumonia developed, no joke for a baby of five months. I could hear his poor little lungs wheezing and squeaking even when he slept. His cheeks were scarlet, and on top of it all, he was teething. No wonder I let the diary slip my mind. All I could think about was that he might die, and that if he did it was my fault. I had even sent him home from Berlin on a draughty train, when he could have travelled in the car with us. I had given in to Anni who, let's face it, isn't a proper nurse, because she was sick of being a prisoner in Moritz's old nursery, spurned by the English couple. She lit a candle for him and cried at night. She felt as guilty as I did (I do, I should say) and now watches him so assiduously that he isn't allowed to cry. Even

Hugo is less anxious to go out in the evenings. For two months we didn't see a single film, and for Hugo that must be a landmark! Marriage may change one's life, but it is *nothing* compared to the change that parenthood brings. I would die for Michael.

Apart from all the worry, it was an uneventful summer. Once Michael was well enough to go out, we went on the usual picnics, and there was one memorable one when a flight of butterflies rose up from the long grass like flowers defying the pull of gravity. I wished (a) I had a camera and (b) I had concentrated more on nature study at school. Had they, in that moment, all wriggled free of their chrysalises? Michael laughed and pointed. It must have seemed like magic. But then, if one considers it, everything must be magical. He has no explanation for the wireless, the milk appearing in his bottle, an aeroplane, the wind blowing the tree outside his window.

September 22nd
Hugo in Berlin for three or four days, and M and I are staying in the *Gasthof* and being *cossetted*.

September 23rd
The most amazing meeting with Christel Neudecker. I was on my way to the shops when I saw her going into the station. She had a suitcase and a haversack, and the elderly lady with her carried a big box tied with string. I called out her name, and Christel turned, and I must say that I had a shock. She had always been pale, but she looked almost emaciated and drawn. She seemed pleased to see me, and said, 'Liese, how good to meet you like this.' I asked her if Karl was with her. The elderly woman said, 'Karl is still in the camp at Dachau.' I said 'What for?' Christel smiled and said harshly '*Schutzhaft!*'* She introduced the woman as her mother. 'We're clearing up the apartment.' I asked Christel where she was going, but she said she didn't know. I felt that she didn't want to tell me. Her mother appeared about to contradict her, and to give me the information, but Christel stopped her. 'We don't want to miss the train.'

When I went back to the *Gasthof* I told my mother, and she said she had heard that Christel's parents had paid enormous sums of money to have her released. I wonder what they did to have been arrested in the first place. Karl wasn't even a proper communist, so it couldn't have been that. No doubt one day the truth will come out.

* Protective custody.

September 25th

Hugo has decided to join the Party! He is home, having had several meetings with Dr Goebbels and other ministry high-ups. The new Reich Protective Custody Chamber of Culture has just been formed, and a place is going to be found for him although in exactly what capacity and *when* is uncertain. The idea (of Dr Goebbels) is to bring all the arts into a single organization so that standards will rise under government supervision. There are to be seven chambers – fine arts, music, theatre, literature, radio and films. (Have just counted – six! I'll have to check with Hugo on the seventh.) Hugo surely will have something to do with films, such a passion couldn't be overlooked even by ministry officials! He will have to break the news to his father.

September 30th

Well, I've joined too. The moment I had made the commitment I felt tremendously relieved and *free*. It was not unlike my emotions when I was confirmed, but that was a matter of course, and this was a positive decision I took for myself (and for my son). I know absolutely that it was the right thing to do, and as soon as I was a member 'on paper' I realized that I had been a *non-signatory* member from the moment our class said 'Heil Hitler' at the meeting in 1931. We'd all heard that Hitler was an emotional speaker and before he arrived we were giggling and doing our imitations in the back row of the lecture hall (it was at the Technical College). He spoke so simply that even Heidi understood, which is saying a lot, and everyone was impressed. We'd been encouraged to go (but not compelled) by our headmistress. I suppose about half a dozen stayed away (Klara pretended she was there and met her boyfriend instead!) and I cheered at the end. I hadn't given much thought to politics – one doesn't at fifteen or sixteen, which was the age of the class – but the Führer imbued me with hope for the future, an achievement when you consider that I hadn't felt a need for hope before. I actually *thought* about unemployment and inflation and communism, and National Socialism. A couple of days after I went back to trying to spot Hugo in the coffee house on his vacation, and forgot my intention to read the papers and buy a copy of *Mein Kampf*. I can only say that today I had no doubt that my inspiration 'matured' in the two years which have gone by, and I am proud and happy and confident to be a member of the NS Frauenschaft!*

* Nazi women's organization.

October 1st
He has broken it to his father. They had a stormy meeting in the office. Herr von S refused to understand. Of course one is bored at times, he said to Hugo, that's part of life. He said Hugo had a duty to carry on in a family concern, for the workers, for the memory of his great-grandfather whose hard work built up the empire it is today, and for himself. He said Germany relied on men of ability and leadership to bring industry up to the standards set by the government. When Hugo said he hoped to bring those qualities to a new profession in films, his father was momentarily speechless.

'Are you mad?' he said eventually. 'Films? Consorting with actors! And worse still, actresses!'

The seventh culture is *the press*.

October 7th
Another week has gone and no word from anyone. Hugo is irritable and restless. Having had the row with his father, he is anxious to hand over and *go*. It is humiliating to hang on, or at least not to have a date of departure. I told my parents, and they, contrary to Hugo's, are excited. Mutti's first thought was the money, but Hugo isn't going to be cut off without a penny. He inherits under his grandfather's will, and in a long, agonizing conference, he has agreed to continue as a director, attending monthly meetings. (I hope Dr G won't object!)

Michael says 'Mutti' and 'Vati' and 'Kuchen' . . . or sounds which I recognize to that effect.

October 20th
A call on the telephone from Moritz, a letter from the Ministry and Hugo is again in Berlin. I went to the doctor for the jelly for Michael's gums (they are very inflamed and it worked for the last tooth!) and decided to take the contraceptive bull by the horns. Hugo is so amorous of late I must do something.

Me   Heil Hitler!
Doctor Heil Hitler. Well, Frau von Stahlenberg, what can I do for you?
Me   I want something for birth control.
Doctor How can you greet me with Heil Hitler and ask for something like that?
Me   I'm frightened of getting pregnant again.

Doctor	To have another lovely son is the finest gift you can make to the Fatherland.
Me	I might have a daughter.
Doctor	(ignoring that) I have just received an official instruction from the Ministry to encourage family growth. By the beginning of this year the birth rate had dropped by a quarter from the figures at the beginning of the last decade. Official policy . . .
Me	It's very important for me to . . .
Doctor	You must forget *me* and think of *us*, of Germany. Large healthy families are the germ cells of the nation.
Me	I need some teething jelly for the baby.
Doctor	That I give you with pleasure.

October 21st

Vati's birthday. I gave him a pipe and Michael gave him tobacco! There was a party at the *Gasthof* in the evening, a *surprise* arranged by Mutti. All their friends were there (except for the Goldbergs, who have 'vanished'* to Holland) and I felt relaxed and happy to be there among all the acquaintants of my childhood. I was glad in a way that Hugo was in Berlin. I am conscious of our status difference, especially with Vati. Mutti comes from a good family, her father is a teacher, but Vati doesn't know much about *culture*. He is a kind, down-to-earth, practical man, and the best *host* imaginable. I wouldn't be so well-educated if it wasn't for Mutti, she was determined that I should go to the school I did, it was why we moved to the district. Hugo has never run down my old life, but I like to keep my worlds apart. It isn't easy for me to cope with all *their* snobbishness alone, but I *can* manage if Vati isn't there to remind them!

There were toasts and speeches and chicken and strudel, and the car to take me home at the end of the evening. Michael was awake and I took him into my bed until he fell asleep.

October 22nd

Hugo is asleep beside me, he doesn't stir when I get out of bed and put on the light to sit and write this at the dressing-table. It is stormy outside, wind and rain are extremely noisy. The moon was there earlier but now it is shining invisibly behind thick clouds.

Hugo takes up his post on January 2nd. We are not going to Berlin

* German: *untertauchen* lit. 'dive under': an expression current at the time.

46

BUT TO MUNICH! A new department is being set up there to compile a kind of newsreel library of party activities in Bavaria; these will be available for incorporation into all types of film, *even fiction*. If, for example, a director wants to make his story more realistic, he will be able to use footage of an actual youth rally, or a crowd cheering the arrival of a minister. Hugo says Goebbels is visionary about propaganda, sees it as a creative art. Reality alone does not 'stir the hearts of the people', a phrase Dr G used four times during their meeting. Hugo will be responsible for selecting subjects, directors, cameramen and so on. In a way he is disappointed because I know he hoped to be involved in the actual filming, and this is an office job. Dr Goebbels told him that everyone engaged in film-making must, *by law*, belong to the Chamber, so that Hugo will have the pick of the profession to choose from. 'Imagine,' Hugo said, 'being able to invite Pabst or Lang to work for us.' The Führer is personally interested in the formation of this department, he is conscious of the importance of the medium in building the new Germany, and *will want to meet those in charge*. How about the *wives* of those in charge? I feel weak at the prospect. What would I wear?

Not going until the new year is a tremendous advantage. It will give all the parents time to adjust, and for Hugo to hand over to his successor. I have only been to Munich once, but I loved it as much as I hated Berlin. It will be the first time in my life (except for that one week on the Obersalzberg) I will be living away from my mother and father. I feel that I will be a mother *in my own right* at last.

October 23rd
A visit from my sister-in-law. The olive branch! Well, well!

November 7th
Yesterday the Führer made a speech which has made *me* think about education. He said that the children of Germany already belong to the State. We, as parents, have had our education and we will 'pass on'. Our children, and *their* children 'now stand in the new camp. In a short time they will know nothing else but this new community.' I talked about it to Hugo and he read passages from *Mein Kampf* to me. Knowledge for its own sake is useless, he says. 'Stuffing with mere knowledge' is the actual phrase which appealed to me. 'Miss' did her best to stuff me with her favourite English poets, and mere knowledge it was, I didn't understand two thirds of what I recited. 'John Anderson

my Jo John, we clamb the hills together', one begins, and what a Jo John is I do not know to this day! Hitler stresses that physically healthy bodies are an important part of teaching, and also service to the State.

I'm not sure I want Michael to put the State first. On the other hand, it's a wonderful idea if we all do our best to make Germany great again. Healthy bodies *are* important, and no children look stronger or more beautiful than those little blond angels one sees in the country. It's a terrible confession to make but I honestly think that if Michael hadn't shed that dark hair he was born with, I wouldn't feel so proud of him. He might be mistaken for a little Jew!

November 8th
We invited the parents-in-law to dinner. Of course it all came out, the resentment at Hugo's decision, the stupidity of changing career in mid-course, the *social* mistake of joining a film department, even if it is for the Ministry. The wrong type of person is always attracted to enter-tainment!!

'I shall be working with one of the Hohenzollerns,' said Hugo.

They were *confounded.*

Then I said – and I congratulate myself, I am not known for the *mot juste,* or for proving myself apt in argument – 'The Party policy is to encourage young men of the upper classes to take administrative jobs not usually associated with their rank in society.'

'It is degrading for Hugo, nevertheless,' said my mother-in-law, spooning up the cream. She wears lipstick and it left a smear on the cream and the spoon!

'No,' Hugo said, taking his cue from me, and giving me a look of intense gratitude. 'It is the reverse of degrading. It is uplifting. Men with qualities of leadership have a duty to move out of traditional fields. When I was at the Ministry in Berlin, I met Max . . .' (Max is a prince! '. . . in a corridor. I asked him what he was up to, and he said he was in quite a junior position in the Chamber of Fine Arts.'

'If men like Hugo don't set the example,' I added, 'the Führer will be unable to carry out the task he has set himself.' (I admit I sounded a pompous and a bit like a newspaper editorial.)

'Oh, I know you can't wait to leave this house and move to a city,' said my mother-in-law.

'Hedwig, that is unfair.' Imagine my father-in-law actually defending me.

'Elisabeth sees her duty with me,' said Hugo.

48

And so it went on, finally reaching a general truce, reluctant but necessary if relations are to be continued.

When they left I went to bed. I felt exhausted, and had a bad headache.

November 11th
I *can't* be pregnant. I must be imagining it. Even feeling sick (and I'm feeling sick with fear) could be *in the mind*. My period is only one day late. It doesn't mean anything. But I have that odd sensation that made me certain I was having Michael, impossible to describe but a conviction that my body isn't the same as it was. I'm going to surprise the entire local population by being in church on Sunday. Last time I prayed to God to make certain I was pregnant, this time I'm going to pray that I'm *not*.

November 12th
Still nothing!

November 13th
My breasts hurt. I said to Hugo 'Wouldn't it be awful if I became pregnant just when we're going to Munich?' and he said 'Why?'

November 14th
If I haven't started by this time next week I'll know for certain. I *can't* have another baby. If we weren't moving I wouldn't mind so much.

November 15th
I told Klara. She's writing to Heidi who knows how to bring it on.

November 20th
No doubt. God didn't listen to me. On the other hand I know that if I am pregnant, no amount of prayers are going to make it untrue.

November 21st
Klara met me for coffee and cakes at Konrad's. She had Heidi's letter, we decided not to risk talking over the telephone. The operator is the mother of one of the girls from school, and things have a way of getting around in this town. Anyway, with the Party pressure on child-bearing, it wouldn't do to talk about *my problem*! Heidi knows a nurse in Munich who will *attend* to me if I can somehow manage to get there.

She has offered to put me up in her place – very nice, she says, paid for by her lover. She says she will lend me the money if I can't get it (100 RM), for which I am grateful. It will be difficult to get it from Hugo without telling him why, and he would never never agree.

November 22nd
A brilliant idea – and all agreed. I said to Hugo that I thought I should go to Munich to look around and find an apartment for us to move into after Christmas. I said it might be necessary for us to take a furnished place temporarily until the right one came along. I said Heidi had invited me to stay with her. He remembers her from the school camp. I said I would go in about a week's time, for two or three days. I wrote to Heidi.

November 24th
I suddenly thought of Grandmother Stofen's brooch. No one cares about it, I never wear it, it won't be missed if I sell it. I'll take it with me. It has sapphires in it and the drop pearl must be worth quite a bit.

November 26th
Heidi telephoned, we giggled half the call. We talked about my dress-fitting! The appointment has been made. H is going to meet me at the station. I'm excited about going, and terrified at the same time. But *relieved*. I don't know if it's my imagination but my breasts are bigger already.

December 10th
I'll begin at the beginning. I forgot to pack the diary but probably wouldn't have written it. Anyway, Hugo took me to the station on the Saturday morning, early, and being on the train alone gave me a heavenly feeling of independence, even though I dreaded the 'dress-fitting'. It's funny, I always thought being married would make me feel independent! The countryside looked so beautiful, that real winter look, thin black branches against a grey sky, and nice and warm in my first-class compartment! The silence when the train stopped between stations gave me a thrilling feeling in my stomach. Then the hiss of the steam and the jolt when we started off again. The only other people in the carriage were two nuns who read the bible and never spoke to one another. Their feet looked huge in their black boots. I had brought a magazine and a book with me, but didn't look at either. I knew absolutely that I was doing the right thing about this baby. Our first year

in Munich is going to be important, and I want to be a *hostess*, not a fertility symbol. I see only too well how I could be left behind by Hugo, and I want to meet the people he's going to meet.

Heidi was there as she had promised. Well, her hair looks marvellous, very *chic*, like an American film star. She wears blue on her eyelids, and rouge. When I think of her at school, those mousy-brown pigtails, and here she is, blonde and coiffed, it is like two different people. We took a taxi to her apartment, which is off the Kaulbachstrasse. We passed the Munich University hostel for girls and Heidi said that Elsa and Mimi (Adler) are there. I never thought they would go on to University, but apparently Mimi wants to be a teacher. Heidi says they are hard-up and the hostel is only 60 marks a month. You can get a meal for one mark!! We meant to invite them, but didn't.

The apartment is small, but extremely comfortable, with a huge double bed!! Insisted on by Herr Levi – but which I shared with H for the next nights! (He was told that her *sister* was visiting and that he mustn't show his face!) It took hours to get the bed up the stairs, Heidi said! In the end the base had to be cut in half and reassembled in the bedroom. The rest of the furniture is smaller – and modern. Heidi likes the latest, whatever it is, clothes, hair, chairs or songs. Herr Levi (who is married and has five children) gives her an allowance, and she also has a job as a secretary in the Brown House. She said, 'They don't know I'm being kept by a Jew!'

We passed the Brown House, which is the headquarters of the Party, very grand and impressive, like a palace belonging to a powerful king. I wonder if that is where Hugo will have his office? He doesn't know himself yet, but he has to go to Berlin again and presumably will find out more about *everything*.

Heidi had made my appointment with the 'dress-fitter', Frau Anna Goedbi, for the next afternoon. 'You might as well enjoy yourself to-night,' she said, and so we went to the Café Heck and had the most marvellous chocolate cake with mountains of whipped cream. When we got back to her apartment I brought it all up! After tomorrow, I thought, I'll be able to keep my food down!

Heidi telephoned Herr Levi at his office so that I could hear his voice. It sounded pleasant enough to me, but I know Heidi despises him. I told her that if she accepted his money she should try to respect him, but she plays terrible tricks on him, pretending she needs clothes or household repairs, and instantly he sends her *cash*. She makes up 'official' stories about the closing down of Jewish businesses in certain areas, so that he is afraid he is going to be selected for retraining. He is in the antique picture business and has a gallery. His partner isn't a Jew, so Heidi says in all probability he is perfectly secure. The gallery was once called Levi and Faulhaber. Now it is called only Faulhaber. She suggested to him that he should put *'Juden sind hier nicht erwünscht'** on the door as an added protection! She said he became angry with her and said he wasn't prepared to go to such lengths.

We took a taxi to Frau Goedbi's establishment, a ground-floor apartment in a quiet street in what looked to be a very respectable residential quarter of the city. Heidi made the taxi stop at the end of the street, we were not allowed to drive up to the house on instructions! When the taxi had gone we walked to the door and rang the bell. I must say I felt extremely nervous, and thought a baby would be preferable to the ordeal ahead. I had a small attaché case with nightdress, washing things, towels, etcetera which Heidi had written on a list. She, of course, had been ministered to by the 'dress-fitter'.

The lady came to the door herself, dressed in a dark grey costume and white blouse. She said 'Heil Hitler!' and we replied, and followed her into her apartment at the end of a long, dark corridor. She remembered Heidi and said, 'No more troubles?'

'Thanks to you,' said Heidi.

'You may safely leave your friend. Telephone me in about four hours' time, after she has had a rest.'

So there I was, deserted by anyone familiar! No words can express my horrified anticipation. Frau G led me into a bedroom with an iron bedstead and a washstand and two huge still-life pictures on the wall of dead pheasants and fruit. 'Wash your privates,' she instructed me, 'and put on your nightgown. No underthings. I will fetch you in ten minutes when I have prepared for your little operation.'

The ten minutes were like ten hours. I waited, shivering, in my nightdress, until she returned. She had changed too. She wore a big red rubber apron and a proper nurse's cap, very stiff and white, with all her hair tucked inside. A formidable sight. First she asked for the envelope, opened it and counted the notes. Then she took my arm and guided me into the *kitchen*. The big wooden table had been covered with a rubber sheet. Everything else in the room was draped with sheets, and on top of a shrouded table was an ominous little collection of enamel dishes and bowls.

* 'Jews are not welcome here', a Stürmer slogan.

She instructed me to lie on the table, with my nightdress hitched to my waist. Then she trapped my feet wide apart from each other with some awful piece of apparatus I couldn't see.

'Your lover doesn't want to marry you, eh?' she said, to the sound of swishing water. Heaven knows what was happening to me below.

'I'm married,' I gasped.

'You shouldn't be a naughty girl and take boyfriends.'

'It's my husband's baby, I just don't want it.'

'You prefer this?' It was certainly painful. There was a strong smell of disinfectant. She sounded disappointed.

'I thought I did!' I bravely made my little joke.

Her voice changed. 'Is he good between the blankets? What does he like to do best?'

'He's just ordinary.'

'You've plenty of experience?' She was definitely eager for revelations. I murmured that I found it difficult to talk in the circumstances. 'Your muscles are nice and tight,' she said. 'A man must find you exciting. When I was your age I had lovely firm thighs like yours.'

There was a moment of such excruciating agony that I screamed.

'Don't make a noise like that. We'll have the other tenants coming down to see what's the matter and then we'll all be in trouble.'

She released my feet. 'Up you get, Madam.'

She put her arm under my shoulders and heaved me into a sitting position, then peeled off her wet rubber gloves.

'I've douched your womb. Enough to poison the baby you don't want. Feel like a murderess? I wonder if it was a boy or a dear little girl?'

She took me back to the room with the bed and helped me to get under the dirty white *Daunendecke*. 'Sleep a bit while I clear away the traces.' Her face, devoid of hair, framed only by the starched white cap reaching her shoulders, reminded me of a picture we had in our history book of an ancient cardinal of Rome. From the angle above me she had hair growing out of her nostrils . . . not that they were in the picture! It was the lined forehead and the small eyes and the nostrils themselves, black caverns!

'I don't enjoy doing this,' she said. 'I like to deliver healthy new babies, not kill them in the womb.'

'Then why do you?' I asked with as much strength as I could summon up.

'Because girls like you do yourself damage when you try to bring on a miscarriage yourself.'

She left me and I slept. Heidi woke me. She was wearing a lambskin coat and hat, her blonde fringe curling from under it. 'Wake up. I've got a car outside.'

In a daze I managed to dress, catching sight of my white face in the mirror. My nose looked curiously pinched and I had bags under my eyes that were literally purple. Frau Goedbi, back in her grey skirt and jacket, hurried us off the premises. 'You'll have the miscarriage within twelve hours. Don't panic. If you bleed too much call a doctor, say you had a fall. He'll know you've done something but there's no proof. Just deny it. Heil Hitler!'

I could scarcely lift my arm in salute. Heidi grasped the other one, took my small case in her free hand. 'Wait till you see him. His name's Max.'

We walked down the street to the corner where the taxi had dropped us. A handsome uniformed SS man sat at the wheel of a Mercedes. He climbed out to open the doors for us. I almost fell onto the back seat. Heidi sat beside the driver, and I could hear her voice, brightly flirtatious, all the way back to her apartment. Inside the front door, he kissed her passionately, then left. 'Isn't he devastating?'

I nodded. 'I must go to bed.'

She waited until I was lying down, and supplied with a tray of food and drink, neither of which I wanted. Then she said would I mind if she went out with the handsome Max. 'I love these SS types. They're so exciting. I suppose it's the uniform.'

I said 'I think you love all types, Heidi.' She giggled and said yes, she supposed she did.

'If only the good-looking ones had the money, though.' She stopped at the door, looking at herself in the wardrobe mirror. 'You don't think I've got too much make-up on, do you? The Party is all for unadorned womanhood. But I feel naked without stuff on my eyes.'

The excruciating pains began before she returned. I was in the bathroom, clinging to the bath edge and practically passing out when she burst in, radiant from the night's success. The whole thing was a dream. I haemmorhaged over the floor and over all the towels. I fainted twice, and was convinced I was dying. I begged her to phone for the doctor. She remained miraculously calm. As she supported me, heaving me from the lavatory to the bed, she tried to tell me details of favours she had divided between Max and another glorious SS god called Erich. 'When you're better we'll have an evening out, just the four of us.'

Even in my hideous state I couldn't help smiling. 'Heidi, the last thing I want is to go out with a man!'

Eventually the bleeding subsided, and I lay back on the high bolster feeling depleted, drained dry and incapable of lifting my arm. Heidi had to hold the cup of coffee to my mouth.

'Honestly, you'll feel fine in twelve hours.'

I didn't. I said 'We must call a doctor.'

She reluctantly agreed, but wouldn't ask her own doctor to attend to me, afraid that she would 'get a bad name'. She inquired at the Marie Antonie Haus (the student hostel down the street) and was given the address of one used by the girls. She insisted that I get dressed, and we took a taxi the half-mile to his house. He was a big, stalwart and unsympathetic gentleman. He knew perfectly well what had happened although I refused to budge from my story. His narrow, gold-rimmed spectacles had thick lenses, and when he looked at me I felt he had the extra sense of seeing through my patently thin facade and into my mind. He said I was lucky not to be dead, I had a minor infection and I was anaemic but I deserved worse. He gave me red iron pills as big as buttons, and a medicine which tasted disgusting and told me to eat steak and spinach. As I was leaving, he suddenly called me back.

'Fräulein . . .' He obviously believed my wedding ring was a phoney. 'You'd better not let anything like this happen again.' I waited, my hand still on the door handle. 'You'd better let me give you some inner protection.'

I couldn't believe my luck. He clearly had a heart of gold under the large ribcage. I tried to thank him, I was weak enough to sink to my knees with gratitude but I clung to the door handle instead.

'Don't thank me. As a matter of fact I don't think the Third Reich is the place to bring children into, only you needn't repeat me.' He handed me a box. 'Put that in your handbag, read the instructions carefully, and come and see me again in about three months' time, when I can measure you more accurately. And for God's sake, if you find yourself pregnant another time, come to me and not to a back street butcher.'

Outside, in the little office, his secretary (no doubt his wife) presented me with his bill. Another thirty marks!! No *Mutterkreuz** for me!

* Mother's cross: awarded to fertile mothers by the authorities – bronze for three, silver for five and gold for ten children.

December 25th
How Michael enjoyed his first Christmas! He eats proper food now, and had his first taste of roast goose. I feel really fit again, I stayed with Heidi longer than planned because of an attack of influenza!! Mutti insisted I see the doctor here, and he prescribed a tonic. My tonic is in the expensive box given to me by the doctor in Munich!!

The pastor spoke boldly against the 'German Christians' under Reichs Bishop Müller, and against the resolutions drawn up after the rally in the Sportpalast in Berlin last month. Something about converted Jews not being allowed into the church and rewriting the bible. Hugo says he counts the days until the pastor is replaced after his outburst!

Anni is in love – unrequited I think. The chauffeur is the object of her affections. She knitted him a pullover for Christmas, and always manages to push Michael across the courtyard of the big house when her beloved is cleaning or polishing the car!

1934

January 10th

Last night in this house. It is still ours – 'for when we come home' as *Schwiegermutter* put it. The apartment we have taken in Munich is furnished. When I'm there I shall look around for something better. Still, all the cupboards and drawers here are empty, and the boxes have gone ahead. Thank God I have Anni to help me unpack. No room for a living-in servant, apart from A, but I shall soon organize daily help. Heidi assures me that there is no problem. She has a Jewish teacher (a friend of Herr Levi's) who is only too glad to be allowed to scrub the floor. I wouldn't want that, myself. I would find it embarrassing, but Heidi says it is doing a good turn.

January 11th

An *exhausting* day. But I am going to love it . . . a view of rooftops and the sense of being in a city even on the top floor! M cried and grizzled the entire journey. He's a country boy!

January 12th

The whole point of coming here was for Hugo to work close to home . . . and now he's off to Berlin again for two weeks. Even the location of this apartment (which I like rather less than I did) was chosen because it is near the Briennerstrasse and the Brown House. I miss Mutti! Nowhere to go for a chat or a meal. Heidi is no substitute for parents and friends. Anni complains about the noise at night and says she can't sleep. She doesn't accept my argument that the noises in the country are far more disturbing. The owl versus the motor-car! I think it's the chauffeur she misses, not the bird-life.

January 15th

I'm bored! I thought that I should be caught up in a social whirl, but I haven't met a soul. I didn't like Berlin but it was *exciting*. I wouldn't even mind Moritz. If I have to hear about Max's virility once more I shall scream.

January 16th
I must keep away from the Café Heck and the compulsive chocolate cake.

January 17th
I've done it! I've had my hair cut! I look like the American actress Carole Lombard. It was a terrible moment when I looked down at the floor and saw what had been my braids lying there, lifeless! I've had it curled too, just a little, and waved. No doubt that I look far more sophisticated. The hairdresser's shop is the most fashionable in Munich ... Heidi made the appointment for me, of course, and accompanied me during her lunch break. Inside it's all pink and gold, with mauve cubicle curtains. It was cut by a *man*, all very different from Frau Helga's attentions in the room over the post-office. What's more, the man was American, very dashing, with black hair and a moustache, like a film star himself. Anyway, I've had my 'old' hair plaited so that I can wear it pinned on if I feel I want to. It's extraordinary how light it feels without it. Quite strange. Now I need to go somewhere to be seen. Very flat sitting here in my bedroom with an elegant coiffure and my husband in Berlin.

January 18th
Took Heidi to tea in the Carlton Tea Rooms and indulged in three cakes. If I don't stop I shall be enormous by the time Hugo returns. But I had to take my hairstyle somewhere! Heidi wants me to make a foursome with her, Max and another SS boy, but I won't ... she doesn't understand me. I said 'I really do love my husband, and I wouldn't dream of going out with another man.' Any male friend of Heidi's would expect a flirtation at the very least, and probably a great deal more. H said 'Why are you worried, we could drive out to the Starnberger See for dinner, and you can't get pregnant, you're equipped.' As soon as I meet some new people I shall drop Heidi – gradually, of course.

January 20th
Michael walked! Four whole steps, and then fell into my arms. Anni cried, but M laughed and insisted on standing and tottering all after-noon. Lovely long talk with Hugo. He hopes to be back in four or five days. He was going to 'Maman's' to dinner tonight, and thought

Richard Strauss was to be one of the guests. 'Maman' had been very secretive about it all but had dropped hints. I *wish* I was there. I feel so provincial and cut off!

January 21st
I don't think I can stand this furnished place much longer. The bed is hard, and the lift broke down for the second time today. The view of the rooftops becomes monotonous after a week, and the couple who live below us have terrible rows on the landing! The front door slams as one or the other leaves in a rage every night. I haven't yet seen them. They lead a nocturnal life. In the day there isn't a sound.

January 22nd
Looked at two apartments today, one in the Ludwigstrasse, the other in the Kaulbachstrasse, but didn't really like either. I suppose it's silly to look, even, with Hugo away. The Ludwigstrasse one was the better of the two, quite spacious rooms, and the central heating was divine after the freezing outdoors! Red damask curtains throughout – *and* over the bed! The stout little widow in residence told me she planned to join her sister in Cologne ('Widows should be together for mutual comfort, don't you agree?') but that she was reluctant to leave her home. 'There are friendly spirits within these walls.' I wanted to ask how they demonstrated their friendliness.

When I reached home I was confronted by Anni who said she had made up her mind to leave. I told her we would soon be moving to a nicer apartment and begged her to stay until then before she committed herself. She agreed and also promised to find some kind of club she could join in order to meet people. She doesn't have a Heidi in Munich, and Michael's vocabulary doesn't allow even simple conversations.

January 30th
Hugo home the day before yesterday so he was here for Michael's birthday party. Didn't like my hair! Then had to admit it was fashionable and today said he was getting used to it. He *did* meet Strauss. He played to them after dinner, something from the first act of his new opera which he hasn't even completed. Most of his time was spent at the Ministry working out the year's itinerary, and selecting possible personnel for the new department. Everyone has to be 'investigated' before being approached, which annoys Hugo. He says the quality of

the work is what matters, not whether you have a Jewish great-aunt twice removed! He felt that half his time had been wasted, not the meetings with the Doktor, but those with lesser luminaries, busily justifying their positions! He found Albert Speer 'interesting, very cultured', and apparently the Führer's new architect, since Professor Troost died when Hugo was there. Hugo says he was in the Ministry, waiting to see the Doktor and overheard Herr Funk (?), another Minister, say to Speer 'Congratulations. Now you're the first.'

I wanted to hear every detail of the visit, but Hugo was more interested in playing with Michael and making love to me. I must say the apartment seems better now he's back, but we'll have to move if we want to keep Anni.

February 4th
My social life begins! Hugo has been working very late the last two nights, but breaks for dinner. Yesterday his colleague, Peter Ranke, an ex UFA man, suggested that *the wives* join them. Frau Ranke turns out to be English, only a year older than me, and very politically committed. Her German is fluent, only a trace of an accent and that rather charming. We are both Elisabeth! (Hers has a z.) But she is called 'Liz' or 'Lizzie'. She suggested she call for me in her car, she is very well-connected with lots of money from her family. She came to Munich eighteen months ago to 'be finished' as she puts it. She was at a small select establishment, but managed to escape at night to meet Peter. The governess was a Baroness, and sent a telegram for Liz's parents to come over and remove her from the school, she said she couldn't control her. The father (in the British Foreign Office) came in an aeroplane, but by the time he arrived, Liz had married Peter in a secret ceremony, and defied her father to have it anulled. He said he would have nothing more to do with her, but changed his mind and gave her a house for a wedding present. It's in Schwabing, the Bohemian area of Munich which I haven't yet visited, but *will* in the near future, as Liz has invited me to lunch. All this I learned on the way to meet the husbands in a French restaurant where we ate frogs' legs. I tried not to think of that clammy speckled skin. The little bones were like chicken wings. Peter is tall, thin, with a beautiful mouth, a perfect cupid's bow. His hands are long and thin and he wears a gold ring with a swastika, a present from Liz, she made him take it off and show it to us. Their initials are linked on the inside. He is at least ten years older than she is, and I think, from the conversation, that he was married before, and I

think it was to an actress. He worked on *Der schwartze Husar,** which I remember seeing (with Conrad Veidt kidnapping a princess) and the last film he was involved with was *Morgenrot,*† which everyone talks about but I missed! He met the Führer and von Papen after the première, which was indirectly how he came to be involved with the Doktor and this whole project. He and Hugo get on very well, and I feel quite uplifted by both of them. By *them* I mean Peter and Liz and not Peter and Hugo!

The men went back to the Brown House, and Liz and I stayed on at the table talking for another half an hour. She collects for the *Winterhilfe*‡ and I have promised to help her with the street rounds in Schwabing.

I have found a church with a social group for Anni to join. Probably all old women, but she might fall in love with the pastor!

February 7th

Lunch with Liz and three other English girls. They kept forgetting I could only speak school English, and so I was left out, until Liz remembered and translated. Afterwards we divided up and did some door to door collecting. Some very artistic types in the Maria-Josefastrasse, one girl had hair down to her hips and bare feet. She said she hadn't any money and needed charity herself! We did quite well, but I felt certain that we were watched from windows even when the front doors weren't opened. No response, no door plaque! Liz returns relentlessly until *satisfaction gained.* There's a clothes collection later in the month and I said I'd help again with that. I could give some of Michael's things, but I think I'll do that in my own district, otherwise it will look as if I'm not contributing.

February 15th

Parcel today from the convent with my table-cloth and napkins! Had completely forgotten about them. But they're very pretty.

February 16th

Went with Liz to the restaurant (Osteria Bavaria) where the Führer often lunches, but he didn't come today although we hung on in hope. Both husbands in a state of frenzy preparing for the first assignment,

---

* *The Black Hussar,* directed by Gerhard Lamprecht for UFA.
† *Dawn,* directed by Gustav Ucicky for UFA.
‡ The official Nazi charity.

the processions on the 24th. We called in on them on our way home, but were clearly unwelcome, so we left! Heidi phoned when I was out yesterday and again today. I'll see her in a day or two.

February 17th

Started apartment-hunting again. Hugo agrees, or rather he said, 'I leave it to you.' Long letter from Mutti with all the local news. There's some kind of hen disease and all the bantams have died. Vati says if it goes on it will be cheaper to buy one's eggs and chickens in the shops. The youngest Brokdorf child has broken a foot. He thought he could jump from one wall to another with his eyes shut! How remote it all seems.

February 20th

Met Heidi for lunch. She is in a great state because Herr Levi is threatening to go to the United States. It isn't so easy to find rich protectors as undemanding as Herr L. Who will pay her rent? She's going to suggest he might like to take her with him, she says she has always wanted to go to America, but suddenly he's more concerned with his family. Perhaps he's not so unaware of the SS procession up the stairs to the bed he installed.

February 24th

Today commemorated the foundation of the Party, and Hugo left at five in the morning. He had an official car, and four film units in different parts of the city, in order to cover the local celebrations which ranged from school displays to the old ladies in the hospital wards listening to the Party leaders on the wireless! Liz and I decided to go along about 10.30 and watch the men at work! As she said, not exactly Hollywood style. The infants marching, and raising their tiny arms in salute, was touching. I admit to a lump in the throat. I don't know if they had been selected expecially, but they all seemed gloriously blond – Heidi's *bottled* colour! The teacher who drilled them was a staggeringly beautiful young woman, and Peter said, when we managed to have a word with him, that they had *combed* the schools for one of the perfect Nordic type, feminine but strong. When I think of our Fräulein Willfried (and the students had thought *her* glamorous) I realize it must have been a task. Gymnastics instructresses are frequently strong, even blonde, but not always *feminine*. 'Wait till Goebbels sees this sequence,' Peter said, 'and he'll be turning up for morning assembly!'

We took Anni with us in the afternoon to see a procession of shop-workers marching past the Denkmal,* and then gave her tea and cream cakes in the Heck. She must savour the joys of city life if we are to keep her! I notice that she is writing and receiving more letters and I'm suspicious that she is arranging alternative employment. Michael was very solemn as the procession passed, but rapturous over the cake he actually chose for himself. He stuck a finger into the cream, claiming it!

A couple at the next table had said that they had spotted Eva Braun in the procession. There are rumours that she is the Führer's mistress – information by courtesy of Frau Lizzie Ranke, needless to say. I hadn't even *heard* of E.B. until this afternoon. She is a sales assistant to Heinrich Hoffmann, the photographer – and *more than sales assistant* – and it is said that Hitler took her up after Geli Raubel's suicide and then dropped her – when *she* tried to kill herself. I don't know whether I should believe it all or not. People always like to speculate and invent love affairs for the celebrated. Look at all the gossip about film stars! Anyway, the next roll of film from my camera is going to be developed at Hoffmann's, and I shall look at the lady for myself.

February 25th
Hugo pleased with the results of yesterday. He has a first-rate editor, Fritz something, but Hugo is doing it with him. Says he wants to learn all he can about actual film-making, not to be only at the administrative end. This means he is out until *all hours*, but he is so happy I can't object. Besides, I understand the importance of making sure that the first filmed record made by the Department is perfect. There is a great difference in making something for your country as well as for yourself. Hugo has always been conscientious, but this gives an added pride.

March 31st
A whole Sunday to myself. Anni has made friends through the church, and has been invited (with Michael) to visit a family of excruciating dullness and plainness, but with marvellous intent! I was introduced to the mother when Anni brought her here with the youngest baby one Sunday afternoon. This is the return hospitality. I can't help reflecting how selfish employers are. What Anni wants most in the world is a husband, and it's the last thing I want for her. I want her to remain a spinster with a few undemanding friends, so that her loyalties lie with

---

* The memorial erected to the victims of the abortive putsch in November 1923.

us – until Michael is old enough to look after himself. Even then I would like her to sink gradually into general housekeeping duties, a 'family retainer' of the Helga type, to retire only when she is incapable of doing what I want! No wonder the Marxists condemn the capitalists, yet Christel managed to justify that Italian with the black hair on the arms (and visually apparent *under* the arms on summer days! Italian women seem to have more underarm hair than any other breed, and despite their curly head hair, it grows horribly straight!)

Hugo is out riding with Peter and Liz, but I elected not to go. They all ride so well. Liz says all English girls know how to *'sit a horse'*. She has taught me a few good English expressions and I slip them into my daily conversation:*'to the manner born'*. Apart from making a fool of myself – and anyway, I don't have elegant riding clothes – there are so many things I want to do today, keeping this diary up to date for one thing. I find it such a bore to sit down at night, especially after a good dinner out, or a concert (we have been to several lately) and scribble away, when I want either to make love or go to sleep. And sometimes the days are too dreary to write about. What is the point of putting down visits to the butcher? I *did* mean to write down all about Dr Goebbels's three days in the Department, but as I never met him myself, I lost the urge! I thought there would be a dinner with the wives, but they were all-male affairs, although Liz says the Doktor spent his *late* evenings with a very minor film actress.

All the preparations now are for the Führer's birthday. Hugo says life becomes art when the propaganda record is made! Already shopkeepers are being approached and told that if their window decorations are especially good, they'll be filmed and not only will the public see them (incorporated in the national newsreels) but the Führer himself will be aware of their tributes to him. *And* it is archive film, so that in fifty years' time their patriotism will still be there to see. I never thought about it before, but films are able to angle the truth in such a way that it can help a cause. Dr G sees this. Ours is the first Party to make real use of the techniques of our age – film and radio. I have cried at radio programmes when Hitler speaks. What a wonderful way to reach the hearts of the people. *Now* I really understand why Hugo wanted to be involved, and couldn't spend his life in the family business, even though indirectly it contributes to the German prosperity we are beginning to enjoy.

Have just read that through. How ponderous it sounds! Not like me at all, and yet it *is* how I feel.

Heidi telephoned. Herr Levi has applied for his emigration papers. He has contacts in New York who will help him to establish himself and has told Heidi that he sees no future for Jews in this country. The grocer wouldn't serve Frau Levi yesterday. In my heart I can't blame them for going. I wouldn't like to be refused by a shop assistant. Hitler *wants* the Jews to go. Making it uncomfortable for them is a way of getting them to make the move.

April 4th
Michael not well. He has a cold and seems to have difficulty in breathing. If he's no better in the morning (it's morning already now I come to think of it . . . he has just fallen asleep) I will call a doctor. But what doctor? Not the one who attended me! Liz will know of someone, or the woman on the ground floor, who greets me enthusiastically whenever we meet on the step!

April 5th
He was no better this morning. The woman on the ground floor turns out to be the sister of the doctor whose door plate I read every time I go to the Heck! He called within the hour and diagnosed *asthma*. I disgraced myself and burst into tears. I could only think of Frau Brokdorf's father, who sits in the doorway of his cottage in a wooden chair, with rugs tucked round him. If he tries to walk he almost collapses, and listening to his breathing makes one's own chest become tight in sympathy. Such awful squeaking and grating sounds come from his lungs, and his breath is so tight and short one wonders that he survives the hour. The doctor told me not to be a stupid woman! In those very words. He asked many questions and said that the illness after Berlin obviously weakened those little lungs. He said that I must keep M propped up, not lying flat, and that he mustn't be taken out, or have the windows opened in his room. He said the attacks won't last more than twenty-four hours, but M is too young for medicines to help him. Later it will be a different matter, he said. Make sure he has nourishing food – soft eggs or milk, but no fruit, nothing acid. After he left I cooked an egg for him, and tried to feed him, but he pushed the spoon away, and when I managed at last to get some in his mouth, he gagged and refused to swallow it. I felt so helpless. I don't know what to do. Hugo is so busy he can't do anything and I can't worry him. Not only are the birthday films being prepared, but the Doktor has indicated that as soon as they are completed, work begins

for the May Day rallies, and for Nuremberg. I *thought* it was going to be Munich only, but now it seems otherwise. Which means more time on my own again.

I feel so guilty. The asthma is the result of my sending him home from Berlin. The person I love most in the world will suffer all his life from that action.

April 19th
Tomorrow is the Führer's birthday. Everything is so *festive*. What a pity the films tomorrow won't show the colours – the houses are festooned with flags, and the scarlet, white and black dazzle one. The *shades of grey* that will be seen on the cinema screens can never be so breathtakingly exciting. The Führer's photograph is in every shop window, garlanded with flowers. Liz and I spent the afternoon walking round the streets, just *admiring*.

April 20th
Too tired to write more than it was a day to remember, the new members of the Corps initiated at the Königsplaz, with torches, music, singing and hundreds and hundreds of flags caught in the searchlight beams, with the effect that they didn't look like flags at all. I'm not good at describing things but when the drums were beaten, and the columns moved into the light I felt it was like a heart beating, and all those people and all those flags became *one* living body.

April 21st
Exhausted. Spent the day in bed. So did Liz. We communicated by telephone.

April 22nd
Afraid Michael was going to have another of his attacks but it passed. Maybe just my imagination. I'm so frightened of it. The doctor came, obviously irritated at being summoned. Assured me that M isn't a bad case and that I should stop fussing. Fussing mothers, he said, make matters worse. I won't any more.

April 23rd
Liz rang to say it is Shakespeare's birthday. I said 'Are we going to celebrate it with parades at the Königsplatz?' She said personally she didn't celebrate it at all, she only remembered because she was given her first pony on April 23rd and he was called Hamlet. Reminds me of

'Miss' and having to learn 'To be or not to be' which I can recite perfectly (I did, Liz was in hysterics) but I still don't know what it's about. At least, only the first two lines which I can translate!

April 28th
Hugo just back from Berlin. Met Roehm at a cocktail party with Moritz. All to do with Nuremberg (not the cocktail party, the sudden visit) as the Department is going to film the *preparations*. Hitler has asked Leni Riefenstahl to make the official film. Hugo said 'If only I could be involved in *that*. It makes my contribution so feeble.' Speer has been asked to redesign the Zeppelin Field where the rally takes place. Hugo said he saw the drawings and they are wonderful.

April 30th
Good start to the week. I have found an apartment! A chance in a thousand, as I haven't been looking seriously, Hugo away so much. I had intended to wait until after Nuremberg. Liz and I decided to go to the Residenz Museum – but never got there! (This isn't the first time that's happened . . . H says it's my sub-conscious, I'm not really interested!) We met one of her English girlfriends as we were window-gazing, and she said she was upset, she was going back home, her parents insisted! She was hoping to finish her year at finishing school, but her family are anti-Nazi. She said that her uncle and aunt were also returning, the uncle being a newspaper correspondent for a London paper. The aunt has Jewish blood and is also communist in *leanings*, though not a member. Phyllis said 'I don't know how they can bear to leave their lovely apartment.' Well, Liz looked at me and I looked at her, and we grabbed P by the arms and said 'Come and have coffee with us.' There was a small café nearby – not the *best* cakes in the world, but passable. So we said 'Choose whatever you like and tell us about it.' It ended with her promising to speak to her aunt on the telephone – luckily she was in – and we all went round there after lunch.

One look and I *knew* it was for us. Three good bedrooms and a maid's room off the large kitchen. First floor, too, so if the lift breaks down it isn't like an ascent in a Riefenstahl mountaineering film! The aunt said she would leave the curtains and carpets, much too grand for the small country house she was going to buy in England. The bathroom is modern, and the kitchen has an *American refrigerator*! Milk doesn't go off in the hottest weather. She even keeps meat in it although there is a meat-safe in the pantry. (Will Anni trust it, though!)

I went straight to the Brown House to see Hugo. He and Peter were in conference, but we waited. When they came out (4.30!) we both talked at once, Liz is as excited as I am about it all. We had planned to go to a movie tonight, but cancelled it, Hugo came with me to the apartment and instantly fell in love with it. We settled it all over cognac . . . and by May Day we will be installed! I can't believe it.

May 2nd
It was a day of National Labour – and *personal* labour too! We actually moved in two days before, but I was still unpacking, and naturally Anni had to have the day off. The church family had invited her to go with them to see the parades in the morning, and to go to a fair in the afternoon. I missed *everything*, but had the wireless on. I was lining drawers to cheers and fanfares! The speeches were thrilling, but needless to say I wasn't able to give my full attention, Michael was *everywhere* and as fast as I would put something away, he would get it out!

Now we have a spare bedroom I hope Mutti and Vati will come to stay, though how they will be both able to leave the *Gasthof* at the same time is a problem to be overcome. Anni and Michael have the room overlooking the gardens, which already has lovely flowered curtains (chintz, in the English style) and a pale blue carpet. *Later* she can move to the maid's room, *if* we don't have a living-in servant. We can certainly afford it, but as we don't entertain on the grand scale, there doesn't seem much point, as Anni cooks our simple evening meals, and I have the woman to come in and clean.

It is 10.30, and Anni has just come in. Hugo has the midnight crowning of a May Queen to film – one of the factories on the outskirts came up with the idea, and it is too good to miss. He says the May Queen has legs like sausages but a pretty face, so he certainly won't be in until about three. I am in bed, admiring the order I have created out of this morning's chaos. I have put Hitler's photograph on the dressing-table. I would *like* one on the wall somewhere, but Hugo won't hear of it. He says it will spoil the decorations. He doesn't *like* photographs out – odd for a film man, I say – only paintings. I have to stop now or I shall fall asleep mid-sentence.

May 12th
A great drama. A dog was run over right in front of the house. Michael saw, I thought he would be upset, but he is too young to know what is happening, he just pointed and said 'Doggie'. The poor

creature howled and collapsed, and continued to live until a telegraph boy passed and put it out of its misery with a blow on the head from a road worker's spade. The road worker had stood leaning on it, bewailing the poor animal's misery! A great pool of blood was left, but someone has put sawdust on it. It's so upsetting. I've felt sick all day. Seeing animals suffer is one of the worst experiences to endure.

May 14th
Lunch with Heidi. Herr L not finding it as easy to dispose of his property as he had expected. No one will give him a fair price for pictures, furniture, house and so on and he cannot go without sufficient funds. She, of course, is delighted.

May 23rd
So much has happened that I must try and put it down. Not just for my personal memories, but because it *is interesting* and one day Michael and any other children we might have (!) might like to know that their their mother saw the Führer in the Osteria Bavaria. I wanted to write it while I still had a clear picture, but days go by and instead of writing it immediately I wrote letters to Klara and Mutti and went to the movies and suddenly I realized this morning that I had better put off everything else and settle down for a good hour.
So, here goes! Liz and I met at the hairdresser's, and afterwards decided to go for a cheap lunch at the Osteria. Liz goes there quite often, and the owner, called (I think) Herr Deutelmoser, greeted her like an old friend. He said, 'I have just had a telephone call to say that the Führer will be here for lunch. I'll give you a table with a good view.' I nearly *fainted* with excitement. I know he frequents the OB but on the few occasions I've been there I've always been surrounded by ordinary citizens, likewise at the Carlton. Liz has had the same experience, she said once she is always hearing where he's been and where he's going but never where he *is*. She said it is like a book she read as a child, jam yesterday and jam tomorrow and never jam today being one of the most quoted extracts. It appealed to me so much I wrote it down! Anyway, the owner put us at a table where we could see the door and everyone coming in. 'This is where the other English girl always sits,' he said, and Liz says she'll ask among her friends and find out *who* it is. We ordered soup and some cold meat and salad, but found it difficult to swallow, and my eyes were on the door (in fact I *spilt* some soup!).

Eventually the party arrived, and I tried not to stare but failed in the attempt! I recognized Gauleiter Wagner, and Liz whispered 'Hoffmann' but apart from those two, and Hitler of course, we couldn't identify the procession that passed only *inches* from our table. They went behind the wooden partition where there is a bigger table. Hitler looked at us as he went by and we at once pretended to be interested in one another and talk. He wore a raincoat, and he had an Alsatian on a short lead, and a dog whip in his hand with the leash. His eyes are *wonderful*. Very penetrating. I felt quite weak even though his glance at us was of the *briefest duration*. L was likewise affected. I tried to hear what was said, but it wasn't possible. Also tried to see what they ordered to eat. We hung on as long as we could so that we could see them as they went out, but in the end we had to go as Liz had a dental appointment and I hadn't the courage to sit there alone. When we paid the bill Fräulein Rosa, one of the waitresses who Liz also knew, said the Führer came in practically every Friday for lunch. We decided *we* would come again next Friday. I like the Osteria Bavaria in any case . . . not only is it not expensive but it is simple and reminds me of the *Gasthof*. I like smart restaurants too, but they intimidate me, and although I manage to put on the right airs and appear to be used to high places, an inn like the OB is more my (secret) style.

Hugo came home early for once, and I said that one day *he* might be part of the lunch group behind the partition! He said, 'I shall certainly meet him at some time, I imagine before Nuremberg.' I can't really believe that we could ever *know* the Party leaders, it doesn't seem any more possible than meeting famous film stars. It has always been *another world*, something one reads about in newspapers and magazines. I thought when I'd married Hugo I'd reached as high as I could ever go, but this move to Munich (to think I opposed the job once upon a time!) opens up such possibilities. It all depends on how well the Department does, but Hugo is clever and works so conscientiously that I think with *a little pushing from me* to encourage him we might move into one of the inner circles, if not the centre. One day I may read this over and think I was mad to presume that a lower-class girl could dream of such possibilities. But Hugo's only fault is that being born into a high social realm, he sees no value in attempting more. He is content if he likes his work and does it to the best of his ability.

Just eating in the same room as the Führer makes me see that anything is possible.

While I wrote all that before lunch I kept the other event out of my mind because one was so exhilarating and the second so horrifying. I had a quiet meal with Anni and the baby. He ate well and said 'Schokolade' when it came to the dessert! I played with him and put him in his cot for a rest, as this is Anni's afternoon off (which she spends with the church family regularly) and now he is asleep.

It happened at the weekend. We decided to go for a picnic in the hills if the weather was good. Saturday wasn't fine, but Sunday was, so I spoke to Liz and we decided who would do what for the lunch; she said she'd bring the wine and fruit and cheese, and I had some cold pork chops, salad and bread, and some beer too. Hugo prefers beer in the day. Anni was at church, so we took Michael with us. The Rankes arrived in their new car and we all packed in, feeling very festive. The sun was really warm, virtually no clouds, and a distinct summer feeling which took me back to childhood as we drove out of the city. We found a perfect spot, spread the cloth that Liz had put in the basket, poured the alcohol (milk for M) and basked in the hottest rays since September. Peter and Hugo talked about the conservative element in society which wants to restore the Hohenzollern monarchy when the President dies (which can't be long). I said, surely that couldn't happen, and they said they didn't think the Führer would let it. We had lunch, and Michael fell asleep on the tablecloth as we cleared away. He looks so beautiful now, long lashes and his hair so blond it is almost white. He was wearing a blue romper-suit and I said we were mad not to have brought the camera.

We drove back around three, reaching the outskirts of Munich about thirty-five minutes later. As we turned into one of the small shopping streets we were flagged down by a Brownshirt, and could see others stopping the traffic at the other end, at the crossroads. Although it was Sunday, there seemed to be quite a jam of cars, and a small crowd in the middle of the street. Michael began to cry, I suppose because he was awakened by the sudden stop, and I felt quite afraid for no reason. I don't like the unexpected, it makes me agitated. 'Probably an accident,' Peter said.

Then we heard the most ghastly screams, so high I thought (if one actually *thinks* in such circumstances) it was a woman in terrible pain or distress. Liz clutched me, and we clung together in the back of the car. She went absolutely white. Michael stopped crying, and then began again, louder than ever. At that moment the crowd parted and we saw a man falling to the ground. It was like curtains pulling back to reveal it, and almost at once the people drew round, blotting him from view. Hugo said 'My God,' and Peter went to leap out of the car, only Liz leaned forward and grabbed him, yelling 'No, no.' Then three or four more Brownshirts appeared from God knows where, and ran into the people, battering them aside with some sort of weapons, and we saw the man lying on the road, blood streaming from his face and head. As he lay there, without doubt dying, one of the storm troopers struck him in the stomach, and two others dragged him by the arms out of the road where he had run, and back on to the pavement. The crowd seemed struck dumb and immobile by the arrival of these other men, watching with staring eyes. I saw one young man in particular, his mouth hung open and tears ran down his face, but he didn't move even a hand.

Suddenly the Brownshirts pushed the people off the road, and called the cars on from both directions, and as we passed I found myself absolutely drawn to look at the beaten man. He was about my father's age, his moustache was grey and he was going bald, although he wasn't more than fifty, if it is possible to judge when someone has been attacked so hideously. The cars moved slowly and it seemed like an hour as we passed one horrorstruck face after another. I was shaking from head to foot, Liz was weeping, and the men were silent and shocked. Our happy picnic shrank to the size of a snapshot, a paper image of the past, long gone and now insignificant. Does that make sense? I had been so carefree until fifteen minutes before, and all at once I was severed from my emotions and overwhelmed by new ones, deluged, half drowned. I can't explain propertly. Writing about it even three days later makes me start trembling. What had that poor man done? I could only think that whatever it was, he had probably got up that morning and had his breakfast and talked to his wife, having no idea that he would be maimed and then dead by the end of the afternoon. The Rankes went home, we all wanted to be in our own tiny family units to recover. We couldn't eat that evening. Hugo said 'Röhm commands a horde of roughnecks, criminals themselves.'

I cannot bear to think of them in our midst – and they are everywhere – although I'm sure there was a reason for attacking that man. I had always thought of them as *protectors*. What made it even worse was that when we got out of the car I saw that there was still some sawdust left in the road from the dog.

June 30th
A ghastly day. The telephone wakened us. Hugo answered and said,

'God, how awful.' I thought – my first thought – that something had happened to my parents. Then his. When he put down the receiver he said 'It was Maman. Moritz has been killed.' He sat down on the edge of the bed. He wasn't able to speak for some time, and I kept asking how, how. Eventually he said 'Murdered. Shot.'

I couldn't believe that anyone would want to murder Moritz. Heaven knows, I never liked him, but who would want him dead? Hugo sat with his head in his hand. I knelt on the bed beside him and put my arms round him. He looked terrible, his whole body sagging as if all his strength had gone when he heard the news. Eventually he said 'She said the Führer.'

Well, I almost laughed, it seemed so ludicrous. Moritz didn't even know the Führer. I shook him, and said 'That's impossible, darling, she must have it wrong. He probably isn't dead at all.' It was difficult to conceive the death of anyone so forceful and affected as Moritz. He wasn't like the man bludgeoned by the storm trooper, an ordinary person living on the outskirts of the city.

Hugo stood up and went into the dining-room where the radio stands on the sideboard so that he can listen to the news when he has his breakfast. I followed him in, I didn't even bother to put on bedroom slippers. He said in a choked voice 'She asked me to find out what I can when I get to the Brown House.'

When we heard the news it was frightful. No mention of Moritz, only of Röhm arrested, and a mass round-up of the SA. There had been a plot to overthrow the Party, and Hitler had flown to Munich during the night.

When Hugo had recovered from the first shock, he telephoned Peter, and some other colleagues. He said there was no doubt that a number of SA leaders had been shot, but since Moritz was not a member, and worked in the Ministry of Propaganda, there may have been a mistake. He spoke again to 'Maman', who admitted that she had acted only on an hysterical telephone call from a young man, an acquaintance of Moritz, saying that the SS had burst into the hotel where he and M were staying, and dragged everyone from their beds, shooting anyone who didn't manage to escape. This young man said he had hidden in a linen closet, and then climbed out of the window onto the roof, and jumped to the ground, hiding again in an outhouse until the attack was over.

H hadn't intended to go to the Department today (we were going to spend a day quietly at home) but he dressed and left quickly, promising to phone me when he had something definite to impart.

I couldn't get hold of Liz, who had gone out early with her English friends, but I didn't want to be alone and asked Heidi to spend the day with me. She was delighted, and very excited about the rumours of the Röhm putsch. Her landlady, who had the basement apartment, had knocked on all the doors, shouting out that there had been a plot to kill the Führer but that he had foiled it, and now the plotters were dead.

All day we had bits and pieces of news, and the wireless communiqués were given regularly. Peter called in on his way home at lunchtime, and filled in more details. Apparently Röhm was a known homosexual, and so were all those in the plot. When Hitler reached the hotel where they were staying, they were all in bed with their boys, who were taken outside and executed. He said news had come from Berlin that about another hundred SA leaders had been executed by the firing squad, under orders from Himmler and Göring. Later we heard that General von Schleicher and his wife had been shot at home, and that Röhm had been executed in prison. At first we heard it was at the Führer's hands, but later this was denied.

Hugo came home in the early evening, and Heidi left. She had been thrilled by the events. 'Thank God, thank God' she kept saying. 'Imagine if they hadn't discovered the plot in time.' We were deeply shaken, although nothing yet had been confirmed about Moritz. 'He knew Röhm well, and he certainly spent weekends with him and all the handsome young men they could get their hands on. So it is possible . . . but I hope not.'

We were exhausted, and were on the point of going to bed, at about eight I suppose, when the telephone rang again. I'd had enough of telephones for one day. It was Frau Schmid, the wife of the music critic who lives in the Schackstrasse (we were invited to go there for cocktails next week; Dr Willi Schmid has been advising Hugo on music for the films) to say that four SS men had rung the doorbell only half an hour ago, and dragged her husband from his study where he was playing the cello, and taken him away. The poor woman was distraught, she didn't know who to turn to for help. Hugo said he would go round there at once. I begged him not to, after all Dr Schmid could have been in the Plot, but he took no notice, said he had to do what he could. So I was left alone again, listening to the wireless. And I still am, although it is now nearly midnight, but the news is repeated over and over again.

July 1st
Hugo cannot account for Dr Schmid's arrest. He says he is a charming man, was never politically involved and only cares about his family and music. He writes for the *Münchener Neueste Nachrichten* and is highly respected. His wife was preparing supper, and the three little children were playing when the SS came to the door. It is a mystery. In my heart I feel that there *must* be more to it, the SS don't make mistakes. I cannot be sorry for the SA either, when I remember that man on the pavement after the picnic. They were brawling brutes and Hitler is right to extinguish them, just as they extinguished *that* life.

July 2nd
It *was* true about Moritz. His body was found in the grounds of the Hanslbauer Hotel at Wiessee. Hugo drove out there today, to arrange for his remains to be taken to Berlin for burial. He says he will go himself to be with 'Maman' on the day of the funeral.

July 4th
We have just heard that Dr Schmid's body was returned to the apartment in a sealed coffin, with orders that in no circumstances should it be opened. It has come out that the SS thought he was Herr Willi Schmidt, one of the local SA leaders. He has also been arrested and shot.

I long with all my heart for this hideous time to be over, so that we can return to normal life. The only good thing that has come out of it is that the Führer was alerted in time and is unharmed.

July 5th
So many versions of what actually happened. Some say Rohm was ill and had gone to the Hanslbauer to rest (it seems it was some kind of sanitarium); others that it was a cover up for a homosexual orgy; others that he was using it as headquarters to organize the plot. I heard today that the SA troops shot in Berlin were killed at such speed that lumps of flesh clung to the wall, to be seen by the next batch. Circles were drawn round their left nipples to help the executioners shoot on target. It makes one lot seem as bad as the other, but one has to be realistic, and this was a revolution nipped in the bud. If it had been the other way round I dread to think how ordinary people would have fared – memories of the man after the picnic. As Hugo says, we have to accept a certain amount of violence to achieve peaceful ends. And

it is to *preserve* the good things in life, after all. I said to Liz, I just wish that everything could be done by the Ministry of Propaganda.

July 6th
A letter from 'Maman'. She writes that the official letter says that Moritz *killed himself* out of shame. They admit he wasn't a member of the SA, but had linked himself with Röhm as a means of practising sexual perversions. Why should he be ashamed? 'Maman' says. *'Name me a great man who hasn't practised some kind of so-called "perversion". Even the great Michelangelo liked boys, so why not a civilized and cultured German of distinguished parentage, who chose to work in the twentieth-century art of radio communication?'*

Hugo says it is no good defending homosexuality in the present moral climate. I heard that Göring is *that way*, but Liz says it only is on account of the way he dresses, and that he is mad for women.

July 7th
Hugo in Berlin for Moritz's funeral. The coffin sealed and strict instructions not to open it. H didn't even see the remains in Wiessee. Evidence concealed. Can a man shoot himself in the back? Poor M and Dr Schmid were only two of the victims who died inadvertently for their own cause.

July 14th
Yesterday Hitler made a marvellous speech in the Reichstag, saying that in future only the army will bear arms. He said that he acted as he did because at that moment he became the supreme judge of the German people, that anyone who attempts to 'strike the State' faces certain death.

Heil Hitler! Thank God.

August 2nd
Well, poor old Hindenburg died this morning. He was 87. Heidi rang me with the news. She thinks it is wonderful. 'The last of the old cobwebs!' I promised to see her tomorrow for lunch. I listened to the wireless on and off most of the day. Now the Führer is Reichs Chancellor. I asked Hugo what he thinks about it, and he said '*I* think about my work and about films.' Dr Goebbels has announced that he didn't leave a will. By *he* I mean the old man, not the Doktor! H says it is very *odd* and he doesn't believe it.

I am a bit depressed, Hugo is going to be away a great deal between now and the Rally. He is either in Berlin or in Nuremberg, and has actually met the famous Leni Riefenstahl and talked to her about the way she is going to direct the film at Nuremberg. *Our* Department film will be the film about the making of the film! 'It won't be art but it will be damned interesting,' said Peter.

It won't only be about the *film* but about all the preparations leading to the Rally. Albert Speer (the architect) has stupendous ideas and some of his drawings and plans will be used. The platform will be ready by September, but many of the new buildings will take years to complete (what does it matter in a thousand-year Reich?). Hugo says he thinks it is going to be staged more theatrically than any Wagnerian opera – or anything devised by mad King Ludwig. Talking of *him*, we *had* hoped to go and look at his castle Neuschwanstein, this summer, but now I wonder if Hugo is going to be home on the weekends. After September the weather won't be so pleasant. I do like outings to be sunny!

August 3rd
Liz, who is much more literary than I am (I'm not), arrived with her Shakespeare. Insisted on reading parts of *Julius Caesar* aloud to me, and said that there were parallels with the Röhm Putsch. In a way she was right. She read (she should have been an actress) a scene in which a poet is killed by a street mob in mistake for someone else of the same name. The name was Cinna, and the poet kept saying, 'I'm Cinna *the poet*.' Well, of course, poor Willi Schmid! I said 'I'm Willi Schmid, *the music critic*.' Liz said 'Shakespeare said everything there ever is to say.'

August 16th
Hindenburg's will has turned up. (Hugo said 'What did I tell you?') His son found it and it has been given to the Führer by von Papen.

August 18th
Colonel Oskar von Hindenburg broadcast today, saying that his father had wanted the Führer to be his successor. We vote tomorrow. I will vote *yes*. Of course he must take over the President's office.

August 19th
Voted. Tea at the Carlton, with Liz and the English contingent who envied me my voting power! The place was packed.

August 20th
90 per cent said *yes*. Anni was one of those who didn't. I think she should go to a different church or she'll be in trouble.

August 21st
Michael has one of his attacks, but not a bad one. Didn't call the doctor this time. I know what to do, but it breaks my heart to see him so pale and struggling for breath. It passes, though. And the doctor said I must keep calm and that helps M. Calmness is essential in the treatment of asthma.

August 22nd
M quite better again, although I had a sleepless night, as I had to sit with him. He fell asleep around 4 am. Was glad Hugo is away, because I can give all my time to the baby. Actually I *like* to be occupied when Hugo is away, because I feel very frustrated thinking about the people he is meeting, and all the interesting things that he does. I ask him for details of his talks with L. Riefenstahl, but he tells me only bits and pieces. That's because when he's home he wants to relax and not to think about work which is *very demanding*. I gather there is general antagonism towards her because she is a woman. Doesn't surprise me. It shows Hitler has more commonsense than most men, since he is the one who asked her to make the film. When I think of my father on the subject of women in command, and when I think *how much Mutti has done* to make his life and work run smoothly, then I say Heil Hitler for yet another reason. He takes the best from Germany, whether it is from the male or female.

August 23rd
Liz wants to get pregnant and can't. She may go to London to see a specialist there. She has taught me how to make English Trifle (a dessert), she says you need the special ingredient 'Bird's Custard', and is going to ask her mother to send me a tin, and if she goes to London will bring me one back herself. We're all going to go to Nuremberg for the Rally, so she won't go until after that.

August 25th
Went to Herrenchiemsee with Liz and the English girls. Heavenly day. They wanted to go tomorrow, but mad to go on a Sunday when *everyone* is out and about. Also Anni has her increasingly trying (for me) day

with the church family, and I can't take M on outings like that. I begin to feel really sorry for peasant women (and others not so low) who cannot escape from their children. Thank God I didn't marry Hans M, who has just risen to the dizzy height of postmaster. His wife has three babies (a year apart, and not a Catholic either!) and the treat of the month is a meal at my father's *Gasthof*!

We drove out by the Rosenheim Road. There was an ancient train by the lakeside, and I imagined King Ludwig and his retinue arriving there and stepping out on to the narrow platform. We then crossed to the island by paddle steamer. It began to drizzle, so we took the covered horsewagon up to the Palace. Breathtaking! The Hall of Mirrors is like something in a fairy-tale. The American lady doing the rounds with our 'tour' kept asking Liz to translate and only wanted *numbers*. How many candles to light the place? How many chandeliers? How many hours to polish the floor? She liked the dining table which descends through the floor to the kitchen, so that Ludwig could eat there alone. What a poor mad creature he was, and yet how *romantic*. Such a handsome man in his youth – a head full of rotting teeth and bad breath when he was middle-aged and mad. I remember all sorts of stories about him, we once had a woman at the *Gasthof* (I was about ten or eleven), an old lady who said that she had met him when *she* was a child. She was related to his valet – I forget the name if I ever knew it. She also said she had seen him on one of his night rides, it seemed to me like a fairy-tale. She had woken one night and looked out of her window – she lived not far from the castle at Berg – and in the moonlight had seen a gilded sleigh glide past, drawn by six black horses. The only sound had been the harness bells. There was snow on the ground and the hooves were silent. In the morning she had run out to see if it had been a dream, but there were the hoof marks in the snow. 'He wore furs,' she said, 'and he journeyed alone.' She also told me about his funeral. The streets were lined with troops and packed with mourners. I have thought about it when I cross the street near the Residenz. That was where it all happened.

After we had seen those parts of the castle open to the public we walked around the grounds. A tall bespectacled man appeared to be listening to our conversation – a mixture of German and pigeon-English and pigeon-German and English! I was telling them about the sleigh-ride – admittedly fascinating account – and I became aware that the man had ceased paying attention to the small group he was with and had ears only for us.

'You shouldn't admire the romantic for its own sake,' he said, joining in. 'King Ludwig lived in a dream. I know a lot about your King Arthur and his Knights of the Round Table,' he said, addressing Liz.

We were all rather surprised at his intrusion, but not averse to it. He looked at us all admiringly, and he had two very handsome men with him.

'Why are you interested in King Arthur?' Liz asked.

'Why not? As a matter of fact I am well acquainted with all ancient heraldry. It's a hobby of mine.'

Time was pressing, and we all had to get back to Munich. The man asked us if we would care to join him and his friends in a meal and a drink at the small restaurant by the quay, but we could see that our steamer was approaching, so we refused. The gentleman clicked his heels, bowed, and insisted on kissing the hand of each one of us. We got the giggles, especially as his companions followed suit. An attendant ran over to us as we boarded. 'Do you know who that was, Fräuleins?' We all said we didn't. 'A pick-up,' added one of the girls. 'Heinrich Himmler!'

'You can keep him,' said Liz in English, translating it for me as soon as we were on the deck. 'What an egocentric bore.'

'I liked the curly blond one,' said Pam, who – according to Liz – has a roving eye that doesn't stop at a passing glance!

When we were back in Munich we decided to have a cake and a coffee together before separating for home. There was a telegram from Hugo, saying he had to stay another few days in Nuremberg. I think I might take Michael and Anni and go home.

September 4th
Nuremberg. I forgot to take the diary home with me. Not that there was much to write, visits to *everyone*, including the in-laws, with *Schwiegervater Hubert* becoming increasingly anti-Party, or so it seemed to me, although Hugo's mother assured me that he still gave handsomely to the Funds. Relationship with her is much better now that we live apart, although she cannot resist those little digs about Michael being the image of the von S ancestors, with nothing in his features of *me*! As a matter of fact I feel less inhibited and more at home there since living away, and being less attached to my own origins! We *all* develop! Hugo's idea that I should leave Anni and the baby with his parents while we are at the Rally. Liz and I drove there together to join our husbands, hard at work!

I like hotel life. We are very well set-up, in *great* comfort, and all expenses paid for! Everyone who is anyone arriving tonight. It's all tremendously exciting. And nightly parties – some official. Some unofficial. Thank God I brought some new clothes. One spectacular 'cocktail' dress of lemon chiffon, second-hand (Pam has got too fat on whipped cream!) made in London by (so she says) the Queen's dressmaker. Some people say blondes shouldn't wear yellow, but – I say it myself – I look sensational in it!

Heard that the Führer is at the Deutscher Hof – why aren't we?

September 8th
Such a whirl, no time to write (not even postcards to parents!). Met the Doktor at last. Funny little crippled creature – yet very dominating, sure of himself, piercing eyes, and *curiously sexual*. Amusing introduction, Liz and I together. Peter and Hugo with the Doktor. 'May we introduce you to our wives, Elisabeth!' He said to me 'Your husband shouldn't hide you.' Nobody else heard. Afterwards he congratualted Hugo on having such a beautiful wife.

H & P very busy during the days – extremely jealous of Riefenstahl who has the pick of the cameramen – but some good shots of her *directing*. The Führer as Film Star! Liz pointed out the two English sisters who follow him around. One lives in Munich – still at school I think.*

The most exciting moment so far (non-social that is) was the first morning in the Luitpold Hall, thirty thousand people saluting as Hitler came down the centre like a God. Flags, music, such an atmosphere of *adoration and glory*. (Albert Speer was responsible for the flags – what inspiration. Hugo has film of the women *making* them, and the workers hanging them with AS supervising.) Gauleiter Wagner of Bavaria read the proclamation. No more revolutions for a thousand years. The Age of Nerves is past. (Not for Liz, she says. She trembled when she met Goebbels!!)

September 17th (Home)
I couldn't have kept it up much longer, it was exhausting.

September 19th
Michael has made such progress, speaking a great deal. Hugo at home,

* Diana and Unity Mitford.

editing the films, but getting back in time for dinner, and Sundays free. A new friend! Todd Phillips, a New Yorker, correspondent for a radio news programme – not handsome, but a very *amusing* kind of face, thin, sharp, lively eyes, doesn't miss a trick. We met at Nuremberg, he bought us lunch (Liz and I), and he told us all about those lovely American kitchens we see in the magazines and on the movies – all gadgets, there's one for every task. He made us laugh, it wasn't just the beer! Hugo and Peter like him tremendously, and he's sending a report on their work, with interviews. Liz and I feel quite proud, having found him. He came to dinner with us (soup, fried chicken, strudel) and we had a somewhat heated – but friendly – argument about the significance of the *Blutfahne** and whether symbols should be used to create feeling. Hugo said symbols are a part of our spiritual life – the Cross, for example (which I thought very clever, it never occurred to me!) and eggs at Easter time. And the Jews at Passover, said Liz! Their symbol is a big nose, said Peter. Todd said, exactly! Symbols were dangerous. When Hitler holds the *Blutfahne* in one hand and consecrates the Party colours with the other, he arouses emotion by association. Blood (dried or wet) is highly emotive. I kept quiet. It took me back to the days with Christel and Karl when I felt such a fool not being able to join in. These things don't interest me terrifically, but I do see that I have to be informed, to take part in my new environment – if I am to be of any consequence that is! Important for Hugo. Who knows who might become our friends in the future. He can't be married to a 'country bumpkin'. So I store it all up like a squirrel, to bring out when needed.

November 10th
Who would have thought there were so many important occasions for future eyes to see. Hugo hadn't thought the Bückeburg Harvest Thanksgiving would have come into his brief – but it *did*. Ceremonies all over the country, with decorated harvest altars and much drinking! Hugo had instructions from the Doktor himself on the 'angle' he was to take – the ownership of farmland for *all time* for those true Aryan Germans with an unbroken line back to 1800. Germany will be self-sufficient in due course, the farmers no longer poor. Mutti wrote that there was much jollification in the village, and the 'harvest gates' were a picture. The harvest crown was awarded to the Ernst Brokdorfs. The

---

* The 'blood banner' with bullet-holes and dried blood, purported to have been shed by Nazi martyrs during the 1923 Putsch.

whole family were photographed for the paper. I wish I had been there.

Yesterday was less joyous – but deeply moving. The anniversary of the Munich Putsch (thank heavens *some* of the events actually occur on home ground so that Hugo is between the marital sheets at night!) with a silent march to the *Feldherrnhalle*.

The *Winterhilfe* collecting has begun, and I have agreed to be the leader for our street.

1935

January 31st
Michael is two! Walks. Runs. Has a vocabulary which ranges from
'mehr Wurst' to 'Heil Hitler'. Is incredibly beautiful. The family are
all converging at the weekend, so I have much *to do*. *All* the von S's
are staying in a hotel; Mutti and Vati here with us. I would so much
prefer to have them *separately*, there's that terrible social juggling with
the two grandmothers, both of whom vie for M's attention. I suffered
it those few days before the Nuremberg Rally and became a nervous
wreck. Still, you're only two once. . . .

February 4th
Anni reluctantly gave up her precious 'Sunday'. I have heard that her
pastor is in trouble with the Party, but dare not mention it to her. She
would have hysterics. She is in love with the pastor (the chauffeur who
once enjoyed her affections is now married!) and quotes his sermons to
me until I think I shall go mad. I wish they would kick him out and
close down the church. The 'Niemöller Wing'* might do the employers of Christian servants a favour. If it continues to resist the Reichs
Bishop, we might have someone to do the housework on Sundays!

Anyway, she did her best to make Michael's party a success.
Michael comes close second place to the pastor! All the relations enjoyed themselves, ate heartily, kept the sneers to the minimum, raved
over the infant and brought *splendid* news. (Splendid is my new English
word from Liz. She is in England seeing the gynaecologist.) Herr
Julius Streicher's presence in Munich and some well phrased speeches
have had the desired effect of making the astute Hebrews realize they
aren't welcome. Including one Viktor Bernstein, owner of three small
flourishing hotels. He is selling, and selling *cheaply*. Papa von Stahlenberg is buying them at a favourable rate (negotiations concluded while
they were here) as an investment, with the sole intention of installing
Vati as manager as soon as he is able to dispose of the *Gasthof*. Vati
will also have the opportunity to *buy* them at any time, and *in his own*

* Pastor Niemöller led the resistance against the Nazified Church. He was ultimately
imprisoned in Dachau until liberated by the Allied troops.

85

time. All this is due to Mutti, who has been pining to live near to Michael . . . and to me. She has apparently been working behind the scenes, and my father-in-law was duly impressed. She wrote to several agents dealing with commercial property in Munich; made an appointment at the foundry – via a secretary – to see *Schwiegervater* and put the position to him. No favours, she said, strictly a business proposition. She did add that she felt that as Hugo's wife, I should be free to act as hostess and to accompany him, which I couldn't do, having their grandson's welfare at heart! My mother-in-law would have thought I was anything but an asset to Hugo but fortunately she wasn't consulted. Now Herr Bernstein has signed the papers and departs for Warsaw, and within the next month or so my parents will be installed in the *Goldener Hirsch*, in the extremely comfortable apartment that Herr B had adorned for himself and his fat little wife. She cried all the time we were there (of course I couldn't resist going along to oversee the arrangements!) saying she felt her roots were being torn from the ground and that she was a decent citizen, it was a national shame that they were being forced to leave. My father-in-law was unnecessarily gentle with her, he patted her shoulder and told her it was in her own interests to make a new life in Poland (where apparently they have family) and that conditions made it difficult for people of her race to live here. Mutti said 'What beautiful bedroom fitments,' which brought forth fresh floods. A vast number of pots, pans and plates in the pantry, all to do with those ridiculous dietary laws.

February 12th
An extraordinary visit from Mr Todd Phillips, our American reporter. Would I like to assist him in a report on the Winter Relief? He would interview me (my replies, in English, would be written down, and we could have several rehearsals) and I would advise him. If Liz was back in time, she could take part too.* He added I would also receive a small payment. Of course I said yes. We have arranted to meet for lunch (Osteria Bavaria) Wednesday week to discuss it further.

February 13th
Hugo against the idea. 'Todd's a delightful fellow, but devious. I'm

---

* The Todd Phillips broadcast entitled 'No Relief' was heard by listeners in the United States on March 2nd 1935. His own commentary changed the emphasis given by Elisabeth von Stahlenberg. He saw it as an intrusion on privacy (the collectors were insistent and persistent) and a form of blackmail.

86

afraid you might get tricked into saying something against the régime.'

I pointed out that I was no fool and quite capable of answering any questions. Hugo made me promise to let him see the translation, and to have it vetted by an Englishman or someone fluent in the language. Nuances of speech are very deceptive. I think he's stupidly suspicious, but I agreed. I cannot let any situation occur in which Hugo's position could be made vulnerable. I suggested that he might like to get 'permission' (I was being sarcastic) and he said it was a sound idea, and he would clear it with the Ministry.

February 14th
The Ministry think it is a *good* idea, and are going to vet the interview. I telephoned Todd (hard to get hold of him, he is never in his lodgings and the landlady is a sour bitch who agrees to give messages and doesn't) and explained what had happened. He said it is fine by him, he'd rather have cooperation from authority. All of which I reported to Hugo as evidence of his poor judgement of his fellow men!

February 20th
Liz back with custard powder (trifle tonight!) and promises of pregnancy from her English doctor. She says the English are openly anti-Jew.

February 22nd
The lunch with Todd. We wrote the interview at the table. Rather *I* wrote it. I told him about the clothes collections, door plaques, one-pot meals. ('Perhaps we shouldn't have had this lunch,' he said. 'We should have eaten a sausage in the street and contributed the money saved.') Made the brilliant suggestion of asking a film star to take part in the broadcast. He is going to find one who has made some sacrifice for the Relief. (I know I read in the *Münchener Zeitung* about some actress giving her fur coat.) We got quite drunk. He said I was a born script writer. He is going to type up two copies in the morning, one for the Brown House to approve, and one for me to practise with!

We sat in the Osteria until after three.

February 23rd
Todd round with the 'script'. I gave a 'read-through' over coffee, while he played with Michael. Michael very taken with him. I made some funny mistakes with my pronunciation, and I wrote words out for myself with hyphens, like in a children's book. And those *Ws*! It

turned out to be an hilarious morning, especially as Liz turned up and the three of us improvised a broadcast on the contents of those one-pot dinners. I'm glad their German is better than my English. The day for my acting début is the 28th. Todd says if it works I can do others, if I come up with bright ideas.

The Bernsteins have moved out. I'm going to arrange to have the walls painted and the curtains cleaned. I went over this afternoon, Fräulein Müller, the receptionist (I've never seen smaller eyes or tighter curls) is going to run things until Mutti takes over in March. She has worked there since she was fifteen and must be in her mid-forties. She says Herr Bernstein never allowed her to say Heil Hitler in his presence, but she was afraid of being reported by customers and had perfected a gesture which looked to him as if she was patting her coiffure! Told to me with total seriousness! I said she could now swing her arm up like a gymnast. Otherwise she had nothing but praise for her departed employer. She said she cried when he left, but felt his livelihood would be safer in Poland. He is going into business with a cousin. I have to admit I had twinges of guilt at the price paid for his excellent hotel. In all honesty, he should have had more. Even Vati could not do better, the rooms are spotless, the staff efficient and the menus reasonable and sustaining. But what could I do in such circumstances? Stand up and shout outside the Brown House that it wasn't just? Hardly. So I must just be glad of our good fortune. Of course I didn't like the B's – but that doesn't alter the situation.

February 24th
Another of those dreary Sundays. I must try and get Anni to take a day in the week instead sometimes. I feel absolutely trapped by her fervent attachments. She spends all Saturday evening washing and ironing her best clothes. I know I shouldn't grumble, she's so good really and M adores her, BUT . . .

February 25th
Todd telephoned and suggested we go to the Residenz. He is preparing a programme on Munich's theatrical tradition, and has asked me to write part of the script! *For a fee* – in dollars! 'Miss' would be proud of her ex-pupil . . . and perhaps not too surprised. After all she chose *me* to write the 'Pageant of Germany' for the parents' entertainment in 1931! I found the programme and showed it to Todd – *Scene dialogue – Elisabeth Stofen. Commentary written by Elisabeth Stofen.* I asked if my

name will be broadcast in America. He said, 'Of course' . . . then added 'As von Stahlenberg or Stofen?' I said *Stofen*. My pen-name.

He collected me at about noon. He had never been to the Residenz before – neither had I! It is *heavenly*. We sat in the empty front row and I looked up at the Royal Box and thought of 'King Ludwig the Mad' sitting there (Todd's name for him) listening to a Wagner opera all by himself. The auditorium is gold and pink and very ornate. (Of course, the Führer loves music, too.) There's a performance of *Don Giovanni* in a couple of weeks' time, and Todd has asked me to go with him, but I don't suppose I can.

February 26th
Hugo away. Lunch with Todd in an Italian-run restaurant in Schwabing. The radio was on the bar, there was a speech by Dr Ley* broadcast from a Württemberg factory, but the place was full of Italians who wouldn't keep quiet, so it was impossible to listen. In the end the proprietor shrugged and switched off and burst into song as he served our spaghetti.

Proprietor: My voice better than the politician's?
Todd: Much better. But isn't it the law to listen?
Proprietor: I had a leaflet from the Ministry of Propaganda. If the customers don't shut up, then I turn off. Politics spoil the appetite.

An Italian boy (son of the proprietor?) came over and admired Todd's American suit. 'If you want to sell, I buy. Good to catch the German girls.' I laughed, Todd looked at me and said, 'Is it?' I said 'I've been caught already, by my husband.' He said 'Your husband's away.'

The shaming thing is that my heart was pounding, and I simply couldn't help looking into his eyes, my own were *drawn* there. I never thought anyone could make me feel romantic except Hugo, and I never thought I would have this feeling for Todd.

I don't love him, absolutely *not*. But I would love to kiss him. Nothing else. They use the term 'magnet' and it was really like that, I felt I was being pulled towards him by strings. Not that magnets have strings, but it's all the same thing – compelling. I suppose it is a bit to do with him being American. He speaks German with such a wonderful accent. He calls me 'Babe' and 'Kid'. He's like someone out of the

---

* The Labour Front leader.

movies – and he wears his hat on the back of his head. It starts out on his forehead, but he pushes it back – sometimes I tell him if he tips it any further it will fall off altogether.

The proprietor began to sing *O Sole Mio*, and Todd put his hand over mine. I took it away and said 'Todd, no.' He said 'Okay babe, I'll wait.' We ordered Italian ice cream, and afterwards we walked slowly back to where we caught the tram, and he put his arm round my shoulders. As we were in a district where I don't know anyone I didn't stop him. We walked along one street – the Maria-Josefastrasse I think – and Todd said 'The King had a girlfriend who lived here, a lady sculptress, your name, Elisabeth. I did a programme on her. She was what we might call Bohemian.'

I said 'Foreigners always know more about your country than you do.'

Todd said 'Okay, you tell me what you know about America. I bet I know more than you about that, too!'

Well, I thought, and there isn't that much I do know when it comes to it. I said 'Hollywood, Greta Garbo, Charlie Chaplain, hot dogs, New York, and I know a lot about the cotton plantations, because we did that at school. And sheep farming in Australia.'

'You win,' Todd said. 'I don't know as much as that.'

I didn't get home until after four, Michael was having one of his wheezy days, which of course would happen when I was out when I shouldn't be, enjoying myself, and making me feel horribly guilty. I *won't* see him until the day after tomorrow when I do the broadcast.

February 28th
Did the broadcast, went to the studio and sat at a table and there was a light which told me when we were 'on the air' (recording really – I should say on the *record*!). I was nervous. . . but I only made one false start and then it went beautifully. Todd said my accent had improved and no one could possibly tell I was reading a language I couldn't speak! Hugo is back from Berlin, so I couldn't stay long with Todd, and I was very glad. Hugo looked so good-looking and tired I was *overwhelmed* with a mixture of deep love and *pity*. I said 'I can't bear to see you looking exhausted.' He said 'I don't mind being exhausted from the filming, which is interesting, but these endless policy meetings are hell. They are worse than the foundry. Anyway, I was congratulated by the Doktor. One of my colleagues said no doubt there will be a special medal issued for film-makers in the Propaganda Ministry!' He

made me promise not to tell anyone, but General Göring has just become engaged to Emmy Sonnemann, the actress. I remember 'Maman' talking about her. I asked Hugo if he had seen 'Maman' and he said 'Where do you think I hear the hot gossip?' In fact he told me later he hadn't had *that* piece of news from her, but from an official source (although the engagement isn't yet, of course) because *his* Department is going to be involved. I suddenly thought how wonderful it would be if I could go with Hugo, and I had quite a little fantasy about becoming a friend of Emmy Sonnemann, perhaps through 'Maman'. If the *wives* are pally, then the husbands usually get together too. I said to Hugo 'Perhaps one day you'll have a splendid uniform like Hermann Göring!' He said 'Shall I have pink satin or white suede?'

Even though he was tired we made love, and I was *so glad* I hadn't been silly enough to get carried away with Todd. I truly believe that wives should be faithful, although I know that *certain people* (i.e. Heidi) would not agree. I don't want to tell Liz because it could get back to Hugo, and then he wouldn't want us to be friends with Todd. But I will tell Heidi when I see her. She'll say 'Introduce him to me.'

March 1st
She did!
I have received my 'writing fee'. My first earnings ever.

March 22nd
Göring's wedding has now been officially announced. Hugo is in Berlin (for some reason, although he is not involved with filming it, the Doktor wanted him there for a banquet being given by the General to introduce his fiancée). Todd heard from Liz that I was on my own, and invited me for dinner. I refused. Wasn't I *strong*? So that I shouldn't be tempted to change my mind I did the noble thing and asked Fräulein Müller to eat with me here. She was flattered and all of a flutter, and arrived in a silk dress, quite hideous, puce and black diamonds on a white ground. Huge white shoes. She has the largest feet in Munich. And a *brown* handbag! She bought a picture book for Michael, and flowers for me . . . so expensive at this time of the year. She has to thank Todd indirectly for the invitation. I have to admit that as we sat in the dining-room alone together I wished it was that attractive and amusing gentleman across from me. 'Do you take wine, mein Fräulein?' 'I am teetotal, Frau von Stahlenberg.' 'This is an English dessert called trifle, Fräulein Müller.' 'How interesting, Frau von Stahlenberg.'

I put on gramophone records after the meal, at least we didn't have to talk. She hummed and drummed her fingers, and stayed until eleven. A good deed.

March 24th
My dream has come true. We are invited to attend the Göring wedding! Hugo says it will be an extravaganza. The Berlin people are doing the filming, but the Doktor has asked Hugo to be on call to *advise*. I am so excited I am breathless, *literally*. Hugo said the banquet was fabulous – all the ambassadors there. The dinner was served in a white marble dining-hall (does Göring breakfast there alone with his mistress?) and there was a hidden orchestra. Hugo said the tapestries and pictures were art treasures – some of them pinched (Göring calls it 'requisitioned') from museums! There was a concert after dinner, and then two extremely boring films 'starring' General G and *stags*. Hugo assures me that the splendours of the occasion are *nothing* to those in store for us on April 10th. 'Maman' has offered to put us up. *She* has also been invited – of course!

March 25th
The dressmaker first thing – then the milliner. I have decided on moiré silk of the palest apricot, a sleeveless dress with self-belt, with matching coat lined with emerald. Emerald hat and apricot shoes, the silk dyed to match the main ensemble. The hat is being made by Madame Maurel, who is 'creating' for me! 'Creating' at great cost, I should add. She is debating on alternatives, a cloche (less fashionable) because it suits my features better, or the sweeping brim. She has decided on emerald dyed feathers as decoration whatever the basic shape. She even asked me to leave a photographic portrait for her to study!

I can think of *nothing else*. I have written to *Schwiegervater* about the wedding gift. I suggest crystal goblets, especially designed and blown. I have done this rather than leave it for Hugo, because when I mentioned a present, he said 'My darling, it won't even be noticed among the booty; a secretary will open it and send out a gracious acknowledgement.' *He is wrong*. It may not be noticed, but if it is, it must be remarkable, and if it is remarkable it will be noticed. 'Who sent that?' Emmy will say. 'The von Stahlenbergs,' answers General Göring, looking at the card. 'Who are they?' 'The brilliant young film-maker in charge of the Bavarian Propaganda Unit, and his beautiful wife.'

I said to my father-in-law that I felt it might be instrumental in

Hugo's career, and that in case the foundry is famous, and it would be good for business! I also suggested that the actual design might be executed by one of the Bavarian artists in favour with the Party.

March 27th
The *Gasthof* has been sold. It gives me great satisfaction. Now my old life has been truly left behind . . . and Mutti will be here to supervise Michael's daily routine while I am in Berlin. The wedding is on April 10th. It was to have been the 7th I hear, but Prince August Wilhelm wouldn't have been able to attend, as it is the anniversary of the death of the Empress.

March 28th
Dress-fitting.

March 29th
Hat.

March 30th
The goblet designs have been approved. The young artist (Hans Stennes) sat up all night, to complete the commission. My father-in-law *thanked me* for the suggestion. There are to be twenty-four glasses, engraved with swastikas and the linked initials of bride and groom. They are to be dispatched direct to Berlin, and so I must, on Monday, post the card to be included. The foundry itself is to make a further presentation of two dozen glass plates and six serving dishes bearing the same design. I have had the idea of informing the newspapers, and told Stefan he should film the artist at work. *He agrees* – wonder of wonders – because it so happens that Goebbels has ordered the Unit to cover the preparations for celebration in Munich. There is a baker who has Emmy Sonnemann's portrait in chocolate icing! The artist is only twenty-two (lives in Rosenheim), handsome and Nordic and a Youth Leader, as well as being a brilliant graphic artist. Apparently the Führer saw some of his work at a local youth rally, admired it and asked for one of the designs to be sent to him at Berchtesgaden. So to use him for *our* gift to the Hermann Görings is *inspired*. I wanted to be in the film myself (after all it is our present) but Hugo refused. 'It's not an advertisement, I'm doing a job for the State, not promoting my family.'
I said I hadn't thought of it that way. I've done very well as it is!

April 2nd
Final hat-fitting.

April 3rd
Final dress-fitting. Some trouble with the hang of the coat but I am assured it *will* be perfect.

April 4th
Mutti arrived, met the train. The furniture and Vati due on the 8th. Just in time! (She stays with us until then.)

April 5th
Dress and coat delivered.

April 6th
Collected hat. Heavenly. Gave dress rehearsal to Mutti and Hugo. Terrifying moment when Michael grabbed the hat! Hugo said fortunate he hadn't just had chocolate cake! Mutti and Anni not exactly in harmony. (Whose baby is it?)

April 7th
My lovely Liz came to admire my wedding attire. I would be jealous in her place, but she genuinely is not.

April 8th
Ghastly day of meeting Vati, waiting for the furniture to arrive and getting the piano up the stairs! Fräulein Müller had arranged to have leaf decorations round the main door – one guest thought it was in honour of the wedding! She said that business had already improved as it became generally known that the Bernsteins had gone and ownership was now in Aryan hands. *My* aim is to have Party officials as regular guests. We leave for Berlin at dawn, I haven't yet finished packing and it is already 1 a.m.

April 9th
Thrilling thrilling thrilling night. Crowds round the Staatsoper when we arrived for the reception in spite of the rain. We were in 'Maman's' car, I wore my yellow chiffon, and *she*, in defiance of her eighty-odd years, wore scarlet satin with an ermine wrap!

I was presented to the bride and groom to be! The reception was in the foyer, afterwards we were ushered into the theatre itself for a performance of Richard Strauss's *Die agyptische Helena*. Dare I admit it? I was so exhausted, *I fell asleep!*

April 10th

Thank God the rain had stopped and the sun came out. The street decorations were positively *royal*. Worthy of Ludwig, I said to Hugo, who seemed to disapprove of so much celebration. *All* the traffic was suspended and (so we were informed) there were over thirty thousand troops lining the route. The couple drove in an open car, first to a civil ceremony at the City Hall, and then to the Cathedral where *we* were already waiting. I only wish we could have been in several places at once. When the united Görings left the Brandenburger Tor, the Führer's car led the procession, and the bridal car came last, almost hidden by flowers. There was an overhead salute of two hundred warplanes! (These we *heard*, even in the Cathedral!)

The guests! Hohenzollerns, Saxe-Coburgs, Field Marshals, Generals and every prominent German in the State. I felt quite underdressed – most of the women wore evening dresses, tiaras and jewels that made the whole dark interior sparkle! Talking of tiaras, 'Maman' told us that Göring's present to Emmy is one of diamonds and amethysts!

The Chancellor sat in an *armchair* below the altar, and when Emmy and Hermann entered he kissed the bride's hand and shook hands with the General. He did it again at the end of the service. Imagine having such a person as your best man! There were four little girls at the head of the bridal procession, in charming pink satin dresses. Two cherubic small boys of the Hitler Jugend held her train. My new ambition is for Michael to do the honour for the *next* important wedding. How heavenly he would look! I have to be patient for the next three years! The bridesmaids wore various, toning shades of blue.

The music and singing were *celestial* – not surprising, since a large proportion of the singers and musicians came from the *Opera*. I had tears several times during the ceremony. Reichs Bishop Müller (Anni's object of hate . . . the silly creature is fed lies by her beloved pastor – a Niemöller man!) conducted the service and made a moving address.

The doors were opened, the couple descended the carpeted steps to a fanfare of trumpets and the rest of us shuffled our way to the daylight as best we could. I have never seen such delighted crowds . . . Göring is often mocked because of his figure and elaborate uniforms, but there is no doubt he is held in great affection. I think everyone wishes him happiness after the death of his beloved Karin . . . and an actress is always a public darling! (Even if she is 42!)

We eventually got to the Kaiserhof for the reception and banquet. We were placed with the lower orders at this starry affair, far from the Princes and Party high-ups, but we WERE THERE. Emmy *seemed* to recognize me from last night, and smiled charmingly, the Doktor kissed my hand, and I stood within six feet of the Führer.

April 14th

Home again. Discussing the menus of the *Goldener Hirsch* with Mutti is quite a come-down! I am still mentally with the boars' heads and quails, and it was difficult to talk of sauerkraut and sausage!

(The entries made by Elisabeth between mid-April and June are sporadic and mainly concerned with her parents' hotel, the *Goldener Hirsch*.)

June 4th

Hugo has selected the 'typical Bavarian family' for his film of midsummer celebrations at Hesselberg. There were some two hundred family applications to interview and visit – suggested by various Labour leaders, school heads, Kulturbund officers and so on. The idea is to show the family setting out for Hesselberg, watching the displays, listening to the speeches, picnicking, dancing, etcetera.

Hugo insisted on a family of *simple origin*. He found the Trauters; mother (factory worker), father (municipal gardener), grandmother (at home looking after the children), children (boys, 14, 13 & 10, girl 4). All healthy, nice-looking (except for Granny who is like a frog) and all good German citizens. I can't decide, myself, whether to go along. It's pretty much a peasant outing – but Julius Streicher is to address the crowds, and the Görings are supposed to be going along. Hugo would like me to be there (Liz, still not pregnant, is driving up with Peter) and I no longer have the excuse of not being able to leave Michael. So I suppose I shall . . . but I do prefer more elegant occasions! What does one wear? Peasant dress! I shall take out the embroidered blouse I once so coveted!

June 22nd

An interview with Unity Mitford – the English aristocratic girl who hangs about in the Osteria hoping Hitler is going to notice her – in the

Münchener Zeitung – about British Fascism. She wasn't *named* as the author, but her photograph was there for all to recognize, and she certainly isn't unknown in this city! Some of Liz's English friends know her . . . she's in love with the Führer. Along with several million other girls!

I drove to Hesselberg with Liz and Todd (how could I ever have found him attractive?) as Peter and Hugo went yesterday. Liz decided she would rather wait for me. Todd, of course, is doing one of his talks about the weekend. I think he's after Liz now . . . I can tell he has cooled towards me just as I have towards him.

We're all staying in an inn just outside Dinkelsbühl. Without Brown House influence we wouldn't have got in anywhere. There are traffic-jams and café-jams and people-jams, the hill will look like an ant-hill to any pilot overhead. We managed to station ourselves on the Hesselberg in time to hear Streicher giving the case against the Jews. It was very dramatic. It was dark by the time he ended, and the night came alive as bonfires were lit to commemorate the dead from the war. I was with Hugo and his crew, and the firelight illuminated the faces of the pretty Trauter children, whose eyes were brilliant with excitement. There was dancing round the fires and coupling in the shadows! Bread and ham were handed out free – the Trauter daughter couldn't get her mouth open wide enough . . . a funny, sweet moment that I am glad the cameraman caught. She was wearing a peasant costume, and a little swastika armband and with her huge blue eyes above her sandwich, and yellow pigtails, she made a symbol of the future . . . well-dressed, well-fed, beautiful and German.

June 23rd

We are staying tonight – the inn is very comfortable, although extremely simple. The rooms are cool and the breakfast and evening meal adequate. We were up early today, and back on the hill to watch displays on both ground and in the air. Later Streicher arrived with the Görings and Fräulein Mitford. He seemed to push her towards the loudspeaker, which surprised everyone who had been told that Göring was going to speak. She spoke of the link between the English and the Germans and their fight against the Jews and how Streicher fought ceaselessly against this enemy. (Is she his mistress?) Then Göring addressed us, stressing the holiness of these mid-summer celebrations – and turned towards Mitford and Streicher, affirming the Anglo-German solidarity, and saying that the Prince of Wales (who will be the next

English King) had made a speech favouring the new Germany. Afterwards they all left the platform and Hugo got some marvellous shots of the three Trauter boys by Mitford and Emmy Göring. Liz and Todd made jokes about national unity and Unity Mitford and unity of purpose!

June 25th
Liz confessed that during the midsummer revels she 'gave herself' to Herr Todd Phillips. I said how ironic it would be if she became pregnant. I also felt smug and a little jealous at the same time. I couldn't have meant that much to him, could I?

July 1st
She *is* pregnant! No one will ever know whose baby it is, but I think it is Todd's, and so does she. The doctor in England said there is no reason in the world that she couldn't conceive. Which looks as if it's something to do with Peter. The doctor had said it was a possibility, but when she mentioned it to P he got into quite a rage and said his stamina and virility were beyond criticism! Anyway, she told Peter he is going to be a father, and he is boasting to everyone about it!

July 3rd
I made a ghastly mistake. I told Hugo. I hadn't meant to, but we were in bed, and I felt so close I saw no reason to have any secrets from him. It started when he said how Peter had bought drinks for everyone in the office to drink the health of his baby . . . his *son*, I think Hugo said. Anyway, I made one slip without thinking, and then found myself telling the whole story, including Todd's pass at me (I didn't say I had had some responses, though just that nothing would ever make me unfaithful). If I am totally honest with myself, I think my jealousy is a little to do with it. I resent Todd's affair with Liz because I know her and because she's pretty. I never expected him to remain solitary or celibate because I rejected him – but I didn't want to *know* anything about his girlfriends.

I felt Hugo *shrink* away from me, not just bodily, but mentally. He was cold and angry in a way I hadn't experienced before. He said 'You should have told me before.' I said there was no reason to tell him, he would have been disgusted with Todd and spoilt the friendship. He said 'I'd never blame a man for trying it out . I blame you for not having told me before.' I began to cry. It was desperately unfair since

I hadn't done *anything*. In the end I got out my diary and *read* him the bits about Todd, so he could see that I was telling the truth. (I had to leave out *some* bits, of course.) He finally relented, but I could tell that Hugo was emotionally drained by the whole episode. I suppose it had just never occurred to him that there was even a possibility that I might be *courted* by another man. Then he said 'Michael is mine, isn't he?' I couldn't believe my ears . . . that he should think *that*. I said 'You know I was a virgin when I met you, and I haven't so much as been kissed by anyone else. How could you demean me and yourself by having such thoughts?' Then he said he was sorry, and he was close to tears. I thought never never never will I tell him anything like this again. 'But what about Peter?' he said. I said Peter would never know, and Hugo said it was wrong that he wasn't told, and that *he* should be the one to make the decision whether or not to father a child that possibly was not his own. He said 'I can't bear to see him so stupidly happy, when he has been betrayed.'

I began to cry again, because I am so afraid that he will feel it is his *duty* to tell Peter. I begged Hugo not to, and he said he wouldn't, but he had to think about it, it was a moral situation that extended beyond Liz's immorality. Eventually he fell asleep, but I didn't, I lay awake all night, hot with horror at my own foolishness. But how was I to *know?* Should I tell Liz? It's better if *she* tells Peter before Hugo does. But then Hugo might *not*. And Liz will *never* forgive me because I had promised I wouldn't tell Hugo in the first place.

July 4th
On top of all the other worries, Mutti has now begun a campaign to make me sack Anni. (a) She says Anni feeds Michael all the time when I am out. (b) He doesn't get enough fresh air. (c) Anni is turning into a religious fanatic, and (d) I should have a proper nurse for Michael and a proper housekeeper, not combine the two in the country manner.

Of course she *is* right. I hate to admit that my mother-in-law was right when she wanted me to take the experienced woman and not Anni in the first place, but naturally I made my decision to annoy her! Anyway, my life was different then. The religious thing is trying – and might in the end reflect on us, because it isn't good for Hugo to employ someone who is opposed to the Reichs Church. I didn't admit this to Mutti, but I dare say I will make the right changes.

July 5th

Liz has told Todd. Todd says he wants to *marry her*, and that if she doesn't tell Peter, *he* will! She is in a terrible state. Spent the whole morning in her apartment comforting her and trying to think of a solution. An explosion is *inevitable*. The only good thing is that it has taken me off the hook.

July 6th

Told Hugo last night. Since he is in the know, he might as well be aware of the latest developments. He said Peter would be better off without Liz. He should divorce her and marry a German girl. I feel almost as exhausted as if it were me.

July 7th

Anni carrying on about her pastor, who I should think is destined for a spell behind bars. He actually had to nerve to *call here* this morning. He has just received a printed version of the Hitler Youth song, with the words 'We follow not Christ but Horst Wessel . . . we are the children of Hitler'. She insisted on singing the wretched thing through to me, then bursting into tears. 'The swastika brings salvation on earth, Baldur von Schirach take me along', something like that, anyway. He has asked Anni to attend a protest meeting. I told Hugo, and when he came home he said she would be very unwise to attend. I was furious with Hugo for not *forbidding* her . . . but he said it was up to her, he could only point out the errors. He has heard that Hitler is going to appoint a Party lawyer to be Minister for Church Affairs, to coordinate the Protestants, and feels that Anni's pastor may come into the fold.

    Todd telephoned to ask me if I thought Liz would leave Peter. I said I didn't know. He asked me to persuade her. He said that she would be *better off in America*. When I asked him why, since Peter is doing very well, he said 'I see the way Germany is going.' Somehow I find myself in the middle of this whole fraught affair. I wish everyone, including me, had kept their mouths shut!

July 8th

I didn't sack Anni. *She* sacked *me*. She said our attitude to the church was *corrupt* (where did she get that big word from?) and that the church family have invited her to live with them free of charge, for help with the children and cooking. Very opportune. I think they have been poaching all along, with this in mind. She said she would wait until I had replaced her before moving out. I was so furious I said she could go today . . . and now regret it bitterly. I should have controlled my indignation and suited myself.

July 9th
Fräulein Müller is asking round for temporary (if not permanent) help for me. Michael crying for Anni all morning. I know he'll soon forget but it is upsetting. Liz plans to tell Peter tonight. He knows something is wrong, he told Hugo, but thank God, Hugo said nothing.

July 15th
Terrible few days, with Liz, Peter, Todd and all coming to me for advice. No domestic help either. Liz has decided to go with Todd, who apparently is *totally* anti-Party . . . he certainly put up a good front. Liz says he has convinced her that as a British-born alien (although married to a German) she is in an invidious position. Hugo says this is utter rubbish, but good riddance. She has behaved in a decadent English manner, and could certainly jeopardize Peter's career. Todd's contract expires in about two months' time, then he goes back to New York, and she says she is going back to England to see the doctor, and then on to America. I am very upset, I shall miss her desperately. I don't have any other good friends. When I said this to Hugo he said I should cultivate the wives of his colleagues. We do meet at the occasional dinner party, but I find them stodgy, Liz has such a spark of fun, *lifts* me out of the dullness of daily life. And it *is* dull if you don't have friends. Peter and Liz were right for us, and now suddenly I have to start again.

July 16th
Yesterday's mood has gone. I know exactly what I will do. I *will* cultivate the Brown House wives – all those whose husbands are useful to Hugo. At the moment I'm stuck in the apartment anyhow . . . Müller hasn't yet come up with anyone suitable, but the daily cleaner has agreed to stay longer and prepare vegetables and even make *simple* meals (boil sausages!). God help us. She cries whenever the Führer speaks on the radio. Shows her heart's in the right place – better than Anni's!

August 1st
Liz went today, a black Thursday. We both cried. I made her promise

to write and tell me every single detail about her new life, and about the baby. She said 'All this has been a funny sort of dream. Perhaps I won't even go to America in the end. At the moment I just long to be home in the English countryside and be able to enjoy my morning sickness in peace!' Todd was at the station – not Peter . . . he moved out and stayed with friends as soon as she had made her decision. When the train had gone, Todd and I went to have coffee, and we felt awfully low. He said 'I hear your Anni's pastor has been arrested. If that's the one at the Confessional Church by the Belgian patisserie.' It is. He said 'I'm going to do my last report on religion. You know your Party Leaders want to do away with Christmas. Himmler's lot celebrate it on December 21st. And there's no compulsion to hold prayers anymore in schools.' I know it's true about the schools but I certainly don't believe him about Christmas. I told him I thought he was wrong to make anti-German broadcasts. He said 'I love Germany, and when I first came here I thought it was just great. But I've changed my mind. If they want some kind of admiration society they'll have to pick a different brand of correspondent.'

Spent the rest of the day with Mutti at the hotel. There's an opera singer staying in Room 27 who has raw eggs for breakfast and sings Wagner at the top of his voice.

August 5th

Our first dinner party for cultivation purposes. Not only did we borrow 'maids' but I had the food cooked at the *Goldener Hirsch*, and pretended it was by my own hand. Much praise. We *dressed!* Herr Smital wore his medals! Frau Smital buttoned gloves of lavender mauve. She is not more than five years my senior but she behaves as if she were fifty. She has a long slender neck, and her hair in old-fashioned 'earphones' and immensely long pointed finger nails. When she rolled back her gloves I was surprised the pin-sharp ends hadn't pierced the silk! She is very keen on music, they go every year to Bayreuth, and know the Siegfried Wagners. I told her the name of the baritone in Room 27 (afterwards I wondered if I should have let on that my father was only a *hotelier*) and she knew his name at once, but said he wasn't at all important, and only sung minor parts. Herr S is a boney creature, but with a kind of elegant style. He has a black patch over his right eye, but when I asked Hugo afterwards he said he didn't normally wear it, *he had a stye!* I had imagined something much more dramatic . . . an eye lost in a duel?

The other guests were the Hans Engels, she is such a mouse, with pale flaking skin – I want to give her a large pot of cold cream – but he is very witty and funny, and is important in the Bayerische Rundfunk, and has the next office to Hugo. I asked him about Todd Phillips and he said that he is very clever, a discerning eye for the telling details and for other people's wives. Frau Smital asked what he meant by that, and Hans regaled him with the story, which led to Frau Smital's recollections of being presented at the English Court (she has aristocratic connections) and said she wore ostrich feathers in her hair, and had to learn to make a special kind of curtsey. She said she would have demonstrated it, but her skirt was too tight!

August 20th
'Maman' has sent us a nurse from Berlin, a sweet girl (had been undernurse at the von Kirchners, and before that with a Russian Princess) who she found through an agency. She *comes* from Munich and is grateful to be back. She *doesn't* go to church, and spends her Sundays (every *other* Sunday – I have learned my lesson) with her family. I had the family checked in the Brown House records, and there is not the hint of a political stain anywhere – in fact her father was a stalwart supporter, no March Violet★ who became involved with local Party activities very early on, and his wife is a street collector for the Winter Relief. Michael *likes* her, what is more, she is always smiling, and plays with him instead of just putting him to play, as Anni did. Of course Anni had other tasks, to be fair to her, and she hadn't the time to devote herself to him. Mutti sends me food over from the hotel almost every day.

August 21st
Letter from Liz. She says she is very glad to be back in England, her parents' garden looks lovely, and they are fussing over her from the moment she gets up in the morning. She has her breakfast on the terrace, and her dog behaves as if she had never been away, jumping on her bed to wake her as he did when she was a schoolgirl! The doctor is pleased with her pregnancy – everything is happening as it should. She has now decided to have the baby in England and wait for her divorce before joining Todd. She says she hasn't heard from Peter, and have I seen him, is he happy? I have seen him, of course, we have had him in for meals on a number of occasions, and he is vindictive rather than unhappy, except one may be an expression of the other. She says, has

★ A derisory nickname for those who took membership in (and after) March 1933.

103

he any girlfriends? I can tell her honestly that he hasn't. He has told Hugo that it will be a very long time before he looks at another woman.

August 26th

Hugo telephoned from the Brown House to say he's doing Nuremberg again – there was an inter-Ministry wrangle between the Berlin people, the major film unit and our lot here. Of course, *The Triumph of the Will* cannot be repeated, that is a masterpiece for all time – and Hugo is not being allowed the thirty cameras of Leni Riefenstahl!! The development of the Speer plans – approved by Hitler, Hugo said today – for the largest stadium *in the history of the world* will be the main theme, together with the general preparations. There are workers going from Munich construction firms, and the flag-stitching women stitch on. Time is short, it is absolutely mad that the decision was only made this morning. I certainly shan't go up for the whole week, just the opening couple of days (how blasé I've become!) because without Liz it won't be the same. But there are bound to be parties, and perhaps this time I will actually meet the Leader.

August 27th

Hugo away now more or less permanently until the Rally is over. Mutti complains she preferred country life! There are some people who are never pleased . . . though she has to admit that the pace of Munich is exciting. 'But vegetables are so much more expensive!' Vati flourishes, however, and has become the city *patron* (if that's the word), enjoying the turnover of commercial visitors, and the Party Members sent via Hugo and the B. House . . . not the most elevated; I mean, Göring wouldn't stay at the *Goldener Hirsch* exactly . . . but what Mutti calls 'the rising class'.

August 29th

Hugo telephones every evening . . . he sounds exhausted. He said that when they begin to build the stadium they'll have to move the zoo!*
The Triumph of the Will is to have a private showing tomorrow, and Hugo has arranged for me to go with Mutti – the tickets are being dropped round here by his secretary in the morning. Everyone else has

---

* The stadium was never built – but the new zoo was!

seen it but me . . . this showing is to prepare personnel for the September enthusiasm that will break out over the nation, and to be prepared to utilize it for the Party good. Apparently there are volunteers for help with the Winter Relief, to help with youth projects, cultural activities, etc. in the afterwave of patriotism inspired by the wonderful sense of strength and unity at Nuremberg.

The curtains have come back from the cleaners *completely faded*! The purples are pale pink, the pale pink roses *white*. I have told them I want money to replace them. *They* say the customer accepts the risk and the material was poor quality. I'm going to get Hugo's secretary to write to them on Brown House paper!

August 30th

What a brilliant film. What stays in the mind? The double row of raised arms as Hitler's car passes between them; the torchlight glittering through the giant flag; the sky as the background for the Führer and the Eagle; all those transfixed faces, the sense of 'one heart' . . . the aerial view of the thousands of tents of the Hitler Youth. The youth itself, so ardent, so fresh, so *strong*. When I think of the boys at home, a pretty aimless bunch hanging around the girls' school, or making up pointless opposing gangs, I can only be glad *yet again* that Michael's age is an age of *purpose*.

He has a little friend, Ewald (aged 3) . . . I rather like the mother. A new friend?

Took Mutti to lunch at the Osteria in the hope that Hitler would come in as it's Friday – but he didn't. We left at 2.30.

August 31st

I wish Hugo could have something to do with the Festival at Bayreuth. Ewald's mother goes every year, and she says it is wonderful. Hitler's presence makes it even more exciting than it was when she was a child . . . her father is a musician and she has gone regularly, since she was Ewald's age. Her name is Annette; her husband is in the army. We met in the doctor's waiting-room and found that we lived only five minutes apart. She doesn't have a nurse, looks after E herself . . . but is very glad when I suggest that he play with M in the care of my lovely Hilde, who proves herself better every day. I suggested to Annette that she could leave Ewald at our place and come to Nuremberg with me. Her husband is taking part. She didn't intend to go . . . but now she's thinking about it very seriously. I hope she says *yes*.

September 12th

Forgot to pack the diary . . . but wouldn't have had time to write anyway. Greeted by Dr Goebbels as an old friend! The Rally as inspiring as last time . . . although I have to admit that in one sense it can't be as thrilling as one's first time. Like a Christmas tree – never as beautiful as the magic moment you first see one, although you can look forward to it. How old must Michael be before I bring him? It might almost be too emotional for a child to cope with. It was almost (once or twice) too emotional for me to cope with – Hitler was thrilling and compelling – somehow one is surprised afresh every time by his presence, his mastery of language and the way he grips your soul. Christ must have been like that. The thousands watching and listening melt into one accord.

Everyone was there . . . including 'Maman', staying with (I think) the Görings. The parties were the champagne and caviar variety – the Führer's own abstemious eating habits are not used as an example by his followers! He might nibble carrots, but his cohorts sink their teeth into the anointed flesh of baby animals and beautiful birds, devouring everything from tongue to liver. I watched the Doktor sink his teeth into a mound of caviar (and contemplate the origin of that!) which looked (in the candlelight) like clotted blood, and almost turned vegetarian myself. The Mitford girl was there – isn't she everywhere – with her saucer eyes gazing after her beloved! When you're on the *inside* – even if it is only just through the door – things appear quite differently. I can't quite believe that these faces are familiar to me – and not merely from the newspaper photographs!

We went to one army gathering at the invitation of Annette's officer husband – Xaver . . . very handsome . . . such a lovely strong and earthy name, and so fitting. He is *rooted* in his origins . . . blond, brown, thick-limbed, and straightforward in the nicest way, good-mannered and honest. Well, that's my impression, anyway, although Hugo found him 'unimaginative' and 'like a farmer's son'. The army affairs are so different from those given for the party élite. The officers' wives are not a very interesting bunch. And their clothes are decidedly out of date!

'Maman' has invited us to stay with her next month for 'some good theatrical entertainment'. She thinks Munich is some out-of-the-way hamlet where you draw your drinking water from the bottom of a well, and the only music you hear is cowbells! She said to me 'I need young people. I feel on an elderly shelf now that Moritz and his friends

aren't dropping in. Not that you're culturally educated, Elisabeth dear
. . . but you do have youthful enthusiasm.'

The Rally and all the publicity have resulted in queues of young men
trying to join the army ahead of conscription. I saw two drunk youths
(one being sick) with coloured sashes and flowers in their buttonholes
– celebrating because they had been passed fit for service. Vati, who
hated every minute of *his* army days, says they are mad! Annette has
found a 'uniform' for Ewald in a toy shop – but there isn't one small
enough for M! Now that I have met Xaver, I see how like him Ewald
is, those sturdy little limbs and firm features. Michael (although I say it
myself) is more *refined!* I play him records on our new gramophone,
and he actually beats time with his little foot.

October 13th
We arrived two days ago, and it seemed like a repetition of my first
visit. Stanley met us at the station, and we went through all that complex
business with the keys and 'Maman' greeting us just inside the front
door, dressed in black with the most heavenly fringed and embroidered
shawl round her shoulders – and jet earrings, which swung with the
fringe! Stanley has become somewhat deaf since we were last here, and
utters his thoughts aloud. I'm not certain if 'Maman' is too deaf herself
to hear him, or if she prefers to say nothing and enjoy his good
attentions. As he lifted our suitcases at the station I distinctly heard him
mutter 'What's she got in here? Bricks?', and at dinner tonight, as he
handed the vegetables to 'Maman's' sister, Blanche, he said 'Greedy
cow!' Hugo met my eye, we didn't know how to keep from hooting
with laughter. Blanche is ninety, and has an appetite like an elephant.

We were coming here just for a short vacation, but there was trouble
with some of the Nuremberg film. Leni Riefenstahl told Hitler the
only thing to do was to re-shoot it, just like a movie, in a film studio.
Alber Speer has made a set of part of the Kongresshalle, and the 'cast'
(including Streicher and Hess) have learned their parts. The studio is
just outside Berlin, and I was able to go with Hugo. I didn't speak to a
soul, just *watched*. Rudolf Hess gave his 'performance' with such conviction I felt the Führer was actually there, listening. I adore film
studios – they were making a costume drama on another stage, and I
crept in when the light was off, and managed to watch that for about
an hour. I didn't recognize the actress, I think it was a minor part of the
story I was witnessing, and as the scene was repeated ten times at least
I couldn't tell what the plot is . . . the actress, dressed in rags, was

discovered under a farm cart by a peasant, who pulled her out by the arm, and called to his wife to come quickly and see what he had found. I couldn't wait long enough to see what the wife did. (Hugo said I might have had to wait several weeks, as scenes are not necessarily done in order!)

Some friends of Moritz's for dinner – Hugo knew them from his university days. A heated discussion about the right to re-shoot parts of the Nuremberg Rally in the studio. Hugo thinks it totally *wrong*, destroying *truth*. So, it seems, does Albert Speer, who had said so today to Frau Riefenstahl. *She* had replied she thought the contrived repetition better than that she had seen on the original film! Hugo felt that if a 'performance' can be switched on like an electric light, it couldn't be from genuine feelings in the first place. One of the dinner-table guests, Walter, accused Hugo of being unsophisticated if he thought the speeches and gestures were ever spontaneous.

October 17th
I do miss Michael. He and Hilde have moved into the *Goldener Hirsch* so that Mutti can supervise the meals properly. I telephone every day, and she tells me all the clever things he has said and done. The hotel guests love him, and spoil him, of course.

I've arranged to have the apartment decorated while we're here. I have chosen peach for our bedroom walls, and the new peach carpet is being put down. Mutti will supervise that too. Thank God she came to live close at hand . . . at 'supervising distance' I should say.

A piano recital last night, a dinner party tonight. They are all talking about the Nuremberg Laws for the protection of German blood and German honour. All 'Maman's' friends are against them, of course, because they deprive the Chosen Race of German citizenship. I am bored listening to them. There's nothing we can do to change the *law*, we'd better accept it. Also I feel slightly uncomfortable, especially when, as tonight, there were Jews at the table. There was a music professor married to a *non*-Jewess (now against the law but leaves *them* in a safe situation*) and some female relation of Strauss's daughter-in-law. They were also discussing his resignation as first president of the Reichs Chamber of Music. Officially this was because of his *age*, but 'Maman' said it was because of the collaboration with Zweig. The Strauss relation (Semitic features but the best possible kind, not at all

* In 1943, however, the Gentile wives of Jewish husbands were rounded up in Berlin for deportation.

grotesque) said was she going to be deprived of her maids – thirty-year-old twin girls, one an excellent cook, one a parlour-maid – since the new laws forbid Jews to employ Aryans under the age of thirty-five. 'Maman' said to her 'Go to America, Hanne, and employ a black girl from the south.' Everyone laughed but I didn't see the joke. Then they started on about the Jewish musicians being sacked from the orchestra. A Dr Dressler said 'Even without them, our orchestras are the finest in the world.'

It is much nicer for me here with 'Maman' now that Moritz is dead. It sounds a dreadful thing to say, but it means that Hugo doesn't go out without me in the evenings and we do everything together. Also, because we're on holiday, he's more relaxed . . . in the most important way, as Heidi would say!!

October 20th

I don't know where to begin. I don't know my own feelings. The whole Jewish thing is getting me down, I feel I should make up my mind, but I can't. I don't like them. Then I don't dislike them either. 'Maman's' friends are all charming. Other Jews I find offensive. But I honestly don't want them to *suffer*. The laws won't hurt them, laws are only words after all. It's the *effect* the laws are having on insensitive people. No one was hurt physically this afternoon, but it was like watching a rehearsal. Or a child's cruel game. You see, I can't even put down my thoughts properly on paper, and that hasn't been one of my failings before.

About 3.30 we decided to go out. 'Maman' has a rest all afternoon. She snores terribly as a matter of fact, and you can hear her through the thick doors! Hugo couldn't stick it another moment. The sun was quite strong for the time of year, so he suggested we walk or take a U-Bahn* to the Kurfürstendamm and sit out in one of the cafés.

Well, we arrived there, among the strollers, and picked our café. We ordered coffee and I have to admit that it was very pleasant indeed sitting out among the Berliners – a sharper, more sophisticated crowd than you find in Munich. I can't say I'd want to live among this lot, they aren't gentle as we are in the south. You hear amusing and acid comments if you listen to the conversations around you. Anyway, we were shutting our eyes against the sun, when we heard this singing in unison. And it made my blood curdle. At first it sounded rousing and

* The underground railway.

inspiring, like the singing at Nuremberg. Then one heard the words. I can't recall them exactly, but it was all against the Jews. 'When Jewish blood spurts from the knife, things go twice as well' we heard. It was a marching song, and it was being sung by storm troopers. Did I say sung? It was shouted, and in the most chilling manner. I looked at Hugo and he looked back at me, and I said 'Let's leave', and he said 'I'm not making that kind of protest with these louts around.' They were the worst kind, the really low kind, crude peasants, but without the humanity of even the simplest peasants. City peasants. I thought of Mrs Bernstein crying because she had to leave the *Goldener Hirsch*, and although I thought she should go, and was glad she was going, I wouldn't have wanted her handed over to this mob.

I looked round at the people sitting at the small marble tables, with their drinks and coffees and cream cakes, all very civilized, the men in nice suits and the women dressed up for Sundays. They all looked appalled, even the ones who smiled. One storm trooper came right up to our table and bawled out 'String up the Jews, put the vermin against the wall.' He glared into my face and said 'Don't you find my song humorous?'

I felt myself nodding, and giving a kind of smile. I was shaking from head to foot, terrified. He turned away then, thank God, and thrust a clenched fist close to the face of a thin, dark-haired man, who *could* have been a Viennese Jew. 'Where were your grandparents baptized?'

The man was extremely dignified. He said 'I'd like to drink my coffee in peace. My ancestry is no concern of yours.' The storm trooper pretended to stumble against the table, and knocked the cups and coffee pot on to the pavement, where they smashed. He then ground his heel on the china, laughed and joined his companions who were still singing the same refrains over and over again. Then they went a few yards down the street to the next café and started all over again, jeering, pushing against the tables, menacing the customers without actually harming them.

Then we got up, Hugo paid the bill quickly, and we left. The astonishing thing was that the rest of them, even the 'Viennese Jew,' went back to their conversations and refreshments. Hugo said as we drove back to the apartment in a taxi 'I don't know why any of them want to stay, they must see the situation can't improve.'

We told 'Maman' over dinner (just the three of us tonight) and she said 'Emmy gets Hermann to help her Jewish friends. He doesn't agree with the Streicher gang, you know.'

I'm glad we're going back home tomorrow.

October 19th
A note from Heidi pushed through the letter-box on our return
yesterday, saying she must see me. She had also telephoned (a message
left by one of the decorators) and called in on my mother, who said H
was in a dreadfully nervous state, smoking non-stop and very thin. She
also said H looked longingly at Michael, as if she wished she had a
child . . . but I think that is my mother's own interpretation! She's a
proud grandmother who thinks everyone envies her! I rang Heidi's
number but no reply. All day. I'll go round there in the morning.

October 20th
No need. She turned up here before we were dressed . . . still eating
breakfast. I gave her a cup of coffee and we went and sat in the drawing-
room, which always seems so bleak in the morning, before the sun
reaches it, and before the cushions have been shaken and the ashtrays
emptied from the day before. She certainly did look ghastly, her hair
was less blonde at the root ends, she had rings round her eyes and she
has lost pounds. I had to help her, she said, she had no other real friends.
She had been reported to the police for living off immoral earnings, as
though she were a prostitute. I said 'But you don't.' 'I do,' she said
'I earn my keep by sleeping with a Jew.' ('If only it were just sleeping,'
I said, 'there wouldn't be a problem.') In other towns they had shaved
the heads of girls who gave themselves to Jews, and they hung placards
round their necks and dragged them through the streets in carts.
Suppose they did it to her? I said I thought the Münchener were too
civilized. I didn't tell her what I had seen in civilized Berlin. I asked if
Herr Levi was still intending to stay in Germany. Yes, she said, he had
given up the idea of going to America, he felt it was the duty of Jews
to stay here and fight, in spite of the fact that his children were no
longer allowed to go to their school. Frau Levi was teaching them at
home (and they'd probably be better educated, he had said to Heidi).
She had been told that she had been put on file somewhere in the Brown
House records . . . she has dreams of finding the card and destroying it.
I asked her how she knew. One of the clerks met her in the cloakroom
and whispered it as they washed their hands side by side at the basins.
I said I thought she should give up working there at once, and move
out of the apartment, go back *home*. And not communicate with Herr
Levi ever again. She said she couldn't bear the prospect of going back

to that deadly life. I had a better idea. I said she should *prove* herself a good citizen, *redeem* herself. She isn't 21 yet, so why not join the BdM*. She said she couldn't bear the thought of all that physical exercise. I said 'You can't seem to "bear" the idea of anything I suggest, so why come and ask me to help?' After that she calmed down and said she would think over what I had suggested. I had given her hope. When she had gone (Hugo had left for work long before I managed to get her out!) I wrote to Klara telling her what a mess our old school-friend had got herself into. It is amazing when you look at us all, once united by 'Miss', now all separate and so very different. I wonder where we will all end up? Will I do the best of all?

October 28th
Herr Levi's photograph, together with Heidi's, on the *front page*. He has been arrested for 'seducing' Heidi at the age of 17, and enticing her away from her family. She was 'saved' from attempted suicide by the arrival of an SS patrol called by a neighbour, who had heard the terrible screams from the apartment. She had a knife in her hand when they burst in. She was going to cut her wrists. Herr L had denied all this. He said Heidi had left home willingly two years ago, and had merely been his 'tenant'. Inside there is an interview with Heidi, saying she had been defiled, she could not go on living with such a moral stain, she had, through innocence, let down her country and her Führer, and now she was going to make amends by working for the future of Germany in any way she could.

October 29th
Everyone is talking about the case. A mob had to be cleared from the street by the Levi house, and the children were stoned. I couldn't even see Heidi again, let alone speak to her. Hugo says she is still working at the B. House, and is being treated as a heroine, the redeemed sinner. I asked him what will happen to the Levi family now. He said 'If they're wise, they'll get out. Quite a lot of Jews are going to London.' I am very upset. I found myself actually crying this afternoon when I was playing with Michael. I had to hug him so that he couldn't see my tears. Poor Herr Levi. His lust was the end of him. How terrible to be imprisoned for something men have always done, kept mistresses. I never knew what she could see in an ugly parrot-nose (even more so

---

* Bund deutscher Mädel – German Girls' League.

since I've seen the photograph) but I wonder what he could have seen in *her*. I *despise* her. If I pass her in the street I won't even look at her. Before we know it, she'll be given a medal. I would go and see Frau Levi if I dared. But I don't have the courage.

I feel even more depressed now, because Todd has just rung to say goodbye. He is going to England to see Liz and then on to America. 'If you ever come over, you know you'll be welcome.' The year began so well, and as it begins to close, horrible things are happening. Not to me personally, but all around me. First Liz and Todd, now Heidi. I put down the telephone and thought to hell with my figure, and ate two rolls with lots of butter and jam. Mutti sent me over six pots of jam . . . I like the cherry best, lots of fruit.

1936

January 10th

We are at Carinhall, the Göring residence! Yes, Hugo was asked for, actually asked for *by name*, by Hermann himself, to film the wild life around this fantastic house. I said to Hugo that if he didn't get me included in the invitation to discuss the project, I'd leave him. There wasn't a problem, when the letter came with the convenient dates, there was the magic sentence. *The General has asked me to say that if Frau von Stahlenberg wishes to accompany you on this preliminary visit, she would be welcome.*

What does one wear as guest of the Görings? I consulted the Brown House wives who all gave different opinions. I made my own decisions in the end – and bought a coat with a fur collar!! Red fox. Hugo has his good leather one, we both have boots – and how necessary they are as we tramp through the game reserve!

The Görings could not be more hospitable, and we are quartered in considerably luxury, indoors there are huge wood fires burning, outside it is *freezing*. The house has been built on the shore of the Wuckersee – remote from civilization, except that the Görings bring civilization with them in food and art! We have had blinis with caviar (HG's favourite dish), eggs benedict, masses of champagne and pâté de foie gras. Frau G told me that after her husband has had a meal with the Führer, he comes back starving, and she has to feed him! 'Appalling meals,' said HG, gloomily. 'Warm stale beer and limp vegetables.'

We are here for three days. The first thing that happened after we arrived (the General was wearing dark green suede hunting-tunic, like something I might have seen at the film studios, he really is *enormously fat*. They both seem very middle-aged, I can't believe I thought them romantic lovers at the wedding last year!) was a tour of the house and grounds and to the *mausoleum* where the body of his first wife is interred in a *pewter coffin*, big enough to take him, too, when he dies. Isn't Emmy jealous? The body was transported from Sweden with much ceremony a couple of years ago (I remember reading about it) and the gravestone is above the vault, which you descend by stone stairs. The light comes through blue glass, and I must say gives one a funny feeling. We all had to stand in reverence and pray! After that we were allowed to rest, and when we met for dinner (changed formally, as instructed). Göring was in white suede, a kind of uniform, his chest glittering with medals. He became very hot and breathless by the end of the meal. Afterwards I said to H it was the weight of the medals!

I like the house. It fits into the countryside. You see the lake or the trees from every window, and there are oak beams inside, and high wooden roofs and huge fireplaces. It has *strength*. It is rural but absolutely not humble!! The gardens are fantastic, especially now, covered by frost, and the lily pond a sheet of ice, with the goldfish visible below. Hard to believe they aren't dead, down there, in their own mausoleum. No other buildings are allowed within a hundred thousand acres!

It was too cold for me to go out, and I stayed by the fire and read magazines while Hugo was escorted round the domains of the wild life. He came in *exhausted*. I hadn't realized that Göring was Master of the Forests – what a fairy-tale title – and Hugo is impressed by the things he has done and is doing, to plant green areas around the cities, and to make it law that all animal hunters should have trained dogs with them so that wounded animals are not left to suffer. He has also forbidden cruel traps and poison, and no one is allowed to hunt by car. I didn't know anyone ever did! He showed us a sign he is going to hang in his office in Berlin. '*Wer Tiere quält, verletzt das deutsche Volksempfinden.*'* I like him, he is a very humane man, even if his clothes are rather comic.

January 11th
The cameraman came today, with Peter Rande, to decide the 'scenario'. While they were there some bison were delivered from Canada. Later everyone had a ride in the General's racing car, and we had another sumptuous meal awash with champagne. The Görings left for Berlin, and we will go in the morning. The servants are all country folk, and adore their master. The maid came and asked me when I would like her to pack for me!

January 12th
Berlin. Here with 'Maman' – the weather was so bad we thought it

*'He who tortures animals wounds the feelings of the German people.'

better to come to Berlin and stay overnight, and take the train home tomorrow. Stanley and Gladys have pictures of the Führer on every wall of their room. They were out at a Party Rally, and 'Maman' showed us their 'shrine'. There were also pictures of the English 'Führer', whoever he might be, and of the English King and his family. The room *stank* of mothballs and that stale smell I have discovered lingers in all servants' rooms. Anni's was the same. Perhaps they don't open the windows. Perhaps it's the cheap clothes. Or don't they wash?

January 13th
Home. Smiling Hilde, smiling Michael waiting for us. Everyone telephoning to ask what it was like at Carinhall. I've never been so popular.

February 8th
We are harbouring a secret romance at the *Goldener Hirsch*! An attractive young woman, one Fräulein Gruhn from Berlin (I think), has been booking a double room on occasional weekends . . . and some week nights too. We all suspected she had a lover, but no one has seen him come or go, and there has been much speculation on the parts of Fräulein Müller, Mutti and me! It was only *today*, when Hugo told me that he had to be at the aerodrome to cover the arrival of Field Marshal Blomberg for the newsreels, that I began to wonder! I said, 'Was the Field Marshal here the week before last?' Hugo said 'Only for one day.'
Well, well! From now on, Detective Elisabeth von Stahlenberg will keep an eye on the movements of that gentleman.

February 9th
Fräulein Müller informs me Blomberg became a widower in 1932 and has five children. Fräulein Gruhn took her lunch alone (an omelette, salad and an apple) and I put myself, Michael and Hilde at the next table. We reached the coffee stage, and Hilde took M upstairs to play with Vati – they have a daily 'assignation' with a clockwork train set – and I smiled at the young woman, and she smiled back. I said 'It's very cold. I hope you don't have to go out.' She said she didn't, she was going to listen to the radio in the bar, she wanted to hear the speeches made by army chiefs when they arrived in Munich. After that she had a hair appointment, but she only had to go to the salon across the street.
I reported this to Fräulein M. The first name, she said, is Erna.

February 11th

Fräulein Gruhn departed, and we are none the wiser. Her 'lover' has also left Munich . . . if he called at the hotel, no one saw him. He isn't exactly a film star . . . and so much older than she is . . . but there is no accounting for taste. An aristocratic *mien*, I suppose. If you like it.

March 7th

The mystery lover (I am almost sure it is Blomberg) took the world by surprise today and has sent German troops into the Rhineland to protect our frontiers and establish 'garrisons of peace' – the official words, Hugo said. The Führer arrived by train this evening. He stepped out, holding a telegram which had been delivered to him on the way, and announced that he had had a communication from the English King and that they would not intervene in our military action. I went with the Unit to the station. It was 'unofficial' but all these events have to be put on film. 'Who knows,' said Peter Rande (I went in his car, Hugo had been there an hour already) 'if there was an assassin waiting. We might provide the evidence. We like to film the Führer whenever he is in a public place.'

I was some distance away, but I thought he looked tired (although triumphant). Peter pointed out Albert Speer (the architect) with him – and The Lover.

March 8th

I must be right. Erna Gruhn is back in Room 12!

April 10th

Hugo is disappointed that Leni Riefenstahl has been appointed to make the film of the Olympics. 'Maman' has already issued the invitation to us to stay with her . . . I don't know what else Hugo expected really. Berlin isn't his 'province'. Of course he is covering the training of the local athletes. And he has had orders from the Doktor to show the freedom of the Jews. It is a relief to see those notices being taken down from the shops and cafés. If Heidi had only *waited*, she could probably have left Herr Levi alone. I wonder what *did* happen to that family. The laws presumably haven't been changed, but Vati has been told that he can accept *Jewish foreign visitors* at the hotel, and ordered to take down the 'Juden unerwünscht'* notices in the beer garden and in the

---

* Jews not welcome.

hotel lobby. The bookings are sensational. If Fräulein Gruhn wants to make her assignments she'll have to apply rapidly, or go elsewhere!

April 11th
Letter from Liz. It made me realize again how much I miss her. Annette is quite sweet (and useful to have a friend with a son to play with M) but cannot compare to the companionship I had with Liz. She has had a daughter. Six pounds. The image of Todd, which clears up the last little doubts. To be christened Helen Mary. Todd is staying there, and they are going to America together at the end of the month. Peter is divorcing her, and as soon as the papers are through they are going to get married. Todd says they can go to Reno, where all the film stars get instant divorces, if there is any hold up. I do *wish* it hadn't happened.

(Frau von Stahlenberg's few remaining entries for the spring and early summer refer only to trouble with her hairdresser, her son's progress and lists of food and guests at the few dinner parties she gave and attended. Hugo spent much of this time travelling to and from his office in the Brown House, to Ministry meetings concerning the Olympic Games coverage in Berlin.)

August 1st
BERLIN OLYMPIAD
We're here for the whole sixteen days. Michael too – back in Moritz's gloomy nursery. Hilde is thrilled to be in Berlin again, and has friends, so it won't be like the time with Anni and all that gloom. What is more, her friends are nannies too – so Michael has a contingent of waiting friends. I might even take him one day to see some of the events. We are in one of the Ministry boxes! Not far from the Führer's so I can see his expressions. He wasn't too pleased today, I have to record, when the Americans marched past! They didn't salute, and *they didn't dip their flags!* This was all the more insulting as the French (in spite of the Rhineland) gave the Hitler salute. The cheers nearly shattered the stadium. The Yanks got boos.

The whole opening ceremony was tremendously thrilling. Richard Strauss conducted the orchestra – and what an orchestra! – and a chorus of thousands of voices. They sang *Deutschland, Deutschland über alles* and the *Horst Wessel* song, and there was a new Olympic hymn composed by Strauss. I noticed that Emmy Göring was actually crying with emotion – and I had tears too. Hermann's uniform was sky-blue (!), his airforce one . . . and he looked large and splendid, especially as Hitler was in his Brownshirt attire which is dreary. I thought he should have had something more spectacular for such an occasion.

If you knew where to look you could see the Riefenstahl cameras working away, and Hugo had *his* cameras on Leni herself. After today, he is concentrating on our Bavarian contestants.

It is going to be the most wonderful two weeks. 'Maman' is giving a party for some of the American athletes, including the dashing Negro Jesse Owens. We have been invited to the Goebbels party (work for Hugo) and the Göring one (which he – Hugo – may or may not film, as yet undecided). I have bought some heavenly new clothes, a black pleated chiffon cocktail dress, *tiny* pleats, all over, with one bare shoulder. Then I have a white evening dress (for the Göring 'do') with a tiered skirt, and I have borrowed my mother-in-law's triple string of pearls, with the diamond and emerald clasp to wear with it. For the Goebbels party I am going to wear the emerald silk I had made last year. I think I look my best in plain colours and simple lines – but I like the material to be beautiful. How my taste has changed since we moved to Munich. Even Hugo said to me the other day 'You certainly aren't the country girl I married, are you?'

August 2nd
The great scandal is that the American swimmer Eleanor Holm has been dropped from the team. She drank champagne on board the SS *Manhattan* on the way across the Atlantic – instead of being a good girl in her cabin. She preferred to have fun with the reporters in first-class, and the result was she was (after warnings) *dropped*. Anyway, someone pulled some strings, and she's now a reporter herself – and I saw her sitting in the press stand today, looking *devastating*.

We heard that yesterday, when the Americans crossed their arms over their chests in the march past, Hitler said 'Not only do they have Negroes and Jews in their teams, but they spurn us as well.'*

Dinner tonight in a small and very exclusive restaurant – and who should be at the next table but Field Marshal Blomberg – *not* with

* This story is also told by Göring's stepson, Thomas von Kantzow, who gives slightly different (and probably accurate) wording. 'Not only do they put Negroes and Jews in their team, but they insult us too.' Von Kantzow was in the box reserved for the Führer and other important Nazis. He added that Göring whispered back, 'It's an American tradition, mein Führer. They never dip their flags to anyone.' (Reported by Leonard Mosley in *The Reichs Marshal*.)

Erna Gruhn, however (she must be reserved for Room 12) but with Colonel General Freiherr Werner von Fritsch (so said 'Maman' in her introduction) and some other army big-wigs. This was a French 'cuisine' and we all had frogs' legs. I don't know why we always have them pressed on us. Dagmar Potowski,* who is being escorted to the Games by Hitler's nephew, showed me how to eat them. (I knew already.)

August 18th
I was just too busy to write – too tired when I came home, too tired in the mornings, and too *involved*. Now I just have to try and remember everything *in order*. To start with 'Maman's' party was cancelled – she didn't want to become involved with politics, she said, and following Hitler's lead (he left the stand rather than shake hands with Jesse Owens) she decided not to shake hands with *anyone*. 'How could I invite Party officials if they are going to walk out because I have black guests?' She is right (according to the life she wants to live, middle of the road) but I was disappointed. Still, just as well, it might have reflected badly on *us*.

The other parties made up for it. They were *incredible*. The Goebbels one was an 'Italian' night – must have been about two thousand guests. He built a bridge to the Pfaueninsel (in the Havel river) and all the delegations from the Games were there. I heard that Gladys's 'English Hitler' (Moses? It can't be!) was there with Unity and Diana (her sister) Mitford – but someone else said Hitler didn't think much of Gladys's God, and he wasn't there. Who knows? (Who *cares?*) There were film stars, and ladies who would like to be *thought* film stars, and fantastic food and drink. Dr G kissed my hand (he isn't as tall as me, but does have an overpowering *presence*) and said he wished all his employees had such desirable wives. Before I had recovered, he was bowing over some other female fingers!!

The Göring party was even more spectacular. I knew from the visit to Carinhall that they had wanted to give the event *there*, but it was too remote from Berlin, so it was held in his palace (on the Leipziger Platz) which is like a film set. In the vast gardens there was a *fairground*, with beer on tap – potatoes, sauerkraut, and much more elegant fare such as game and champagne. I went on the roundabout until I felt sick ('Maman' actually took a turn, in a sedate carriage. I sat astride a

* Probably Godowski, a sociable film star who played opposite Valentino.

horse, and a beautiful creature it was, dappled, decorated with gold and scarlet) and won a prize at the shooting gallery. Of course all those SS men were on target, but it was an achievement for a girl like me.

As if this wasn't enough, the principal dancers from the Berlin Opera Ballet entertained us brilliantly, and there was a 'sky ballet' too, with Ernst Udet in a biplane, right over the lawns! Many of the guests were dressed 'down' for the occasion, having been told in advance that there was to be a beer garden . . . our host wore leather shorts, frilled shirt and edelweiss in his hat! We stayed until about 4.30 in the morning. Hugo and I went on a tour of the house, and there was a naked girl swimming alone in the indoor pool. She had a bottle of champagne at the side, and I suppose from time to time she took a drink. When we were there she didn't even see us, she seemed in a kind of dream.*

When we finally left, there were still couples dancing on the lawn. I flopped into bed and didn't wake up until three in the afternoon, and missed vital events at the stadium.

One night we went to the theatre to see the Olympic Festival of Youth, with a cast of *ten thousand*, a wonderful spectacle, a visual feast. We were going to see a Schiller play but never got there. 'Maman' also wanted to take me to the Opera, but there wasn't time for that either. Michael made four little friends, and saw Jesse Owens win for America. (The people sitting around us said it was unfair to use Negroes, who have animal power, and are not like human beings.)

Still, we white Germans did better than the American blacks. We won hands down – 33 gold medals, 26 silver, 30 bronze. What triumph . . . and although Hugo wishes *he* had been in charge of the major filming, Leni R's *Olympische Spiele* is going to be a small ambassador for our way of life. (Should I say ambassadress?) I secretly confess that Hugo wouldn't be able to make a film like Riefenstahl, who to my mind is a genius, an artist. Well, to Hugo's too – he just has *dreams*, and sometimes it must be frustrating to deal only with minor aspects of the big events.

September 8th

Back in Nuremberg . . . how it has become a way of life! The national events are like Christmas and Easter, and since the Third Reich is going to last a thousand years, Christmas and Easter may fade into history while the Rally goes on. We may have missed the opera in Berlin last

---

* This was Eleanor Holm, the disgraced American swimmer.

month, but made up for it this evening with *Die Meistersinger.* Opera
bores me . . . but never let it be said. I enjoyed dressing up (had another
new dress for the event, told Hugo I *must*; oyster satin, extremely low
cut!); Blomberg in a box with others. Bowed to me! Ah, Frl. Gruhn,
if you but knew, your secret lover looked down the front of my dress
from his lofty seat! Amazing moment when the two Mitford girls (are
they everywhere?) appeared in the Blomberg box wearing cotton
shirts and skirts! The Führer there, of course, and I *thought* I saw him
looking at me.

September 14th
Eva Braun and Unity Mitford sitting side by side at the Zeppelinwiese
for the March Past. Tonight Miss England was back in the third row,
crying at Hitler's speech and at the singing. I'm not mocking her, I
cried too. You can't help it. EB seems to be *established.* No more gossip,
but acceptance that she is his mistress. We are driving home in the
morning.

October 10th
The event of the week was the 'secret' wedding of Diana Mitford and
the English Führer, named not Moses but *Mosley. We* knew. Hugo
was in charge of some very secret filming. It took place in a house not
far from the Reichs Chancellory, and the Goebbelses were witnesses.
Hitler gave a private dinner in the evening for them. I wrote to
'Maman' and told her to tell Gladys and Stanley!

1937

New Year Celebrations with the von Stahlenbergs. A family gathering. Can I be accepted at last? Both sisters-in-law treated me (almost) as an equal. Michael was the hit of the party. Not only the youngest cousin but the most beautiful. Of course. His hair is almost white, and Valerie's offspring (who began blond) have darkened to boiled potato-skin brown. With all their 'breeding', I'm the one who produced the true Aryan.

Our house is now used by both sisters and families as a holiday retreat. Valerie graciously offered it to me at any time they weren't using it themselves. 'Now that your parents have moved' (she couldn't resist!) 'you have nowhere to stay here. How is the new hotel doing? I understand Vater invested in your father's professional expertise.'

I said it was doing very well, and that *her* father had already benefited from the outlay. I mentioned that Blomberg stayed there, and later managed to bring in a casual reference to Emmy G.

Visited various old friends. Klara still husbandless, and was so envious of me (kept saying how lucky I was) that I felt guilty. Still, she has a good job (now regrets not going to the university) as head florist with the nursery gardeners, her lover is the boss, fortyish but not bad looking. A beer stomach though! She runs the village Winter Relief . . . tells me my *Schwiegermutter* is very mean, and tried to get away with giving the maids' cast-off uniforms last month! Klara said it didn't qualify for a door plaque, so she had to add cash.

January 7th
Home. And glad to be home. Letter waiting from Liz in New York. She has German neighbours. Jews of course. Says the weather is terrible but the apartment centrally heated. Wants me to go for a holiday. How I wish I could.

January 31st
Michael is four. We gave him a toy car big enough to ride in (a Mercedes)! Ewald gave him a trumpet. Grandparents gave him endless kisses and a party at the hotel.

February 1st

Horror of horrors! Last night, amorous (as *I* was) after the birthday champagne we drank in Michael's honour, Hugo asked me to have another child.

I have to face it. My maternal instinct is satisfied.

Maybe when I'm forty, a final flowering? But not NOW. We'd have to move. I'd have to have more help. Not that Hilde isn't a mother's answer, *she's* the maternal one, but I simply don't want anything more to do with napkins, breast-feeding (and they say it *hurts* with a second child, labour pains every time it sucks) or regurgitations down my lovely clothes.

The trouble is, Hugo is filming a thing called *The New Generation*, the climax being Mothering Sunday. The glory of giving birth and all that stuff. I've done my bit of mothering for the Fatherland, I've produced a son. Hugo has been following Frau Trauter's pregnancy (yes, another little Trauter on the way!) and is quite caught up with woman's function ... more than he was with me and my production of Michael. I've seen the first reels of film (unedited), all bulging stomachs and little blond heads and the revolutionary sight of actual feeding. I'm not sure I like the idea of all those bosoms being bared for my husband.

February 16th

1. Told Hugo I'd have a baby, but don't want to start it until after the Party Rally. He understands *that*. I want to go to Bayreuth anyway, this year, and I can't enjoy it if I have morning sickness.
2. Made an appointment with the doctor to be fitted with a new contraceptive.
3. Will think up another excuse when the Rally's over.

February 20th

The doctor obliged, but gave me a lecture on my *duty* as a German woman to bear children! Quite a change from the last time.

February 30th

The inescapable Heidi has turned up again, and in the most extraordinary way! The Unit is filming in the *Lebensborn* Home just outside Munich. Hugo has been raving about the lovely grounds, calm atmosphere, etc, and begged me to see for myself (his own personal propaganda!) and I must say I was curious. There are all the jokes about the 'stud farms' and plenty of rumours about the girls who go there –

Annette has heard they are *paid* – so I put on my tightest dress which makes my waist look like a mannequin's and went with him this morning. The camera equipment was already there at the lakeside. *And so was Heidi!* She arrived yesterday, a month to go. At first I didn't recognize her, no make-up and all wrapped up in a thick grey cloak, but she gave a shout of joy at the sight of us. I would have cut her if I'd met her in the street, but I couldn't exactly create a scene among all those bovine women who had been put out to graze in the morning mist like sheep. Suppose I upset them, and brought on miscarriages!

Heidi: Oh Liese, I've thought of you so often. I'm so happy to see you.
Me (truthfully): I've thought about you.
Heidi (whispering): I know you despised me when the Levi thing happened. But I had no alternative. You'd have done the same. Anyway, I heard he was released. They went to Holland or England or somewhere.

Hugo then decided he would use Heidi in the film! Fortunately we went indoors, as it was very chilly by the water. The other mothers- to-be continued to take their daily exercise obediently. It wasn't a beautiful sight.

Hugo and the Director sat Heidi underneath the *Lebensborn* red and white flag, and asked her to talk. It was a fascinating testimony. This is it, more or less.

I decided that I would like to make the Führer a gift of a child.

I had also committed a sin against the Fatherland by giving myself to a Jew. At the time I didn't realize what a disgusting act this was. But now I realize it and want to atone. As a racially pure woman in good health, I believe the finest thing I can do is to produce a child that will contribute to the future strength of Germany.

I got in touch with *Lebensborn*, and was told to attend a hostel near my home ten days after the commencement of my next period. I went along as arranged, and after a medical examination I was introduced to my 'procreation helper'. He was an SS man, carefully chosen for this function. My baby cannot fail to be strong and beautiful. I stayed at the hostel for a few days, and then returned home. I was admitted to this wonderful Home yesterday, and I will stay here until my baby is ready to leave me. It will be adopted by a good Aryan family. I accept that illegitimacy is acceptable in this way, and I would not want to bring up a child without a husband.

Well, Herr Levi, you are atoned for!

When we got back to Munich I couldn't wait to tell Annette. She said she can't understand it, because all illegitimate children are unacceptable. She has a cousin who was expelled from the Kulturbund because she had a child last year – and that was by her (then) fiancé, not just anyone.

March 7th

Hugo in a great state. The Ministry have cancelled the film. He is going to Berlin to talk to Goebbels. It is such a disappointment, so much work has been done. And it *is* to do with illegitimacy. Annette was right.

March 11th

Hugo back. The film is *on* again, but without Heidi. It's too early for her statement to be released – but is to be kept in the secret archives. Himmler's scheme is half-secret, but *officially* births must be legitimate. The Doktor hinted to Hugo that it won't be long before unmarried mothers will be allowed to call themselves 'Frau', an honorary title. Heidi's *Hitler-Gift* should be about to face the world. She referred to it as 'he' but suppose it's a girl? Does she have to find another 'procreation helper'?

May 15th

Well, the film's finished, and I'm very glad. It has had me in an emotional turmoil ever since it started. Now Annette's pregnant. I'm surrounded. It's ghastly. Michael and I went with Hugo for the final day's shooting last Sunday – Mothering Sunday – to a small village between Munich and Nuremberg. Some of the houses were elaborately decorated with flowers and wreaths because there has been '*Kindersegen*'* during the year. There was an exhibition of a kind in the little church hall, mainly photographs and portraits of men who were famous and fathers of large families (or sons of large families – like J. S. Bach). All this went into the camera, plus an open-air ceremony praising God for the gift of parenthood. A number of large ladies, whose bodies gave evidence of their fertility, were blessed and presented with crosses. (It's all very well for the peasants!) We were asked back for

* Blessed with children.

Hitler's mother's birthday (August 12th) when there will be more praise for the prolific. But I've had enough!

June 28th
Dr Goebbels in Munich. Conference called at the Department. Hugo at the Brown House all day, and not even accessible by telephone. (I tried! I thought Michael had a bead stuck up his nose, but it was a false alarm!) The result – PROMOTION. Good or bad, I don't know. Peter Rande is to take over Hugo's job of organization. Hugo is to oversee – but not be involved daily – with the Bavarian folk film. Unless it has political importance. He is to form a special group attached to the *War Ministry* to make a highly secret record of the build-up of the armed forces. He *says* that he won't even tell me and that my days of watching the filming are over. He says he should not even have told me this much.

When he *did* I got quite a horrible feeling in my chest. Firstly because he is obviously going to be away much more, and I will be *cut off*. Secondly because the idea is frightening. Does it mean we may have a war? Hugo says no, it is a purely protective measure and that armed strength prevents war. No one attacks a strong country. Erna Gruhn is in Room 12 again, so Blomberg must have been at the meeting. I asked H, but he wouldn't tell me.

The good thing is that it does mean we have more money. And with the price or coffee rising (and not only coffee) I'm not regretful about *that*.

But no Bayreuth. I did so want to go, and had already bought a couple of new dresses. I said, if the Führer finds the time why can't you?

July 1st
Hugo is in Rome. How I envy him. I would love to go to Italy, and especially to Rome. Everyone says you can buy the best gloves in the world there.

July 4th
Hugo back – with three pairs of gloves and some lovely Italian cheese. He was very funny about the Duce and did an imitation. He said he would like to see Göring and Mussolini side by side in a small elevator! I asked if Hermann was there . . . he wouldn't say. How *silly* to be secretive over a thing like that. I find it *very* irritating.

Annette is moving. Xaver is being stationed on the Ruhr, and she is going too. How sad Michael will be without Ewald, they are like brothers. I asked Hugo if Xaver's move has anything to do with the things he's involved with. He said, 'They are making a number of changes, generally.' That tells me a lot!!

Actually, I don't think he knows a *thing!*

August 4th
It has happened!

Hugo has been in conference with *the Führer*. He tells me it was to discuss the filming of the Rally. I don't care what it was about. Only that it happened. And will happen again. He has been invited to the Berghof *
next weekend. Perhaps it's just as well Annette is going. An ordinary officer's wife is too low a companion for the wife of one of Hitler's associates! If anyone should ever read this diary, I can assure them that was a joke. I shall miss her. Somehow I seem to lose all my girlfriends in one way or another. I moved away from Klara, Liz moved away from me, Heidi became impossible and now it's goodbye to Annette. She's such a jolly, open girl, and I can hardly discuss intimate matters with Frl. Müller or the Brown House wives!!

August 9th

It is 3 a.m. And I can't possibly sleep. I AM IN THE BERGHOF. I AM HITLER'S GUEST.

It has to be the most exciting thing in my life. Excels even the night I lost my virginity in the summer house, even the birth of Michael. I've had some marvellous days, but nothing can compare with this.

Two days ago I didn't even know I was going to be here. It was Hugo's conference weekend. I had planned to go with Mutti to the pictures and had asked the drab Frau Smital to take tea with me this very afternoon, while her husband played golf.

Then I had a telephone call from Hugo's secretary. Very brief.

Fräulein S: Is that Frau von Stahlenberg?
Me: Yes.
Fräulein S: Your husband has asked me to tell you that you have been invited to join the party at the weekend.
Me: You mean . . .?

---

* Hitler's house on the Obersalzberg.

Fräulein S: He suggests you arrange for Michael to stay with your parents, and that you make a hair appointment for tomorrow.
Me: Is he there? I'd like to talk to him.
Fräulein S: I'm afraid it isn't possible. He's in conference for the rest of the day.

I can only say that when I hung up the receiver, I could scarcely breathe. I had to sit down. Then I rang Mutti, and she had to sit down too! Hilde's hand flew to her heart, then she *kissed me.* Then apologized! Michael didn't know why we were in such a state and burst into tears. I hugged him, and got a huge lump in my throat. I have never been more impatient for Hugo to come home.

It was rather flat when he did. He hadn't even taken the call inviting me. Fräulein S had been given the message that I was expected to be with him, and he'd told her to ring me. I had just the faintest suspicion that he was worried that I was going to be there, that in some way I might let him down. He kept saying things like: 'You won't be able to wander about the house' and mad ideas like that. I said 'I wouldn't want to.' He said 'You may find you have to be with the other women.' I said 'Don't worry, I'll do whatever is expected of me. I won't belch at the table and I won't go to the bathroom in my underwear.'

He realized that he had been stupid and slightly *insulting.* I said 'You may remember that you were the one to fall asleep after dinner at the Smitals'!'

I had my hair done, but I was careful not to look too smart, because the thing nowadays is to be as natural looking as possible. I had the green silk suit at the cleaners, and collected that, and also looked for some 'country' clothes, skirt, shirt and flat walking shoes. I *did* buy a new nightdress. No one will see it but Hugo, but I couldn't sleep in the Berghof in anything but the best.

I told practically everyone I know what was happening, and they couldn't believe it.

We drove up in the afternoon (Friday) and I have to say I was shocked at what has been done to the countryside round here. It is so beautiful, but has been built up hideously, concrete roads through the forests. Hugo says this is Martin Bormann (who has a house there on the top of the mountain) who is a philistine. A pity Göring couldn't have been in charge, he loves nature. To get to the Berghof, you have to go through two checkpoints and into a barbed wire enclosure – like being at or rather *in* the zoo!

When we arrived the door was opened by a bodyguard, and then a maid showed us to our room, on the upper floor. There was a fantastic view from the window – you could see Salzburg – but when I opened it there was a smell of petrol, which must have come from the garage below. We had nothing to do until dinner, the Führer was in a meeting with Bormann, and we didn't see any of the other guests. I unpacked, and Hugo read through a file of papers he had brought with him. We had been told to go down to the anteroom at eight. I didn't know what to wear, but Hugo said he had asked and it was definitely formal, but not dressy. . . . I had brought two with me, one with long sleeves and a high neck so I wore that. We went down as arranged, and Eva Braun greeted us, and was clearly the hostess. The Führer came in with Bormann, shook hands with Hugo, and was introduced to me. My legs went to water. He bowed over my hand, and said how delighted he was that I had been able to come. There was no one that I recognized among the guests, and Hugo told me later that they were all connected with the Rally organization, and that Goebbels and his wife were arriving in the morning.

The dining-room has panelled walls, and there is a long table, and chairs covered in red leather. Hitler sat in the middle, facing the window, with Eva B on one side of him, and a dark-haired woman on the other. I was on the opposite side, but too far away to talk. We were eighteen in number. We began with a barley and carrot soup (all white china by the way, nothing grand in either food or setting), then had a pork dish and vegetables (Hitler only ate the vegetables, and drank Fachinger,* the rest of us had wine) and an Apfeltorte to follow. The waiters at the table were part of the bodyguard, Hugo informs me.

I was too nervous to enjoy the dinner, and the conversation was stilted. I couldn't help noticing a shaving cut on Hitler's neck which had bled onto his collar. I was glad when it was over, and we all reassembled in the salon but horrified to see that I had dropped some wine on my skirt . . . a small purple stain which I tried to conceal by arranging my dress as I sat down.

The salon is amazing, like something out of a fairy story, and I don't mean beautiful! It is like a room for a giant. An enormous window, a vast clock with a terrifying bronze eagle crouching over it, a table which has to be twenty feet in length, a sideboard at least ten feet high

* Mineral water.

(it turned out to conceal gramophone records!), huge paintings, tapestries . . . one of which hid the movie screen which I was astonished to find as part of the evening's entertainment. The room seems roughly divided in half, the window half and the fireplace (very very big) half. We began in the window half, the tapestries were lifted (the projector was also hidden behind one) and with some slight rearrangement of seating (Hitler by Braun) we were treated to what seemed like five hours of La Jana* – not exactly Hugo's choice, or mine. We all applauded at the end, and made appropriate comments. The screen was once again disguised by the wall hanging, and at the Führer's suggestion, we removed ourselves to the fireplace section of the room. Hitler planted himself in a comfortable chair, beckoning EB to sit beside him, and then, to my astonishment and some embarassment, asked me to take the chair on his other side. The fire was stoked by one of the male servants (every inch a bodyguard!) and poor Hugo found himself in the middle of a self-conscious row on the long sofa, which was (he said) back-achingly low. For a few moments we talked about the film (not much to say) and then about other films. Hugo's opinion as an expert was sought on such things as camera angles, but I had the feeling his answers fell on deaf ears. *I* thought he spoke very well. Hitler then took Eva's hand in his – a very *ordinary* hand, with only one small and uninteresting ring – and talked to her so softly, that I couldn't hear. Then he went into a sort of trance, fiddling with his shaving cut and staring into the fire, and I stared too, and so did Eva, and one or two of the guests murmured remarks to one another. It was *most peculiar*. A relief when the manservant brought round wine – the sparkling variety. I grabbed a glass and clung on to it like a lifebelt. Neither AH nor EB drank, but continued to sit with their hands loosely linked. The hours DRAGGED. My eyes went from the awful eagle clock to Hugo's watch and my face was continually stretched by suppressing yawns. It was after one when to my unspoken deep gratitude, Eva stood up and said goodnight. Whether it was a pathetic attempt to indicate that she wasn't his mistress, or merely that he wasn't yet tired, Hitler didn't leave with her. Another terrible twenty minutes before he stood up again and said goodnight. As soon as he had gone, everyone yawned and stretched, then remembered themselves, and said formal goodnights.

'My God,' said Hugo, 'if the new job means many more of these evenings, I shall request to go back to the old one.' I said I thought it is

* Popular musical film star.

a small price to pay for the GLORY of being here. How many people have the chance to say it is boring spending an evening with Adolf Hitler!

We didn't get up early. Hugo had a meeting with two of his colleagues at eleven, but I didn't appear until we were summoned to a late lunch. *It was exactly like the previous night!* Same seating and almost the same meal! Once it was over, we went up to our rooms to prepare for a walk, and assembled again downstairs, all wishing we could sleep off the meal.

Two of the SS men took the lead, and we followed in pairs – even a pair of dogs! Hitler and Hugo walked behind the bodyguard, and I found myself with Eva Braun! Our talk was superficial and dull, but she seemed quite envious of Michael, and questioned me about him. She asked if I could ski, and when I said I hadn't had the opportunity, she became briefly animated in describing its joys.

Our aim was the Teahouse – Hitler's favourite spot, and I was very thrilled by the view and said so. ('Yes,' said one of the other guests, 'if you don't have to go there every weekend!')

We filed in, and were taken to a round table, where we could see out of the windows. I was again asked by the Führer to sit by him (E of course was on the other side of him) and several of the guests went into the other room, since there wasn't room for everyone here. Hugo was beside me, and I pressed his knee under the table, as we drank chocolate and liqueurs and ate cakes!

Hitler began to talk of his early years in Austria, which should have been interesting, but was told so monotonously I found my attention wandering. At one point *his own eyes closed* and he stopped talking, and I thought he had fallen asleep. However, he began again, and Hugo's knee pushed against mine, and we tried to look interested.

Eventually we left the Teahouse, and walked to the parking area about twenty minutes away, where (thank heavens) there were cars to whisk us back to the Berghof, where we had a couple of hours' respite before dinner . . . the *same* again, plus a different but equally *indifferent* movie. It is now Sunday morning, and I write this before our final meal, and departure.

How I long for supper at home. The greatest man in the world, possibly *for all time*, and the weekend has been a drag from the moment we arrived. Who would believe it?

Next time – if there is a next time – may be jollier – but at least I'll be prepared. What a contrast to the Görings.

September 11th
NUREMBERG
The most spectacular ever. When the cornerstone of the Stadium was laid, Hitler apparently said to Speer 'This is the most important day of your life.' Last night 100,000 members of the political leadership corps marched past their Führer, bearing banners. Hugo has the figures, 32,000 of them. Searchlights were directed thousands of feet into the sky so that there was an actual dome – breathtaking. I should think the rest of the world will tremble in awe when it sees the movies.

Annette had lunch with me – so lovely to see her again. Ewald has grown. Wish I had brought Michael with me, next year I will.

September 26th
Hugo in Berlin. I go tomorrow, Italy's unlovable leader is here, with my poor husband part of the entourage, whisking him and filming him from one side of the country to the other, from his reception here in Munich, to the Görings' at Carinhall. Anyway, there's much celebration planned for the day after tomorrow, and I'm always pleased to go to Berlin.

Of course, now the Rally's over I must be prepared to delay my pregnancy yet again! Maybe Hugo has forgotten.

September 29th
'Maman' not really well, and much aged. She wasn't up to going to the Maifeld yesterday to hear the Duce and Hitler. The crowd was enormous . . . a million so they say (not a million and four?). I was relieved to be in a private area. The sky was dark, and grew darker, until the most violent thunderstorm broke, right in the middle of Mussolini's oratory. (The heavens knew not to interrupt Hitler!) The wild applause died away and there was much confusion, as everyone tried to run to shelter. The Duce got SOAKED. I expected to see him snuffling and sneezing today at the military parade but he strutted about in the comic way of Laurel – or is it Hardy – looking pompous and ridiculous and terribly grand! Hugo says it was a great success – he was filming the army and air force detachments – and that Italy has cast her lot with ours. Italy rather appeals to me, I rather like the idea of a link of friendship between all those dark curly heads and our blond ones! I like spaghetti too.

September 30th

Concert (followed by a small private recital) followed by a supper party given by some important Italians. I was swept along without knowing who my hosts were, but the Italian women were very elegant, wearing beautiful silk dresses (as a matter of fact so was I and was complimented on it by Dr Goebbels. Magda G looked very tired and not too happy.). 'Maman' managed *this* party, but stayed in bed all day in order to be energetic enough to attend. She now uses an ebony stick to assist her – but somehow manages to make it chic!

October 22nd

Hugo home again, only to be sent to the Obersalzburg where Peter is filming the Duke of Windsor and his wife (the one he gave up the English crown for) who were visiting the Führer. I wasn't included this time in the official invitation. I had lunch with Peter's new girlfriend (one of many, her name is Cecilie, and I'm sure I'll never find it necessary to enter her name in these pages again) and we talked of nothing but cake recipes and Peter's performance in bed. I couldn't say I'd heard it all from Liz and knew *exactly* his procedure, which never varies.

Hugo says the Duke is a good friend to Germany, he liked him and admires him for having given up the throne for love – his American wife was divorced which was why she couldn't be Queen.

November 19th

Hugo *again* at the Berghof – another English visitor, Lord Halifax. The Führer loves the English. It must be cold in the mountains as it's miserable down here today. I wrapped up very warmly to do my stint of collecting for the Winter Relief. (I look forward to the *Summer Relief*, when I don't have to do my street walking!)

Had lunch at the hotel. *She* was there (of course, Blomberg is at Berchtesgaden!) and we chatted about rising food prices and how the one-pot meals* were becoming a necessity rather than a sacrifice. (I didn't tell her that restaurants and hotels had been issued with instructions on how to use up left-overs, since she was flattering about the kitchen at the *Goldener Hirsch*!)

November 20th

Hugo seems depressed, presumably overwork, since he comes home

---

* The officially inspired saving of cost for Winter Relief.

and falls instantly asleep. (At least this prevents pregnancy!) He talks nostalgically about the days when he was filming the Trauters and not the army. He *did* say he dislikes the idea of 'war footing'. 'Generals get tired of *playing* soldiers.' I said I thought it gave us prestige after the humiliation we had suffered. I'm a bit afraid he might ask to be 'demoted' to the old job. With prices the way they are, we couldn't afford it.

1938

January 6th

It's been a ghastly beginning to the year. Michael's last cold developed and his asthma is so much worse. The doctor says it is the bad weather. He mustn't be *fussed* over, or he'll become girlish, but we have to take care to keep him out of the damp. Often these cases clear up in the teenage years, I hope so, I would hate to think that all the fun ahead, the Youth Camps and so on, the hikes and climbing, will be curtailed because of a weak chest. What bad luck.

We were going to the von S gathering as last year, but couldn't make it as Michael was *in bed*. He was all right at Christmas, but two days afterwards the wretched attack began.

Hugo preoccupied with his work. Letter from Liz, they are moving to Boston, Todd has a job in radio there. She is glad, found New York too hectic. She sent a snap of the baby and Todd. Ironically, in spite of what she says, the baby looks to me like *Peter!*

January 12th

Well, Erna Gruhn's devotion to Room 12 has paid off. Today she and General Field Marshal Blomberg were married, with no less than Hitler and Göring as witnesses! It is said she was his *stenographer*.

January 13th

Who should I meet in the milliner's (Madame Maurel's of course) but Eva Braun! She greeted me like an old friend and insisted I have lunch with her at the Osteria. My hat is a spring straw, hers a black felt, somewhat severe. On the way to lunch we went to Hoffmann's place to pick up some home movies she had taken in and around the Berghof. She 'sprang to life' when she talked about them. She said she started taking films last year, *in colour*. These include some of the Führer's dog Blondie (the Alsatian) and his little Scots terrier. Eva said (it seems so mad I can't believe it) that he won't have official photographs with a small dog – because *it isn't manly*. He is afraid of being laughed at, she says – but I said I can't imagine anyone would ever want to laugh at him. Over lunch E said her dream is to go to

Hollywood and be a film star. She said that some of the film she had with her showed her dancing by a lake. She was dying to see it, the Führer had held the camera!

January 30th
Michael had a happy birthday.

February 12th
What a lazy cow I am! Perhaps one is only a keen diary-keeper in one's teens. I kept meaning to settle down and write the Blomberg story (it turns out Fräulein Gruhn was the daughter of a brothel owner, and had herself been convicted for prostitution and posing for a certain kind of photograph!) for he has been replaced by someone else! Hugo heard that he was offered suicide as a way out, but that he is far too much in love with his young (if not pure) bride, and continued his honeymoon after being dismissed. It's all scandal at the moment. The Commander in Chief of the army is supposed to have had an affair with 'Bavarian Joe', a notorious homosexual. There are many versions and many stories of course. How everyone loves the gossip.

Hugo is up in the mountains again – the Austrian Chancellor is meeting the Führer. I *hope* Hugo is back by tomorrow night, we are supposed to be having the Hans Engels to dinner.

February 14th
Hugo *did* get back, thank God. It was actually quite important for him as the Engels are close friends of General von Brauchitsch (C in C of the army) who I *know* hasn't met Hugo socially. Hugo was very taken with Chancellor Schuschnigg. Says he is very much the Austrian gentleman, charming, well-mannered, courteous – in the mould of his own father he said. Well, my father-in-law *is* a gentleman in the old-fashioned manner. Herr Engel said Austria would never hold on to its independence. I should think a link with us would be better but I didn't bother to say so, I hate these political discussions.

The spinach soufflé was excellent, I 'borrowed' the chef from the *Goldener H* . . . it's his night off, and he's always glad for the extra money. Funny man, no family, broken nose and a cheek scar, long torso and short legs, and a *genius* in the kitchen!

March 9th
Hugo left in a great hurry after telephone calls of secrecy and

importance. He kept shutting the door, and lowering his voice. Who does he think I'm going to tell – it's all so boring anyway!

March 10th

Hugo phoned from Berlin. Says he won't be back for some days, won't say why, only that he's on a government mission. I'm getting used to being a 'grass widow' but I don't like it.

March 12th

We have invaded Austria – the newspapers say that the communists are pillaging and shooting in Vienna. Goebbels has spoken on the radio. My father says it is against the League of Nations. He is depressed, but I am excited, and so is everyone here. The Austrians are welcoming our troops with joy. The Führer is in Linz. I wonder if that is where Hugo is?

March 14th

Hugo is *in Vienna*. The Anschluss has been declared and Austria is now a province of the German Reich. He managed to send me a telegram, he is staying in the Hotel Imperial.

April 3rd

Hugo in a very difficult mood. He came back from Vienna tired and for some reason deeply depressed. He said the Austrian NSDAP were behaving like pigs, the Jews were being made to scrub the gutters and the army latrines, and that they were looting (the NSDAP, not the Jews – looting Jewish homes that is). I have never liked the Austrians, and said so. Hugo absolutely loathes the man in charge at Linz* where he spent some days (Hitler's school town), who should never be in charge of anything bigger than a butcher's shop, a very crude man.

I am longing to go to Austria now – I have made Hugo promise to take me next time he has to go. I know a number of people who have already visited the nearby border towns. The food is *sensational*, and the prices unbelievably low.

April 4th

Learned with some horror that Hugo was actually attached to the fighting forces in Austria. I said 'You might have been killed!' and he

---

* Karl Adolf Eichmann.

said 'That is the least of it,' a silly reply, because it is the most of it, the worst aspect of it.

He really is in a trying state of mind. When I press him, he refers to the behaviour of the Austrians. I said that the Austrians are not the Germans, not known for their finesse. If the Austrians treat the Jews without humanity, we Germans are not responsible. Hugo is by no means for the Jews (except the few) but he must have seen something to make him so intense. He actually *threw away* Michael's favourite book (*Trust No Fox and No Jew*),* as if Michael could possibly *know* what it meant. He just likes (lik*ed* I should say, since it is now in ashes) the pictures. The ugly Jewish children being expelled from school are just 'naughty boys and girls' to him. I told Hugo I didn't even *read* the words to him. In fact, the very handsome blond Aryan at the beginning 'who can work and fight' Michael called 'Vati'. I spoke with more than my usual spirit to Hugo. Nothing makes me more irritated than the way adults try and impose their ideas on children. I want Michael to have an *open* mind. He has all kinds of books, and to make an issue out of this one (given to him, by the way, as a birthday present from Hilde, which makes it all the more embarrassing) simply draws attention to it.

April 6th
Trying to persuade Hugo to take me to the Salzburg Festival. Even Fräulein Müller is going to Austria for her holiday – it is the bargain of all time.

April 20th
BERLIN
I now love this city. Strange, when I consider how gloomy I found it on my first visit. We are here, with 'Maman' again (although now she really is virtually confined to her room during the day, and Gladys has taken over the function of a nurse) for the Führer's birthday. We have been invited to a reception at the Chancellery (quite a step up!) and Hugo has a number of meetings with the Doktor and military chiefs.

I had a long talk with Gladys. She is apparently a country girl, and was sent into service at the age of twelve at the manor house in the next village. Stanley (ten years older) fell in love with her, went off to war, and was wounded. When he came out of army hospital he was put in

---

* This book was published by Streicher and the NSDAP.

charge of German prisoners of war – one of them being a Count. After the war, the Count asked Stanley to come to Germany as his valet – Stanley agreed, but only if he could bring his wife. He then proposed to Gladys (by then seventeen), she accepted, and they came to Berlin! The Count was killed in a riding accident, and they took the post with 'Maman', who had been a friend of the Count's family. Gladys told me that 'Maman' had *never done up her own buttons, or dressed herself,* in her life!

Hugo spends at least an hour a day sitting with 'Maman' and talking to her. I find it annoying – they talk about things which I don't know about, and now she has put him off going to Salzburg, because Toscanini has cancelled his performances there 'in view of political events'. Just when I had pushed him to the point of asking for time off so that we could have a holiday there. I'm dying to go down the salt mine too – Annette told me about it, it's like something at a fair, and *thrilling.* (Toscanini shouldn't mix art with politics, in my opinion – not only did he send a telegram to the Festival organizers, but one to 'Maman' too – he always liked to visit her on his trips to this country, and she sent one back congratulating him on his stand.)

April 21st
The reception was rather dull, though the Führer's presents were on show in the old cabinet room. I talked to Frau Goebbels, and when we got home 'Maman' (who was waiting for a detailed description) told me how unhappy the poor woman is because her husband has countless affairs, and that she is in love with Karl Hanke (State Secretary in the Propaganda Ministry) who is half her age! The Doktor is currently besotted by a Czech film star, Lida something.

I have discovered what has been worrying Hugo. When he saw the atrocious behaviour of the Austrians towards the Jews in Vienna he gave orders for the cameras to be turned on them. All this film has been destroyed *by order of Dr G.* Also Schuschnigg (who Hugo liked so much) is under house arrest, and being badly treated (although this is hearsay). I told Hugo his job is to show the world the good side of the coin – what possible good would it do to let people see that the NSDAP, even the crude Austrian version, behave like thugs at times. Now Germany and Austria are united, it is necessary for everyone to know that it is for the good of both countries. Hugo said 'My job is to show the truth'. There is a blank wall of understanding I cannot seem to break through. The truth often *harms,* as it would in this case. I

143

simply don't see why he *can't* understand. If I can, with my far less astute mind (I'm under no apprehension!) why can't *he*?

April 29th
No coffee anywhere in Munich! Chocolate and tea are *not* the same!

May 20th
Hugo in the Obersalzberg. Sudden telephone call this evening. He just threw his night things in a case and was *gone*. There have been quite a few stories on the radio and in the papers about the Czechs attacking the Sudeten Germans. Hugo said it was the only thing he could think of that would make it necessary for him to see the Führer at this time of night. I made him promise to telephone me when he gets there (he's staying in a hotel, the *Berghof* is full!) just to say he has arrived safely.

Midnight
He phoned half an hour ago. Woke Michael, who has been wheezing ever since. I can see a night up for both of us – possibly *all* three of us, as Hugo was going to an urgent conference as soon as he came off the telephone.

May 24th
Hugo back – just in time because we're going to Fallersleben tomorrow. The cornerstone of the *Volkswagen** factory is being laid on the 26th. For some reason the Doktor wants Hugo to be there, and we promised Hilde and Michael they could come too. We're staying in a small hotel, run by a friend of Vati's. Hugo told me in secret that it was to do with the Czechs – but that it's now calmed down.

May 26th
Quite a nice little hotel, but an exhausting day. Still, I think Hilde and M enjoyed it. The Hitler Youth were out in full and made an impressive sight under the enormous flags. A marvellous speech by the Führer, promising cheap cars for everyone – the Strength-through-Joy car. There is going to be a huge industrial complex of communities called Wolfsburg. What a wonderful name! Michael has begun to buy his first Volkswagen! Through saving stamps. A brilliant idea that Hugo says will not only pay for the car, but for building the factory.

* lit. People's car; the Nazi concept of a standard car for all.

May 28th
Home to find a telegram to say that 'Maman' has died. I feel despairing.
I telephoned the apartment, and Gladys was crying too hard to tell
me much. The funeral is next week (Tuesday) and I suppose we have
to go. I would have gone a thousand times to see her when she was
alive, but it seems pointless to pay those 'last respects'. Am I hard? Am
I without feelings?

May 31st
Michael is ill, and so I can't go to the funeral after all. Hugo will, of
course. The doctor said that M *must* stay in bed for a week at least, and
eat only the lightest food.
   The official law against degenerate art was passed today (so the radio
informs me!). Hugo is interested in art but it bores me. I did go to the
opening of the House of German Art last summer, but couldn't get out
of it quickly enough, and to the reception! I *did* go to the 'Eternal Jew'
exhibition, and bought a couple of postcards but only because I had
promised Frau Smital I would go with her.

June 20th
I have asked our doctor to arrange for Michael to see a specialist. He is
better for a week, then the attacks start up again. We have tried so many
remedies – steaming kettles, burning feathers, sleeping in an upright
position, no eggs, etc, etc. What makes me more anxious is that next
year he will be old enough to become a Pimpf* and so much depends
on physical fitness for recording in the performance book. There must
be some effective remedy. After all, medicine is not in the Middle Ages.
   Klara in Munich for a few days' holiday, staying at the *Goldener
Hirsch* (where else?) and we are having long schooldays reminiscences.
She met Fräulein Willfried the other day – no longer teaching gymnastics, but leader of the local Bund deutscher Mädel. She told Klara
that she was the model for the last 9th of November† poster – the one
with the blonde woman in black holding a banner, and her left arm
raised in salute.
   Vati has given Michael a lot of saving stamps towards his car! I said
at this rate he'll be the owner before he is old enough to be allowed to
drive it! *Michael* says he would rather have a Mercedes Benz like Hitler!

* Young boys served as 'apprentices' to Hitler Youth.
† Commemoration of the Beerhall Putsch.

August 10th

At last we have seen Dr Kordt, the famous chest specialist. We had to go to Berlin, and for the first time I stayed in a hotel there. How I miss 'Maman' – in the end I was sorry I couldn't go to the funeral. Hugo said he had never seen so many celebrated people from all walks of life gathered together. And all in tears. I don't even know what happened to Gladys and Stanley.

Anyway, the hotel was pleasant enough, but our room had gloomy, huge high windows which I couldn't open, and faint marks on the ceiling from the days of gas lighting. Michael was afraid to be left alone there, so after dinner I stayed in the room with him and read a novel about life on the farm – lent to me by Fräulein Müller who is a great supporter of the *Heimatroman*.* Eventually I joined M in the huge double bed but didn't fall asleep until about two (I heard the clock strike one and seemed to lie awake for a long time after that.) Michael woke at his usual hour of six, so I wasn't exactly rested when we sat in the waiting room for the appointment with the renowned Dr Kordt.

I felt unexpectedly nervous. Michael chattered non-stop, amusing the other patients. Finally we were called, and proceeded down a long corridor painted dark yellow (or else the paint was yellow with age). His consulting room was brighter, a wallpaper and several pictures of landscapes, and a signed photograph of Himmler on the desk, together with one of three women, presumably his wife and daughters.

He was in his mid-fifties, and not unlike Himmler to look at. He was very kind to Michael, and gave him a book to look at while he asked me a great number of questions about the attacks, whether they followed any particular food, whether we had a dog or a cat or a pet bird, whether Michael became over-excited, whether he was constipated, whether he was wheezy on rainy days, in the country, whether Hugo and I had arguments (I really couldn't see what *that* was to do with anything!) whether there was a history of asthma in either family.

After all this, he took a throat swab, a nasal swab, a blood sample, and sent Michael off with a bottle for a urine sample and another container with a miniature trowel in the cork for *the other*. I was going to accompany him, but Dr Kordt said, 'My nurse will take him.' Michael trotted off like a lamb, and the doctor explained that children don't perform for their mothers, but will oblige a stranger, particularly a stranger in uniform.

---

* The regional novel.

When he was out of the room he said he was going to take chest X-rays, but he felt that Michael was the type of child to grow out of the disease by his late teens. He said he recommended that I take Michael to a mountain resort in France called Le Mont Dore, which has natural waters and gases beneficial to sufferers. I said I would have to ask my husband – never having been out of Germany I am terrified of going to France alone, I can't speak more than a few words of the language. Dr Kordt said I should make up my mind quickly, because it would be advisable to go within the next month, and one has to stay three weeks. He said the hotels are full, and he would recommend me to a doctor there, who sees his patients.

As soon as I was back in Munich and on the way home from the station with Hugo, I told him about the cure. He said at once that we must go. I asked him if he could take a holiday and come too, but he said 'IMPOSSIBLE. You've no idea how much is going on.'

I wrote off to Dr Kordt and said I would take Michael whenever he could arrange for us to see the French doctor. He wrote back, giving me the names of three hotels and their weekly prices, and told me that Dr Schaeffer would see us at 3 p.m. on September 16th.

I then sent a telegram to the Hôtel Gallia (the middle-priced one of the three) and had the booking confirmed the next day (yesterday, in fact) and now I'm reading a French phrase book so that at least I can order dinner.

September 16th
Le Mont Dore
I have been so busy preparing for the journey and nursing Michael through his worst attack ever, that all Hugo's problems didn't touch me. He had to go to the Rally, of course, but for the first time since our marriage I wasn't there. I listened to the speeches on the radio – Göring called the Czechs a 'miserable pygmy race', and Hitler was at his most formidable and compelling, insisting that the Czechs give justice to the Sudeten Germans. You should have heard the cheers. I wondered that the Hall still stood. Many people seem to think there will be a war, but if there is, how long will it last? I'm perfectly sure Hitler doesn't want a fight.

Hugo is very depressed and *very* overworked. I have a feeling that his work isn't *only* to do with the filming now, though when I ask him he says I'm mad to ask, *of course it is*. He couldn't even see us off at the station yesterday morning, because the English Prime

Minister was coming to see the Führer, and Hugo had to stay at the Berghof.

Now I'm here, and political life is far away, and I just feel that everything will be all right. I can't read the French newspapers or understand their radio, and I'm much more interested in *asthma*. We saw the doctor this afternoon, and we start the cure in the morning (I say 'we' because it seems that I am involved, it isn't just a matter of delivering and collecting M). The doctor is charming (Jewish? Well, I won't think about *that*) and Michael took to him immediately. We had quite a long wait, but there was a little asthmatic English girl and her mother in the waiting room, and we managed to make conversation. The mother spoke fluent French, but also seemed to understand bits of German and my halting English, that came back to me from school. 'Miss' would have been proud of her pupil. We are staying in the same hotel it turns out, but they have been here for a week already, and the English lady has offered to accompany us to the cure centre in the morning.

And it is *the morning!* We have to be there by *seven*. The town itself is picturesque, but nothing like as beautiful as Bavaria. It is right in the mountains, but I have to admit to being disappointed by the general shopping and residential area. We had to go to the shops to buy the special suit to wear to the 'cure' – since the morning air is cold. Michael had one of the smallest sizes, and looks like a gnome in his white trousers and hooded jacket, perfectly adorable. We also bought some French sweets, in a box like a sailor's hat with a red pom-pom in the centre. The sweets are hard 'fraises du bois' with juice in the hollow centre. Delicious.

Quite a mixture of nationalities in the hotel – all linked by asthma. Apart from the English child (Juliana?) there is a little Belgian girl (Lizette) who has an Aryan appearance, fair curls and blue eyes – the English one is dark and rather *frizzy* – and a number of French children of varying ages. There are the adult asthmatics too, one of them in the most terrible state that I feel no cure could affect . . . his chest is literally caved in, shoulders hunched, and just to listen to him breathe makes me agonized. He is attended by a spinster (daughter?) who has to help him to the elevator, and assist his painfully slow efforts to get to his feet from the dining-room table. Others are in varying degrees of health, from a stalwart young man who looks as if he could swim the Atlantic, to a frail American woman in her thirties, accompanied by a devoted husband.

Now Michael is asleep, and I am keeping the boring hotel vigil, as

in Berlin, with the shutters closed (the doctor insists) and hoping I will
be able to go to sleep soon myself, since we are to be up so early.

September 19th

The days seem endless. We are up and dressed and walking through the
mountain mist to the *Thermal* by seven. You hear the phlegmy
coughing of the *curistes* making their way before you are out of the
hotel door! First of all you take the water. Yes, I am drinking it too, I
am assured it can only do me good. For this we have special glass cups,
which we bought at the cure place, mine blue, Michael's red! We stand
in the tiled hall, and I have the sensation of being at a railway station,
domed roof, voices echoing slightly. *Then* we inhale the nasal gases,
sitting round a table with central partitions, each partition having a
little tap and rubber tubing, to which we fit our own wooden tubes,
rather like hollow knitting needles. It certainly clears the head! Michael
has his instructions and is almost able to turn the tap himself, another
day and he won't need help! We keep the 'knitting needles' in holders,
and bring them with us each day. Sitting around the inhaling table is
like sitting in a patisserie! There is one in Berlin in particular of which
I am reminded as I take my place!

I *don't* indulge in the final daily episode – the steam room! Adults
have individual cubicles, but the children go together. Attendants are
there to help to remove the special suit, and Michael wears his vest and
pants and a bathing cap. He disappears into the white fog – swallowed
up in an instant. To while away the time today I had a *Douche Ecossaise* –
a tough lady (of the Bund deutscher Mädel instructress brand) hosed me,
first hot and then cold, with such painful force I had to cover my
breasts. I shan't indulge again – the English mother suggested it,
she finds the waiting so tedious, but she must be stronger and healthier
than I am!

Eventually the children emerge, to be dried down, changed into the
clean underwear we bring with us, and dressed again in the 'suit' which
has been heated on a radiator. We take the car back to the hotel – and
I think in future we will take it *there* as well. It's all part of the service!

Then it's back to bed, and breakfast – at a time when I'd still be
asleep at home! The femme de chambre heats the bed with a brass
warming pan – and leaves black smuts behind! The breakfast is
delicious, croissants, coffee and cherry jam. Michael has to spend an
hour in bed, so we are not really out and about again until after lunch
(which we have early for something to do!) and this afternoon we

went with Lizette's mother and Juliana's mother (and the children of course) to hire donkeys. Michael was ecstatic – though a slight *fracas* (see how my French is coming on) because Juliana lays claim to a donkey by the name of Caroline, and Michael decided it was the one *he* wanted. In the end he settled for a little dark brown beast called Mierette – which I thought prettier.

Both the other mothers are in a state of tension over the political situation. They are convinced there is going to be war, and Juliana's mother, whose husband is a doctor, is considering returning home. She is frightened of being stranded if war is declared – but her little girl had been so ill during the summer, she is loath to cut short the treatment and the hope of a cure.

September 27th
Letter from Hugo. Says the Führer has been in a state of extreme tension and that the British Prime Minister had made another visit. (He was writing from Godesberg, a small town on the Rhine.) He said he had never seen the Führer so out of control of himself. Hugo thinks war is possible, unless the Czechs hand over the Sudetenland. This what the British want them to do – but they have refused up till now.

I rode a donkey myself today, up the mountain paths. All the mothers are in the same state of boredom, although the children adore every minute. We have been up the mountain in a funicular to the roller-skating rink at the top (I did rather well for a beginner) and to the market (where a pigeon relieved itself into Juliana's mother's hair, much to the delight of the children). I bought a dark green cardigan with some embroidery on the front, and some sweet glass brooches (rows of little birds on branches) for Mutti, Hilde, Fräulein M and others . . . I will, of course, take Mutti something more, possibly some French wine –except it is a nuisance to carry on and off the trains.

September 28th
My French-speaking friends tell me that the Parisians think there will be war within twenty-four hours, and are leaving the city. I still can't believe it will happen, but their fear is beginning to affect me, and I sent a telegram to Hugo asking if I should come back. The English people have packed and intend to leave in the morning (it is now 4.15 and I hope to have Hugo's answer before tonight).

A few minutes after writing the above, there was a fierce knocking on my door. One of the guests had been listening to his radio, and had heard that Hitler had invited Monsieur Daladier, Mussolini and Chamberlain to a meeting in Munich tomorrow ... and it *must mean peace.*

I *knew* the Führer wouldn't lead us into war – a peaceful settlement and Michael will be able to complete his three weeks' cure! Thank God.

October 7th
How wonderful to be home – and Michael seems much better. Everyone thrilled to see us, and all in high spirits since war has been averted, *to our greater glory.* I'm not sorry to have been away during the talks. Mutti says Vati was *impossible.* Hugo was away the whole time, rushing from Berlin to Munich to God knows where. He says we had the army ready to invade – he *also* said that the Führer was disappointed (privately) and was reported to have said that Chamberlain had spoiled his entry into Prague!

I am proud of myself – I have travelled abroad and *coped.* I feel now I could go anywhere, do anything. Where next? Prague?

November 7th
A Jew has shot the third secretary at our Embassy in Paris – he thought he was assassinating the Ambassador!

November 10th
Awoke last night to sounds of crashing and screaming. Hugo was already at the window, and Michael and Hilde joined us – I think everyone on the street was at their windows. The sky was bright with fire, everything pinkish, and the noises bloodcurdling. At one point a whole army of people tore down the street making the most ghastly noise, smashing shop windows as they went.

This morning we heard on the radio that rioting started to revenge the Embassy man shot in Paris by that stupid Jew – he should have known what he would unleash on his people. All over the country synagogues have been burnt down, Jewish shops destroyed, Jewish homes burned. Jews killed. We went for a drive to look at the damage. I can only hope some of the poor devils were insured, their livelihood has gone. Hugo said, 'Where is German humanism? I am disgusted.' Who wouldn't be? Why oh why don't those idiots pack up what they have left and just *go* – where they are wanted!

December 1st
Posted a birthday card from Michael to the little English girl from Le
Mont Dore. Her birthday is on the 5th – they exchanged dates. I only
hope they remember to send one to M on January 30th. (She is Gillian,
not Juliana, as I discovered when I looked properly at the address!)

1939

January 30th

I cannot believe that Michael is six today – a happy day. A family party and a whole heap of presents. The little English girl did send greetings from London – and M has taken the stamp off the envelope and put it in the album he received from Fräulein M. Hugo home for part of the day, he is backwards and forwards from Berlin (hates Ribbentrop).

March 18th
VIENNA
At last!

Everything everyone has said is true – a *heavenly* city. *My* kind of city, I love everything about it, from the incredible cakes (went to Sacher's!) to the grand buildings. We came (well, *Hugo* came) for the Ministry, as the Führer is here to look over some treaty or other. While he (Hugo) is working from an office in one of the official buildings, making endless telephone calls of great importance(!) – so they tell me every time I try to reach him on the telephone – I am walking down the wonderful streets, gazing in rapture at everything. The Riding School! I must bring Michael one day. The Opera! That staircase! It's what I want in my own home, I have a private dream of descending stairs like those, wearing a ball gown and long white gloves. And diamonds, of course. I'm not sure who is at the bottom waiting to receive me. Hugo is there, and the Führer – and some very handsome film star, or perhaps the English Duke, the one who gave up the throne.

I found a café near the hotel where I had the most heavenly hot chocolate. I sat for hours, watching the well-dressed businessmen take their newspapers from the wooden stand and read them as they eat the most elaborate slices of fruit tart (worthy of my French milliner!) with an abstracted manner, as though it wouldn't do to be seen enjoying anything so delicious! Hugo loathes it here – he says his last visit at the time of the *Anschluss* has destroyed pleasure in this capital for ever. The marvellously ornate buildings which to me are like a fairy-tale city are hemming in and oppressive to him.

I have, through the hotel concierge, arranged to take a tour tomorrow,

with three other ladies, and much look forward to it. The car, shared
between us, is quite cheap – prices here are so low.

March 19th
We drove out of Vienna to the surrounding villages – even prettier
than in Bavaria. We made a stop to taste the wine (and eat cakes!!) in
one picturesque hamlet – and one of my travelling companions became
instantly drunk, and talked and hiccupped for the rest of the morning.
Our driver told us that Beethoven realized he was deaf when he saw
the bell swinging from the church, and couldn't hear the sound. He
stopped the car, and we all stood and gazed reverently at the offending
bell – he pointed out various other Beethoven associations – he seemed
to have lived in a great number of places, endlessly thrown out by his
landladies. I think our drunk lady didn't see the bell or anything
else!
    Schönbrunn was on the itinerary, and very *schön* it is. Not too
crowded either; the driver said that in the summer the place is jammed
with tourists, although he wonders if it will be as popular this year. I
said, with the prices being low and the food so good, Germans would
be pouring over the border.
    Hugo was back at the hotel, and said as soon as I had had a short rest,
he was going to take me to the Prater. I had a bath (a huge, deep, satisfying bath with an enormous towelling robe to wrap myself in afterwards) and we had a light meal in the café I discovered yesterday, before
taking the tram, my first trip on a tram here, how spoilt I am with my
taxis and private cars!
    I hadn't the courage to go on the Big Wheel – so Hugo went alone.
Afterwards I was sorry, because the view must be wonderful from that
height. But it went so slowly, and I thought I would be dizzy, or want
to cast myself down.
    Not every attraction was open, and the air was quite chilly, but I
found it myseriously romantic as the lights flared in the woodland
setting, and the smells from the fairground food mingled with the scent
of the dead leaves still on the paths and the damp evening air. Couples
strolled and children ran and there was none of the frenzy I have sometimes seen in fairs at home. Perhaps because this is permanent, and not
travelling, there is less pressure to enjoy everything at once. We were
about to turn round and make our way back to the hotel when we came
across a carousel worked by real horses, gentle blinkered creatures with
shining harnesses trimmed with bells. The coaches (gilded, carved,

seats of red plush velvet) moved quite slowly at first, turning a little from left to right, then, as the horses plodded faster, a mechanical organ began to play and Hugo and I held hands and revolved to a wheezing waltz under the branches of the Viennese trees.

It has been a lovely three days.

April 20th
I am home, Hugo has flown to Berlin. Hitler's birthday – *his fiftieth*. He doesn't *look* fifty. Part of the new road is going to be opened, and there's a ceremony at the Brandenberg Gate. I was going to go, but the Vienna trip came up, and I made my wise choice!

I had lots of little presents from Vienna for Michael. A miniature of the Wheel (his favourite) and a china dog Hugo won at the shooting range. I also found some hand puppets in one of the shops, and brought a Hänsel and Gretel and a witch with a huge and horrible mole on her (Semitic!) nose. This, needless to say, is Michael's favourite.

April 30th
Hugo's father here. I like him more and more, a very gentle and cultured gentleman of 'the old school'. He visited a Jewish family (an old banking family he said, with whom he has done much business) who lost most of their possessions in a fire on *Kristall nacht*. I only hope that if he was seen visiting them, there was no connection made with *us*. I don't want Hugo's position jeopardized. *Schwiegervater* is trying to get this family to America, but there is trouble getting the insurance on their damaged property. I said to Hugo 'Don't ask your father too many questions. We don't want to know what he's doing.'

May 10th
Met Eva Braun again today. We had lunch in the Osteria together, and I left feeling sorry for her. She said the Führer doesn't feel he has a long life ahead, and keeps saying that he must complete his plans for the Third Reich before he dies. He made his will last year, soon after his birthday, and he said to Eva, 'I'll have to give you your freedom, why should you be tied to an old man?'

'Fifty isn't old, is it?' she said, and her eyes swam with tears. She talked with great feeling about Geli Raubel killing herself 'before I came on the scene. He loved her much more than he loved me.' (She feels that he keeps her out of things.) She said she couldn't bear the idea of women dying young, and said how upset she had been when Renate

Müller died* and how wonderful she had found her in *Die Privatsekre-tärin,†* her favourite movie. She then confessed that she had once tried to kill herself, and that Hitler had been deeply disturbed, and when she wasn't well he was very concerned. I was also interested to hear about the Führer's doctor, who had saved Hoffmann's life – she had been working for him at the time. Hoffman persuaded Hitler to go to him and Dr Morell gave him Multifor capsules (which I have heard about) and injections from animal testicles! (She said he once told her he had a love-child, a son, but she doesn't believe it.) He made Eva go to the doctor for an examination, but she said he was 'disgustingly dirty' and never went back again.

Michael greeted me at the front door with stars in his eyes. He has been given his Performance Book, he is a *Pimpf.* I said we must cele-brate, and took him off to the *Goldener Hirsch* for a game with his fond grandfather, and a glass of apple juice! The Performance Book goes with him to the very end of his days in the Hitler Youth.

There is a little trouble at school because the PT (which is compul-sory) sometimes brings on an asthma attack. Michael *refuses* to give up even one class – and there are five a week. The drill is not too bad, but the running really affects him. I have written to Dr Kordt, to ask if there is anything he could take on those mornings. I admire Michael's will – not many little boys would be so determined in face of the misery and discomfort of an attack. Of course, much more importance is placed on PT than when I was at school.

Saw a marvellous movie tonight – *Tanz auf dem Vulkan‡* – which I missed when it first came out. It is set in the time of the French Revolu-tion, and one could feel the whole audience stirred to an emotional response – even the girls next to me, with their box of cakes, stopped eating, and at the end, people applauded as if they had seen live per-formers.

May 29th
Michael felt an attack coming on, and so I gave him one of the small ephedrine tablets that Dr Kordt prescribed following my letter. It worked, although he said his heart felt like a fast clock. I must write again to Dr K and find out if this is normal or whether they don't agree with M.

---

* Renate Müller was a popular film idol who died in 1937 at the age of 31.
† *The Private Secretary.*
‡ *Dance on the Volcano.*

June 4th

What do I do? Michael is determined to take part in the Camp arranged by the school for the 6 to 10-year-olds. Our doctor here advises against it. Hugo thinks he *should* go if he wants to so much. Says he can always come back if he is taken ill.

June 5th

I talked to Michael very seriously today about the Camp and his health. Hilde was out (seeing her boyfriend – married fortunately, so she won't be leaving us!) and Hugo at the Brown House. I said that I thought it unwise to sleep in the open, because the damp affects his chest. He was suddenly thrown into the most extraordinary rage. Normally he is a peaceful little boy, but my words 'weak chest' made his face scarlet, his eyes blaze and his fists clench. He hit his chest with his fists and shouted at me 'It's not weak, it's NOT WEAK. It's like everyone else's.' Then he burst into tears, hit out at *me* and rushed out of the room. He leaned against his bedroom door with all his strength so that I wouldn't go in. Of course it wasn't very difficult, but it took a long time before he allowed me to touch him and put my arms round him and lift him on to my lap.

I found I had tears in my eyes when I held him. He said 'I MUST go to the Camp. You can't stop me.' I asked him why it mattered so very much, and he said, through sobs and gulps 'Because if I don't I'll never go to an Adolf Hitler School.'

I didn't even know he had *heard* of the A H schools. I was astonished. They're a new venture, under the direction of the Hitler Youth – but pupils aren't accepted before the age of *twelve*. I said that he had *six years* before selection, but somehow he had got it into his head that if he didn't attend *this* camp, if it wasn't entered in his Performance Book, he would lose his chance.

I was totally exhausted after it all, and had a dreadful headache. But of course I had given in and said yes. How could I prevent him from taking part in something so important to him? A couple of hours later he was his old self, smiling and playing with his soldiers, while I felt as if I had been put through the washing machine.

June 6th

Letter from Dr Kordt. The reaction to the pills is natural. I suppose I can make him take them to the Camp.

June 7th

Hugo told me today that the government has ordered that the foundry must be turned over to rearmament. When his father was here he had discussions at the Brown House. It was the real reason for coming to Munich. I felt rather hurt that I was only told at this late date, as if I wasn't trustworthy. Hugo has a group of new friends – well, new to me. Walter was a fellow student in Berlin, and now works at the *Haus der Kunst*, in charge of some of the exhibitions. Georg (tall and bearded) is a Brown House colleague – married to an intellectual and unfeminine *creature* who reminds me of Christel and makes me feel a fool because I can't quote Goethe – and Theodor, an artist attached to the Ministry. Hugo brings them home in the evenings, so I am not left out ... but I feel left out, just as I did when we were first married, just as I did with Moritz. Not 'Maman' – she had the art of making everyone feel interesting, whatever the contribution. But this lot try to draw me into the conversation, and somehow push me to the outside. My contribution is the coffee, the wine and the cakes. Yet in many ways I think I'm *better* than they are, I dress far far better than the 'creature', and when she dismissed Vienna as 'decadent' and said she loathed the architecture, I could have hit her over the head with the *Streuselkuchen*!

I feel very very glad that Michael is mixing with all types of children. The Hitler Youth is a *leveller*, which is how it should be.

June 8th

Hugo is going to be away for several weeks. He has been assigned to the Luftwaffe manoeuvres and although he will be home some weekends, nothing is planned, so *I* cannot make plans. No dinner parties, because I won't be asked without Hugo (the new friends certainly won't bother to entertain me) and if I'm lucky Frau Smital will ask me to a ladies' lunch. I said to Hugo if he's going to be with Hermann Göring, he can *cement* the relationship. I'd love to go to Carinhall again.

June 9th

Hugo has been given a uniform – and looks very splendid. He has been told to wear it now for all official assignments when he is with the Reichs Marshal. I said to him that he must keep a diary, so that he can read all the details to me. He said he would 'try' but it means he won't. Some of it, of course, is secret, but I don't care about the secret bits. I want to know what the hotels are like, what the Reichs Marshal eats for dinner, and how much money is spent on champagne and caviar.

June 16th

Hugo back for two days. He is going to Schleswig-Holstein* for some meeting or other, then he goes to the Ruhr. I said I was so bored by being left alone I might just as well have another baby. Hugo said 'There's going to be war by the end of the year. It isn't the time to bring more people into this lousy world.' I cried. I couldn't help it. I feel so frightened. Oh God, *don't* let it be true.

June 27th

We're going to have a holiday – of a *kind*. We're actually going to Bayreuth in August. Not *alone*, with Georg and his patronizing wife. They go every year and are Wagner fanatics. It happens that the Festival takes place when Michael goes to Camp – yes, I am quite reconciled to it, he knows when he needs to take his pills, and has become such an ardent little soldier I couldn't disappoint him. He has some paper cut-outs of *Pimpfe* and *Jungvolk*, and arranges them in 'camps'. I am not allowed to touch them, they are set out on the table in his room. Hilde knocked them over when she was dusting and he was furious with her! They all have names. Each day they do some different exercise.

August 9th
VENICE!!!

What a year. This time in 1938 I hadn't been out of Germany, now I notch them up. France. Austria. *Italy*. It's incredible. Now I can't imagine myself *not* travelling. I feel sorry for Fräulein Müller who will never go further than Rosenheim (where her sister lives). I want to write and write and write about Venice, but before I let myself go on its beauty, I must put down the events which brought us here – no one knows the truth. Not even Hugo. I can never tell him.

We drove to Bayreuth in a Party Mercedes. Ours had broken down, and Goebbels arranged that we should have an official car, which puzzled me as I had assumed we were 'on our own' and this was a private holiday. But no, Hugo informed me, it was 'business' too. He didn't divulge its nature, and I have to say that I have no inkling even now, as we behaved like private citizens, and stayed in a tourist hotel.

We inadvertently found ourselves ahead of the Führer's car (we came from different directions, but met on the route into the town).

* Göring met with Swedish industrialist Birger Dahlerus and British businessmen in an attempt to persuade the English to 'see reason' over the Polish question.

The crowds were waiting – the children with posies, with flags. The women thought *our* car was part of the procession (or even *his* car) for they waved and saluted and shouted and *sobbed*. You would think he was Valentino, I actually saw one young woman in hysterics and *urinating*. Where she stood! I don't think she *knew*.

Hitler stayed at the Siegfried Wagners' in Haus Wahnfried (Wagner's house – oh, yes, I did my homework, so that Georg and Frau Georg couldn't crow over me)with the Goebbelses, Albert Speer (he really is very nice looking) and his wife, and a couple of others.

I had read on the operas we were going to see, and had borrowed a guide book of the town and a history of the Festival, and I did rather well at dinner – I spoke three times, and even the 'creature' agreed with what I said (about *Tristan and Isolde* which we were going to see the next night).

I looked at my very best, and I felt self-confident, which helped me to overcome my nervousness. Hugo looked desperately handsome in his evening dress (Georg looked frightful while *she* looked like a scarecrow) and I felt all those yearnings which I haven't been experiencing of late.

I enjoyed the opera more than I thought I would – all that grand passion suited my mood. The Führer was in the big central box with the Doktor and his wife. During the intermission one of the ushers brought a note to Hugo, inviting us to a reception afterwards. By *us* I mean Hugo and me – not Georg and wife. They were impressed and said they would see us in the morning at breakfast, and we planned to take a long walk. I said 'If we're not too tired after the party! You know how late the Führer stays up.' I couldn't resist it. The 'creature' wilted with envy.

The reception was a small private one in a beautiful house belonging to one of the Festival administrators. An elegant room, furnished with heavy antiques, thick velvet curtains, hordes of servants and delicious food. The Doktor was there (Frau Goebbels was not, which will be explained afterwards), and I suddenly found him at my side as I looked out of the windows to the floodlit garden.

'What a glorious night.' I was quite startled, and said 'I haven't been to the Festival before.' He said 'Having come once, you'll never miss it again. It becomes part of one's summer.' Then he said 'Have you seen the garden?'

I said no, I hadn't, and he suggested that he show me the grounds. Full of topiary or whatever the word is – trimmed bushes and hedges anyway – and I said I'd love to see it all. Off we went, through the open glass doors, and not only was there lighting in the trees but a moon like a beachball. Some of the flowers were of the night-scented kind and it was like being in heaven – until I was suddenly clutched by the Minister of Propaganda, pushed into the coiffured bushes and kissed on the exposed part of my bosom. As he is only a shrimp of a man (funny foot and all) his lips were just about level with it! I should add that my dress is low cut and does push me up rather!

I pushed him off, and he said 'Don't reject me, dear Frau von Stahlenberg. Your beautiful body maddens me.'

I couldn't believe my ears. He said 'I want to make love to you. Now. Tonight.' Of course I've heard all the stories.

I said 'Dr Goebbels, I am happily married. I can't . . . you must forgive me.'

The terrible thought crossed my mind that Hugo might be sacked, if I didn't oblige.

He said 'You must forgive me. I was overcome.' (What *relief!*) He seized my hand and frantically kissed the palm which I could just about tolerate. The awful thing was I wanted to giggle.

He then escorted me back to the house, and as we reached the doors (and inside I could see Hitler talking to the hostess, and Hugo stuck with one of the singers, not an important one) he said 'I will always be waiting for you. You know, one day you will be mine.'

We went in and he said to Hugo 'I have just been escorting your lovely wife round the garden. She has beauty and charm. I must congratulate you.' Hugo looked pleased, and the singer irritated. Dr G called over a waiter with champagne, and gave me a glass, trying to look into my eyes. Then, fortunately, the Führer called him over, and I was able to breathe again.

At first I couldn't wait to tell Hugo, and then I suddenly thought he might be too angry, and while not exactly challenging the Doktor to a duel, might feel he had to say something or resign . . . both of which would be disastrous for his (our) future. So I decided to keep quiet about it.

On the way back to the hotel I asked what had happened to Frau Goebbels. Oh, said Hugo, she was in a terrible state. The Führer had just broken up her love affair with Karl Hanke* – this was the 'official' marital reconciliation, and she was in tears all the time. Hadn't I seen

* State Secretary at the Propaganda Ministry.

at the opera? No, I hadn't. Poor woman, said Hugo, she had had to put up with the infidelities all these years, and now she has fallen genuinely in love (an odd couple, but no accounting for tastes) it was cut short.

Hugo: I dare say he's learned his lesson too. He'll keep his hands to himself for a while. The Führer likes a clean Party image.

Me: I expect he will!

We did manage to wake early, because Hugo really wanted to go on this walk. But we would have been wakened in any case. As we reached the dining-room for breakfast, the hall page rushed up to us to say that Dr Goebbels wished to talk to Hugo on the telephone.

I could scarcely swallow my coffee.

When he came back he said 'Darling, we're going to Venice.'

I said 'Venice or Vienna?' I couldn't see why or how.

He said 'The Führer has suggested that *as Frau Goebbels isn't well* they should leave Bayreuth immediately.'

'But what's that to do with Venice?'

'The Doktor has told me he wants me to accompany him and Dr Dietrich to the *Biennale* on the 8th. He said he insists that I bring you with me, he said you had told him how much you longed to go to Italy.'

I just said 'How nice of him.'

'Oh, he can be thoughtful at times,' said Hugo.

I hadn't any idea what the *Biennale* was, but I gathered it was an art exhibition by the time breakfast was over. I was thrilled to be going but terrified that I would be put on a spot by Dr G. I just thought that I would never never allow myself to be alone with him.

So far, I've succeeded.

We went back to Munich after the few days in Bayreuth, and I washed some clothes and repacked them, and bought a bathing suit – I hadn't thought about Venice having a beach until Mutti said 'Are you staying on the Lido?' She went there for her honeymoon.

We went by train, and I will never never forget the extraordinary moment of leaving what seems like a perfectly ordinary station, and stepping out onto a canalside. You can't believe your eyes. Opposite you there's a church with a green dome (copper, I'm told, turned that colour) and you look up the Grand Canal, and there are gondolas and bridges, and it's all, well . . . breathtaking, and that's a feeble word. I thought how lucky I was, Vienna and Venice in one year.

We were taken by boat to St Mark's Square – a *taxi boat* – and a porter there took our cases and we followed him to our hotel. I was stunned by it. The Square is like a huge ballroom – and the Cathedral like a stage set for an opera. Somehow it looks *flat* as if it hasn't a back to it, when you turn to face it. . . . Then there's music playing from the little orchestras outside the cafés and restaurants, and the pigeons . . . and the shops . . . and our hotel. I can't even put a sentence together I'm so excited.

The hotel is near to the Fenice Theatre, and I'd describe that if I could do it justice. But I can't. I have never been anywhere so exquisite. The room we have is on the top floor, and has a chaise longue, and bamboo furniture, and a view over the rooftops, and a cross over the bed, and a cat that keeps coming in through the window from the parapet outside. Amazing. Amazing.

We took the waterbus to the *Biennale* – and that's amazing too, with pavilions for the countries exhibiting their paintings, all in a shady kind of park. I felt very proud of ours, even though it reminded me inside of 'Maman's' bank in Berlin! I thought the paintings were inspiring, and was surprised when Hugo said to me privately that he found it limited. Well, I don't know much about art, but it didn't seem in the least limited to me. I liked Adolf Ziegler's work the best, but I overheard one of the tourists saying it was 'a pale imitation'. He didn't say an imitation of what!

I had to talk to Dr G, who said how charming I looked, and tried to look meaningfully into my eyes. I couldn't help thinking how Heidi would relish the opportunity I'm turning down! Horrid little man – but I'm NOT going to be trapped.

I don't have to go to the exhibition again, although Hugo does. Some of the artists are going to be filmed, and some of the 'decadent' art of other countries is going to be shown. This was the subject of a conversation I overheard on the beach, and which ended with me being invited to lunch by an English woman.

While Hugo was at a meeting in the Gritti Palace (the best hotel) with the Italian propaganda people, I bravely took the *vaporetto* to the Lido, and then walked down the main shopping street (called after me! The Elisabetta!) to the beach. I had to pay to go on the private beach of one of the hotels (Hôtel des Bains, it's called) and I hired a cabin to change into my new black bathing costume, and then I hired a chair to lie on (luckily I'd brought my hotel towel with me or I'd have had to pay for one of those too) and I stretched myself out in the gorgeous sunshine and listened to those Italian mothers calling to the children with the beautiful Italian names – Fabio and Massimo and Giulio. It turned out that what I thought was Giulio was in fact *Julia*, and there was this lovely red-haired lady as unlike an English person as I'm unlike an Italian. We got into conversation and it turned out she was with a group who had come to see the *Biennale*. They weren't all staying in the same hotel, but this family – Paula and her husband and two children – had invited everyone to lunch on the beach, and she said to me, 'Why don't you join us?'

In fact we walked up the beach to one of those little restaurants actually on the sands. It was run by a gesticulating Italian and his Irish wife. Their dog had a name like Boddle. The daughter waited on us. We had fresh fish, which was being cooked with herbs while we ate the spaghetti *pomodoro* (hope my spelling is right) and drank wine. There was a schoolmaster called Clement, very tall and obviously very witty because he made the others laugh a lot (I couldn't catch much of what he said, but I smiled as if I had) and a young woman who said her husband was an art historian. She didn't speak a great deal, but when she did it was with a slight smile and absolutely to the point. She demolished an argument being waged by two of the other guests with one logical sentence. I know it was logical because someone said to me in German 'She has the most logical mind I've come across.' Someone else said 'For a woman.'

Clement said he'd heard the Germans were filming at the *Biennale*. 'Just their own National Socialist exhibits?' asked Paula's husband.

I said 'Of course not.'

Someone said I shouldn't be too sure. I said 'I *can* be sure, because my husband is in charge of it.' (Not strictly true, but it created an impression.)

The lady with the art historian husband (he was at the exhibition and so I never met him) said she thought the film would draw large audiences in that case, as the exhibition of decadent art in Munich eventually had to be taken off because of the attention it caused. I'm not a fool, I knew what she meant, but (a) I couldn't think of a quick answer, and (b) it's impossible to defend something in stilted English to a company only one of which spoke fluent German.

After the delicious lunch everyone went to sleep in the sun, until Paula's little boy brought us all peach and pistachio ice creams from a man wheeling a cart along the sands – striped umbrella shading it. I said to Paula 'I wish my little boy was here too' (hers is around the same age). She said 'Why didn't you bring him?' I explained about the

Camp, and about the whole Youth Movement we have. I could feel (although she never said so) that she loathed the idea. She said she liked family holidays, and she would be afraid of trusting strangers with her children. I said all the people in charge of Hitler Youth were trust-worthy, and had been highly trained and selected with rigorous care. I know she wasn't convinced. There are some unseen walls you can't climb. Her husband tried to ask me about the Jews, but I didn't get into the subject. I just said some of my friends had chosen to leave. I *did* say the Austrians had behaved very badly at the *Anschluss*, and that I felt there was a difference between the attitudes in the two countries.

I couldn't help boasting, and mentioning that I had stayed with the Führer at the Berghof. That was the one moment I had everyone's attention. They fired questions at me . . . I wouldn't dare let Hugo know. I told them what he had had for dinner, and what film we had seen and how we'd walked to the Teahouse.

Afterwards I wondered if any of them were Jewish. The one married to the art historian has a Jewish sounding surname, but from her con-versation I gathered she had completely renounced *the church*.

Paula's husband's name is David, but that doesn't really mean any-. thing. They have invited me for lunch again tomorrow.

Tonight we are going to a concert on an island opposite San Marco, San Georgio I think . . . with THE DOKTOR. Help! Help! I shall hold Hugo's hand all night, and appear *very loving*.

I hear him coming up the stairs now – no doubt exhausted from his working day, which makes me feel horribly guilty, especially as I know why the good Dr G thought the holiday would be so nice for me!

August 19th
Le Mont Dore

The tête-à-tête with Dr G was avoided. When we returned to the hotel after the concert there was a telegram from Mutti waiting to say that Michael had been so ill at the Camp he had been sent home – or rather Vati had collected him. Our doctor had even spoken to Dr Kordt, who had suggested a very strong injection to bring the attack to an end. The only good thing (from Michael's point of view) is that he was praised in his Performance Book for not giving in, and for carrying on in spite of physical difficulty.

The concert had been heavenly – in the open air, in a courtyard. Much more to my taste than Wagner and Bayreuth. We'd had a marvellous dinner first, and I saw Paula on the boat going over, and introduced her to Hugo. On the way back, now a clear starry night, she called out to me that Venice was the most wonderful place on earth – such un-British enthusiasm – but she had said to me that I didn't seem like a German, so perhaps there aren't really true types.

We were planning to return to Le Mont Dore in September, exactly a year from the last time. We managed to get into the same hotel earlier so decided to leave immediately on Dr K's advice

The journey was somewhat eventful. The train separates into two parts which we hadn't been told . . . we were in the dining car, and wondered why we had stopped, and what the jolts and bumps were. We found out when we went back to our compartment, and it wasn't there – with our luggage! We went on to Vichy, and had to take a taxi all the way back. Michael thought it was a huge adventure.

Because of the war scare a number of people had left or decided not to come for the cure, which was how we managed to get accommodation. I'm not scared. I think of last year. A repeat performance.

Quite a few familiar faces – Michael greeted by the attendants at the *Etablissement Thermal*. He recognized one boy he had met in the steam room last September – although how anyone recognizes anyone in a bathing cap in a fog I can't imagine

I decided, bored as I am, that I won't submit to the douches. I talk to a Dutch mother with two sons asthmatic and a German widower who has brought his little girl for the first time (from Ulm), a rather lonely figure. His wife died early this year, and the child developed asthma straight away. What an odd illness it is, so many causes.

August 25th
Telegram from Hugo saying we should come home. The telegram was sent from Berlin. Many of the hotel guests seem to have the same thought, and there is an exodus every day. I half thought of wiring back and saying Michael must complete the cure, but I decided to let him complete the full second week, and make arrangements to leave on the 30th. Which I have done. I have the tickets and have simply sent a telegram to Mutti (no good sending it to the house, Hugo obviously isn't there) to say unless she heard from me again to be at the station to meet me.

August 28th
Someone left a copy of yesterday's *Völkischer Beobachter* at the *Thermal*

this morning. The headline is enormous – *Whole of Poland in War Fever! 1,500,000 Men Mobilized! Uninterrupted Troop Transport Toward the Frontier.*

For the first time I'm terrified. Should we go tomorrow and not the day after? Those hateful Poles.

August 29th
Impossible to change train reservations unless we are prepared to go without sleepers and risk standing all the way. I'M NOT. I shan't panic. It was averted last time. Michael says 'Why do we have to go? I'm enjoying it here.'

August 31st
SAFELY HOME.

September 3rd
England has declared war on Germany. Hugo has just telephoned me from Berlin. I had to have a strong drink, and now I can't write any more. My head is splitting and I feel ill with nerves.

September 4th
I feel better today. The navy torpedoed and sank a British liner. That will show them. I know it can't last long.

September 5th
We have been issued with food and petrol ration stamps. Every minute there is another order on the radio. It is like being in another world. Already young men are being called up. Thank God Hugo has a post that exempts him. I couldn't believe it today when I went to the shops and saw the queues. Surely it is panic, and not necessary. Why should our whole way of life change in two days?

September 6th
Fräulein Müller has been made responsible for the blackout in her street, she wears a helmet and looks *grotesque!* Every night I wake up waiting for an air raid. I suppose I'll get used to it. After all it hasn't happened.

October 13th
The English have *turned down* Hitler's offer for peace. One good thing.

I have a *fur coat!* Hugo arranged it (left by Jews in Berlin, so we were able to buy it at about a third of its real price), it has never been worn I should think. Arctic fox – creamy-silver – lined with satin. Ostentatious on one of *them*, but I look like a film star!

November 5th
Hugo away at Youth and Film Conference. I feel frightened on my own.

November 9th
It all seems very close. A bomb last night at the Bürgerbräukeller, meant to kill the Führer (who fortunately had left) but seven people were injured. The papers say it was the British Secret Service.

November 10th
I find it so difficult to write. In one way everything is normal, Michael goes to school – is much better as he was last year after the cure. The hotel is doing well – a number of Gestapo and official visitors. Because of the hotel I'm able to get coffee. I will also be able to get sheets when I need them – heaven knows why there should be a shortage, but there is.

I wonder how Liz is. I suppose we'll still receive letters from America.

Hugo is in Munich – now wears his uniform all the time. He looks dashing. SS Standartenführer* von Stahlenberg.

Christmas Day
We went to church. The whole family were here together, so we were happy and depressed at the same time. Olga Tschechowa† is visiting the troops at the front line. We went to the Regina Hotel for lunch, we took up three tables! Eating in restaurants – if one can afford it and we can – solves the food shortage problem.

New Year's Eve
Tonight we're going to have dinner in the Vier Jarheszeiten cellar. I wonder what 1940 will be like. Hugo said that Hitler thinks it's more important for actors to entertain than go into the army. I was surprised, but it is good sense if you think about it.

* Equivalent to a Colonel .
† Screen idol.

1940

January 17th
The Poles arrived yesterday at the hotel, and Mutti says already she can tell it's an improvement on the Bavarian 'sluts' who took the opportunity to leave her in the lurch for 'war work'. I'm only waiting for Hilde to go . . . so many domestics are keener to serve their country than their employers. I don't know that I would qualify for slave labour, though. Mutti has been told she need not feed hers beyond the necessity of health. They are not used to a high standard of living. She said she understood, but of course intends to treat them well – and she saves money by not having to give them wages.

January 30th
Michael had a happy day. His first wartime birthday (I hope the last). The Polish workers were very sweet to him. The one I call Frau Bormann (she has his eyes!! He wouldn't like that) lost two children in the fighting, and keeps kissing M – which irritates him terribly. She made him a little cake. Hugo away.

February 3rd
Hugo back from Prague. Very depressed by what he saw there, but wouldn't divulge much except to say that it was worse than his first visit to Vienna. I said 'Well, they asked to learn a lesson.' He said, 'They've learned it too well, I'm afraid.'

March 1st
Wonderful month, Hugo home (although off to Berlin in the morning to attend meetings with an important American*) and much social activity. I had a long talk with Heinrich Himmler at a Brown House reception – he told me about Teutonic types. He said I fitted into the 'Falian' mould. He says there are six pure types, and they must be kept unadulterated, that moral and racial life go hand in hand as the basis of a strong society.

---

* Sumner Welles, United States Under-Secretary of State.

I asked him what he thought about illegitimate births, and he said he was speaking unofficially, but he believed that it was the duty of every German to produce a pure child, and that it is the sublime task of all German women of good blood to become pregnant – particularly from soldiers going to war, since they may die for Germany. He said he disapproved of promiscuity, but such an act should be considered with profound moral seriousness.

I thought of Heidi, and said I knew a girl who had deliberately conceived from a chosen SS donor, and had had her baby adopted. (I haven't seen her since but I assume all went according to plan.) Himmler said this was the greatest gift she could give to the future, and essential. 'You have only to look at the Polish pigs that are coming here to work on the land to see the degradation of the inferior genetic strain.'

March 3rd
Talking about Heidi has made me curious about what happened to her. I have tried to get in touch with her, but no one seems to know where she is. She isn't working at the Brown House, and the old address proved useless.

I don't think my clothing coupons are going to be sufficient. We only get 150, and you have to give forty for a brassière. It seems excessive – my summer coat (being made now) is taking thirty-five. Frau Smital is going to put me in touch with a family who will be happy to sell theirs, or to exchange them for my cast-offs.

March 12th
Russia and Finland have signed a peace treaty.

Michael has a special award for his poem on 'My Country' – it was read aloud to the whole school (three groups – his is the youngest) – I don't have a copy but when I do I will have it *framed!*

March 15th
Hugo back from the Brenner Pass – meeting between the Führer and the Duce . . . and that was all I could get out of him. He is very thrilled to have managed to get his cameraman out of the army, and back on the important job of filming! Goebbels asked for the conscription papers to be sent to him, and TORE THEM UP!

April 30th
Heidi has turned up – back home with her mother! Klara met her with her *daughter* – aged three! She told Klara all about the birth and how, since it wasn't a boy, she decided to keep the child, and now knows she could never have parted with her. Heidi is quite *fat*, and 'cow-like', Klara writes, and hopes to find a *husband*. What a mess that girl is.

Marvellous party to celebrate the fall of Denmark and Norway. Everyone says fur coats will now be much cheaper – and not on the ration either. Shall I have *another*?

There is an official complaint against *Leidenschaft** and about the 'trend' in modern films. Hugo says they may make complaints, but it will fall on deaf ears – we live in a new world.

May 10th
We have attacked Holland. It suddenly becomes very exciting, the way Germany is crushing her enemies. Now I think it was a good thing the English declared war on us – it has *shown them* aggression doesn't pay.

The grocer said that with the collapse of Denmark and Holland our butter shortages will be over!

May 15th
Michael asthmatic again. What can have set him off *this* time?

Holland surrendered today.

We shot down *forty RAF planes*. I am so glad Liz went to America.

May 28th
I suppose I have to record that the Belgians have surrendered – otherwise one day Michael will read my diary and say 'Wasn't she interested in Germany's great victories?' Thank God he's much better again.

May 29th
Hugo has gone off to a secret destination – but *I* think it's Holland. Everyone is in such a good mood, there's nothing like a victory to uplift the spirits. The newsreels are better than the movies – thanks to Dr G (my would-be lover!) and also to my husband, who is pressing for the use of colour. The Polish campaign (seen in our local movie-house) made me feel I had actually *been* there. When I said that to Hugo, he said 'Yes, but when I went to Warsaw the dust hadn't settled. The

* *Passion, a film portraying extra-marital sex.*

smell of burning and the grit in the air made me feel physically ill.'

I said 'Thank heavens Michael wasn't there, dust brings on his asthma.' (I realize now that it was because we took down the heavy curtains – *full* of dust – to be cleaned that he had his last attack.)

Peter Rande (back from the Front) said that newsreel commentaries are being prepared in *sixteen languages*. I am glad Hugo wasn't there at the time of the fighting – 23 war correspondents have been killed, not all film unit men, of course. The films are flown from the Front. Peter says the Führer sees the newsreels before they are released. He has them run silently, and the commentary is read aloud, so that he can approve the way they are linked for the final version. Peter is always full of gossip and false information, so I shan't accept that as gospel!

May 30th
A letter from Annette. Xaver was killed in Belgium.

Poor girl. Poor little boy. And the baby, only two.

What would I do if Hugo were killed? War has seemed so remote from us. Somehow I've only thought of the *enemy* soldiers dying. In a way it's the fault of the newsreels. We see our soldiers alive, strong and jubilant. Smoking cigarettes after a battle. We hear what the enemy losses are – not ours.

I don't know what to say to her. I haven't the courage to phone. I just hope France gives in quickly and then it will all be over.

May 31st
Couldn't sleep last night. I kept thinking of Annette.

June 6th
Well, now we have Dunkirk. It was astonishing to hear about the British escape in their boats – fishing boats, pleasure boats. Vati said you can't help admiring them for it – but it is a humiliating defeat, an army leaving in a fleet of bath toys.

Anyway, we're well into France. It is thrilling to listen to the radio, and read the papers, especially *Das Reich*,* which I get free from the Brown House, from Hugo's secretary. I can't wait for the war to be over.

June 7th
I had the brilliant idea that the Trauter family might like to sell their

* Goebbels' paper, launched that year.

clothing coupons. Such a big family, and Herr Trauter is bound to be in the forces. It takes courage to ask, and I decided I would take some butter (Danish) from the hotel as a gift, and say that Hugo and I had often wondered how they were.

I took the tram – I start my driving lessons this week, with Hugo away so much I might as well be able to use the car – and found only the frog-grandmother and the younger children at home.

I presented the butter and explained who I was . . . she had quite forgotten me! When she remembered (or said she did) I stood on her doorstep feeling a fool, and wondering just how I was going to get the conversation round to rations.

Me: Everyone is short of butter.
Granny: Thank you a thousand times. . . .
Me: How do you manage for other things?
Granny: Well, there's no coffee. Listen to that baby bawling its head off.
Me: May I see the baby?
Granny: If you don't mind risking a cold . . . her nose never stops running.

So in I go, up the stairs, to the bedroom which has the shutters closed and is extremely hot and stuffy. The baby, the Trauters' ugly duckling, cries all the time I'm there. I'm convinced its germs made a direct hit on my nasal passages.

Finally we go downstairs again.

Me (desperate): Do you manage to stretch the clothes ration? It must be so expensive to dress all the lovely children.
Granny: Well, you mustn't tell anyone, but we sell our coupons to the von Zeidlers – and then buy second-hand clothes through the school. That way we benefit twice. The clothes are half the price of the ones in the shops.

So I won't get the red silk suit from Frau Dora, who is making for *everybody*. As Frau Smital's contacts also fell through I may be trapped by my own coupon book! I wonder if Fräulein Müller would consider a deal? I think she stocks up on stockings and woollen knickers – 16 points a pair! She certainly wears nothing new on the top.

June 14th

The Eighteenth Army has occupied Paris. There is a swastika on the Eiffel Tower.

Heil Hitler!

June 16th

Hugo home. He arrived at midnight. He was exhausted and excited. Began to make love to me, and fell asleep . . . and I had a hell of a job pushing him off me to his side of the bed. He snored until ten in the morning. I kept Michael home, and then let him wake his father!

He has the day off – then tomorrow he has to see the film he brought back with him. Dr G is coming to Munich to discuss a new film about our marvellous victories. I wonder if they will ask Leni Riefenstahl to direct it, or work on it? Hugo doesn't want to talk about the war or his work. 'Let me have one day off.'

I would like Hugo to direct it.

June 17th

Was invited to a private showing of *Fezldug in Polen** which I hadn't seen before. Very impressive. I asked Hugo if after the war he wants to direct films. I had a private dream of going to Hollywood! I'm becoming like Eva Braun!

June 22nd

The armistice with France is signed.

We heard it on the radio. It takes effect from the 25th. I can't understand why it doesn't begin at once. I asked Hugo if it meant the fighting will still go on until the magic hour of 1.35 a.m. on that day, but he said no, it has stopped by now.

Surely *this* must mean the war will end? Hugo said 'Göring will want us to finish off the English first.' (He has been with Göring several times recently.) I can't believe that the English won't *offer* to surrender, or make an agreement. They must know how strong we are and that they wouldn't have a hope of winning.

June 23rd

At dinner (at Platzl's . . . I didn't find the cabaret particularly funny,

* Campaign in Poland, first released in February 1940.

I really don't like beer gardens, although the *Brathandl** wasn't bad)
Hugo said to me, very casually 'Do you want to go to Paris?'

I thought he was joking. I said 'Tomorrow or the next day?' He
said 'The day after that.'

'Oh fine,' I said, playing along. 'What clothes should I bring?'

'Just simple things,' he said, 'we will be filming, so there is going to
be a lot of standing about. You'll certainly need a light coat of some
kind for the evening.'

Then I knew it was REAL. I couldn't eat another mouthful. PARIS.
I'll actually *see* the Eiffel Tower. I'll have to be smart in Paris. It's all
very well for Hugo to say 'just simple things'. He probably doesn't
realize that the women in Paris are the most elegant in the world.

June 24th
We're *flying* there. I am in such a state I don't know what to do next.
I've had my hair washed and set, I made the milliner trim the straw
(last year's) in an afternoon. I've told Hilde to take Michael to the
hotel for all meals (he loves the Poles) and I've arranged for the
decorators not to come until the week after next.

I only hope I won't be sick. I've always said I'd never fly.

June 26th
PARIS
I'm there. Little Liese Stofen is in Paris. Frau Elisabeth von Stahlenberg
is staying in Paris, wearing the red silk costume acquired with black
market clothing coupons, and last year's black straw hat trimmed
with silk poppies. She also has a new nightdress and dressing-gown of
peach satin (25 and 18 coupons respectively – thank God for the
'source' provided by Hilde's mother – father killed in Danzig – all they
want is money for food).

The film unit is here, and they are looking at the locations. The
Führer is arriving at Le Bourget airport, and the cameras will follow
him on his 'tour' (that's the day after tomorrow) – and newsreel shots
are to be assembled. Hugo and his director want the Paris scenes to be
the culmination of the glories – and it is a perfect city for it. I have
walked and walked and walked today – the Etoile, the Place de la
Concorde, the Opéra, the Madeleine, the Rue de Rivoli, Notre Dame
. . . well, I relied a little on the unit car for transport too, but I have
corns on my feet! Many of the shops are closed, and people seem to be

* Bavarian roast chicken.

staying indoors except for the queues at the food shops. Not all of *them* are open either. Our soldiers are the ones on the street – and our hotel is full of officers. I'm told the restaurants are reopening, but that thousands left the city when the fighting was getting close. We went to a restaurant tonight, the owner welcomed us – which gave me a good feeling because at the airport I had a sense of resentment, even hatred. It isn't *our* fault, but I understand how they must feel.

The dinner was perfect – and two special bottles of wine were brought up from the cellar. Everything I have heard about French food is true . . . I can't count Le Mont Dore, it wasn't 'haute cuisine' and this certainly was. We were greeted with a 'Heil Hitler' and then told what we were going to eat – no choice. And of course, it was a perfectly balanced meal, the vegetables cooked in butter, the steak tender, the cheese (camembert) ripe, the peaches huge and soft. Hugo has gone to sleep, but as a matter of fact I have indigestion and sitting up and scribbling helps matters!

June 27th

We have to be up very early in the morning, the Führer is landing at about half past five! Hugo is still out making his preparations, and I have nothing to do but sit in the bedroom – I'm getting rather good at sitting alone in hotel bedrooms (or while my son or my husband sleeps). I want to write down what happened to me today, because it was a very touching experience, I was upset by it, and I want to do something to help if I can although I don't know who I should tell to change matters.

I came back to the bedroom during the middle of the morning and the chambermaid was making the bed. I said 'Don't let me disturb you' because she immediately began to apologize and back out. I showed her my camera, which was what I had come to collect.

As I was leaving she suddenly said 'Madame!' I stopped and said 'Oui?' Then she said, half in French and half in German, that she needed help. And she began to cry.

I said (of course) 'What can I do?'

She said it was impossible to buy food, only the Germans were served in the few food shops that were open. She needed milk for her children. Would I go to a shop and buy it for her. She would give me the money. If I pretended it was for myself they would let me have anything I wanted.

What could I say but yes? She then began a torrent of misfortunes.

She came to work on a bicycle, but yesterday the Germans came to the door and asked her for it, gave her a receipt and took it away. Would she get it back? The same thing had happened to her neighbour's car two days ago and it hadn't been returned. Her neighbour's son had by mistake stepped on a soldier's foot, and he had been taken away and not seen since. What would they do to a boy of fourteen? Everyone was saying that innocent people were being shot. Was it true?

I could only say that I didn't believe any German would hurt a child – I hadn't met any, as a race we loved children. I didn't think innocent people would be shot – what was the point of it? I said I had no idea about the bicycle and the car.

Anyway, she then went out of the room, and came back with some francs which she pressed into my hand. She directed me to the shop about forty times (an Italian shop, she said), and she would see me here at one o'clock, before she went off duty. I was to tell no one or she might be shot.

Shot! I said to her, we are an occupying army, but you are being stupid and unjust. No one would shoot you for getting milk for your child. I was shocked that even an ignorant peasant could harbour such dangerous fears and rumours.

I went where she told me, and found the place. It was fairly full of our soldiers, buying wine, cheese, salami and so on. When it came to my turn, I spoke in German (which the proprietor spoke fluently with a very Italian accent) and asked him for milk, cheese and bread. I hadn't enough of the woman's money, so used my own.

The soldiers were very interested to find a young blonde compatriot amongst them, and we chatted – I was even asked out for dinner! I took the stuff back to the hotel, and had to hang about until the hour of my assignation with the maid! When she came, and I gave it to her, she looked into the bag, burst into tears, and took my hand and covered it with kisses. It was ghastly, so embarrassing – and the poor woman has a sore on her mouth!

Eventually she left, still thanking me. When Hugo came in to have lunch with me, I told him, and said he must report to some high authority about the bicycle. He was cynical and said 'She'll never see that again.' When I said if it was reported, she might, he said 'Morality isn't too high on the lists of occupying armies.'

In the afternoon I went to the Bois du Bologne – I'd always heard people picnicked there, but it was deserted, like everywhere else. I'm sorry that my first visit to Paris wasn't at a livelier time.

It was better tonight, a small reception for us given by General Pommer, who is organizing much of tomorrow's security and has arranged for the film crew and the unit officers to have passes. Very good champagne and pâté such as only the French can make.

June 28th

It was tremendously moving to watch the Führer's plane descend from the dawn sky and land in the conquered city.

He made a point of greeting us (even me!) before he drove off with Professor Speer and members of his staff in the Mercedes which were waiting.

We followed immediately, leaving the small film unit to take some further shots of the airport. It was all planned to the last detail, and I could see how efficient Hugo was in organizing and arranging so many different elements.

We drove to the Opéra. The Führer went inside, but we didn't – Hugo promised I could have my own private tour later in the day – and when the tour restarted we did the same route that I had done alone on my first day, ending up at Napoleon's tomb. There were a number of stops, but Hugo said that most of them would be cut out of the film when it finally reached the newsreel screens.

Of course it was very early in the day, but except for a single priest and a few policemen, the city was deserted. Swastikas and banners were everywhere, but I felt that they should be being *waved*. I spoke to one of the cameramen, and he said it was much more impressive this way – the Führer's city. By nine it was over. Hitler went back to the airport, and I stayed with the crew doing close-ups of statues! Later Hugo said Göring had slipped off to an art museum, and he had heard he had in that short time appropriated several treasures for his own walls!

One more full day, and then we go home too. Vive la France!

June 29th
Notes to myself

Remember to find out if Le Mont Dore will be open for Michael's final cure this September. Buy perfume before I leave.

July 18th
Berlin

This is what we should have had in Paris. The whole city turned out for the Victory Parade through the Brandenburg Gate. Everyone was

in a festive mood. I was glad Michael was with us, his little heart must
have felt like bursting with pride. For once Mutti and Vati made the
journey, and they said tonight they wouldn't have missed it for the
world.

July 19th
England has *turned down* Hitler's new offer of peace.
   They must be mad. Why should anyone turn down peace?
   Göring has been promoted, and everyone is laughing about his
newest uniform – gold and silver braid and heaven knows what else!

July 23rd
Hugo and I had dinner with the Smitals – dreary food and company,
but interesting speculation about whether we will invade England.
Herr Smital says that the Führer is still very much for the British and
wants peace with them. It is Churchill who stands in the way.

August 20th
The papers are full of furious air battles over England. Everyone says
it's to soften them up for the invasion. Managed to get some real coffee
today. (Goodbye to that French scent!)

August 24th
Berlin was bombed last night. Will we dare to go there again? Is this a
taste of what is going to happen all over Germany? I telephoned friends
of 'Maman's' and asked them what it was like – they said 'Terrible'.

August 29th
The first of our countrymen killed by the vicious British bombers
(every night this week). I can only thank God it has been confined to
Berlin.

September 4th
The Führer made a fantastic speech today – I listened and felt my blood
race back after my feelings of faintheartedness. (No doubt this is what
our brilliant Chancellor intended!) So strong, so sarcastic about the
night raids (they daren't come in daylight). He said that when the
British drop their 4000 kilograms of bombs, we will drop 400,000
kilograms.

September 8th
LE MONT DORE
It didn't close – I am relieved to have been able to bring Michael here (the time of year doesn't agree with him at home, something to do with the dying vegetation the doctor says) – but relieved too that we won't be coming *next* year. Michael's health improves, but my morale is *very low*. As the British people's must be. Last night London was devastated by bombs.

We are in a small hotel this time, and the town is half empty. I asked the 'patron' about it and he said last year there were 7000 *curistes* but this year he wouldn't estimate more than 1000. The patients seem to be only French. I have yet to meet another German. I can't really see why the occupied countries shouldn't be able to send their asthmatics here. I wondered today about Lisette, the Belgian child we met in 1938. I think she has probably completed the three years. By next year no doubt things will have been sorted out.

We share a table with four other people, all taking the cure. There are twins (brothers) in their forties – one worse than the other. The doctors are very interested in them, as it is quite rare. They say there have been articles on them in medical magazines. Then there are two single ladies, one is an ardent donkey-rider, and has offered to take Michael with her every day – she saw me trudging round the mountain paths yesterday – before we actually disappeared into a low cloud! Michael made me laugh – he said it was like being in the steam room.

September 10th
I'm glad of my fur coat, it has turned chilly, and last night I went out when Michael was asleep. (I had told him and he didn't mind.) I went with the donkey-riding lady to see a French film. She whispered a translation to me (she is fluent in German, English, Italian and Spanish and never stops telling me), but it didn't help, as I missed the pictures half the time because I was craning towards her to hear her voice.

Such a different atmosphere here to Paris. Although it is quiet, I feel as if the war hasn't happened. Except for the lack of people it's much as it always has been for a non-asthmatic! DULL! If the troops *were* here it might brighten life up. I wouldn't mind another little flirtation in a grocer's shop!

September 11th
Michael has found a French friend, Jean-Pierre, aged ten (much admired

by M, who is flattered to be liked by someone so OLD), the son of someone in the Vichy Government. Jean-Pierre is a little *rough*, and there have been complaints about his behaviour to small frightened girls in the steam room (he jumps out on them with terrible shrieks, M tells me) and he *looks* fierce in yellow bathing cap – the thin clinging kind which gives him a *bald look!* The mother is in Vichy, J-P is here with a nurse who has little control.

September 12th
Quiet afternoon, while Michael, Jean-Pierre and the donkey-rider are off on their marathon! The nurse almost wept with gratitude when I offered to take him off her hands. After the ride, I'm taking them all for hot chocolate and cakes. I've just written a long letter to Hugo. I do miss him. It is awful, when we are separated so much by his work, that we have to separate for this – though no better cause than Michael's health. I try not to let myself think that I am responsible by letting him leave Berlin when he was a baby.

Being away from Hugo makes me realize how much I still love him. I am SO LUCKY.

LATER
Michael and Jean-P are convinced that Madmoiselle Mauret is a SPY! I said, what on earth could she have said on their donkey ride that makes them so sure? Michael confided all this to me when I was getting him ready for bed. He was quite angry when I laughed. It is absolutely true, he assured me. Jean-Pierre KNOWS, his father is in the government. There are lots of spies trying to get messages to the French traitors.

Me: What messages do you think Mademoiselle is trying to pass?
Michael: She kept asking Jean-Pierre what his father *did.*
Me: I asked him too . . . it's just conversation.
Michael: No. Not with her. Jean-Pierre says you can see it in her eyes. He knows what spies are like. He says she's only here because it's near Vichy. He doesn't believe she has asthma at all.
Me: Darling, I've seen her at the *Thermal.* . . .
Michael: She's pretending. I'm going to watch her. I'm going to make notes on what she says at lunch tomorrow.

Poor Mademoiselle Mauret – her kind gesture in taking them for the donkey ride has provided them with a burning interest for the next week. Detective Michael von Stahlenberg has now fallen into a heavy sleep beside me – wish we could have had two single beds – snoring like a MAN!!

September 13th
Well – the spycatchers are certainly occupied. We had to buy notebooks and pencils this morning. I do miss staying at the Gallia. The breakfasts were infinitely better, and the beds more comfortable. After the cure, Michael sat up in the *sloping* bed and made notes about the innocent spy and says he wondered if she had a radio transmitter in her room to send messages to England! I said only a radio (I know because she listens to music in the evenings) and he said 'Aha!' and wrote it down with much significance.

A long and loving letter from Hugo. He says celibacy doesn't agree with him.

September 14th
I was furious with the boys today. I found them trying our bedroom key in *her* lock. Thank *God* it didn't fit. They said they wanted to look at her radio. I said they had taken the silly game far enough and I didn't want to hear another word about spies. Imagine if she'd caught them – not I. And she's been so kind. Not only the donkey rides, but she's bought them drinks, and has offered to take them roller-skating before she leaves.

September 15th
Drama at the *Thermal* . . . we lost Michael's clean vest while he was in the steam! It didn't turn up – I suppose some other child went out wearing it! Profuse apologies from the attendants, and the loan of one two sizes too big.

I had to do the donkeys this afternoon, as Mademoiselle M had a headache. I'm glad she wasn't subjected to the boys' silly questions. I've seen them making signs to each other when she's with them, and feel she must be aware. Probably thinks they're making fun of her.

September 16th
Mademoiselle collapsed this morning. We met Dr Schaeffer on the stairs, on our way back from the cure. Everyone was talking about it at lunch-time (her empty chair at our table was filled half way through by a man who arrived last night) and Michael couldn't eat fast enough

to be able to closet himself with Jean-Pierre. It was raining and so the donkeys were out as far as I was concerned. I think the man wouldn't have let them be hired on such dismal day, they would get rheumatism (or wheezy, says M!). I sat downstairs, and talked to one of the twins (the healthier one, the other was resting).

When I went up to see if the boys felt like a walk (it had stopped raining by about four) Michael said they had something very important to tell me. Mademoiselle hadn't had a heart attack – she had been poisoned. Jean-Pierre had told his father she was plotting to overthrow the government. They had *seen* her transmitting messages through the keyhole! When she was having her steam treatment, poison had been let into the cubicle instead of vapour!! Michael said the man who had sat out our table was sent by Jean-Pierre's father to keep a watch!

I said they'd done very well! Hitler should give them a medal. Jean-Pierre said his father knew Hitler. 'So does *my* father,' said Michael. 'My father was with him in Paris.' 'My father was with him when he signed the armistice.'

Sometimes I wish I had had a *daughter*!

September 17th

Woke at about 3 a.m. being prodded by Michael, to tell me something was happening. There were low voices outside the room, and much to-ing and fro-ing. He wanted to look, but I held him *by force!* I said it was *nothing to do with us* and if we were wanted we would be called.

He said hopefully 'Maybe it's an attack by the British.' I said his geography wasn't too good. He said scornfully he didn't mean by land.

In the morning we heard that poor Mademoiselle Mauret had died. Michael was jubilant. I was horrified. 'Serve her right. We caught her. Jean-Pierre and I caught her! I'm glad she's dead.'

I really lost my temper. Thank heavens the awful Jean-P leaves today. He's a bad influence. I told Michael he was behaving like a peasant. The poor woman had been kind to him and what had started as a game had grown out of all proportion, and now that she had died I didn't want him to go on pretending. He shouted back at me that he wasn't pretending. It was true, true, true.

I wish I'd never encouraged them in the silly idea. I suppose it's partly my fault, talking about Hitler giving them medals. I said to Michael that she had been a very nice person, and it was unkind of him to go on. He said (and I must say he sounded very like Hugo in the way he phrased it) 'Just because someone is *nice* on the outside, doesn't mean they can't be bad inside. She was a spy, and we were right to report her. Your country comes first.'

He's seven. He has to be somebody very important when he grows up!

September 18th
Couldn't sleep last night. I thought suppose it had been true. Suppose that ordinary woman had been murdered because two small boys were playing a game.

By the time the call came to get dressed for the cure, I was sane again! You know how things are in the night.

October 30th
Had a row with Mutti over whether or not women should wear trousers! She says *no*. I say yes – and so does dear Dr Goebbels. My champion.

In the winter, when it's cold he says, *why not!* Aping men, says my mother.

November 14th
Hugo in Berlin. Yesterday he was at a party in the Russian Embassy when there was an air raid. We read about it in this morning's papers, and I felt *sick* until I managed to get a call through to the hotel and learned that 'Standartenführer von Stahlenberg left five minutes ago'. I do wish he didn't have to go to Berlin so often.

November 15th
Our precinct warden called today (and walked straight in the moment Hilde opened the door!). 'I have come to check on your blackout.' I said 'You don't have to worry. My husband is an SS Standartenführer. We obey instructions!'

He didn't sound so aggressive after that, but still looked at our curtains. He kept his helmet on all the time! Where do they find these people?

1941

January 19th
Hugo in the Obersalzberg. Thick snow. He had difficulty telephoning, perhaps the lines have been blown down.

January 21st
Hugo back. The Duce was Hitler's visitor. Which I think I'm not supposed to know.

January 29th
Berlin
Michael's birthday treat a day early. The opening of *Sieg im Westen** – a private showing for the press and for PEOPLE WITH BIRTHDAYS! M absolutely thrilled. After he had saluted Dr G, he was wished 'Many more happy and victorious anniversaries'. He was bursting with pride – and proud of his father, who had arranged for him to be there. 'I'm the only child,' he said!

The movie was tremendously exciting and stirring. Of course the Paris scenes pleased me the most, and how interesting it is to see how editing alters even the order of the events! And so much left out. When I think it took three hours – and we saw it in – what? – six minutes?

Afterwards we went out to dinner, and Berlin seemed very much the capital city. I was afraid that the air raids would have crushed that spirit (was a bit afraid to come here because of them) but in spite of the damage and the sandbags, the *pulse beats!* I realize, as I always do, that Munich is a backwater in comparison.

We chose a restaurant with an orchestra and who should be sitting at the next table but Zara Leander† looking ravishing. Michael asked for her autograph, which was given with the famous smile. What a birthday. I hope all the excitement won't bring on an attack.

When he had gone to bed and was asleep Hugo and I did the unforgiveable and went out to a nightclub. (I thought, just suppose there's

* *Victory in the West.*
† Film star of great popularity.

an air raid and he wakes up and we're not there – but there *wasn't* and he *didn't*.) I have never been so irresponsible before. The wines in the restaurant and the nightclub were *all* from France. We were even more irresponsible when we got back to the hotel at three in the morning. We made love (and not all that quietly, although I *tried*) with M sleeping on the single bed across the room. I said to Hugo 'We may have been married over seven years, but you have the perfect Aryan thighs!'

January 30th
Invited by the Görings to the Leipziger Platz. Hugo couldn't get over the collection of paintings. Looted from everywhere, he said afterwards. He is rather shocked. The Reichs Marshal boasted that he had thirty-one Dürer sketches from Poland. 'But I paid for them. Don't listen to rumours. I always pay.'

He said he had advised the French how to protect their art treasures, and to build special bomb-proof shelters. Emmy showed me a wooden statuette. 'Doesn't it look like me? Hermann bartered it!'

'He has good taste,' Hugo said as we drove back in a taxi with a gift of French soaps for me, chocolate for Michael – who had been invited too – and some brandy for Hugo.

'Even in white uniforms?' I said. He looked like a huge decorated ice cream.

The little girl, Edda, is sweet. When she and Michael grow up . . . well, why not? She's about six years younger than he is, not a bad gap! As long as she doesn't inherit her father's figure.

January 31st
Train packed with soldiers. Michael longing for a uniform – not long now, only one more year. He had a long chat with one young man, a Schütze* who looked no more than seventeen although he said he had a baby son. He said he had fought in Holland and France and that it seemed a shame to destroy villages which had been there for hundreds of years. 'That's war,' said my wise child! The soldier gave M a piece of shrapnel, now a *most treasured* possession and in a place of honour on the wall.

Had looked forward to an early night but Walter arrived, and had to provide dinner. He was obsessed with the Göring art collection, which Hugo feels has been wrongly appropriated. Walter says better

* Private soldier.

it should be in the hands of an art lover than have jackboots through Raphaels by ignorant peasant soldiers who simply want to destroy. Göring understands that paintings have to be kept in certain temperatures, and will preserve them for posterity. There are plans for a new National Museum at Linz. Walter said paintings are being stored in Ludwig's Neuschwanstein and at Hohenschwangau, and in the Führerbauten here in Munich.

Was unable to keep my eyes open . . . which Walter fortunately observed. He left soon after saying 'You must be tired after your journey.'

Just about had the power to stay awake to write this – as can be seen by my handwriting – and now I shall COLLAPSE.

March 10th

Hugo left yesterday for Bulgaria, a newsreel story on the troops. I really become so scared when he goes off like this. What would happen to us if he was killed? I couldn't live without him. I keep thinking of when the war is over and we can have a normal life, with him going to work in the mornings and coming home in the evenings like other men.

March 11th

Now Michael wants to go off on another of those camps. I tried to convince him that it would make him ill again (and he's been so fit since we came back from Mont Dore) but he doesn't even listen. He gets into a state of fury and hysteria and impatience and accuses me of trying to make him unpatriotic and soft. If only Hugo was here to discuss it.

March 12th

Spoke to the doctor and to the Youth Leader – both say let him go. Both say if he is really ill he can come home. I have to agree now although it goes against my heart. Anyway, it's not for another month.

April 17th

Can't believe it's a month since I opened this book. Hugo is safely home and Michael is at camp – and no word, so obviously he hasn't had an attack. They are in the Obersalzberg, not far from where I met Hugo . . . I can't believe that's so long, either. Had a lovely letter from

Liz, and she says she has sent me a parcel of food as she thinks we may be short. She sends them every month to her mother in England. I can't write and tell her we're better off than we were just before the war – all the lovely food coming from Denmark and France and Holland – when she is so kind. I wonder what she has sent. I'm sure American food is lovely. It looks so delicious in the advertisements in the magazines. She has sent snaps of her house and her little girl. The house is one-storey, made of wood I think, although it's hard to tell from a snapshot. There is a huge car parked in front of it – *very* American. The little girl looks sweet and is holding a Shirley Temple doll as big as herself

Good news today. Yugoslavia has surrendered and the Greek army has capitulated. Also we have been asked to dinner with the Kurt Troosts, who are bound to have at least one film star as a guest. He is making a musical film at present, and of course, *as always*, she has a part, although she can't act. I've been dying for an invitation, and it's taken a lot of presents for their baby and phone calls when her mother was ill to get it. Only hope Hugo won't be *called away*. I wonder if I could go on my own?

April 21st
Michael back and fit. He looks brown and keeps showing me how to click my heels – a very useful accomplishment!

April 30th
THE DINNER. Not one film star, but two, and a producer. After we had eaten, we had a private showing of the last Troost film – it was like being at the Berghof again, but so much *jollier*. *Their* screen was hidden behind a tapestry too. The baby is frightfully spoilt and was brought in (it is very beautiful, round and blonde and smiling) and sat on the floor gurgling and being fed! I said something about Eva Braun wanting to be an actress, and Kurt said God Help the German Film Industry.

May 11th
Rudolf Hess has gone to Scotland or England (no one seems to know which) – he has gone mad! He flew off in a Messerschmitt. They said on the radio tonight that he has existed for some time in a state of delusion and thought he could bring about peace!

May 14th
Peter Rande has announced his engagement to his secretary. How DULL!

May 15th
Peter's engagement yesterday – and Liz's parcel today.

2 cans of hamburgers
1 packet of drinking chocolate
1 can of salmon
2 bars of Hershey chocolate
2 pairs silk stockings
1 Mickey Mouse
1 can of coffee
1 box of dried fruit
1 can of dried milk

It was like Christmas opening it. She has forgotten how old Michael is – he was very scornful about the Mickey Mouse. Hilde, some twenty years older, seized it and said 'I'll have it'.

June 22nd
We have invaded Russia. Hugo says he has known for some time. I wonder how many secrets he has that he can't tell me.

The Luftwaffe raids destroyed 1800 planes – Hitler had named Göring his successor in the event of his death. The news bulletins are so good I know the war won't last for long. We have thousands of tanks on their way to Moscow and Leningrad.

This is the first time Michael has really been aware of what is happening, and he has a map in his room which he has pinned on the wall today. 'This is what we have conquered' he said, for all the world like a school teacher. He showed me where our troops are, what we occupy, what we are *going* to occupy! He even told me that we needed the *space* in Russia for '*Lebensraum*'* and that their material resources were necessary for us. I said 'Where did you hear all that?' He said 'At camp and at school – but I have a mind of my own!' I said 'An excellent mind – but put it to use on your mathematics too.' His report last term was very poor.

---

* Living space – a Nazi concept for spreading the Aryan race.

June 30th
We are charging ahead in Russia. The news is better and better every day. I have asked the Troosts back – on the 7th, and they have accepted.

July 8th
Party went splendidly. *They* have their sights on Hollywood after the war. Walter said he thought 'after the war' was a long way off. Kurt said it will be over by the winter. 'We've taken so many prisoners already they won't have anyone left to fight.'

I brought the conversation back to America, because the Troosts have been there – he worked on two films at Columbia Pictures and met Gary Cooper and Fay Wray at a party. Also Nazimova who he said liked 'the girls and not the boys'.

July 18th
My father-in-law has been asked to take over a group of industrial works in the Ukraine. Hugo has been given permission to go with him to decide how best 'to exploit them for the Fatherland'. Those were the words on the official permit. Michael said 'When I grow up I shall be doing that kind of thing too. By then, of course, the USSR will be part of the German Reich.'

He's right!

July 25th
Hugo back. Says the Ukrainians are well-disposed on the whole, and only too happy to begin working for the Germans instead of the Stalinists. There was an underground waiting to emerge and help us.

The commissioner is a loathsome man called Erich Koch, a very bad choice, who 'likes to kill'. He told me a funny story about Alfred Krupp, who is responsible for dozens of factories there. Göring once said 'Kill all the men, and then send in the SS stallions', and Koch had actually been trying to carry it out as an order. Krupp said he couldn't really wait for the 'foals to grow up', and he needed the men to work!

August 2nd
Hugo has been asked to go to Roumania – and I am going too! I have arranged for Michael to stay with a schoolfriend, whose brother is a member of the Hitler Youth Patrol Service, which is now Michael's dream. This was *his* idea – he feels trapped staying at the hotel, says my

mother is too fussy! It's a good idea, now I come to think about it, for the young to police themselves. Sometimes I think the Hitler Youth is a bit too military, but there are plenty of good ideas. When they go on an outing, they pool their sandwiches, and everyone has an equal amount – nobody hangs on to their own caviar!! Or gets stuck with a sardine!

August 12th
Bucharest
Not like anywhere else! I hadn't realized how different it was in this direction . . . but the Roumanians are certainly far from friendly. We talked to a young English woman, a writer* (funny to meet one's enemies in a hotel bar!) who is about to leave – and she said it isn't just the Germans who get the cold shoulder – the English do too. She said the only ones she liked had been the Jews, and they were getting out as fast as they could.

Hugo is busy organizing the film – it's going to open with a shot of the flag and then pull back to show that it is on the front of a hotel, and *then* to show the hotel in the street, which is obviously 'foreign', and *then* to show the city from the air.

We are staying in the Minerva Hotel, almost all Germans . . . it is like being at home if you just shut your eyes and listen.

The cakes are lovely – and the women very beautiful. They have deep eyes like gypsies, which I know isn't the type one is supposed to admire but seeing them altogether is picturesque. (The Jews are the blond ones here!!)

August 13th
Met the Roumanian film crew (a German director of course) who were most attentive to me. Dinner at the Athénée Palace (which had been the 'English hotel' when there were enough to fill it. There are English journalists here now, scribbling their reports. I don't think they'll be welcome much longer).

It is defeatingly hot. I have to wear a sunhat, and even this evening (well, late afternoon) I had to walk in the shade. One of the film crew bought a bunch of roses for me from a gypsy – I carried them with me all day – now I'm back in the hotel room, and they are trying to revive in the tooth-glass.

* Possibly the novelist Olivia Manning, there with her husband Reggie Smith of the British Council.

I'm on my own tonight, Hugo has been invited to a dinner and meeting combined, and a wife is strictly on the outside. I've got a book, but don't feel like reading. I went downstairs and had a solitary dinner, and then came up here and stood at the window watching for at least three-quarters of an hour. I find it a depressing city. There are some Iron Guards marching up and down, and I can hear melancholy music being played on a violin which I think comes out of the open shutters four houses up across the street. There's a huge moon, and the sky is still streaky. I can smell the roses, and also the cooking from the hotel kitchens which is floating up to me in a meaty way.

I hope Hugo won't be too late.

August 14th
I like the street cafés and restaurants – sitting out under awnings. I wish I had followed the political events here – but it's no good, I simply never get down to that kind of thing. I have to ask Hugo, and he fills in the worst gaps, so I now more or less know about Barbarossa. No doubt Michael will give me a lesson on his map.

Tonight we had dinner in a garden restaurant and were entertained by a man with a little monkey dressed in satin skirts and a bonnet. He kept her on a lead, and she danced round the tables, and sprang on to his shoulder and took the mouth-organ from him and pretended to play it. He told her she was a bad girl (or so our interpreter told us) and she hid her head in her little black hands. He came round afterwards to collect money and I don't know if I gave too much or too little, I haven't mastered the currency any more than the politics.

By the time we had got to our coffee and sweet liqueurs, a three-piece orchestra appeared and played folk music. They were short stout men, dressed in silk shirts with big sleeves caught at the wrists, and black velvet trousers. When we applauded, they suddenly smiled and played – believe it or not – *Deutschland, Deutschland über alles*, and as the applause doubled, we realized that all the diners were German! I think they did financially better than the monkey (although I preferred the monkey myself).

Only a day or so more and Hugo will have finished. Then the Roumanians can complete the filming (they will have the script set out) and the director (Hans) will bring it home. There's no rush on this one, it isn't HOT NEWS. I suggested they might like to use the musicians, and they thought it was a clever idea. If they can't get those particular violinists they can always *set it up*, as Kurt Troost says. He says they 'set up' a Berlin scene on the Columbia back lot, and it was so realistic he thought he was back home.

August 15th
Wonderful party given by the German General (at the Athénée Palace) who has been so wonderfully helpful to Hugo. There *were* some Roumanians this time – including a Princess, no less, very charming and *very* elegant. The funny thing is the women here are so much more beautiful than the French but on the whole seem less attractive because they dress badly. I suppose the *international set* are the ones who have 'chic' wherever you go.

August 16th
I was hoping we would go out into the countryside – there was some talk of it yesterday – but it was decided to be unnecessary. We met the English writer and her husband (Mr and Mrs Smith) and had drinks with them. They are going soon (they have been told to leave) – and asked them if by any chance they knew Liz. It was unlikely, but the world is a small place (and England isn't that big!). But they didn't.I couldn't help wondering if we would meet *them* again – in England, under German rule – but of course couldn't utter the thought. I don't see why this time next year Hugo shouldn't be organizing the propaganda films in London. How glorious. I should adore to go to London. I might meet the *English* princesses – much better than the Roumanian one last night! After all, Princess Elizabeth and I share the same name!

A cocktail party this evening – this time given by an American newsfilm company which seems to be covering Hugo's ground!They had brought their own gin all the way from America – and made real cocktails with exotic names (shaken in a shaker!) – I had a Silver Lady. Their producer said it was the right choice – my hair was silver-blonde and I was certainly a *lady*. He was thin, tall and had a lined face, but in an attractive way – very blue eyes and *silver* hair – which I pointed out. He said there was no 'Silver Gentleman' cocktail – but he didn't consider himself a gentleman anyway, although he might be called a 'Dude' (but no one could explain what he meant).

Have finished packing, we leave very early in the morning.

September 12th
Saw *Ich klage an** last night, the best film I have seen this year. It really

* *I Accuse*, a film about euthanasia.

193

made me think – not just be entertained. Hugo didn't seem impressed, and said it was angled and melodramatic . . . but I do see the point made by the story, that *sometimes* (not always) it is right to kill, *painlessly*, genetic undesirables. There was a family in our village in which almost every child had a defect, and the father was in and out of prison. We used to say the mother ought to be sterilized – now I wonder if at least two of the children who were mentally deficient and couldn't even go to school, ought to have been 'allowed to sleep' at birth. When I said this to Hugo, he became angry and refused to discuss it, which I think is stupid. Everything should be discussed, *especially* questions like this.

September 14th
All Jews are to wear yellow stars on their clothing so that they can't get away with not being recognized. I think a lot are being hidden and fed and housed by friends – sometimes I even suspect my parents-in-law, I know *Schwiegervater* helped some families get exit permits. How *lucky* I was to be born an Aryan.

October 3rd
Big party . . . one of the best, and all the more high-spirited because everyone says the Russian Campaign has been won. Michael went to a film show – especially for children – and seems to have enjoyed himself tremendously.

October 12th
Dr Goebbels made a speech today about the use of film for teaching purposes . . . which is what we all believe it should do. Hugo has been practising it for several years, as I explained to Mutti, who says *she* believes that films are to 'take your mind off things'! Had a quiet supper with her and Vati, as Hugo was working late.

October 20th
Hugo had an official letter saying that he is to receive a medal for his work for the Fatherland. Well, he *deserves* it, and the Führer knows it. Other people have medals for far less devotion – for saving someone from drowning – and even rescuing dogs . . . sometimes I think *I* ought to have one, for not complaining that my husband is away more than he's at home.

November 30th

Frantically busy with the *Winterhilfe* (street collector again) and with M's school activities – have been helping out at some of the evening meetings, so many teachers have gone into the army – and Hilde daily threatens to leave for more 'useful' work . . . I wish she'd think of me as her war effort. Her brother was killed in Russia and she went home for *two weeks* to comfort her mother – it couldn't have taken that long, I think she is becoming lazy. Her lover has also gone into the army (although a little old for it) so she isn't so contented being here – her prime purpose was to see him whenever his wife went out! There has been a setback in the Russian Campaign.

December 2nd

There is a *Winterhilfe* appeal for warm clothing for the troops – it is below freezing in Russia. We have been asked to give our fur coats – but I'm not going to give mine yet – no one will know. I just won't wear it, even if it gets very cold. I'd never find another like it.

December 8th

The Japanese have attacked the American Fleet at a place called Pearl Harbour.

December 11th

We have declared war on America (I wonder if Liz will be able to send me any more parcels – the coffee was like nectar after the *Muckefuck** we've had to drink) – the Führer has made a tremendous speech. The whole world seems to be fighting now – except Sweden . . . and Switzerland as Michael reminded me, with an account of the necessity of neutral nations!

December 25th

Hugo not home this Christmas – the first he has ever been away from us. Not the happiest day. So many young men being killed in the Eastern Front, and dying from *cold*. I think I *will* give my fur coat. I can't live with my own conscience if I don't. So many poorer people are giving generously – as I know . . . and when I collect the blankets and coats and socks I feel GUILTY.

But oh! my beautiful glamorous Arctic fox. . . .

---

* German slang for ersatz coffee.

December 27th

Saw *Ohm Kruger** – not my sort of film, I prefer modern stories – unless they are historical in a romantic way with beautiful costumes. Michael *loved* this – it's *his* style!

* Film about concentration camps during the Boer War.

1942

January 1st

We ordered coffee today at forty marks (for a kilo) and *bought* it. My new year's resolution – to hang on to my coat! I cheated . . . I bought a second-hand fur from Fräulein Müller – her aunt died – and gave it to the *Winterhilfe*. Even if I don't wear my own until the war's over, I don't care. I LOVE IT.

Am a bit worried about the lack of qualified teachers at the school. I hope Michael will get into a Napola School.* I want him to have the best education possible – the finest teachers teach in the system. I feel Michael's background will give him a good chance, as long as he can keep up on the physical side.

Hilde gave me her notice today. I am going to apply for a Slav. If I show that I am helping with the school and the *Winterhilfe* I don't see why I shouldn't qualify. They're supposed to 'relieve the housewife'.

January 10th

Hugo at today's inauguration of the UFA-Film GmbH.† Hilde departed saying she wants to train as an auxiliary nurse and work at the front. *I* think she wants to get her hands on those wounded soldiers.

January 30th

Michael can now join the *Jungvolk* and wear a uniform.
Michael is the happiest boy in the Third Reich.

February 5th

Youth Leader Axmann spoke today on the war effort of the Hitler Youth. Michael inspired to do all he can – has followed me around telling me how I must understand if he has to do his duty, and that even if it was my birthday and there was something the Hitler Youth needed him for, I would have to take second place. I said I *quite understood*. He said he hoped I would and it wouldn't be because he didn't love and

---

* Schools for the future Nazi élite – selection was at the age of twelve.
† Founding of the State Film Monopoly.

respect me, but the Führer needed the new generation to build for the future. (Not an original statement, I thought to myself!)

February 28th
Goebbels made a very important speech today about the film industry. Hugo said it was a 'milestone' and he doesn't often praise in that way. Some of the things he finds silly – there are masses of rules, one being that every film outline has to consist of thirty-four nineteen-syllable lines on every typed page! What *is* good is that no film will go into production without having been passed by the Ministry, which will stop it becoming decadent as it has in America. I agree that films should entertain – but they should also teach, guide and enlighten. Then you come out of the cinema feeling satisfied, and thinking for yourself, as I did, after the one about euthanasia.

March 8th
Hugo and I both went to an evening given by Michael's *Jungvolk* branch. The meeting-place is in the old synagogue hall – on the wall there is the *Siegrune**, some posters and an artistic arrangement of flags. There is also a library, which Michael runs on Wednesdays, and the Leader told me that M is a very promising young man!

The evening was an entertainment. There was some singing – mainly *Trutzlieder†* – with and without accompaniment. One boy played the guitar, another the piano. Then we were given some simple food (not terribly enjoyable!) and some *Muckefuck* (undrinkable) after which there were readings and recitations.

Before we left we were shown a display of weaponry – from the primitive clubs used by early man to the rifles used today. Michael is going to be instructed in gun handling, which I must say fills me with horror – but of course he can't wait, especially as the instruction is going to be given by the army, after a display of military manoeuvres. That's next month sometime. *Why* do boys love guns so much?

March 13th
We heard today that now the Russian winter is ending, our troops are getting ready for the new and final offensive. The Red Army has been crippled. Since the Führer took over command and removed a General or two there will be no more setbacks.

*The Hitler Youth emblem of a lightning flash.
† Songs of defiance.

I'm glad they managed without my coat. I wish I didn't feel so guilty.

March 14th
Hugo says we are going to Paris again. He is planning a series of short films on the occupied countries demonstrating that we are not 'iron conquerors'. The dates are not fixed. The Führer has shown a great interest in the idea. I am thrilled. I have developed a taste for travel . . . and when most people have to stay at home it gives it an extra savour.

March 15th
I'm sick of eating fish instead of meat! I collected our vitamin pills – these are now distributed officially since we aren't getting enough fruit – and then decided to call in at the hotel. Thought I'd have a quiet lunch with Mutti, but found the place full of SS – there's a special course being given and I'd forgotten that every hotel in Munich is packed. So instead of being waited on, I put on an overall and helped out in the kitchen like an *Ostarbeiter** which was not what I had intended!

Vati hadn't been too well, and had to wait two hours to see the doctor, the *old* man, the young one has been sent to an army hospital. Anyway, the doctor gave him some medicine, says there is a gastric infection going round, and that he has come across many more cases during the war. He puts it down to nervous tension.

April 2nd
PARIS
Michael is staying with the same family as he did when we were away before, and we are back in Paris. And what a difference – the cafés are full and the shops open. The hotel has been taken over by the army for the use of people like us – and we are in the most elegant suite of rooms. There is a wonderful social life, and of all people to meet, I found myself in the elevator with Lili Schmidt, who was in the class below me at school. She is only married to the Oberst† who has been assigned to Hugo!

We stared at each other – neither of us could believe our eyes. She has been in Paris for eight months, and is going to take me *everywhere*. She says I must have some clothes made, and she will introduce me to

---
* Eastern slave worker.
† Colonel.

one of the top designers. All the officers' wives go to this salon, terribly expensive but worth every mark. (I mean franc!) What luck to meet someone I know. She looks so smart and attractive, that I can't believe she was ever spotty with a flat chest.

We had dinner with Lili and her husband, Theodor – he is extremely good-looking, and very strong, both physically and in character. I don't wish to sound vain but I think he was attracted by me, he kept meeting my eye, and when afterwards we went out to a café to have cognac (kept for the Germans – I said to Hugo he'd better not put that in his film), he walked very close behind me as we went to our table, and guided me by putting his hands on my hips.

One of the maids in the hotel has her head shaved – Lili says it is because she slept with a German, the French women do this to girls who 'collaborate'. Poor girl – why shouldn't she go out with a German soldier – they are much better looking than the French. I think the French had better get used to the idea we're here to stay.

April 5th
Have been too busy to write – have been to Versailles, and to the *couturier*. The most wonderful salon . . . white and gilt with a huge chandelier as big as the ones I've seen in castles! I am having an evening dress made – the lace is fantastic, from Chartres (where, incidentally, I went yesterday in Lili's car – with an army chauffeur!). The French do know how to flatter the figure – they have only to drape a piece of material around one – and immediately it looks chic. The designer is certainly Jewish – when I said this to Lili, she said, 'He's just kept out of the way if anyone really important appears.' We were told an extra-ordinary story at the salon, by one of the seamstresses. She said a few weeks ago she and her husband were about to go to bed when there was a knock at the door. They answered it and two Gestapo officers stood there. 'Well,' she said (as if we weren't Germans ourselves – she spoke in German though), 'you know how one trembles at the sight of the Gestapo. So we said what did they want. Immediately we felt guilty although we're good enough citizens. Oh, they said, we want beds for the night. What could we do but take the children in with us and give them the room. We were afraid to speak in case we said something incriminating. We wondered if we had anything lying around that would have us shot.' (I was shocked at the way she spoke, but didn't show it.) 'In the morning I gave them some of our lousy coffee and some bread, and they thanked me, and left. When I went in to make

the beds what should I find but a little British flag under the pillow. On it it said 'With thanks from the RAF.'

'You mean, they weren't Gestapo.'

'Oh Madame, you're as slow as I am. . . .'

Afterwards I said to Lili 'Do you think it's true?'

'I expect so,' said Lili. 'She's quite a character, isn't she?' I said I found it strange that she should tell *us* – and run down the Gestapo.

'Why not?' said Lili. 'How can you expect them to like us Germans really. I find it amusing. I don't take offence.'

I think she *would* have taken offence if she knew that her husband has been pursuing me, even into the bedroom. He knocked on the door yesterday evening, when he knew Hugo wasn't in the hotel – and when I opened it, he almost pushed me in, and grabbed me in a passionate embrace – everything very pressing, if you get my meaning! I had to struggle free, and almost push him out. He wouldn't believe me when I said I *really didn't believe* in being unfaithful. He thought I just didn't find *him* desirable. Who wouldn't . . . he's like a film star. 'Why not?' he kept saying. 'You've been giving me the come-on since we met.'

'A lie,' I said.

'You've made me so excited that if you reject me I'll have to go down to the red light district and find some little French tart.'

Hardly complimentary! Poor Lili!

Tomorrow we go off on our location hunt – as far as Bordeaux. We will have the director and the production manager with us – and they promise me that we are going to stay in some lovely little inns and see some glorious countryside. 'And when they know we're going to put them in the movies, you'll be surprised at the delicacies they'll find to feed us with.'

We come back to Paris for a final day, when I will collect my dress.

April 14th
PARIS

I went without packing my diary – and I had intended to keep a travel notebook so that I could tell Michael all the geographical details, and write down all the menus. Not that they are easy to forget – we had the most amazing food, we went to Rheims (and had *everything* cooked in champagne) and to the Dordogne, where I had my first truffles, and bought some in tins to take home (at great expense, we knew we were being cheated but didn't care) – and saw the vineyards at Bordeaux, and spent a night in a little town called Chalon-sur-Marne, where we had sweet omelettes. None of that is in the right order – we drove part of the way (to Lyons), then we flew in an army plane to Bordeaux – and drove back to Paris, stopping frequently to take photographs and eat and drink. I am still amazed how the French manage to eat so much and not feel full or get fat. At one little farm we had a delicious vegetable, cooked in butter (and butter is supposed to be short!) and when I asked what it was, she said it was the *spinach stalks*. I also had snails. And a very tender and delicious casserole that the girl who served us said was 'poodle'. I hope she was joking – anyway, we all laughed. There *was* a pet poodle (white with runny eyes) waddling round the tables, and Hugo said she was kept for breeding. Anyway, it was a very good dish, with herbs and white wine.

I collected my dress – sensational. I hope I have an occasion to wear it that is worthy of it. It is pale orange chiffon, trimmed with matching ribbon (satin) and the Chartres lace – also dyed to match. It is softer and more feminine than the clothes I usually wear. The skirt is full. What heaven it is to buy without thinking of clothing coupons – *or* of the cost.

April 20th
Michael went on his rifle range while we were away, and tells me he is a crack shot. I didn't like the idea that they were also taught how to throw dummy grenades – it seems brutalizing for a ten-year-old-boy. But as I've said before, he loves it. Thank heaven the war will be over by the time he's grown up.

April 21st
Must make a dental appointment for Michael and myself.

April 29th
The Goebbelses here – a dinner reception to which we were invited. The Führer greeted me as if he knew me far better than he does. Said 'The next time your husband comes to the Berghof, you must join us.' I almost *swooned*. It seems so unfair that Eva should be banished from occasions such as this . . . after all, she has given up her life to him really. It seems so wrong that only marriage gives prestige. Not that I would want anything *but* marriage for myself. I can't bear to think what would have happened if I hadn't become pregnant, and Hugo had married someone nearer 'his station'.

Talked quite a lot to Magda Goebbels, whom I have grown to like, perhaps because I feel sorry for her, having such an unfaithful husband

and her own chance of love cut off for political convenience. I find her pleasant and sensible, and, like most mothers, we talk about our children.

I don't mind the Doktor either, in a mixed gathering. I just don't want to be alone with him!

April 30th
Read through yesterday's entry and was suddenly struck by the enormity of writing about Hitler and the Goebbels in a matter-of-fact way (except for the swooning reference). It really is incredible what we come to take for granted.

May 10th
BERGHOF
The invitation came much sooner than I expected – and here I am back in that same bedroom – going through the same routine. The Führer wants to hear all about the French films, and all about our experiences there. He asks what seem to me to be unimportant questions – like how prominently were the swastika flags displayed in the small villages. I was disappointed that there was no film showing after dinner – partly because I always feel especially privileged to see a film in a private home and not in a cinema – and partly because it passes the time agreeably.

Tonight we had records instead – mainly Wagner! One of the guests asked for Strauss . . . Hitler appeared not to have heard. Later Hugo told me that Goebbels had told him that Strauss was *out of favour* because he dares to criticize the government and the way the war is being fought! If only 'Maman' were here, how she would enjoy the gossip. We drank French champagne, which Hugo said wasn't very good – 'Hermann Göring has had all the best champagne delivered to Carinhall!' The Führer was very charming to me, and asked me to sit by him. He asked if I had gone to the Opéra in Paris. When I said I hadn't, he said it didn't matter because he was going to build an even more beautiful opera house in Berlin.

It is peaceful here – but curiously dull. The conversation never sparkles, and although I am no intellectual, I almost wish for Georg and Walter and the 'creature'. There's something flat and trivial about the talk of films and actors. The Führer makes jokes about his Ministers and everyone laughs. He tells a few stories about his early life in the army. But it is like an apple without a core, which is one of Mutti's expressions, and an apt one. I once heard Dr G say how he would do

203

anything rather than stay at the Berghof, and I begin to understand why.

May 31st

Last night the British bombed Cologne. They sent over a thousand planes. The city must be unrecognizable. How I *hate them*. How frightened I am that Munich might be the next target.

June 8th

Frau Smital telephoned and begged me to come on to the Strauss Birthday Celebrations committee. I protested that I am not really musical but she said that it doesn't matter – it is purely a matter of organizing. Can't get out of it . . . can't plead *Winterhilfe* work, as it isn't winter.

Hugo in Berlin.

June 9th

Michael and his friends making models of guns – M is carving a Luger out of wood, and I must say it is impressive and horrifyingly realistic. He got very upset, almost hysterical yesterday because the paint didn't have the right metallic sheen. He terrified Mutti with it!

June 15th

Hugo back (by air, greatly relieved not to have to face the long train journey, so many stops nowadays because of troop movements) and says he is being considered for some new and secret assignment. Doesn't know what it is, but says he has had intensive interviews, questioned about every aspect of his life from schooldays onwards – even asked about *Karl Neudecker* – wasn't much they didn't know *before* he was called in. Lucky he doesn't have anything to hide.

Went the other day to my first committee meeting. Was told that the whole celebration was almost cancelled, because of the Führer's anger with Strauss – but has now agreed that the *music* can be praised, *but not the man*. The festival was supposed originally to have been this month, but Hans Hotter* has hay fever in June and it was thought better to wait until after Salzburg in any case. The première of the new opera is on October 28th – the committee is arranging a reception. I decided I don't like committee work . . . such pointless arguing, such

---

* Famous baritone (Olivier in *Capriccio*).

consumption of cakes and black-market coffee; such rivalry between the ladies – and so much wasted time. Who should be invited – who should be left off the list – who should approach who about getting the French champagne – should it *be* champagne – and so on and so on, until I had a splitting headache. At the end of three hours all that was decided was that it would take place *after* the opera, not before, and wouldn't go on too long, as the composer's age had to be taken into consideration and that when he left so should everyone else! Frau Smital insists on that! I said I thought it would seem rather flat, and Frau S said anyone who wanted could always go on celebrating privately. I wouldn't mind giving a midnight supper myself – I haven't given anything larger than a dinner since we came here, and I think I've been to enough affairs to know how to do it rather well.

June 26th
We've begun the new Russian offensive. Michael's map is covered by swastikas on pins!

June 30th
Well – the war looks good again. We are on our way to Stalingrad. Michael exuberant!

It looks as if I *am* going to have a Slav *Dienstmädchen*.* I have received the 'Conditions of Work' leaflet which says they have no free time, and can only go out if it is in connection with household tasks. They are *not* allowed to go to church. What a relief . . . I never forget Anni!

I wonder how long before the actual slave follows the instructions on how to treat her.

July 5th
SHE IS HERE. Name of Stazi. A sad creature (from Czechoslovakia), tall but skinny, and scarcely ever smiles. I have introduced her to Mutti's Poles (who are very happy and well) but they can't speak the same language and are curiously hostile. I show her what to do and she does it. If Michael were younger he would have broken the ice, but he is almost impolite to her. I have to keep telling him to say good morning, and to *look* at her. He is behaving as if she wasn't a human being, unpleasantly arrogant. I said to him that if that is what he learns at the *Jungvolk* meetings I will go and talk to the leader. I can't stand bad

* Servant-girl.

manners, neither can Hugo, and I am going to get him to speak strongly to M. German good manners have always been admired throughout the world – and my ten-year-old son isn't going to let his country down. Because she is in our hands, and not free, it is all the more necessary to prove that we are worthy masters . . . or mistresses, as in my case!

July 6th
Oh these committee meetings. I think I'll have to resign. I must find an excuse. *Two hours* discussing the table decorations. . . .

July 20th
Stazi makes me feel so uncomfortable I think I'd rather do the work myself. I had to tell her she couldn't go to church, and she cried. (I think she is Catholic.) She has asked for a cross to put in her room – drew it for me to tell me what she wanted – and I'm not sure if I am allowed to let her have it. She does look healthier though. But I hear her crying at night. I can't ask her about her home and family until her German improves.

Hugo spoke to Michael – who behaves when his father is around but relapses when it is only me here to correct him. He used to be so helpful and obedient, that I can only put it down to bad influence either at school or at the *Jungvolk* centre. The only time he was pleasant today was when he showed me the advancing pins on his map of Russia. . . . I think all children go through difficult stages at home as they approach puberty. Michael is growing fast, and looks older than nine. Hugo said *his* voice broke when he was twelve.

July 21st
Coincidence that I was thinking about Anni – and then should meet her. To my amazement she rushed and embraced me – she has been working on munitions, and returned to Munich last week. She has a new cause! Church bells are being taken on orders, and melted down for war use. Another wrong against Christianity.

I almost began to argue with her, try to convince her that it would be anti-Christian not to help the war effort – then I decided that it was useless. I just said I thought it was terrible. She asked after Michael and I said she must come and see him one day soon. I told her about Stazi, and she said she thought *that* was anti-Christian too! You can't win.

July 30th
Was told today that Eva Braun sent money to Frau Hess. (Hess is now a prisoner of war.) I wonder if AH knows. I have a feeling he doesn't.

August 10th
Hugo has gone to Berlin again. He is pretty sure that he will be given a new assignment, if not a new job. He has not only had the high level interviews, but he has twice been at the Chancellery – and hasn't told me much about it, except that there are no women guests – Bormann has been there on both occasions, and Dr G. I would like to have told Anni what Hugo told me – that Bormann is directing the *Kirchenkampf*★ because he sees a conflict between the Party and the direction of the church (not the Reich Church, of course, but the *other* factions) as being dangerous. Hugo hates M. Bormann, finds him insensitive and unpleasant – harsh words from my husband who generally tries to find good in everybody.

August 11th
Anni turned up – and to my astonishment was greeted rapturously by Michael – he actually kissed her! She cried with pleasure, and they sat down together and he told all he'd been doing since she left. He brought out his ghastly model guns – and she said how beautiful they were, they were the only guns she had ever liked because they couldn't kill. I was waiting for him to hold forth on the necessity of killing the enemies of Germany (he's got a very violent speech about that which is copied exactly from his friend with the brother in the Hitler Youth Patrol Service) but he didn't say a thing. Just laughed. Anni then went to find Stazi, and in very odd broken German, made herself understood. Stazi smiled, and took Anni's hand, and Anni said 'I'm going to take her to my church.' (Heaven knows where she worships now, since the old one was closed down.)
I said 'Anni, the government doesn't *allow* her to go to church. She's a war prisoner – just not in a prison camp.'
'Never mind,' said Anni. 'I will help her!'
I explained that we will be in terrible trouble if she goes against the law. 'Don't worry,' said Anni. And before she left she told me she was going into Stazi's room for a few minutes, so that they could pray together
I can't bear it.

★ Campaign against the Church.

August 13th

Anni turned up with a bible in Stazi's own language – heaven knows how she got hold of it – *and* a cross. Stazi is a different person. I heard her singing while she washed the sheets. I admire the spirit, although I am nervous that I am doing wrong – the Gestapo sometimes call unexpectedly to see that the slaves are working, and I don't want to be in trouble for allowing her the cross. I don't *think* that could be classed as 'attending religious worship' – but I don't want her taken away from me, especially as she is settling down at last. It's impossible to find German girls to work in the house.

August 16th

Hugo back – and there *is* a new job. He is to be made *Obergruppen-führer** of a Special Unit recording The New Order in Europe.

What is the New Order? The redistribution of people and property in the occupied countries apparently. The filming is top secret, and *extremely important*. Beyond that I am to know nothing. Well, I may persuade him to tell me a little more in bed – if not this week, in due course, when he has become used to the *importance* and can relax. He says he has to study a great many documents which are top secret and that this is as confidential as military plans.

Well – it is several steps up the ladder – and several thousand more marks in the bank and extremely *thrilling*.

MY HUSBAND IS AN OBERGRUPPENFÜHRER. When we married he was only Herr von Stahlenberg.

August 20th

Couldn't sleep last night. I suddenly had this daring thought – if I give a supper after the première of the Strauss opera – could I ask the Führer?

I mean, why not? I've been invited to the Obersalzberg twice. He's asked me to *sit* by him. My husband has been to the Chancellery. We're 'in', if not in the *inner* ring.

The minute the idea came to me, I was wide awake. I don't want to seem pushing – and I don't know what Hugo will think (he's away) but I DON'T SEE WHY NOT. Not really.

The committee ladies would be sick with jealousy. It would be one in the eye for my darling mother-in-law, who now writes that she

---

* Equivalent to a General.

won't come to Munich in case there is an air raid – she prefers to remain in the country. Valerie is living with her (in our old house) and it is all cosy. Not bad if the son who married beneath him has Hitler to a party. It's awful, but I can't think of anything else. I will resign from the Festival Committee. I'd rather concentrate on my *own* affair. The last meeting produced a fierce argument about the rewriting of one of the opera parts so that Hildegarde Ranczak can sing it. One silly woman said creation was sacred, and if it had been conceived for a contralto originally, it should never be changed.

They don't know anything about it, really – just like to make themselves self-important and knowledgeable. I find this is often the case with women from rich families.

August 30th

I delivered my bombshell to the assembly, as they drank the coffee we always manage to procure! I said it was for *domestic* reasons – which is true! – and they all said how much I would be missed and what a splendid contribution I had made. Utter nonsense.

I still haven't said a word to Hugo about *our* party after *Capriccio*. He has been busy and, when home, rather distracted.

Excellent report today from the *Jungvolk* leader. Everyone who has instructed Michael has said how impressed he has been to see so young a boy overcome his disability. In spite of asthma he has never sought to be excused from the compulsory boxing or the running, both of which make him unwell. In fact, he has redoubled his efforts, and has always come top of his group on the averaged assessment marks.

September 2nd

Anni turned up again – and was embraced by Stazi. I think they have had their strange communications on the telephone when I have been out. How they understand each other, God knows. Stazi looks much fitter than when she arrived. Anni told me all her family were killed, including her pregnant daughter who had lived in a small village near Prague, which (Anni claims according to Stazi) was totally destroyed by our occupying forces because of Reinhard Heydrich's assassination. That I don't believe. Maybe the girl was one of the assassins. I told Anni to ask her.

The news is still marvellous. We have reached the Volga, just north of Stalingrad – and Rommel has launched an offensive which everyone believes will break through to the Nile.

September 4th
   Me: I thought we might give a party after the opera next month.
   Hugo: Sorry. What opera?
   Me: Strauss's new opera.
   Hugo: Of course. Of course.
   Me: Shall we give a party – a select one?
   Hugo: If you like. I never know where I'm going to be though. You
   may have to give it without me.
   Me: I'll trust to luck. Hugo?
   Hugo: Yes?
   Me: I wondered if we might ask the Führer.
   Hugo: Good God!
   Me: I'd like to. After all, I've been invited to the Berghof with you.
   Hugo: True.
   Me: Well? Is it so crazy?
   Hugo: He may turn down the invitation. You mustn't be upset if
   he does.
   Me: I'll risk it.
   Hugo: It's up to you.

September 6th
I'm going to have the invitations printed formally. I can get them done
through Hugo's secretary.

September 14th
Now that all the foundry is given over to munitions, my father-in-law
is employing Russian prisoners of war . . . including Jewish women!
(He was here for a few days – has just left. Michael says 'We don't get
on anymore.') How ironic that Russians should be making weapons
to kill their own countrymen. It must be a terrible thought – *if* they
think.

Hugo and his father believe the slaves should be treated humanely,
and that to overwork them – as some employers are doing – defeats its
own ends. I'm sure they are right. I know some very ordinary house-
wives who don't treat their one woman much better than their dogs.
Sometimes I think the dog does better! I can't say anything, it isn't
my business, but one of the women on the Committee called hers 'My
Second-class White' and I honestly believe thought of her as less than
human.

September 15th
I've made my guest list – eighteen people. I wish it was possible to ask Eva B, but it simply isn't done. Frau Smital – but no other committee lady. I want them to be *jealous*. The Goebbels' (if they're here) and some of the singers. Peter Rande, of course. Two of Hugo's Brown House colleagues, and Ernst, the director. Mutti has promised me help from the hotel, *even* if they're frantically busy. I'm going to have two waitresses, and one of the Poles is going to make the desserts – she has turned out to be a sensational cook. Oh, I'm so excited. I dream about it every day. Please God let the Führer accept.

September 20th
HE HAS.

September 21st
Managed to get to the new Zara Leander movie – had to queue. Letter from Klara. She's engaged! He's an *Oberleutnant** – was on leave when they met. Love at first sight, she says. He's gone to join his unit. She doesn't know where, hopes it isn't Russia.

September 22nd
Two children from M's school have died from scarlet fever. I am terrified there's going to be a bad epidemic. I wish I could keep him home . . . but he wouldn't stay, even if it was allowed.
   The meat ration is going *up* a whole 350 grams a week, but – clothing down to only 80 points. Jews are to have *their* food ration cut.
   I suddenly remembered the truffles we brought back from the Dordogne. We'll have them at the party.

September 25th
Hugo telephoned to say that he was bringing a Dr Rascher† to lunch. Panic, until I arranged for Stazi to go over to the hotel to fetch some cold stuffed pork. It was a pleasant but dull occasion – not over-impressed with Dr R – who is doing some experiments for the Luftwaffe on the ability to withstand high altitudes. He has three children – the most interesting thing about them being that his wife gave birth to all of them after she was forty-eight!!

---

* Lieutenant.
† Dr Sigmund Rascher conducted experiments at Dachau.

September 30th
The Führer said in a speech today that this war will bring about the destruction of all European Jews. I wonder if he is right?

October 1st
Michael has made the most brilliant model of a Tiger tank. He could be a sculptor if he wanted, I imagine. I asked him if he had thought of being an artist of any sort, and he was *scathing*. 'You know I'm going to be a General!'

October 10th
Hugo at Sachsenhausen* for discussions for a film. I shall wear my Paris dress at the party. Everyone has accepted. I haven't told a soul that the Führer is coming – in case something happens and he doesn't – I don't want to be made a fool. Imagine what they will feel like when they walk into the room and *see him standing there*. They won't believe their eyes. I'm going to let Michael stay up. I want him to meet Michael. You never know, in the future. . . . Oh, I'm a scheming mother! Well, why not?

October 11th
Suddenly occurred to me that I must have a variety of vegetarian dishes for Hitler.
   Have told my mother-in-law – because I want to borrow the Meissen. I will get Hugo to fetch it if necessary.

October 12th
Herr Rust arrested for serving Jews with more than their ration. Hope this doesn't mean the shop will be closed down. I rely on him for extra fats.

October 15th
My mother-in-law says we can't have the china. Selfish bitch. She says it might get broken but she just wants to spite me. Can't wait to tell Hugo. He should be back tomorrow.

October 17th
Hugo back – he said 'My mother isn't as devoted to the Führer as you are.' I'm *furious*.

* He must have gone to the labour camp established there.

October 18th
Watched part of a rehearsal of *Capriccio* . . . it's amusing to see them in their everyday clothes on a stage without the scenery. I didn't stay too long (Frau S arranged for me to go) as to be honest I was rather bored.

Hugo very uncommunicative. Won't tell me a thing about the new film – I suppose this is the 'Highly Confidential Official Secret' attitude he likes to take! I am irritated. I don't like feeling excluded.

October 19th
Anni brought some woman round to meet Stazi. I suppose it's allowed. Told Michael he will probably meet the Führer *one day soon*. Didn't say when, as I don't want him boasting at school.

October 20th
The Rust grocery *has* closed. What a nuisance. Now I am stuck with going to the *Konsum.** I must give a present to Frau Hann, some chocolate for her little girl. Georg gave me two dozen bars, so I can spare a couple . . . for future services to be rendered.

October 22nd
Found some photographs in Hugo's desk (he's in Berlin) of prisoners in a workshop – they look rather comic with their heads shaved – all men at *sewing machines*!

I made Hugo promise to fly back and not come on one of those creeping trains; he must tell them he needs to be in his office in Munich on the 28th. Surely he's important enough?

October 23rd
Rearranged the furniture in the dining-room, so that there is plenty of room to stand for the buffet.

October 24th
Am terrified some war crisis will mean that the Führer will have to fly off to Russia or France or Egypt on the 28th. I suppose he *knows* I'm not inviting Strauss . . . he might not come if he thought he was going to be there.

* Cooperative store.

October 25th

Hugo not back. Frau Smital said the Führer is *not* attending the opera. My heart stood still when she said it. Perhaps I should have chosen another occasion – when there's Wagner. Changed the menu – the *Apfeltorte* too ordinary. I persuaded Mutti to let me have the preserved raspberries. *She* knows all about the guest of honour. She said 'Does he have false teeth?' I thought she'd taken leave of her wits! But she was thinking about the raspberry seeds. Vati can't eat them, they get behind his upper plate!

October 27th

Hugo back – thank GOD. I said 'I'd have divorced you if you hadn't come to your own party.' He said 'It's your party' . . . he's not what I would call full of life at the moment.

Everyone says Stalingrad will surrender by November 10th at the latest – and then it will *all be over*. England will surrender.

I am terrified something will go wrong tomorrow. I'm having my hair done early – first appointment. I want to have a rest in the afternoon, even if it's only an hour. I've told Michael he's allowed to stay up. I *think* he has guessed. I've told him to wear his uniform and his PT medal.

Every time the telephone rings I think it is going to be a message to say that *he can't come*. I don't care if the Goebbelses don't turn up – but I will DIE if AH isn't here. I am sure it will be the turning point of our lives.

October 28th

I know how the Disciples felt when Jesus picked them!

The summit of my life.

First Strauss's *Capriccio* – the poor old fellow looked very frail – then the official party.

Afterwards *my* supper. The Führer ate the Dordogne truffles and *a great deal* of raspberry dessert. (No dentures?)

The whole evening was a triumph. The opera was received with nothing less than rapture! Everyone said it was a pity the composer couldn't have conducted. The scenery and costumes were heavenly . . . and it *wasn't too long*.

Word had gone round that the Führer was to be at the official gathering . . . which was unlikely, considering his feelings about RS. I had one glass of champagne, then left – everything perfect at home –

I had candlelight mainly, and lit them at five to eleven. (My guests were due at eleven.) The table looked glorious – in spite of my own plates not being from Dresden! – and the food like a Roman banquet.

Michael was waiting – and I told him 'As far as I know, the Führer is going to come.' His eyes were brighter than the footlights! I told him not to be disappointed if he didn't arrive – but I thought he would.

He did. He was charming. The guests were *stunned*. He talked to Michael about school – and afterwards said to me 'What a handsome boy – it makes me feel overjoyed when I think of the new generation. We are producing fine men of the proper type.'

He spent time talking quietly to Hugo – one sees who is an 'intimate' and who is not by the greetings – no 'Heil Hitlers' from those who know him well, just friendly handshakes.

He left at 12.17 – and the others had all gone by one o'clock. I sent Michael to bed at midnight – he said it was the finest day he had ever spent – and *thanked me!* He was still awake fifteen minutes ago when I went in to make sure he hadn't kicked the covers off – and hugged me, and when I tiptoed out, he shot up his hand and said 'Heil Hitler', and we both laughed. Hugo is in his study – I'm waiting for him so that we can discuss all the details – and I can hear Stazi in the kitchen washing up.

Even the collapse of Stalingrad won't compete with tonight.

A triumph.

I did it,

October 29th
Hugo left early, before the post.

I received an official letter – one of the blue ones without a stamp, which usually come for Hugo. It simply requests me to appear before the Gestapo the day after tomorrow.

Why?

I hope I haven't done anything wrong. It can't be about the black market coffee – everyone does that. It's silly to feel that it's trouble. Especially when I entertained the Führer last night. It's probably to ask me to do something official – or to keep an eye on someone – Frau Smital was asked to watch her janitor. He was arrested three weeks ago.

I wonder if anyone has said anything about my hiding my fur coat. I don't think I *told* anyone. Only Mutti, and she wouldn't say a thing. Anyway, it isn't a *crime*.

Phone been going all day with thanks for last night – it would have been a *perfect* day if only that letter hadn't come.

Hugo came in at ten and went straight to bed, but I feel strung up and know I'd only lie there wide awake. I said I wanted to listen to the radio – it's on, but I'm not paying attention.

I'll be so relieved when I've seen them and know what it's all about.

October 31st

It was very strange. Unnerving. And yet nothing terrible was said. I had told Hugo. He didn't seem interested. 'Wait and see. Don't speculate.'

The address I had to go to turned out to be a house converted into offices. I had to ring to get in. It was answered by an ordinary looking woman, a cleaner, and as soon as I entered, a door to the left opened and a man in civilian clothes came out. I showed him my letter and he directed me to an office down the corridor. I could hear a typewriter going, and a telephone ringing briefly.

When I reached the right door I knocked and a voice called out to come in. I opened it – and there was a second door inside the first, padded with leather.

I opened that one too, and found myself in a large office. There was a young man sitting behind a desk. He stood up.

'Heil Hitler!' I said. 'I hope I've come to the right room.'

'Heil Hitler! Frau von Stahlenberg?'

'Yes.'

'Please sit down.'

I sat and tried to seem at ease. Believe me, I was not!

'Forgive us for bothering you, Frau von Stahlenberg. There are one or two minor matters I wanted to talk to you about.'

I thought: *The Coat.*

'Frau Rust . . . Frieda Rust.'

'The grocer's wife?'

'We have her in custody. There have been complaints against her.'

'I knew her husband had given the Jews double rations.'

'How did you know that?'

'Everyone was talking about it. He was my grocer . . . it was no secret.'

'The wife pleads innocence. Do you believe she knew nothing?'

'It's probably true. She didn't work in the shop.'

He put down his pencil. 'I hope it's true. One doesn't want to hold an innocent woman. It's difficult to reach a decision in these cases. Wives are usually in full knowledge of their husbands' affairs. I'm sure you know what your husband does, for instance.'

I said 'As a matter of fact I don't. Since he changed his job.'

'Changed his job?'

'Well, he's still with the Ministry of Propaganda. In the Film Section. But now his work is secret.'

'Secret even from his wife?' The man smiled.

'Even from her.' I smiled back. 'I ask him frequently but he doesn't tell me a thing.'

'Let me give you a cup of coffee. *Muckefuck*, I'm afraid.'

I thought: *That's it!* The black market coffee! He rang a bell and the cleaner who had answered the door came in. He asked her to bring some coffee. It was all very pleasant. He opened the window. 'Such a warm afternoon, Frau von Stahlenberg. We might as well make the most of the sunshine.'

The coffee arrived. While we drank it, he asked me how I had enjoyed the opera. 'I saw you there. Forgive me, but I must tell you that you looked ravishing.'

I have no recollection of seeing him until today – and he must have read this in my face, because he said 'We know most of the important citizens here. It's our business.'

When we had finished the perfectly ghastly coffee, he stood up and thanked me for taking the trouble to come in. (As if I would have dared to refuse the summons!) As I walked to the door, he suddenly stopped me.

'Oh. One other thing.'

I turned back. I felt terrified. It was the coat after all.

'Did you know that your servant goes to church?'

'No.'

'On Sundays, when you go with your son to your parents' hotel. . . . She meets another woman.'

I said 'Anni!'

'That's correct. You're surprised?'

'I'd no idea.'

'It's against the law, Frau von Stahlenberg. I suggest you put a stop to it or she'll find herself in prison.'

'As long as I don't!'

'Oh, we won't hold you responsible.' He smiled. 'Heil Hitler!'

'Heil Hitler.'

It's absurd, but when I got out into the street I was *trembling*. I haven't done anything to be afraid . . . to be ashamed of (possibly the wretched coat. God, if they ask again this year I'll be the first one to donate) . . . but it's the *manner*. Charming yet full of implication. I told Hugo word for word. He said it was nothing but routine. But I'd better tell Anni to lay off and Stazi to stay in.

My head is splitting.

November 12th

Hugo is away (in Eastern Poland) and Stalingrad hasn't fallen in spite of the promises. I have a feeling that it is going to go on and on and on, and this winter is going to be like the last. The Führer was here as usual for the November 9th celebration and spoke with great confidence. I can't think why we didn't make the all-out effort in the summer to finish the Russians off.

December 12th
BERLIN

Risked the raids to come to the opening of the *Staatsoper*.* They've made a fantastic job of the rebuilding. Everyone looked splendid too, all the uniforms (Göring's the most glorious, of course) and evening dress – you wouldn't know there was a war on. The opera was *Die Meistersinger*. Food after was marvellous – everyone in high spirits saying it will all be over soon. Our air force is going to supply the soldiers temporarily cut off in Stalingrad. Thank God for the Luftwaffe and twentieth-century engineering! Saved again!

December 25th

Although Hugo was away we managed to have a good Christmas. Sometimes I am really depressed by our separation, and then I tell myself that it is only temporary and once the war is over we'll move out of the city and live a relaxed life. I certainly don't want to go back to 'the family seat', but I would like a house in the hills round Munich. I think it would be better for Michael too. He is such a 'city boy' now, and not at all interested in nature.

I hope Hugo will be back for the New Year.

December 30th

Hugo here overnight with Dr Hirt from Strasbourg University – I

* State Opera House.

218

gave them breakfast this morning, and off they went. I imagine I won't see Hugo again for at least a week. I gathered from the few remarks made at breakfast that Dr H is engaged in research (anthropology, I think, is his subject) and that Hugo is filming the results. At least he's not at the front.

December 31st
Was invited to a small party for New Year's Eve, but decided not to go.

1943

January 12th
Letter from Hugo from The Institute of Military Scientific Research.
So I was right. Husbands may not tell their wives everything but if the
wives have an ounce of brain matter then they put two and two together and find out! He says he is there for some weeks more and is
missing home dreadfully. In a way I'm glad we've been kept apart,
because it has proved how much we love each other. I don't like
Michael being without him, though. When he was small it was easy
for me to make all the decisions, but I find it difficult now. He is so
headstrong, and so *determined*. The asthma is under control at the
moment anyway, which is one problem out of the way. I took him for
a check-up (a different doctor again – there's a new one each time I
make an appointment) but the records are there and this one said too
much fuss is made about asthma. The right mental approach is a cure
in itself.

January 30th
Michael had a nice birthday today. Hugo was here, though he was not
his usual self. He is tired, and looks it. Thank goodness he has 'leave'
for fourteen days. We celebrated with a small family party, and meas-
ured M against his bedroom door. He has grown seven centimetres
since last summer. Anni came round – I do *wish* she'd stay away. (She
promised not to interfere after I was at the Gestapo offices. I told her she
would get herself into trouble as well as us – and that if Stazi disobeyed
again, *she* would be dealt with.)
　　Michael said she'd made his birthday by coming . . . and seemed more
enraptured by the hideous scarf she'd made him (army grey) than by
the model submarine from us. Those early childhood bonds are in-
destructible unfortunately.

February 3rd
Such a shock today. I was listening to the radio – when the programme
was broken into, for a special announcement. There was a roll of drums,
which made my heart feel quite cold. Then they played the second

movement of Beethoven's Fifth Symphony (one of the few things I recognize!) and then it was announced that the Battle of Stalingrad had ended. *We have been overcome.* I couldn't believe it. I cried. Hugo held me and said it was a terrible set-back, but it was only one battle lost in so many victories. We can't expect to have it our way all the time.

But it was such an *important* victory. Hitler knows. There are to be four days of national mourning – cinemas are to be closed.

February 18th
Dr G made a speech today – on 'total war'. It was uplifting and cheering – and at the same time made one (made *me*) feel that any sacrifice is worth the suffering in this final charge to defeat the enemies.

February 20th
Eva Braun telephoned and asked me to have lunch with her in the Osteria. We had a quiet table, away from the front. She was more het-up than I've ever seen her – about the ban on cosmetics production. 'And permanent wave apparatus.' I couldn't care less about the last – I'm growing my hair again, I've decided I like to be able to put it up – but I wouldn't be able to *exist* without lipstick. Even if I didn't wear it every day I would *have* to use it for parties. She says she is going to speak to 'Adolf' about it. 'I've never interfered with anything before, but this time I'm going to have my say.'

February 28th
We have been asked not to use too many light bulbs, and luxury restaurants are being closed. Thank God the *Goldener Hirsch* doesn't come into that category. Mutti has had new instructions on how to use up the left-overs! I have a cold. The student riots are over.*

March 3rd
A terrible air raid on Berlin last night. Thank heavens we weren't there. 20,000 houses destroyed by the loathsome British – and how many dead and injured?

Some amusing stories going around about Göring – he tried to stop Horcher's† being closed and Goebbels arranged for some youths to throw stones through the windows when Hermann was there – he

---

* Anti-Nazi riots triggered by Gauleiter Paul Giesler's speech to the students resulting in trial and execution.

† Berlin restaurant.

was of course in some fantastic uniform and *gobbling away*. The place was closed the next day!! Also he has taken to putting on *rouge*. Is that why Goebbels has stopped the manufacture of cosmetics?!

March 4th

Twenty-fifth anniversary of UFA – celebrations, in spite of 'total war' and Hugo and I had one of our most relaxed and happy days for a long time. He said 'You've no idea how I long to be involved in fiction instead of reality. When the war's over, I shall make nothing but happy romances.'

March 10th

I find it difficult to write. Life is so flat. If only we could go off to Paris or Venice again. I'm afraid I am quite *discontented* confined to Munich. I know Hugo goes abroad – Poland, Czechoslovakia and I think he has also been to Denmark (although he hasn't actually said so). I would love to go to Prague. I don't really see why I shouldn't go too. Even if he is working at research institutes, I could look around the city.

March 21st

I asked Hugo if it wouldn't be possible for me to go with him now and again. He said 'Even if it were possible, I can assure you that you wouldn't enjoy it.'

When he makes love to me now it isn't ever *fun*. I don't know what's happened to him.

March 22nd

An unexpected party – some film people we met in Paris arrived, telephoned, and invited us to dinner. They had all kinds of French delicacies – including cheese and *snails* – and we sat in their hotel room and made absolute pigs of ourselves, and became quite drunk on the two bottles of wine and one bottle of cognac they had brought with them.

I am my old self again. And so is Hugo. What I wrote yesterday isn't true. It *was* fun . . . and very loving too.

(*There are no entries for April 1943.*)

May 10th

Schwiegervater stayed with us last month on his way to a meeting of industrialists at the Obersalzberg. He looked older, but was as courteous as always. He asked me to make sure that Michael was receiving sufficient instruction at school. He said there are plenty of elderly teachers around who would be happy to coach M in the evenings, and that he would be happy to pay. I didn't dare tell him that Michael was too busy every evening with the *Jungvolk* and had no time for academic work. Of course I could insist – I tried to discuss it with Hugo, but he said I would have to cope with it myself. He (*Schwiegervater*) stayed a night on his return too – said he thought Göring was ill, and that he had *fallen asleep* in the meeting. 'We all pretended it hadn't happened, and went on with our discussions. But he looked rather comic, I must say, with all those medals and whatnot all over him, snoring with his head on the table.'

May 14th
Things are very bad in Tunis.

May 15th
Hugo telephoned from Berlin. His father is there for another meeting of the industrialists – without the sleeping Hermann I imagine! They had just been to dinner at Horcher's, which is now a club for the Luftwaffe – and just as good as it was when we went there together. I wish I could have been there with them. I feel like a celebration. There's nothing to celebrate in this dead place.

May 16th
So sad, Klara's fiancé was killed. Mutti had a letter from *her* mother. She so wanted to get married, too, and it had taken so long to climb out of the 'mistress' blockade.

June 26th
I had Klara to stay for three weeks, and have done my best to cheer her up. She is to receive a medal for her fiancé's bravery. He was taken prisoner by the Russians and died (she thinks he was shot). She left yesterday, feeling much brighter she said. Today Dr G is here and made the usual speech for the opening of the Seventh Great Art Exhibition.

I was invited to the opening – and did my rounds of the pictures. My favourite (Eduard Grützner) is the Führer's, so I am in good company. Dr G made his usual proposal – and as usual I made a kind but negative reply. I said 'If I looked at anyone but my husband it would be you.' An outright lie, but it doesn't do to aggravate one's husband's boss. He took me to one side and asked me if I thought Hugo was well. 'He seems to have lost some of that early enthusiasm.' I said I thought he was just tired. He asked me if Hugo ever discussed his work with me, and I said 'Not any more.' It reminded me of the Gestapo gentleman. I can't help wondering if they are worried and trying to find out. Fortunately for them, my husband is completely honourable.

June 30th
Hugo back. He has lost weight. I suggested he see a doctor while he is home, but he said 'I have seen enough doctors. I am working with them most of the time nowadays.' He mentioned later that he had been to a lecture at the Berlin Medical Military Academy with Dr Sauerbruch* – and even I've heard of him – so I suppose if there were visible signs of ill health Hugo wouldn't go unattended. He met his Uncle Gustav (a heart specialist) there which astonished them both!

I managed to unload a whole lot of Michael's clothes (in very good condition, just too small for him) on a friend of the woman downstairs, so am *rich with coupons*. Will keep them for the winter, as I have enough summer things to keep me going.

July 11th
Have just learned that allied forces have landed in Sicily. I hope that they'll be defeated quickly. There was a talk on the radio, which makes it seem unimportant. You never know nowadays.

July 27th
Mussolini has resigned for reasons of ill health. No one can believe it. Vati says it doesn't look good. Badoglio, who has taken over the government, is anti-German.

July 29th
Mutti has asked Aunt Gerda to come and stay here until the bombing is over in Hamburg. This is their fourth night of raids. I don't like her, but I suppose she has to come. She's so *critical* of everything I've ever done. I don't remember a hotter, drier summer. Everyone is wilting. Aunt G would be the final point of exhaustion!

* A famous lung surgeon.

August 1st

A terrible day. Hugo paced the room almost all last night. Wouldn't say what was the matter. Was he ill? No! Was he worried? No! Was there some sort of trouble? No! Did he love someone else? No! I heard our clock strike five, and he finally got into bed. I put my arms round him, and I suddenly realized *he was crying*.

I didn't know what to do. He's so strong. I begged and begged him to tell me what has happened, but he didn't – won't. All day he has stayed in bed, and has eaten next to nothing. Tonight I said 'You have to tell me *something*. I must be able to help!'

I was still terribly afraid it was to do with me, that he wanted to leave me. I cried a bit myself, which I was very ashamed of, as he needed me to support him.

He said of course it wasn't anything like that. He loved me more than he had ever done and couldn't live without me. It *was* to do with his work. He didn't think he could continue. I said *in what way*. Was he given too much to do. He said no, *too much to take*. I said he must explain, but he said he couldn't. It was a moral decision that he had to make and it was terrifying to make it. He said there were certain medical experiments being carried out on prisoners, and he felt that the Führer didn't know. He didn't know whether to talk to Dr Goebbels, or to try and see Hitler, or even approach Hermann G, who is more approachable.

I said I thought Dr Goebbels was the best one, because he was responsible for all the films made. Hugo said yes, I was right, and he would talk to him. He said meeting his uncle had shocked him, because his uncle is a well-known physician, and should have spoken against these experiments, whatever they are. I wanted Hugo to tell me, but he wouldn't.

Then he broke down again, and said I was the most wonderful wife any man could have, and that I had helped him so much. I gave him bread (albeit the horrid bran bread which is all I seem to be able to buy) and some of the American dried milk as if he was a child!

He's been asleep ever since. I had to write it all down. I can't sleep myself.

August 15th

Hugo has his appointment with the Doktor today. He is going to tell him what he knows – he has been working all day and every day on a dossier – and ask for a full investigation.

I'm sure it will work out all right.

August 16th
Anni was arrested last week. I only heard today via Fräulein Müller who knows everything eventually. Anni gave bibles to all the Eastern workers and encouraged them to break the law by going to church. If *only* the silly misguided woman had listened to my warning. I'm not surprised – but I am very very sorry. I told Michael, and I *was* surprised by his reaction. He didn't seem at all upset – and he loved Anni very much. He said 'She shouldn't have done it, that's all.' Stazi cried, and went into her room – no doubt praying all evening. I wonder if I can do anything to help. It was done in good faith and for the best motives, and wasn't *such a crime*.

August 17th
Have waited in all day in case Hugo phoned. I had expected to hear from him, perhaps he didn't see Dr G after all Terrible air raids all the time.

August 20th
Letter from Hugo. Nothing about the meeting.

August 21st
Met Aunt Gerda at the station and took her to the hotel. Her house is still standing, but not much else. I hope it continues to stand. If she's homeless, God help us all. At least she's clever enough to have stored her furniture in four different places.

August 22nd
Row with Michael about swimming. They say polio is spread by water and I don't want him to go to the pool. There have been quite a lot of cases. He says he won't go – but I have a feeling he will. Half the time now I don't know what he's up to. If he says he is going to the *Jungvolk* meeting, how am I to know if he's lying? I can't check up on him like a spy – it's too degrading. Oh, how I wish Hugo was here.

August 23rd
Michael came back with damp hair – so I gave him *Stubenarrest*.* I've

---

* Room arrest.

never done it before. It's very upsetting. But I can't let him get away with things.

August 24th
Tried to make inquiries about Anni, but drew a blank.

August 30th
Hugo back. *He never said a thing to Goebbels.* WHY?

September 9th
Yesterday Italy capitulated. I felt sick when I heard. Vati, who takes everything in his stride, says we're better off without them, they're only good for making ice cream.

September 13th
A brilliant coup. We have rescued the Duce! They found out where he was, whisked him up in a plane, took him to Rome and to Vienna tonight. I wonder if he'll come to Munich. His daughter is already here.

September 15th
Mussolini has today proclaimed the new Italian Social Republic! Will he be reinstated, or is it his end?

September 20th
I spoke to Hugo about his failure to speak to Goebbels. He said, 'I lacked courage when it came to it.'
I said 'You should, you know. You won't be happy until you do. And from what you tell me, you have a duty.'
He said he would find the opportunity. He goes away again tomorrow, and not to Berlin, so he won't have the chance. He is meeting a Dr Frank Bláha at the camp at Dachau. I took the telephone message. The plane is leaving at 7 a.m. – another restless night!

September 25th
Another row with Michael. This time because I found him in Hugo's study with the desk open. He *said* he was looking for some glue – for his models. But there is glue in his own room, and he hasn't finished the pot, because I went to see. There is nothing in the desk – all the

official papers are in the office – but I can't stand prying. I said I would tell Hugo, and that if I ever caught him there again I would punish him. And I *would*. I'd stop him going to a meeting or to a camp, something that really matters.

September 26th
We have lost Smolensk, but we are forming the 'Winter Line' which the Führer says will be impregnable.

September 30th
Hugo writes that he will be away another two weeks.

Felt like going to a movie, but the queue was so long that I gave up the idea. As I turned away, some greasy old man came up and offered me a ticket – for three times the price. I said I'd report him, and he just melted away. A grand note for one to take – who spends half her time searching for black market coffee!

October 2nd
Last night our lovely opera house was destroyed. We were in the cellar and I thought it was our *own* house. *Capriccio* was only a year ago. Somehow it's like the end of everything.

October 13th
Italy has declared war on *Germany*. When I think of Venice I could weep.

October 15th
At last Hugo has pulled himself together. He has spoken to Dr G. Says he wasn't unsympathetic and he would give the matter thought.

Tried to get Hugo to speak to Michael over the desk incident and the swimming, but he wouldn't. Said if he had been involved personally at the time he would have punished him, but now it's history.

October 16th
Hugo is to edit the films *here*. Hurrah! Have arranged two small dinner parties to celebrate.

November 1st
So satisfying to be a 'family' and to entertain again. Party a great

success. Did the cooking myself – chicken cooked in wine. Georg said he thought the Führer was thinking of negotiating peace with England, which turned into a fierce argument, with Herr Smital shouting 'Utter nonsense, if he negotiates with anyone it will be with Stalin.' Mussolini, I learned, is doing nothing, except to cling to his mistress who was delivered to him at Lake Garda. What DID people talk about before the war?

November 5th
It's so ghastly I don't know what to do. A blue unstamped letter – which I gave to Hugo without even *thinking*. He's had them so often for one official thing or another.

He opened it. Read it. I saw his eyes go back to the beginning again. We were still at the breakfast table – M had left for school.

Hugo said 'My answer.' He gave it to me.

I took it, and I felt so drained, as if my blood was being dragged down to my feet – it was the sort of sensation I had on the beach in Venice, the tide dragging the sand from under me.

It said he had been *relieved of his present post*. That he would be responsible for a small unit filming the progress of the German Seventeenth Army. There was also a code name, Hugo has the letter with him and I can't remember it.

He said 'That's Russia.'

I said 'But *why?*'

He said 'An expedient way of stopping my protests.'

I said 'You can't go . . . you'll die of cold.'

It was at this point – staring at each other – horrified – that we heard Michael's voice at the door saying 'I was sent home. I was too wheezy to do PT.'

I don't know if he'd been there for long. He looked peaked and hunched and his breath *scraped*. Hugo picked him up and carried him to his room, and I propped up the pillows. The worst attack since before the last visit to Mont Dore. I telephoned for the doctor – not in, out on his rounds, won't be back before two. One of those terrible mornings. I know people don't die from asthma, but he really couldn't breathe – it sounded as if his intake of air went down five centimetres. And then it was a fight to expel it.

I rang Mutti – she knows a doctor personally, an old man, retired, but who does help out nowadays. He said he'd come if we could fetch him (no gasoline) so Hugo drove round and brought him back and he gave M an injection of adrenalin, and the results were instant – he lay back and his breathing eased, and he looked white and exhausted and said 'Feel my heart. It's racing.'

Hugo said 'I'm going to the office to clear up my things.'

I said 'You mean you're not going to *fight* it.'

He said 'No!' as he went out of the door.

I read to Michael all afternoon – Kohl's *We Fly Against England*, not exactly my choice! – and while I read I found I was thinking all the time about Hugo, and not knowing what I was saying. That's how some women knit and listen to the radio at the same time – two functions, one automatic.

I can't believe they mean to send Hugo *there*. It must be a mistake, an error made in some official department. *Why* would they want to send him to Russia? Anyone can do a film job like that. He's an *Obergruppenführer* – not some dim SS-Mann, to be shunted around. I don't believe Dr G even *knows*. The Führer came to my party – Hugo's been to the *Chancellery*.

If he won't speak to Goebbels, I WILL. I *know* it's a mistake.

November 6th

Hugo came back late last night, and refused to discuss it. Michael is much better this morning – but has to stay home. I said to Hugo, 'Are you going to speak to the Doktor?' He said 'I told you, no. He's too busy. They know what they want me to do, and I'll do it.' *I just don't understand his attitude.*

November 7th

Another letter, telling Hugo to report to the Ministry Offices in Dresden for briefing.

And he's going. Accepts it. Like a *mouse*.

I lost my temper. I don't often. But I can't stand seeing someone I love being so *passive*. Does he want to freeze to death, or be taken prisoner by the Russians? Or shot? Or wounded?

He said 'You don't know what you're up against.'

I didn't answer. But I'm not leaving it. I'm NOT. He can say what he likes.

November 8th

Hugo has gone. He left at 5 this morning.

I telephoned Dr G. Not there, but I left my name. If he doesn't call me back, then I'm going to GO THERE. I have no intention of getting a widow's medal.

November 10th
This time he *was* there, and took my call.

> *Dr G:* My dear Frau von Stahlenberg, what can I do for you?
> *Me:* I need your help.
> *Dr G:* In any way I can.
> *Me:* May I come and talk to you?
> *Dr G:* Do you want to come to Berlin?
> *Me:* Anywhere.
> *Dr G:* I'll send a car for you. You can fly from Nuremberg. I'll have you informed of the arrangements.

I said to myself when I put down the telephone, remember to wear your French perfume, your crêpe de chine underwear and your Dutch cap.

November 14th
BERLIN
I felt like Clara Petacci* – the Mercedes arrived. SS driver. I wondered if the neighbours were watching. In fact I flew from Regensburg – in a private plane. I know it's dreadful to admit it, but I was excited. Even the ghastliness of Hugo's situation was somehow subdued. I've never done a thing on my own before, not like this.

I was met by another car in Berlin, and taken to the hotel. I was told a number to telephone in the morning – *not* the one I'd used before.

I had something to eat and went to bed. I did ring home to speak to Michael, but he's fine.

After breakfast I called that number, and although a secretary answered, the Doktor took it immediately. He said 'Why don't you come here at about two? I'll arrange a light lunch.'

I walked round the streets. The damage is heartrending. When I think of the city when 'Maman' was alive and we stayed with her, I am so sad. I used to be pleased when I heard of the raids on London, but now I know how they felt.

I arrived at the Ministry at ten minutes to two. I was shown into the office at one minute to the hour. It is like going aboard an ocean liner –

* Mussolini's mistress.

or being in a movie. He got up from his desk, and greeted me by taking both my hands in his. There was really no pretence. He said 'Now you must tell me what I can do for you?' But what he meant was 'What can you do for me?'

I said 'Hugo has been sent to the Eastern Front, Dr Goebbels.'

'Joseph. For today at any rate. Perhaps not officially.'

'I thought it might have been a mistake.'

He went to a cupboard and took out glasses and a bottle of vodka. 'From our more successful excursions in Russia.'

I thought I had better drink.

'Dr Goebbels, I don't know why you've sent him there, but I'm afraid he'll die.'

'This is wartime. He has a job to do for me there.'

'Please, won't you give him another job?'

He sat down facing me. I hated him. I knew what he was thinking. He sat so that he could see my legs.

'I'll tell you the truth. Your husband is too squeamish. He was upset by filming necessary experiments designed to prevent our troops from freezing to death, or suffering from gas burns. Who do you put first? Our brave soldiers and airmen, or the prisoners and second-class citizens we have in our camps? The doctors know what they're doing. They have assured me that unless the experiments are carried out, we're going to lose our men. We use only criminals, who would have been shot in other circumstances – prisoners who would have starved to death probably or died from exposure. Anyway, our doctors aren't inhuman – every care is taken to reduce suffering.'

He put his hand on my knee.

'And you mustn't forget – your husband came to me to ask me to transfer him to some other field.'

'I thought he came to you to ask you to instigate an inquiry.'

'Absolutely not. There's no inquiry to be made. The state has authorized the use of selected TPs . . .'

'TPs?'

'Test persons . . . in specified cases.'

He leaned forward and undid the two top buttons of my cream silk shirt and slid his hand inside. I said 'Are there no other fields than the Eastern Front?' I thought I'd better say it *now*. It is a bargain after all.

He laughed. 'I'm sure we can find one nearer home.'

And that was it. He was like a rapacious ferret, all over me. In such a hurry he didn't take off his clothes, only mine. The horror was that he was skilled, and detesting him as I did, I was aroused. By 2.15, I was on my way out – not having had any more light lunch than the glass of burning vodka which had dehydrated me.

I went back to the hotel, ordered tea and a sandwich, and put my feet up on the bed, astonished at my own behaviour. Why, I could be a Mata Hari if circumstances demanded it!

A call came through. The plane would be leaving tomorrow at 9 a.m. The car would be here at eight. I would be flying back to Munich direct.

I wonder whether that's it – or whether he'll want to see me again. It's lucky Hugo isn't home yet. There's a bruise on my breast like a prune.

November 15th
Home. And no one knows.

November 16th
All day I've expected a telephone call from either Dr G or from Hugo. But nothing.

November 17th
Nothing.

November 18th
Nothing.

November 19th
Nothing.

November 20th
Nothing.

November 21st
2.30 in the afternoon – a ring at the door. Hugo there. Bursting with the good news. He swept me into an embrace. 'I've been transferred.'

'How wonderful.'

'I'm needed in Berlin.'

'I'm so glad. . . .' I was genuinely crying. I felt weak and relieved and overjoyed and triumphant.

'Now all I need is to be bombed in Berlin!'

'You mean you'll be in Berlin *all* the time?'

'Isn't that better than Smolensk?'

'We've lost Smolensk,' I said, sobbing. 'I listen to the news bulletins.'

'I'll be able to come home – we can meet there.'

But I decided. The *new strong me* made the decision. 'Hugo, I am lonely and unhappy when I'm away from you. We'll move to Berlin.'

'The raids . . . I don't think it would be . . .'

'We'll risk the raids. Munich's had raids. I'd rather be with you. I'd rather *die* with you. But we *won't* . . . we'll . . .'

'You sound like one of those terrible films . . . *Die grosse Liebe** . . . one of those.'

I *did!* I said 'But I will come. We'll find an apartment in the suburbs. Anyway there isn't much left to bomb. I should think they'll realize that.'

We told Michael we were going to move, and he was upset, as I'd anticipated. His friends are here, and he's doing so well. I half thought of leaving him with Mutti, but in the end I knew I couldn't. I can't live without Michael any more than I want to be without Hugo.

When we were in bed for some reason I found myself pretending it was Goebbels. Now Hugo is snoring – and so is Michael, two wall-thicknesses away, it's like an orchestra!

December 20th

An exhausing month. First of all we had to cope with my parents' distress that we were going – and I understand because they came here to be with us. We can hardly expect them to go to Berlin. Then there has been the business of letting the apartment, packing, winding up all kinds of trivial matters, sorting out, throwing out, saying goodbye.

Hugo is already there. He has found us somewhere to live – not easy, as there are so many homeless, grabbing up whatever is vacant, and the exodus of Jews which made life easy before is over. We go early in the New Year. I dread Christmas – everyone is so depressed about the way the war's going, and because we're leaving it will be depressing.

December 28th

Hugo back for just a few days. It helped to keep the spirits up, and in fact we had a good time, a huge party at the hotel, lots to drink and everyone sang everything from hymns to waltzes! Hugo sorted out his

* *The Great Love.*

own clothes and papers, to my relief, which was one job less for next week's final clear-up of the apartment. He gave me a great pile of papers and said 'Burn them'. I said 'Are you sure!' Once before he had thrown away an insurance policy. He said absolutely. He then added another wad, and said 'The dossier I never gave to Dr Goebbels.' I couldn't believe that he'd kept it – not shown it. When I said what had been the point of producing it, he said it had helped him make up his own mind.

I put the lot on the fire, and tried to remember if I'd made a fool of myself with Dr G – because what he had said was true. Hugo *had* just asked for a transfer. Not an inquiry. And of course I couldn't let Hugo know why I was upset that he'd changed his mind and not told me.

1944

BERLIN
January 30th
Michael hasn't been accepted for Adolf Hitler School because of the asthma. He blames us for not letting him go to all the Camps. This means his chances of getting to an Order Castle* are remote. But at least he has joined the local *Jungvolk*, and has settled in. Hugo went to see the leader, and had an excellent report for the first two weeks.

Hugo's work is dull and local. He is merely recording the buildings that are standing, street by street, in detail; photographing those bomb-damaged; going through the architectural archives for plans. All this for the major rebuilding (by Speer, I suppose) after the end of hostilities.

I nearly died with guilt when Hugo said 'Even the Russian front would be preferable to this. It's nothing but an office job. Surely they could have found me something more demanding.'

The apartment isn't bad, smaller than the one in Munich, it wouldn't take all our furniture so we left some with my parents. No study for Hugo, but we've put his desk in our bedroom. It won't be for ever.

It is depressing here.

February 5th
Saw Dr Goebbels for the first time since November, and I blushed. I suppose I expected him to make some private remark, or meet my eyes – but he didn't pay me even the attention that he had *before*. It makes me feel as if I failed. I *didn't* – because Hugo is here and not dead of frostbite. But I must have failed sexually – unless that's his way. Just once with everyone. But I do know he has had affairs, there was that one with Lida Baarova. He was supposedly in love with her.

I mustn't make it too important to myself. It certainly wasn't for Goebbels. He said to me that day 'I knew if I waited long enough . . .' which was humiliating too. It is only important to me because I was taught that sexual experience is only permissible with a husband – or at

* Institutions for training the Nazi élite.

least with a man one loves. But in my heart I know that's an implanted guilt. I'm not religious. I did it for a purpose. And that's that. Elisabeth von Stahlenberg – forget it! It meant nothing except that it saved your husband's life.

February 20th
Very busy. I am working for the *Winterhilfe* – we need anything made of metal. I have even been at the depot sorting through the debris brought from the bombed apartments and houses (all the things that haven't been looted! Quite a problem).

I realize that I wasn't aware of the war in Munich. The few raids, the black market meant nothing compared to life here. Night after night we go to the shelters – we go to the one on Wilhelmstrasse (below the Adlon). The one under the zoo has room for 10,000 people! Going home at four in the morning after the all-clear has a curious peace about it. No cars, no trams, no nothing. The sky is usually red from fires, and the houses look like a child's cut-outs – especially the ones that have been sliced in half. The trees have gone and we stumble through valleys of rubble. People live in the most extraordinary circumstances – and treat it as if it is normal. Sometimes they have only two rooms left out of a big apartment, the ceilings in dust-heaps on the floor! I won't mention the stench.

Everyone behaves like old friends – inviting us in to share whatever they have left. We have found some old friends actually – and some new ones. One of the *old* friends (Hans T – 'Maman's' godson) was arrested yesterday because he was listening to a foreign radio station – his landlady reported him. Hugo is going to try and find out if he is to be fined. He doesn't have a great deal of money, but a number of us would club together. What we are afraid of is imprisonment.

We go to the cinema twice a week – the queues are eight times longer than the ones in Munich, and there's little hope of getting in *without* paying the black market prices. My scruples are gradually being overcome in so many fields!

Hugo has met a number of University friends, either working at one of the Ministries, or at the General Staff Headquarters. We go to concerts. Two-thirds of the seats are generally given to soldiers on leave. We are going to hear Furtwängler conduct in the Admiralpalast.

February 27th
What is exciting is that all our friends here are *hochgeboren* – well – not

all, but many. Much more select that in Munich. Isn't it funny how things have turned out so well? I think I'd rather like to live here permanently. There's something about the *Reichshauptstadt**! The people are more sophisticated.

Tonight we're dining with Hugo's friend Peter Yorck (really *Count Peter Yorck von Wartenburg* – a direct descendant of the famous Prussian general. I remember the name from history lessons at school!). Tomorrow we're going to a new movie with Oberstleutnant Freiherr von Heiden and his wife (a beautiful Swiss). We're going to have dinner at the Eden afterwards.

February 28th
I met an officer at dinner who was just out of military hospital, and he has *a silver shoulder*.

(There are no entries for March or April 1944.)

May 12th
Those British 'mosquitoes'! Michael has models of them too. I said to him, why on earth does he want models of *enemy* planes. His room is so cluttered I can barely get in to dust. Stazi is doing well at the hotel – but I miss the help. If we manage to find a place with one more bed-room I'll fetch her myself – about the one thing that would get me back to Munich. I can't believe how in love with with Berlin I've become.

Hugo is desperately bored with the work – but is happy with his group of friends. They come to us – or he goes to them – two or three times a week. It's like being back at University, he says, they talk philosophy and politics and literature and films. I'm so happy here myself I'm not even jealous!

My friends are the Swiss wife, Danielle – and Helene, who I met through the *Winterhilfe*, a movie addict. She has sons who are at school with Michael. The kind of friends I like him to have. Polite and well brought-up and with some *background*. I used to think it was ideal for all children of all social classes to be together in the Hitler Youth – now I feel that this is right for *part of the time*.

Am going to see Schiller's *Die Rauber*†. Everyone is talking about it.

* The capital of the Reich.
† *The Robbers.*

Gustav Gründgens wears his hair like the Führer – and plays the villain!

May 24th
Met a very interesting actor in the air raid shelter! He has been touring with a small company, and has given performances to the SS guards in various prison camps! Had a wonderful reception in Auschwitz, and were given *a banquet*. They were waited on by the prisoners, which he said made him feel uncomfortable – couldn't help wondering what they had for dinner!

Helene is a member of a theatre-booking organization, which means she can see plays at half-price – ten, I think she said, each season. In spite of the bombing, and in spite of the fact that some of the theatres have no roofs and some are rubble, Berlin is still the *theatrical centre*. I am just discovering its joys.

May 30th
Went shopping on the Unter den Linden. In the few stores left, nothing but bales of hideous grey material and *Filzpantoffel*.* They've stopped making anything attractive.

June 1st
Letter from Mutti – took ten days to get here! Everyone is well. The hotel is full. Mostly official parties. Hamburg has been badly bombed again. But Aunt Gerda talks of going back! Says she would rather be in her own home, even without her furniture (all *four* storing places were bombed!). I can't think why they protest – I'd let her go without a murmur!

June 2nd
Hugo's cousin staying with us – have made up a bed for him on the living-room floor. He's on leave from Russia. It took him eight days to get here – and he won't talk about the war!

June 3rd
Michael persuaded our guest to talk about the battles. He said the Germans are loathed by the Russians. ('That's only because they are Bolsheviks' said my eleven-year-old son!) He is a doctor – and says

---

* Arab slippers, still available.

he has never seen anything like the carnage – he said he attended both Russians and Germans. Michael *prised* the details out of him – deeply interested in amputations!!

June 4th
'Maman's' building had a direct hit.

June 5th
Hugo bartered our precious schnaps for a bicycle to go to work on – and to make his endless survey of the changing streets. It's a different city each week!

June 6th
Went out around midday – saw groups of people in the street. I thought there had been an accident, but it was far far worse. The English and Americans have invaded France.

Hugo's cousin had a telegram about the same time – I saw the boy delivering it as my neighbours were telling me the news and my heart nearly *stopped* – it was bad news for him, not me. He had his leave cancelled and had to return to Russia.

Hugo and his friends talked until after midnight. They say it is the beginning of the end. The enemy have superiority on air, sea and land. What will happen? What will happen to us?

June 7th
Michael's school cancelled all lessons. An SS officer talked to them on home defence. Surely they can't believe the invasion will happen here?

June 16th
We have a new miracle weapon to save us – *a flying bomb*. No plane, no pilots . . . it will devastate London. Michael, of course, knows exactly how it works!

June 17th
An amazing escape for the Führer. A flying bomb, destined for London, went astray, and landed on top of his bunker. If he had been killed it would really have been the collapse of Germany. There has to be a God. *No one was even hurt.*

June 28th
Everything is going very badly for us. The Russians are on their way to
Poland. I wonder if we should go back to Munich? I am terrified.

July 4th
Went to a wedding. So many important people – so many of the
nobility. For a time it seemed as if everything was normal . . . until we
went to the reception which was in the only part of the hotel that was
usable (it had been blasted last night!). I was astonished that so many
people would brave the journey (one family came from Austria) but
there was bottle after bottle of champagne to bring them there.

The bride was young and beautiful, and the groom on leave from
the Eastern Front. I couldn't help thinking that he was as likely as not
to perish – what a way to begin married life.

When we got home Michael was listening to the *Luftlage* broadcast,*
and said we were okay for the time being. He had the map out. 'Gustav
Friedrich' is the code which tells us that the alert will be sounding for
us in about ten minutes! I don't understand the system, but M (and all
the children around here) have it pat.

Hugo received a telephone call and said he had to go out . . . so I am
now waiting nervously for his return. At least there hasn't been a raid.
Michael has gone to sleep, so I don't know if we are expecting one.

July 5th
Gave dinner to Peter Yorck and Colonel von Stauffenberg. (Michael
fascinated by the fact he has only *one* arm!) I do miss being able to give
my orders to Mutti's hotel cook, and to collect a delicious meal that
everyone thinks I cooked!

July 12th
Saw Joseph and Magda Goebbels in the theatre – I don't think they
saw *us*. I smiled at him and then felt rather a fool when he didn't
respond.

July 17th
Michael missed his 'small arms drill' – my fault, and he was upset.

July 18th
We've been adopted by a stray dog – I feel the owners must have been

* A service which gave the route of enemy aircraft.

bombed out or killed. A gentle, nervous creature – not a prize winner!
I have a suspicion that before long it will have moved in altogether.
We're too soft-hearted.

July 19th
Having said that, the dog didn't arrive for its daily meal! And I'm
worried. Hope it turns up tomorrow. I've kept a succulent bone!

July 20th
I write the 20th – it is really the *21st*. It is two in the morning. Since
four o'clock there were rumours something was happening. I went
down to get some bread (and look for the wretched dog!) and there
were people standing about in the street. At the shop, Herr R said that
he'd heard that the army had taken over and that Hitler had been
killed. No one really believed it. (They are used to rumours of assassination!) And *of course* it turned out to be untrue. Hugo was home, hot
and tired (first day on the bartered bicycle) and pouring himself a glass
of the weak beer (there's a bigger outcry about the quality of the beer
than in anything else!) when there was a radio announcement saying
there had been an attempt to kill the Führer, but it had failed.

Michael then arrived *with the dog*, who had been waiting on the step
for him – the dog panting and Michael breathless. It really has been a
ghastly hot and stifling kind of day – asking if it was true that Hitler
was dead. I was happy to be able to say we had just heard that he was
safe.

We were glued to the wireless. Around nine o'clock we heard that
General von Hase had been arrested and that the SS have taken over
command of all the troops in the city, under Reinecke – and were
about to storm the Bendlerstrasse. We were promised that the Führer
would speak to us later in the evening

Hugo suddenly said over dinner that perhaps it would have been a
good thing if it had come off.

I was shocked, and Michael, fresh from a meeting, couldn't believe
his ears.

I said 'How can you say that?' and Hugo said he felt that some things
were being badly mismanaged, and that power was too concentrated.

I can't bear it when he talks like that. I won't let myself think for a
single second that we might lose the war. In my heart I *know* it's a
possibility, but I love Germany and I love Hitler (he has done so much
for us all) and I don't want criticism *even* if it has some truth in it.

I changed the subject. We talked about the dog, who had received the bone with rapture – it obviously doesn't get fed anywhere else. Michael asked if he could stay up to hear Hitler. If I'd known he wasn't going to speak until *one* I certainly wouldn't have said yes. Every few minutes we heard that he was going to speak shortly. It took so long to happen I had begun to think he had been hurt or really was dead.

Anyway, at last he was announced. It was so hot the whole of Berlin had their windows open – and everyone had their radios on. It was as if Hitler was the voice of God, heard indoors and out!

He said he was speaking so that we should know he was unhurt, and that it was a crime unparalleled in our history.

Then he said 'The bomb planted by Colonel Count von Stauffenberg...' Well, Hugo leapt to his feet. Michael and I stared at each other.

I said 'Not our . . .'

And Michael said 'HIM!'

Hugo said 'Good God.' We were all so STUNNED that we didn't hear the rest of the speech. I could only think that he ate the casserole I cooked a few nights ago and said it was delicious.

I said 'What will happen to him?' Hugo looked drawn – quite ill. He was shattered by the revelation. He said 'What do *you* think?'

I packed Michael off to bed – wide awake, of course, and dying to tell his friends he *knew* the Count.

I've just realized that I wrote 'knew'.

July 21st

Hugo has been arrested. He had *nothing* to do with it.

They came and dragged him out of bed – well, he had got up to answer the door, at *six o'clock*. We were sound asleep and they hammered and rang. They took him 'for questioning'. All day I've tried to find out where he is, and can't.

I'm exhausted. We only had four hours' sleep – and then this. Like a nightmare.

July 22nd

Michael and I were playing cards – we don't know what to do. We take it in turn to listen for the door and the phone. These two SS men came. My first thought, so help me, was that they were going to arrest *me* (there have been thousands of arrests since the attempt) but they just came in and questioned me. It was mad . . . I said 'You're making a mistake, my husband doesn't know anything about it.' Ah yes, said the thin one. But you have entertained the late Count von Stauffenberg, and Count Yorck von Wartenburg.

I said 'They were only *acquaintances*. You can't *know* what's in people's minds. My husband was as horrified as anyone else when he heard who had done it.'

'Let's have the truth, Frau von Stahlenberg.'

'I swear it's the truth.'

'Your husband met Count Yorck von Wartenburg as often as twice a week.'

'He *liked* him. He said it was like being back at the University. They talked about films . . .'

The loathsome man actually *laughed.*

The other one said 'Did your husband express his *views* on the Führer?'

I said 'His views were my views. He knew the Führer well at one time.'

'But not lately?'

'He has changed his job within the Ministry.'

'Oh we know all about that.'

I said 'I don't know how often I have to tell you, but he had nothing to do with the attempted assassination. I would have *known*. He couldn't believe it when he heard that Count von Stauffenberg . . . we were here together, Michael . . .'

'Michael!' said the thin one. 'Well, Michael, let's hear you tell us what happened.'

The one with the three rings smiled at Michael, stood up and said, 'Why don't I talk to Michael in the other room?'

They weren't long there. While they had gone, we went through the whole rigmarole again, about how well Hugo knew them, when he met them, what he said and didn't say.

Then the other one came back, Michael following him, and they thanked us and left. I sat down and burst into tears. When I heard the car drive away my strength just left me. Michael was marvellous, so sweet, he kissed me and said if I wanted to go to bed *he* would cook our supper. (It was bread and herb tea!)

Now I'm in bed, and I can't possibly sleep. I feel I'll never be able to sleep again in my life. Could I speak to Dr Goebbels? We haven't really seen him properly since we came to Berlin.

July 23rd
No word. Where *is* he?

July 24th
I telephoned Dr Goebbels at the special number. At least he spoke to me. He said 'I'm sorry, there's nothing I can do. I got him off the hook last time.'

I felt so *cheap* – I had hoped he would have asked me to see him at least. I was prepared to go through the whole thing again. But he's not interested in me – or in Hugo.

Oh God, what shall I do?

July 25th
He's in the Lehrterstrasse prison. We heard today.

July 26th
The trials are beginning on August 7th.

Peter Rande telephoned. It is even more terrible. He has been assigned to the unit *filming* the trials.

July 27th
Hugo is not being tried yet. We heard that there are at least 5000 arrested. It's going to go *on and on* all the year.

The dog has moved in. In a way it's a comfort. It barks when people come to the door.

July 30th
Peter Rande is staying with us. He has been to the People's Court to arrange about the cameras. Having him here makes me feel better. At least I know what's happening.

July 31st
Peter Yorck and seven others are to be tried first. *I can't go.*

August 5th
I have seen Hugo. It is terrible. He looks twenty years older. I am in despair. I have no feeling of hope.

August 7th
Peter says they are all broken men. They are dressed for the trial in old

246

clothes, and Field Marshal von Witzleben has had his false teeth removed and was given trousers too big for him so that they almost fell down.

Freisler* yelled at him that he was a dirty old man and should stop fiddling with his trousers. I cry every time I hear such ghastly tales.

August 8th
Am waiting for Peter to return. I heard on the radio *all* eight are condemned to death. Poor men. Poor wives.

August 9th
He came back terribly late last night. *White. He cried.* He was *there* at Plötzensee. *He had to film it.* Hung from meat hooks. The nooses were piano wire. I wish he hadn't told me but he had to tell someone. As they struggled the beltless trousers fell off.

Hitler has asked to see the film the same night – it was developed immediately. Suppose it had been Hugo. It isn't human. I feel so sick I haven't been able to go out all day. Michael fetched the bread.

August 10th
Peter says there is some hope. He is going to talk to someone today who knows Freisler socially.

August 11th
Peter spoke to the man today. He is going to do what he can.

August 30th
We still have no word from Peter's friend.

September 10th
Hugo is to be hanged.

September 11th
I keep telling myself it isn't true, that I'm going to wake up and find that I'm in Munich – 1934 or 5, when we were happy and Michael was a baby.

I'm back in the shelter. It must be two or three o'clock, we came down at midnight. 'Gustav Friedrich' gave us time to get down here

---

* Ronald Freisler, President of the People's Court (Volksgerichtshof).

before the alert. God, how I hate that sound. You can't hear it so well here, under the hotel. Arriving early gives one a chance to get a bunk. Sometimes I think all that will be left of Berlin will be the shelters, Professor Speer's shelters strong enough to survive the 1000-year Reich. Will the Third Reich hold out though, I wonder?

I have to be careful that no one reads this over my shoulder. I am terrified that I might fall asleep, and the diary drop onto the floor. Anyone might pick it up, the old man who watches me from the opposite bunk, the baby that crawls up and down, up and down the narrow aisles all night. Or *Michael*.

He sleeps so peacefully now. How angelic he looks. Just occasionally I have discovered him in the bedroom. Oh, there's always an excuse, he wants a comb, a handkerchief, the compass from the desk. Hugo's desk.

His name makes me weep. Not outwardly of course, down here in the crowded shelter. I weep inside my head. The tears drip down behind my sore eyes to my thick heart, to my sick stomach. I try to think where it went wrong – for us (because it did, it hasn't been the same for a long time now), for Hitler and for Germany. For some reason I think of the Trauters at Hesselberg, the little girl wearing her armband, her eyes as big as the cornflowers that Liz lay down in with Todd. What a summer! If we had known the future then! Why, the war hadn't even started, wasn't thought of. Except by the Führer perhaps.

People say terrible things about him now. I can't believe them. They say he's mad, that he doesn't care about anyone, only himself. I say they forget the wonderful things he's done for us, the feeling he gave us for our country. They won't remember what it was like before 1933, before Michael was born. Michael grew up in Hitler's Germany. He loves him.

Is that why he steals my diary? Reads it when he thinks I'm out? Creeps in to put it back? I think he read it in October 1942. Two weeks before the Gestapo called me in to talk.

Three bombs so close I can't help thinking we will have to dig our way out. No, it's all right! Someone has gone up to the street to have a look. The buildings across the road are down. The sky looks like a sunset, not a dawn he said.

I shouldn't have written that. It isn't true. Not Michael. We're all so afraid nowadays, so full of suspicions.

But what did he say to the officers after the arrest? What did he say in the other room?

When he heard the last bombs he stretched out and took my hand. 'Mutti, don't worry, we're safe.' My dear child. My sweet boy. 'Mutti, we're safe.' Hugo isn't safe. There's a meat hook waiting. God, I'm going to vomit. It gets so hot down here, so stuffy, all of us breathing the stale air, the children urinating, the smell from the chemical worse than the stench it's intended to conceal. That cold sweat breaks out on my face and palms. Another bomb. Oh God, oh God. Let this raid end. Make the planes go away. Save Hugo. Save Michael. What will become of us?

September 12th
Mutti is staying with me, she wants me to go back to Munich but how could I leave Hugo in Berlin. They haven't set a date. This could go on for months.

September 30th
I was allowed to see him. So thin. Those strong thighs like hambones under the beltless trousers. He says there is no hope. Nothing we can do. Mutti has gone. There is so much work in the hotel, everyone is leaving Berlin and going south.

October 9th
Peter has gone. He kissed me goodbye. He said 'Who would have thought we would have ended like this?' The hangings and the trials are no longer of interest for the newsreels. There have been too many. They have gone on for too long. No one cares except us.

CHRISTMAS DAY
Michael and I went to Helene's. He enjoyed himself with the children. I made the best I could out of the sad day.

1945

January 30th
Michael said 'Only one more year and then at last I'll be in the Hitler Youth.'

I couldn't tell him. The Russians are 100 miles from Berlin.

February 2nd
My darling Hugo was hanged this morning. I wish I were dead.

February 3rd
The courthouse was bombed. Judge Freisler was killed.

True Justice.

I hope he rots in hell.

February 10th
Freezing. We have run out of coal.

March 19th
They are taking boys of fifteen and sixteen to fight. Thank God Michael is too young.

March 23rd
The Americans are near Mainz. I know from the BBC.

April 20th
Hitler's birthday. Dr G spoke to us. He promises victory – but how can there be victory? The Russians are east of the city.

April 30th
He said – Michael – 'I have to fight.'

It was the most terrifying thing. I grabbed his arm. I shrieked 'You're thirteen. A LITTLE BOY.'

He said 'I don't care. We're all going. We PROMISED WE WOULD.'

The dog was barking. It gets so excited when we raise our voices.

'Do you want to get killed? What good will that do anyone, you, me . . .!'

'Germany.'

I said 'You stupid idiot. Germany's finished.'

He was wearing his uniform, and he *had a gun*. God knows where from.

He said 'You don't have to worry.' Shrill and scathing. 'I know how to shoot.'

Then he burst into tears and the dog jumped up and nearly knocked us down. I shoved it into the dining-room and locked the door.

I held Michael, and he clung to me, saying 'I don't want to go. I don't want to leave you.'

I was so relieved. I stroked his head, and promised him. 'I won't let you go.'

But when I went to let the dog out to stop the persistent whining, Michael was at the front door. We just stared at each other.

He said '*I'm* not a traitor like my father. I'm not afraid.'

I have never hit him before, but I did then. Across the face so hard he stumbled. He lifted his gun and pointed it at me. I thought, he can't kill me. I screamed his name. It was a nightmare.

With his other hand he opened the door. He shouted 'Yes, he *was* a traitor. So was Anni. And I'm glad they were caught. Heil Hitler!'

And he ran down the stairs. I flew after him, but he rushed into the street ahead of me. It was dark except for the fires. You could hear the guns.

Then the dog bounded out barking, and I cried at it to come back.

The dog came back.

Michael hasn't.

It is 11.30 now and we have been told that the Russians are in Berlin.

May 1st

I dare not turn off the radio. I have just learned of Hitler's heroic death.

My Michael hasn't come home.

1948

FRANKFURT
January 30th
Michael would have been fifteen today. Sometimes I pretend he could
still be alive. It doesn't have to be a pretence. He could have come back
and not been able to find me after the apartment was shelled. He could
have lost his memory, one does hear of cases all the time, still be in
hospital somewhere.

A procession of machinery from America has just gone by. The new
building programme. My reception desk faces the window. It's sunny
and the whole thing looked like a parade – it reminded me of the old
Nuremberg days. There was quite a crowd (we Germans love a turn-
out) and I went to watch. Why not? There's no reason that Ilse can't
cope with the switchboard, she's not a total fool.

It was colder than it looked from inside. I was glad of my fur coat.

There are days when I *make* myself unhappy. It isn't right to forget,
but I think I have become a person who lives in the present, it's really as
if it all happened to some other lady. When I took out my diary last
night, I had to keep saying 'That was YOU. You were married to
Hugo. You actually had a son.' Without those pages would I remember
anything at all?

It's odd, when a person is in extremity, the things that become
important. 'Don't pack,' said Peter Rande. 'If you want to get out of
Berlin alive, you have to leave now.' So what did I take? An orange
chiffon dress, the coat, Peter's model gun, the diaries. At that moment
they seemed as important as my own life. Now I know they are my
life. The truth is, it is only when I go back to the *Goldener Hirsch* and
that wretched dog – oh yes, I took the dog – jumps up at me that I'm
badly affected. Which is why I try not to leave Frankfurt. It's fine here.
I have a two-room apartment in the hotel, and the pay is good. There
are the tips, too. The Americans are always generous.

I had to stop there. New arrivals came with a mass of luggage and
then made a fuss about sleeping in north-facing rooms! Not easy to
switch around but I sorted it out. I'm very efficient. 'Cute' the Americans call it. I hope they're going to be as friendly as the first batch, Ian

and Bro, Pete Holamby and Ken Mac (the best dancer in the world – he taught me how to jive) and the Australian stenographer Debbie, who sent me a huge and glittering Christmas card from New York which must have cost as much as a pound of coffee, and has *promised* to try and trace Liz. (I wrote to the old address but the letter came back 'Not Known'.)

There's a photograph of us all pinned up in the Bar, our Marshall Plan Christmas party the night before they left for the USA. 'One for the road,' they kept saying. But really it was one for the sky because they were flying. 'I'll take you along in my pocket,' said Barry from Cincinatti. 'You're a pocket-sized blonde. Hop in.' How I longed to go with them.

Once again I had to stop. This time one of the new arrivals came down for a map of Frankfurt and to ask if he could have drinks sent to his room. He's a Mr M Gelder from Dallas – *Morris* I think. I'll look in his passport when the manager brings it back. He stayed chatting for a long time! He asked my name. For the record I call myself von Stahlenberg-Stofen nowadays. My in-laws wanted me to drop the von Stahlenberg once Hugo was dead, but I had no intention of doing that. Widows often add a hyphen and their maiden name. I think it has style.

Mr M Gelder asked me if I were married, and then regretted it. Americans are always embarrassed when they find out the situation because they think that one of their soldiers could have killed my husband. I said that Hugo had been murdered by the Nazis, and that put him at his ease. He says he just can't believe I am thirty-three. Well, although I say it myself, my new hairstyle *does* make me look a lot younger, like Veronica Lake.

July 31st

Already the new money has made a difference. I don't understand these things, but *why* didn't they do it before? It's so simple, knocking off the zeros. Morris tries to explain, but I'm what he calls 'dumb' when it comes to financial matters!

It's a wonderful summer. One wing of the new factory is already in operation, but I hope we're not self-sufficient too soon. *I don't want the Americans to go.* When I told Morris he said, 'You don't want the supply of nylons to stop!' I said he wasn't being fair! 'What is it then, the coffee or the chocolates?' I said 'You know I'm not like that.' He makes me laugh. He teases me all the time.

Ilse just knocked on my door to give me my mail. A postcard from Klara, a bill from Madsen's for the mattress, and A LETTER FROM LIZ. Well, happy, mother of three, *still* Mrs Todd Phillips. She writes that she thinks of me often. She couldn't believe her ears when Debbie called from New York and told her we'd spent last Christmas together. We must never lose touch again.

Have just looked at the time. Must bathe and change. We're going to the movies tonight. I'll write some more when I come home.

Elisabeth von Stahlenberg did not continue her diary. Two months after the last entry she married an American business-man and moved to Texas where she still lives. Her first daughter was born in January 1949, her second in December 1950.

Her former identity is not generally known and for this reason all names except those of public figures have been changed.